SPEC

Hell's Handlers Florida Chapter Book 2

Lilly Atlas

ISBN-13: 978-1-946068-40-8

Other books by Lilly Atlas

No Prisoners MC
Hook: A No Prisoners Novella
Striker
Jester
Acer
Lucky
Snake

Trident Ink
Escapades

Hell's Handlers MC
Zach
Maverick
Jigsaw
Copper
Rocket
Little Jack
Joy
Screw
Viper
Thunder

Hell's Handlers Florida Chapter
Curly
Spec
Tracker (coming Soon)

Blue Collar Bensons
First Comes Loathe

Shock and Aww

Audiobooks
Audio

Join Lilly's mailing list for a **FREE** No Prisoners short story.
www.lillyatlas.com
Facebook
Instagram
TikTok

Table of Contents

Prologue

Sweat drenched every surface of his body.

It poured from places he didn't know produced sweat.

Between his toes. His earlobes. His eyelids.

His T-shirt and military-issued underwear were beyond soaked and smelled like a decomposing animal. He'd shed the uniform days ago. Too goddamn hot. Hell, even his internal organs had to be swimming in perspiration inside his overheated and starved body.

The heat intolerance came as a surprise. He'd trained in the desert hundreds of times for this very situation. SERE training wasn't for the faint of heart, and he'd not only survived it but rocked that shit. Sleep-deprived, dehydrated, and roasting in one hundred fifteen degrees of burning Texas sun. He'd taken it like a champ.

During the torturous training, he'd been able to disassociate. To crawl inside a hidden corner of his mind and ride out the discomfort. It was how he'd muscled through all the near barbaric training exercises during his military career.

Wasn't fucking working in real-time.

Five days ago, he'd been taken hostage in enemy territory. Their helicopter, flown by one of the best pilots he knew, had been shot out of the fucking sky like a skeet target. Only two of the team survived—Scott and one other.

How? How the hell had it happened? How had the fucking low-tech terrorist group known they were coming? Was it shit dumb luck that had his unconscious body dragged from the helicopter and shoved into a box somewhere in a Middle Eastern desert hellhole?

"Fuck!"

He was literally baking to death inside a four-by-four wooden box, crate, whatever the hell. Everything hurt. His knees ached like a motherfucker from being curled for the past twelve hours. His neck killed him from half a day bent at an unnatural angle. Both shoulder blades burned with a searing agony that threatened to overtake the heat for the worst discomfort. Though he had no way of seeing or reaching behind himself to check, he was pretty sure the skin over his shoulder blades had been abraded down to the bone after so many hours of pressure against the wooden planks.

Twice a day, the terrorists opened his prison. Someone would drag him out by his feet and toss him in some kind of shack. There, his captors gave him one cup of cloudy water and what amounted to a slice of bread. The first few days, he'd fought like an animal, but weakness eventually won, and now he could barely lift the water to his cracked lips.

Every day he thought of upending that cup and refusing the meager bite of food. If it'd hasten his death and end the torture, it sounded damn good at this point.

Two things kept him from choosing that route. First was the notion of 'returning home with honor.' The goal of every POW taken hostage. What his team stood for. What he'd trained for. Resisting the enemy and staying alive until he could return to US soil, having not disgraced his country. Though no one would ever find out, he'd know if he failed that mission by not trying his damnedest to stay alive until he could be rescued.

Secondly, he wasn't alone. As long as another team member suffered alongside him, he'd never abandon them. It didn't matter that the man captured with him was his closest friend in the world; he'd do the same for any other soldier.

The fact it was his closest friend did ramp up his mental anguish to an unbearable level. Thankfully, their captors were unaware that Scott and Deke were tighter than some siblings. If they knew, they'd use it to their advantage, making the torture worse than it already was. Scott worried his psyche couldn't handle more than he'd already been forced to endure.

So much for being a badass Army Ranger.

Footsteps crunched along the sand nearby his box, growing louder each second. Time for his daily mind fuck. His heart rate ramped up, as did his breathing in the parched, dusty air. Even though he lacked the energy to freak the fuck out anymore, his subconscious still panicked and tried to get his body ready to fight or flee. Unfortunately, he'd fall flat on his ass if he tried to swing a fist and wouldn't make it ten feet running before they shot him dead.

Besides, he'd endure this torment for the rest of his life before abandoning Deke.

"Wake up, shithead," the guard shouted in heavily accented English, pounding his fist on top of the box.

As the wooden box jostled beneath his captor's heavy fist, pain rippled through Scott. His raw shoulders rubbed across the rough wood. He bit down on his lip to keep from crying out and giving his captors any ammunition to use against him. The dry skin of his lip ripped open further. Blood seeped into his mouth and coated teeth he hadn't brushed in ages.

Metal clinked and jingled seconds before the lid of the box opened. Harsh sunlight flooded his torture chamber. Early on, he'd learned to keep his eyes shut tight or be blinded for a solid five minutes.

Five minutes of increased vulnerability was a dangerous thing.

Rough hands grasped his shoulders and yanked him from the box. Splintered wood from the box's rim scraped down his raw spine, drawing a grunt of pain from him. He'd have fucking screamed if he had the air.

He scrambled to get to his legs beneath him, or at least it felt like he moved fast, but his brain and body weren't on the same wavelength anymore, and he sagged in his captor's hold as his knees gave out.

After blinking a half dozen times, he forced his eyelids to remain open. Bright sunlight seared straight through his eye sockets to his brain. Everything appeared fuzzy, from the tan sand to the armed men dressed in sandals and robes. They yelled what he recognized as slurs in Arabic as his body was dragged past them.

Moments later, he crumbled to the ground in the hut he'd become all too familiar with since being captured. He lay in the heap they tossed him in, waiting for the throbbing to pass.

"Scott?" Deke's frail voice had him lifting his head despite excruciating pain in his neck.

"Jesus fucking Christ," he whispered when he saw his friend.

Deke let out a barely audible chuckle. "I look that sexy, huh?"

Scott swallowed a burning trail of bile. "Deke..." His friend looked like a rotting corpse. There was no nicer way to describe it. The cuts their captors had inflicted all over his skin oozed with thick green puss. Both his eyes were blackened, his lips were split, and his hair was matted with blood. He'd lost an alarming amount of weight for such a short time. He sat, slumped on the ground with his left leg

4

bent at an unnatural angle. A dislocated knee maybe from when their interrogator had taken the butt of his rifle to it yesterday.

This is how it had been for the past five days. Twice a day, their captors dragged Scott into this hovel for interrogation after a dozen hours in that fucking box. They wanted to know what intel the US had on them. They demanded he film a video denouncing his military and his country. Instead of using physical coercion to get his compliance, they did something worse.

They tortured Deke while forcing him to watch.

The number of times he'd almost caved hit into the thousands. But he'd kept his mouth sealed shut, honoring his country, and destroying his friend. In the process, the guilt thrashed his soul beyond repair.

"Scott?"

He closed his eyes as now-familiar despair washed over him. "Don't make me say it, Deke. Please don't make me say it." From experience, he knew they had about five minutes before the sadistic fuck they called an interrogator came to play.

"I'm sorry, brother. I have no choice."

"Yes, you fucking do," he snapped. Guilt slammed into him. He was such an asshole, sniping at the man who'd been tortured for days because of him. "Shit. I'm sorry."

Deke snorted. "Like we've never lost our shit on each other before. You don't scare me."

Scott's laugh was full of sorrow. Nothing would scare either of them after this. They'd stared into the face of the devil and lived. So far. Or hell, maybe everything would scare him moving forward. Maybe he wouldn't be able to leave his house—if he ever made it home—too afraid of the evil lurking behind every smile he came across.

"Scott, I'm going to die soon."

The words terrified him more than the thought of returning to the box. "No! You're not. No fucking way. You're too strong for that shit." Deke couldn't die. He wouldn't allow it. Who would cruise the bars with him? Who'd roll their eyes at the ridiculously lavish life Deke's estranged father lived with his millions of dollars and narrow-minded beliefs? Who'd suffer through trainings and miserable missions with him? They both could've retired from the military last year but decided to stick it out for a few more. Grab a little extra pension. There was some irony in there somewhere, but he couldn't muster the strength to figure it out.

"Scott, please. You know it's true. No one can survive this indefinitely. Not even a perfect specimen like me."

Christ. Deke was the one suffering unimaginable torture, but he still managed to joke while Scott was acting like a little whiny bitch. His shoulders slumped. He'd give his brother whatever the fuck he wanted in his last hours. Even lie to his face. "Go ahead. I'll say it." Deke forced this little ritual on him after the first time their captors made Scott watch them slice into his brother's skin.

"This is not my fault," Deke said in a weakened version of his voice.

As he stared up at the cracked mud ceiling, Scott repeated. "This is not my fault."

Except, it sure as fuck is.

"I honored my oath and my country."

Maybe, but I got my best friend tortured and killed.

He repeated the words though he knew they were lies.

"This is not my fault."

Fuck Deke for always making him say that one twice.

"I did not kill Deke."

He froze, then raised his head to meet Deke's pain-filled gaze. His neck screamed at him, but he ignored the searing pain. "That's not the line, Deke." It was supposed to be *I did not hurt Deke.* His empty stomach cramped.

"Say it." Deke coughed. The sound rattled Scott's bones. For fuck's sake, he sounded like he was dying from emphysema. Along with the lacerations, bruises, burns, and blood loss, he probably had a fever. Maybe pneumonia. His life was down to days, maybe hours.

Where the fuck was their rescue?

Scott stared at his friend and saw the acceptance, maybe even peace with his impending death. His soul ached. Only once before had he experienced this brand of emotional pain. A few years ago, Scott's sister had been kidnapped and brutally raped by a psychopath who now rotted in hell. He'd felt the same helpless rage he experienced then and the same guilt for not being able to save someone he loved. But there was one major difference between the situations. His sister survived. She'd been given a chance to heal—as much as one could from a trauma like that. She had a life with a man who fucking worshiped her. She was happy and thriving.

Deke wouldn't get that chance.

Scott's shoulders slumped. How could he deny his friend anything in his dying moments? "I did not kill Deke." The words tasted bitter on his tongue. They were a goddamn lie.

The door opened, and the same three assholes who'd conducted his 'interrogation' strode into the room. The leader, a man with a dark beard and wicked scar on his cheek, smiled.

He always fucking smiled.

Given a chance, he'd be the last one Scott killed after he watched Scott burn his entire compound to the ground. But Scott was too weak to do anything but hang limp as the other two men lifted him under his arms and propped him up.

"What does your government know about our operation?"

He always started with the same question.

"Fuck off." Scott would've spit on him if he'd had even one drop of saliva in his mouth. They hadn't bothered giving him a drink today.

The sadist drew his knife from a sheath on his belt. Wearing the sinister grin that would haunt Scott's nightmares, he rotated the blade's tip against his finger. "Your friend can't take much more."

Scott shifted his gaze to Deke. He hadn't moved an inch.

"What does your government know about our operation?"

The answer danced on the tip of his tongue despite his promises to his country. Despite his training. Despite his internal revulsion at giving these men even one word that could help their cause. Every ounce of honor he possessed fought between trying to save his friend and remaining loyal to his country.

"Don't," Deke rasped.

They'd both been at this game long enough to know the harsh reality. Even if he spilled every single detail he'd learned about this particular terrorist cell during hours of intelligence briefings, it wouldn't spare their lives. These men had no code. No principles. No integrity. Nothing short of a miracle would save Deke now.

So he straightened his shoulders, despite the burning pull of his muscles, and locked out his knees. The joints screamed in pain. After twelve hours of being curled up, his body didn't want to straighten. But it hadn't failed him yet. He looked his tormentor straight in the eye. "Fuck. Off."

The man tsked, then turned to Deke, who lay with his eyes closed. Only the flaring of his nostrils and rapid rise and fall of his chest showed his anxiety.

Scott's breathing sped up too, and his heart raced, which felt like unfair bullshit. It wasn't his skin being flayed off his body. What right did he have to feel such dread?

The asshole crouched over Deke's mangled body. He

waved his knife near the skin, choosing where to carve. Acid burned in Scott's stomach and up his esophagus.

When the tip of the knife pressed into the thin skin of Deke's forehead, Scott froze. But not Deke. Deke's body began to tremble, and Scott felt in his soul how much his friend hated showing weakness.

The bastard turned and smiled at Scott before drawing the knife across Deke's forehead. His friend hissed out his pain as Scott watched, helpless and with an indescribable amount of guilt, while blood oozed from the fresh wound.

"You know how to make this stop. What does your government know about our operation?"

Sweat poured down Deke's face. He lay panting and twitching occasionally but with no other outward reaction. For fuck's sake, was he even aware of what was happening?

Best if he wasn't. Maybe he couldn't feel the pain anymore.

Scott swallowed an excruciating lump in his throat. The asshole moved the knife to Deke's chest, carving a line across one filthy pec.

Jesus, he was going to fucking cry. Deke was the one on death's doorstep enduring inconceivable agony, and Scott was the one near tears.

Man the fuck up.

For Deke.

"Fuck off," he said to their torturer, nearly vomiting as he sentenced Deke to more cruelty.

This went on until the torturer grew bored and Scott was a whole lot more fucked in the head than he had been a few hours ago. At least for the moment, Deke had the sweet relief of unconscious oblivion.

The terrorists dragged him back to his box, where he spent the next half-day losing a little more of his sanity. Then, again, he was hauled back to Deke's hut and dumped on the floor for another round of psychological torture.

This time, the world around him wavered, fuzzy and unsteady. Worry for Deke and pain had kept him from anything more than a fitful catnap. Exhaustion muddled his thoughts and vision, making him feel as though his brain couldn't process the input from his eyes any longer. He'd learned about heatstroke. How long before he started having delusions? Stroked out?

He forced himself to push aside the gruesome thoughts and focus on Deke. As always, they'd only have a few minutes to speak privately. No doubt Deke would run through the words he always made Scott repeat. And he'd give them to Deke, no matter how much he disagreed with their truth. He'd give his brother-in-arms and best friend anything the man wanted to give him an ounce of relief.

"What do you think, man?" he asked Deke in as strong a voice as he could muster. "Steak or burger when we get home?"

Silence met his question.

"Deke?" When his friend didn't respond, Scott's insides iced over. It took him a solid minute to struggle to a sitting position. "Yo, Deke, wake the fuck up, brother." Using his absolute last morsel of energy, Scott dragged his aching body across the grimy clay floor. He froze about two feet from Deke.

"No," he whispered.

His friend lay on his back, eyes wide open, staring at nothing. Flies buzzed around, occasionally landing on Deke's gangrenous wounds.

Scott's stomach lurched. He turned his head and vomited stomach acid on the ground. "God, fuck," he whispered when the excruciating abdominal contractions ceased. He collapsed to his back as tears slipped from his eyes.

Despite all the odds, he'd held hope they'd be rescued.

And now Deke was dead. The man who'd had his back

every day over the past twenty years was dead.

I didn't kill Deke.

Bull-fucking-shit.

He may not be as guilty as these shit-ass terrorists, but Deke's death was a stain on his soul he'd wear for eternity.

Chapter One

Olivia scanned her fiancé's desk as she settled her hands on the keyboard.

Home row. Ready to type in the cryptic combination of letters and numbers that would grant her access to his personal computer, searching her fiancé's computer for evidence of cheating.

What a cliché, and not somewhere she'd ever thought she'd end up.

But there she was.

"Come to mama," she whispered as though Lance's password would magically flow from the ether into her fingertips.

Nothing came to her. Big surprise.

She blew out a frustrated breath and sagged against the oversized office chair with the buttery soft leather and extra-wide armrests. What else could she try? All the usual suspects had failed.

Her name.

Her birthday.

Lance's birthday.

His mother's maiden name.

The name of his favorite golf club—that's right, it had a name. Casper.

Hell, she'd even tried his childhood dog's name. He'd hated that dog.

For the past week, she'd slipped into this office each evening while Lance was 'at the gym' and tried two passwords. Three strikes would lock the screen and give away her sleuthing. So when her two tries failed, she left and impatiently waited for the next night.

He was cheating on her again. She knew it in her bones despite his repeated professions of loyalty and love. Six months ago, he left for work and forgot his phone. Like the sweet partner she was, she'd decided to bring it to him at his office. His day would suck without it, and if she could help, why wouldn't she?

Well, the joke had been on her when at five minutes after nine, a text came through from his secretary saying how she could see him sitting at his desk and how she couldn't stop thinking about what he'd done to her on that desk the day before. There was even mention of how hard it'd been to keep from screaming in pleasure and alerting the staff to what happened.

Oliva may have grown up spoiled rotten by her single-parent father, but she wasn't nearly as soft as the men in her life believed her to be. She'd thrown Lance's engagement ring in his face, stormed out the door, and driven straight to her father's house. No way in hell would dear old dad let Lance humiliate her by eating out his secretary. On his desk. During the workday.

That'd been the worst part. Her fiancé didn't have enough imagination to cheat with someone original. He'd chosen the most cliché woman in his life to fuck. His secretary.

There was no way in hell Olivia would put up with that. Neither would her doting father. He'd rip Lance a new one, complete with cutting all business ties. The man would burn down a forest if she got a papercut.

She'd been heartbroken as hell but ready to dance on Lance's unfaithful grave.

That was the day she learned what her father really thought of her. He'd patted her hand and told her she had two choices—look the other way or do a better job satisfying her fiancé. He reminded her how she loved Lance but also how intertwined they were due to her father and Lance's business dealings. Their careers were too important and lucrative to sever over wounded pride. He'd told her to finish throwing her fit, go home, accept whatever gift Lance purchased to appease her, and give him a reason to be faithful.

She'd stood there, jaw on the floor, as her father rolled his eyes. "Come on, princess, you're not a child anymore. What the hell did you think I'd say? Lance has the youth, money, and popularity to practically buy me a Senate seat." He'd patted her shoulder like she was the child he'd claimed she wasn't.

"We all need to do our part. You included. So go home and make up, okay, princess?"

She'd left in a daze and arrived home to find gaudy rose bouquets taking over the house, a bubble bath in their oversized jacuzzi tub, and a naked Lance waiting to make up.

With a whole host of sorrowful words and renewed promises of loyalty and love, he'd slid her engagement ring back in place and presented her with a tennis bracelet even more sparkly than the ring.

She'd let him back in, telling herself everyone made mistakes. She really did love him. And no relationship was perfect. He'd promised it wouldn't happen again, and if she loved him, shouldn't she believe him?

With Lance's convincing apology and her father's

prompting, she'd forgiven him.

But she hadn't forgotten, and a small part of her wondered if there'd been other women she hadn't known about. Or if he really did love her as much as he said. As much as she'd loved him.

They quickly fell back into their routine and to the outside world, looked as happy as they ever had, but something had changed inside Olivia. She found herself unable to give him the trust she'd so blindly handed over before knowing about his cheating. Though she kept her concerns to herself, she began to wonder if he was lying when he claimed to be golfing, or at the gym, or staying late for a meeting. She'd tried to push the doubts away. They'd only destroy her relationship, but they lingered. And they began to poison her love for her fiancé.

Olivia found herself pulling away emotionally and physically. For years, she'd been happy to be the smiling woman at his side, meet up with her friends for lunch, hit the gym at ten in the morning, plan parties, and play the glamorous hostess. She'd done those things because she loved her fiancé, and he wanted her home instead of working. But it meant giving up on her dream of becoming a veterinarian. After the cheating episode, she signed up for online classes to finish her veterinarian school prerequisites.

Lance had no idea, and she couldn't imagine him agreeing to her applying for veterinarian school in a year or so, but it felt so good to have something for herself. So good to have a purpose. A goal to strive for.

She'd considered ending the relationship but clung to the hope that with time and Lance's continued faithfulness, she'd return to the love she'd had for him not long ago. He'd given her no concrete reason to suspect continued cheating.

Until last week.

She'd been gathering clothes for the dry cleaners and

found a receipt from his favorite restaurant. It'd been from the previous night when he claimed to be at the gym. When she slyly inquired what he'd been up to the night before, he'd laughed at her poor memory. "You already forgot I had a session with my trainer last night? We talked about it this morning." He'd shaken his head and kissed her cheek on his way out the door.

Her heart had dropped, but she didn't feel the same crushing pain she'd experienced the first time she discovered his cheating but more of a resigned disappointment and embarrassment. Did that mean she'd fallen out of love with him?

"One more try tonight," she mumbled.

On impulse, she opened the center drawer on the desk. Lance didn't keep much in his home office. A few Montblanc pens, a pack of cigarettes he claimed to have quit, and, oh look, some Trojans.

Classy guy.

"God, I hope he didn't screw some trashy skank on this chair," she mumbled. It'd be a shame to sully such a quality piece of furniture with his pasty ass. She was moving on from disappointment to anger at being taken for a fool yet again. "Least he uses condoms."

She pursed her lips as something sparked in the recesses of her brain. Wasn't there some stupid story he'd told her from his fraternity days about Trojans?

"Shit, what was it?" She closed her eyes and pressed her fingers to her forehead. "Think, Livy, think."

Something about accidentally leaving a box of condoms at his grandmother's house when he'd road-tripped through her town on spring break. She mailed them back along with a few more boxes and some homemade cookies. His frat brothers called her the Trojan Fairy and him...

"The Trojan Kid," she said aloud. He'd loved that stupid

nickname and wore it like some ridiculous badge of honor. What a stud. The guys from his frat still called him by the stupid label when they got together once a year for a weeklong Vegas bro-fest. She could only imagine how many condoms he went through during those weeks.

Could it be that easy? Her thirty-five-year-old fiancé reliving his glory days through his password? Unfortunately, even if she guessed the correct phrase, she could still fail. There were capitals, special characters, and numbers to consider.

"Here goes nothing," she whispered as she clicked the keys. She capitalized the 'T,' changed the 'o' to a zero, and capitalized the 'K' as well. They seemed to be the most obvious options, and since she'd already established his lack of imagination, she'd assume he'd choose the obvious.

Closing her eyes, she hovered her finger over the enter key. "Please work."

She smashed the button as she squeezed her eyes tighter. The sound of his operating system booting up filled the office space.

Olivia's heart shot into overdrive. "It worked," she whispered as she opened her eyes. Sure enough, the screen shone bright with a grid of their security cameras. "Oh, my God, it worked!" she shouted. "Trojan Kid. Of course."

Now that she'd cracked the code, the real mission began— find irrefutable proof of Lance's cheating.

Where to look first? The calendar, maybe?

Her gaze roamed over the grid of images on his large monitor. He'd left the security app open as he often did. Lance had cameras everywhere—inside the home, around the property, at the office, in the garage.

Huh.

She frowned. Three of the grid squares were darkened. Did that mean the cameras were broken? Lance would have a fit if that were the case. The malfunctioning squares were from the garage beneath his office buildings in downtown Chicago. Three cameras focused on the garage area with his designated parking spot. It made sense to keep an eye on his car, considering how much he paid for the Lamborghini.

So why weren't they on?

She clicked around, trying to diagnose the problem, which didn't appear to be major. In fact, it seemed someone had merely shut the cameras off. Maybe the office had some sort of power glitch, and they hadn't kicked back on.

No matter, easy fix.

She selected the three dark cameras and, with a few flicks of the mouse, had them up and running again. As she was about to minimize the application, movement from the garage camera caught her eye.

Lance climbed out of his car with a scowl and then approached another vehicle parked two spots away. Frowning, Olivia leaned in closer. She didn't recognize the other vehicle, a black SUV with opaque windows.

As Lance neared the SUV, the driver's door opened, and a man stepped out. He was as unfamiliar to her as the car. Shorter than her six-foot-two fiancé by at least three inches, the newcomer was thin with a thick head of light-colored hair and a mustache to match. He wore jeans, a dark hoodie, and a frown.

"Who are you?" Olivia asked aloud.

This wasn't some evening rendezvous with an airheaded mistress.

She watched, captivated, as Lance spoke to the man, who nodded then opened the back door of his SUV. Narrowing her eyes, Olivia leaned in even closer as though that would help her hear the soundless video. "What are you up to?" she whispered as she tapped her lower lip.

Was this something shady? Illegal? Lance seemed so

polished and concerned with his image to engage in drugs or guns. He was way too worried about his socio-economic status to risk his livelihood with illegal activities.

Wasn't he?

So what was in that vehicle?

The man reached in and yanked a woman from the back of his car.

"What?" Olivia reared back, making the wheeled chair roll away from the desk.

Shit, she looked young. Maybe eighteen or nineteen. And was she drunk?

The young woman stumbled and swayed as the unknown man set her on her feet. Her eyes were slits, and her head lolled as though too heavy for her neck. Alcohol wasn't the issue. At least not the only issue. This woman had been drugged.

The guy shoved her toward Lance with little to no care for her balance. She tripped and hit the hard concrete ground.

Olivia winced. With nothing but a miniskirt on her bottom half, the poor woman would've certainly torn up her knees. She held her breath as she watched this scene play out with a pit in her stomach.

Something was seriously wrong here.

Lance grabbed her upper arm and yanked her to her feet. The girl teetered on her spiky heels, then leaned into him for support. He spoke back and forth with the man—she'd kill for some freaking sound—then handed over what appeared to be a thick wad of cash.

Jesus, had her fiancé purchased a drugged woman?

The guy got back in his car then disappeared from the camera's range. Olivia shifted her gaze back to her fiancé. They were supposed to be married in less than a year in a small wedding at an exclusive Tahitian resort. Every woman's dream turned into a nightmare.

Still holding the drugged woman by her upper arm, Lance steered her to his car. She staggered along beside him until they reached the Lamborghini. Then Lance crowded her against the driver's side window.

Olivia had a full view of the side of his face, and the girl's as well. He leaned in and kissed her neck as he mashed his body against her.

"No," Olivia whispered. The pit in her stomach bloomed into a lead brick.

The girl shook her head and made a weak attempt at shoving him away. He ignored her, knocking her arms out of the way before he grabbed the hem of her skirt. As he began to work it up, the woman tried again to swat him away. The attempt was beyond ineffective.

Lance laughed, then grabbed her leg and hiked it up over his hip.

"No!" Olivia shouted this time. Her stomach turned. God, he was about to rape this woman right before her eyes. She grabbed her phone off the desk and scrambled to open the call app. "Pick up, pick up," she murmured as his phone rang in her ear.

Her eyes remained fixed on the screen, watching as Lance's face changed from lust to annoyance. He fished his phone out of his sports coat pocket and then glanced at the screen.

"Answer it!"

With a shake of his head, he shoved it back in his pocket.

"Dammit!"

The police. She needed to call the police.

"Nine-one-one, state your emergency," a calm woman's voice stated.

"I need to report a rape. Please. You have to hurry. He's about to rape her."

"Ma'am, are you safe?"

"Yes!" She smacked her hand on the desk. "I'm fine. I'm

not there. I'm watching it on a security camera. Seventeen-twenty-two Sixth Street. Downtown Chicago. The Delmont building. Fourth floor of the parking garage. Hurry!"

"Okay, ma'am. I'm going to need to ask you some questions, but I'm dispatching officers right now. Okay?"

She nodded, gripping the phone as she watched the drugged girl swat at her fiancé in vain.

"Ma'am?"

"I'm here. Ask anything." She answered all the questions while helplessly watching the woman struggle against Lance. When she'd given all the information she had, the dispatcher asked her to stay on the line. "Please hurry," she whispered.

Lance reached between him and the woman, who'd stopped struggling and slumped against the car. He pulled his belt open.

Olivia's stomach lurched, and her eyes filled with tears. There wasn't a single thing she could do to stop these events from playing out five miles across town. "I'm so sorry," she mouthed as she squeezed her eyes shut, unable to bear watching.

Large tears leaked from beneath her eyelids. The cops would never get there in time to stop it. Would the woman remember anything tomorrow? Would she wake up confused and sore, unsure what the hell happened, or would she recall the way Lance violated her in a dirty parking lot after she'd been drugged? Which scenario would be worse? God, she hoped this woman had support and would be able to find peace and healing after Olivia's fiancé hurt her.

What was she going to do now? She couldn't stay with Lance, that was for sure. She pressed a hand to her head, still holding the silent phone to her ear with her eyes squeezed shut. My God, her fiancé was a rapist.

The man she'd loved for years. Had she ever truly known him? Had everything he felt for her been a lie. All their plans?

All their dreams? They'd mostly been his dreams, his plans, but she'd loved him enough to make them her own.

She'd been a fool to love this man.

Scratch that. He wasn't a man but a monster.

If only her half-brother, Deke, was still alive. He'd not only know what to do, but he'd make sure Lance was punished. With fourteen years between them, she'd never been close to her older brother. When Olivia was a toddler, their father wrote him out of their lives. Deke hadn't wanted any part of their father's business but instead dreamed of joining the military. That wasn't acceptable to their father, and he'd cut Deke off in the harshest of ways. Back then, he'd told her Deke had left of his own accord and hated their family. It was only when she was in her late teens she'd learned the truth. She'd wasted so many years thinking the worst of her half-brother.

Deke had been a good, honorable man and soldier who fought against injustice and would've helped her without question even if he thought her a spoiled, selfish brat.

And she had been to him many times. Teenage girls given any and every material possession tended to turn out that way. Now it was too late to apologize for the brat she'd been when Deke was alive.

"Ma'am, the police are arriving."

Her eyes flew open to find Lance scrambling to right his pants. He shoved the drugged woman to the ground and then scrambled to get in the driver's seat. As he began to pull out of his parking spot, police cars appeared on the scene, surrounding his car.

Olivia blew out a breath of relief. They hadn't been in time to stop him, but at least the woman would get the help she needed, and Lance would be arrested and not able to hurt anyone again.

Oh God, had he done this before to other women? She

shuddered at the thought. Then another sobering thought popped into her head. Would the arrest stick? Lance had money coming out his ass and a whole firm of lawyers at his disposal. Would he even spend a night in jail?

She needed insurance.

Blowing out a shaky breath, Olivia got to work emailing herself the footage from the minutes she'd been watching.

As the file compiled, she stood. Soon as it finished, she'd send it and get the hell out of there. Tapping her foot, she stepped closer to the desk, then leaned in and stared at her fiancé bent over the hood of a police car with his hands cuffed behind his back.

How had she missed this? How could she have been in a relationship with a man for years without knowing the dark, monstrous deeds he was capable of? Was there something obvious in him she should've noticed? A glimmer of evil in his eye? A sinister smirk? If so, she'd missed it entirely.

Did that make her stupid or plain oblivious?

And which was worse?

Lance's gaze scanned the lot as the officers spoke to each other. As his gaze passed the camera, she shuddered, suddenly unable to imagine being anywhere near him again.

He kept up his visual journey until he darted his eyes back, staring straight into the camera. Shock and fear crossed his face for a fleeting second before a hard mask morphed his features into a fearsome and ugly warning. An icy shiver skittered down her spine. She swore he could see straight through the camera lens to her standing in his office.

The cameras hadn't been off by accident. Lance had done it. He knew. He knew she was there and had witnessed what had just happened.

One side of his mouth turned up into a grin of evil promise. He narrowed his eyes and mouthed three words she made out clearly, even through the grainy video. "You'll be sorry."

Olivia lurched back, stumbling over the chair then falling to the ground as though he'd shot her.

Her heart hammered so hard, her ribs ached. Pressing her hand to her chest, she trembled.

The computer chimed, making her jump so hard she levitated an inch off the ground. The file finished uploading. She clambered onto unsteady legs then sent the file to herself as fast as humanly possible.

She had to get away. Now. Right now. He was going to kill her. She knew it in her bones.

Where the hell could she go? Her friends were Lance's friends, and she wouldn't risk her father. Besides, the man loved Lance. Could her father be trusted? Was he aware of this?

"You're spiraling," she whispered to herself.

A hotel? An Airbnb? Should she head out of town? All of those places were so easily tracked by credit card.

"Cash. I need cash." Hell, he could track her car with the vehicle assist system. She'd have to ditch that too. Maybe she needed to lose her phone as well. And her smartwatch. Shit, there were so many ways her fiancé could keep tabs on her. Would he do that? Did he know how? She had to assume he did. Clearly, he had friends in low places.

First things first, she had to get the hell out of the house. She ran from the office to the main bedroom. She'd have to give up everything. Stop taking classes, leave the only city she'd ever lived in. She'd be on her own for the first time in her life. Fear settled low in her gut. Had she ever even eaten at a restaurant alone? Her brother had been right. She was a pampered princess without any knowledge of how to survive without someone rich propping her up.

Pitiful.

"Deke, help me," she whispered.

Wait… Deke. He had a friend. One he raved about. A guy he claimed was the best man he'd ever met. A friend from the military.

Scott, Scott something.

After stuffing as much as she could fit in a Louis Vuitton suitcase, she ran to her car. Tonight, she'd stay at a no-name motel, and tomorrow she'd find Scott.

He'd help her. Protect her.

He had to. It was a matter of life and death.

Hers.

"Thank you, Deke," she whispered.

Chapter Two

"Spec," Curly shouted from his recently constructed office. "Get your fucking ass in here."

Scott sighed. Time to pay the piper. He'd been waiting for his president to lose it on him for a while now. Bunch of horseshit if you asked him, but he'd known it was coming. The rest of the guys had been giving him the damn side-eye for weeks, as though he were a ticking time bomb waiting to detonate.

But Curly had stayed quiet. Relatively.

Guess last night's bar fight had been the straw that broke the camel's back.

"Uh-oh," Tracker said with a laugh. "Somebody pissed off Daddy. Better go in there and take your spanking like a man, brother."

Rolling his eyes, he flipped Tracker the bird and ignored Lock and Pulse, who snickered behind their beers. If they weren't a bunch of fucking pussies, they'd be the ones about to have their ass drilled by the prez.

"What's up, Prez?" he asked, pausing to lean against the doorway. The office was about ninety-five percent complete. He'd thought it was done, but Brooke insisted it needed to be decorated or some shit, and since his prez couldn't say no to his woman, she'd be stopping by later to drop off some candles and pictures of babies in flowerpots or whatever the fuck it was woman liked.

Curly glanced up from the computer then gestured to the empty chair across from his desk. "Grab a seat."

Scott did as instructed, propping his ankle on the opposite thigh. Damn, he wanted a few fingers of that half-empty bottle of whisky on Curly's desk. It was the good shit the prez hoarded like it was his chest of gold.

The walls of the office were white and bare. Aside from a desk, computer, and a few chairs, the whole room was plain and boring as hell. Huh, maybe Brooke had a point.

"Scott, I heard—"

Shit, he's bringing out the big guns with the real name. He held up a hand. "Look, Prez, how the fuck was I supposed to know that chick and her man got off on that shit?" Shrugging, he continued, "If I'd known they were doing some kinky role play and she was into it, I wouldn't have beaten the guy's ass."

"Spec, you can't keep—"

"The fuck was I supposed to do, Curly? They were in an alley behind the bar. I went out to take a piss, and I heard some woman whimpering and clearly saying no. The asswipe wasn't listening, so I made him listen."

Curly sighed. His hair had grown over the past few months, brushing his shoulders now with the spirals that gave him his name. After claiming he couldn't wait to get out of the Army and have something other than a fucking buzzed scalp, Scott still kept his hair a quarter inch in length.

Old habits. And maybe something to keep a connection to Deke. It'd been nearly two years since his death. Sometimes, the army-short hair seemed the only remaining physical connection.

"You beat the man to a bloody pulp while his hysterical girlfriend screamed at you to stop."

She screamed? He blinked, unable to recall anything beyond the roaring in his ears and the white-hot rage that tunneled his vision to one point—make the motherfucker pay. But Curly didn't need to know he'd been in a semi-trance when he'd kicked that weak punk's ass. Just like he hadn't needed to know about it when Scott had fucked up two guys from his prez's old MC in a gas station a few months back.

Bottom line, he wouldn't stand by taking a piss while some jack-off abused a woman. Not after what his sister, Chloe, had suffered. "Prez, my sister—"

It was Curly's turn to cut him off with a raised hand. "I get it, Spec," he said with deep understanding. Last year, the prez's woman had nearly been killed by her ex-husband. Scott had put a life-ending bullet in the bastard, but the traumatic memory lingered in Curly's eyes.

Probably would for the rest of his life.

Chloe was Scott's sister, not his woman, but she'd suffered a brutal attack he hadn't been in the country to protect her from.

"There are other things you could've done besides break four ribs, his cheekbone, his nose, and give him a concussion," Curly said, reading from a sticky note on his desk.

Damn, he'd done good. He fought to keep from smirking. He whistled. "I do good work. I'd only heard about two of the ribs." It'd felt fantastic to let his beast out on that guy. Sometimes his anger felt like a living creature inside him. It needed time out of its cage to stretch its legs and wreak its havoc.

Curly leveled him with a cold stare, but his own lips quirked.

He shrugged. "They call 'em bedroom games for a reason,

Prez. They shoulda kept that shit between their sheets and behind a closed door."

His prez grunted, which he'd take as an agreement and the sound of forgiveness. Until Curly said, "It fucking stops, Spec."

With a nod, Scott began to rise. "Got it." If only it were that simple. Maybe more time with the heavy bag would help pound some of the fucked-up feelings out of his head.

Curly speared him with a look full of disappointment. For the first time since they started talking, a bit of shame wormed its way under Scott's skin.

"I mean it. I know it ain't fair, but I've already got the cops sniffing at my asshole because of my past. Can't be giving them more reasons to be after us. You gotta get that temper under control. You're part of this brotherhood now, and your actions can affect all of us."

Fuck, when he put it like that...

Felt like disappointing his fellow Rangers, and it sucked.

"I got it, boss," he said with sincerity. "I won't be responsible for fucking shit up here." This was too important to him, to most of them. This was his family now. He wouldn't fail them as he'd failed Deke. Besides, he couldn't handle anything else to feel guilty about.

And fuck, now he was thinking about Deke. Goddammit, he'd made it nearly a full hour.

"All right. Get outta here." Curly waved him off as someone knocked on the door.

Scott pulled it open to find the mohawked and tatted Tracker smirking like an idiot. "The fuck's wrong with your face?" Scott asked. He reached out to wipe that grin off his brother's face, only to have his hand smacked away with a laugh.

"Someone here to see you, Spec," Tracker said, still grinning.

He frowned. To see him? Who the fuck did he know in Florida? None of the women he'd fucked around with would be darkening his door. A few said he was too intense, and another cried because he'd left her bed two seconds after coming. Sorry, but even one minute was too long to linger. Gave those clingy bitches ideas. He was too screwed up for anything more than a few hours of bedroom gymnastics, and he made that very clear upfront.

"Who the hell is it?"

"Said her name was Olivia." Tracker's grin grew.

"Olivia?" He shrugged. "Don't know who the hell that is. She's got the wrong guy. Tell her to fuck off."

"Nuh-uh. Do your own dirty work, man. And she specifically asked for Scott Hughes, so that's all you." He pressed his lips together and rocked back on his heels.

Scott rolled his eyes. "You're dying to say something else. What?"

The idiot was having way too much fun. His eyes practically danced. "She's a looker. All fancy and shit. Have a feeling she's the type who doesn't hear the word 'no' very often."

"Don't be a pussy and deal with it, Spec," Curly said without taking his attention from his computer.

"Fine." With a groan, Scott strode out of Curly's office. He had shit to do, and dealing with a deranged chick he'd fucked once upon a time wasn't on the list.

Lock pointed toward the bar where a woman stood with her back to him and ramrod straight. She wore a pale pink dress that looked like, shit, what was that? Silk? Who did he know with enough money for a dress like that? As she waited, she delectably lifted a leg and scratched the back of her calf with one foot. Scott at least knew enough about women to recognize the telltale red bottom of those heels as some designer they all flipped their shit for. At least, his sister always drooled over that nonsense. So did her friends.

He racked his brain but couldn't place the woman from her back or spectacular ass. Her hair gave him no hints either. Light brown and twisted in some classy knot, she could've been any brunette he'd met. Maybe he'd fucked her a decade ago? But why come here now? Maybe it was the bike. It seemed to attract more women than diamonds.

He cleared his throat. "You looking for Scott?" What had they said her name was? Olive? Alyssa?

The woman spun on those expensive four-inch heels. It might earn him a slap to the face, but Scott couldn't resist trailing his eyes up those long sexy stems. Damn, that dress fit her like a glove. Her shoulders were bare like her legs, revealing smooth, creamy skin. She wore a single strand of pearls around her neck. Nope, he'd never fucked her. A pearl clutcher? Not his style.

Hell no.

He continued his shameless inspection, taking a good look at her perky tits way too covered by the dress. She was much younger than he'd originally assumed. Her face was slender, her makeup flawless, and her eyes a gorgeous shade of green.

Air whooshed from his lungs as a ghost's gaze connected with his.

Impossible.

"The fuck is this?" he spat out, stumbling backward. A loud screech sounded as he backed into a table, dragging the legs across the concrete flooring.

"Hello, Scott," she said in a low, smoky tone. "I'm Olivia, though you probably heard me called Liv or Livy." She smiled, presenting a row of straight, gleaming teeth, and held out her hand, also perfect with pink manicured nails, a shade darker than her dress. "I've heard so much about you from D... uh..." She cleared her throat. "From Deke." Those two words came out in a whisper.

He stared at the hand as though it held an unpinned grenade. Images bombarded him from all angles.

Deke in basic training, sweating and filthy.

Deke, drunk off his ass the night he turned twenty-one.

Deke, saving him from a bullet by slamming him to the ground.

Deke, beaten, bloody, and tortured.

Deke, lifeless on the filthy ground. Dead.

Because of him.

Guilt pressed so hard on his chest, he couldn't draw in a breath.

"I... uh, I'm Deke's sister," she said, her forehead wrinkled. "Well, half-sister."

Of course, she seemed confused by his reaction. All her family had been told was that Deke was killed behind enemy lines by a terrorist. Nothing more. Lucky for them, they'd never know the details. Never know how Deke fought or how he suffered. They'd never know his best friend was the one who signed his death warrant.

PTSD. Survivor's guilt. Anger issues. Neat little labels the Army's psychologist pinned him with. Yeah, no fucking shit, he was angry. Those buzzwords did squat to scrub the memories from his brain. Same with all the bullshit tricks and techniques that hack had tried to teach him. It wasn't his fault she recommended pointless nonsense like journaling. Wasn't her fault a lobotomy would be the only way he'd ever scrub the horror of Deke's death from his nightmares.

"Are you okay?" Olivia asked when he did nothing more than glower at her. She glanced to the right, where Curly had stepped out of his office.

No, he wasn't fucking okay, and he wouldn't be okay until she got her swanky ass out of his clubhouse.

"I know who you are," he said, straightening as he advanced toward her. She needed to leave before he lost his shit.

Her eyes widened, but she held her ground. "Oh, good." She tried for a smile, but it wobbled.

Most men cowered under his glare, so he wasn't surprised this snowflake couldn't hang.

"I'm p-pleased Deke mentioned me. May I... um... may I have a word in private, please?"

So formal. So fucking stuffy. "You're Deke's half-sister." He tapped his chin, coming to a stop a few inches from her. She wasn't tiny, maybe five-foot-eight, but she had to lift her chin to see him at his six-two. "How did he describe you? Oh, right, the pampered princess living off your daddy's golden teat. Never had to work for shit. Never had to fight. Never abandoned by your family. Yeah, I know who you are, Olivia." He smirked. "Now get the fuck out of my clubhouse, princess."

He had to give her some credit, though he'd never admit it aloud, she only sputtered for a second before squaring her shoulders and affecting a haughty smile. "Excuse me?" she asked, her tone dripping with ice. "Who do you think you are to speak to me that way?"

He sprang forward, crowding her against the bar. Satisfaction flashed through him when her eyes flared. "I was Deke's best friend. The one who was there for him when your precious Daddy Moneybags kicked him the fuck out of his home. Was it fun being the only child? No competition for Daddy's attention. Or his money." He grunted. "Spoiled fucking brat," he said as he turned to walk away.

"Uh, Spec, maybe you should back off a bit."

"Stay the fuck out of this, Tracker."

Just the thought of her and everything she stood for disgusted him. So maybe Deke hadn't been nearly as harsh when he described his sister, but what was a best friend for if not to stand up when Deke couldn't. This princess had no idea what her brother endured after their father kicked him to the curb. He'd lived on the streets for months until meeting an Army recruiter in a food bank.

"My relationship with Deke was complicated, yes," she said, cold as fuck. "He called me a pampered princess?"

"Sure did." Kind of. He said she'd been raised as one, but he'd also admired her grit and determination to remain as grounded as possible as an adult.

"Well, he told me you were the best man he knew. That if something ever happened to him and I needed help, you'd be there, no questions asked."

Ouch.

"So," she continued. "Clearly, he was a shit judge of character."

He snorted out a laugh that quickly turned to a growl. No way would this woman get on his good side with a joke or a quip.

He whirled around and charged toward her.

"Spec!" Curly called.

He wasn't going to hit the bitch. Just get her to fucking leave.

"Get the hell out!" he screamed in her face.

Fear flashed in her eyes. Deke's eyes. Though it was only for a second, he took satisfaction in knowing he got to her.

"Get. Out," he said again in the measured tone he'd been told terrified anyone who heard it.

He'd be seeing those eyes in his nightmares tonight right alongside Deke's disgust at how Scott treated his sister. One more thing to torture the few hours of sleep his body granted.

"Fuck it." He was the one who needed to get out. Maybe a ride would clear his head and relax his body.

Though nothing could redeem his soul.

Chapter Three

Cold washed over Olivia. She was frigid to her bones.

If he'd slapped her, she wouldn't have been as stunned.

This was the man Deke called brother? This was the best friend he'd boasted saved his sanity after their father disowned him? The one he claimed women threw themselves at? This neanderthal in faded jeans and a too-tight T-shirt that made his muscles bulge like he was about to film a thirst trap. Well, he could save that shit for his OnlyFans site. She wasn't impressed, and she wasn't intimidated.

She wasn't attracted either.

Mostly.

Just because she hadn't saved a million people in the Army like he and Deke had didn't make her a lesser person.

Didn't make her a damn princess.

God, she hated that nickname. Her entire life, people called her a princess. First as a term of endearment, then as an insult.

It was part of the reason she'd started taking online classes with the goal of going to veterinarian school. At twenty-five, she was still incredibly young but already felt like she'd wasted so many years on fluff. Lance's infidelity shocked her out of her cushy existence and made her realize she'd been coasting along without contributing to society. Marrying rich and becoming a trophy wife was what was expected of someone like her—a woman raised with privilege, money, and an easy life. Looking at it now, she felt like such a fool. So she did what she always did when those strong emotions wanted to take over.

She acted as frigid as she felt. Her go-to shield to protect her from the judgment and criticism of others.

"Don't worry, I'm leaving," she said to the jerk's retreating form, forcing herself to sound superior. As though she were a queen—not a freaking princess—talking to a peon. Words were the only weapon she had against him, and like any cornered animal, she struck back. "If I'd known you were a dirty biker in a gang, I never would've wasted my time coming here. Good thing I've had my shots."

He mumbled something that sounded a lot like 'bitch' as he stormed outside.

What the hell was she supposed to do now?

Where could she go? She was tired, hungry, and very much done with sleeping in seedy motels. The drive from Chicago had taken days, and the decade and a half old Chrysler she'd traded in her BMW for didn't quite measure up as far as comfort and amenities. But Lance would never suspect she'd get a crappy car, so that's what she'd gone with because the texts she'd received before ditching her phone chilled her spine and made her wonder how on earth she'd ever spend a minute in Lance's presence, let alone loved the man. He'd threatened her with every vile act in the book and truly terrified her.

The door slammed behind Scott, making her flinch. Now that he'd left, a hush fell over the room. Olivia felt the weight of numerous judgmental eyes on her.

Men she'd just called dirty bikers. She swallowed a rising

lump of fear and kept her face as unaffected as possible. They stared at her with varying levels of disgust, and she gave it right back with a superior glare of her own.

They'd never know she trembled on the inside.

Wrinkling her nose as though she couldn't stand the smell any longer, she tossed her hair over her shoulder, then strutted toward the exit Scott had just disappeared through. Let them stare. They didn't need to know how broken she was beneath her expensive clothes.

With each step, her Louboutins clacked on the concrete floor like gunshots.

Hopefully, the noises weren't foreshadowing her fate if Lance found her. He'd made it perfectly clear he wanted to find her and make her life hell.

You'll never escape me, and I can't wait until we're back together.

She shivered. As she reached the door, a woman's voice yelled out, "Wait!"

"Christ. Brooke, not your business," one of the men called out.

Olivia turned as the woman she assumed was Brooke ran up to her. "Hi!" she said, slightly out of breath. "I'm Brooke. Curly's ol' lady."

Olivia guessed Brooke as older by fifteen years at least. Pretty in a natural way. In fact, she couldn't spot a stitch of makeup on Brooke's face. Who knew the last time she'd left her house without makeup? Probably when she was thirteen. Hell, she rarely had a naked face in the comfort of her own home. The mask of concealers and color gave her strength and confidence.

"Babe, stay out of it," the guy who'd come out of the office spoke. Must be Curly. But what was an ol' lady?

Brooke waved off the man with shoulder-length curly hair. "Don't mind him. He's growly, but he doesn't bite." The man snorted, and Brooke turned pink. "Anyway, let's talk outside where this nosy group can't spy on us."

"Thank you, but that's not necessary. I'm just going to go."

Brooke linked her arm through Olivia's as though they were long-time besties. "Then I'll walk you out."

As Brooke tugged her toward the door, one of the guys chuckled. "Looks like your woman's collecting two-legged strays now, Prez."

She frowned, but Brooke rolled her eyes. "Ignore them."

Together, they strode out into the hot Florida sun. Olivia had parked her car in the unpaved area beside a few huge motorcycles. Trudging through the dust and dirt again wasn't high on her list of fun activities. Her poor shoes.

"Let's walk a little."

"No, I—"

"Come on." This time it was more of an order than a suggestion. Brooke steered her around the side of the building. Olivia gritted her teeth as she wobbled along in the grass on her four-inch stilettos. Keeping her spikey heels from sinking into the ground gave her legs more of a workout than she'd had in ages.

Many chickens ran around, unaffected by their presence. If she stepped in chicken poop on top of everything else, she was going to flip her shit.

"Hope you don't mind dogs," Brooke said as a huge brown, tan, and black furry friend walked into view.

She gasped and locked out her knees to keep from throwing herself at the beautiful animal. "Love them," she whispered.

As a child, her father had two ferocious guard dogs she wasn't allowed near. They never came into the house and were cared for by a handler. "They're not pets, Olivia," he'd always said when she'd asked to play with them. "They'll take a man's arm off with one bite." That had terrified her but didn't destroy her love of animals. For a time. Throughout her entire childhood, she'd wanted to be a veterinarian and had never outgrown the dream. She was the kid who ran up to every dog she saw and begged her father for all manner of pets. He'd never permitted it. She'd given up on her dream of veterinarian school when her father basically forbade it.

Lance hadn't been much better. The man would rather die than have a stray animal hair find its way to one of his bespoke suits. He'd never flat-out told her not to go to veterinarian school, but when they talked and planned for their future, it always included her at his side in a supporting role rather than having her own show. She'd been starry-eyed enough to go along with it.

And then he stuck his dick in someone else. The start of her life going off the rails. Though now she was grateful for it because the idea of marrying him while being blind to the kind of man he really was chilled her to the bone.

"Well, Ray is the sweetest boy you'll ever meet. C'mere, buddy," Brooke called, and the dog immediately ran toward them with his enormous tongue lolling out.

Olivia laughed as she crouched down to greet the enormous German Shepard. All it took was one adorable dog to have her forgetting she'd worn heels. They sunk into the ground at the same time Ray reached her. His big face nudged her chest, sending her teetering backward.

"Shit!" Brooke yelled. "Ray, sit." Somehow, she managed to catch Olivia under her arm before she landed on her ass in the dirt. "Oh, my God, I'm so sorry."

The monstrous dog sat at her side with his fluffy tail thumping and his drippy tongue hanging, oblivious to the fact he'd nearly barreled her over.

Olivia chuckled. "No worries. My fault for trying to balance with these shoes." The nine-hundred-dollar shoes that she'd never get clean. Worth it for a few moments of furry distraction from her problems.

Brooke grimaced. "I really am sorry. You can meet him more formally later when you're dressed for the farm. "Ray, go play." He bounded off with a woof.

Dressed for the farm? What the hell did she have that would work on the farm? And later, she'd be back on the road, heading... somewhere.

Thankfully, the other woman didn't harp on the issue. But she did relink their arms and continue their stroll. Dressed in cutoff shorts, sneakers, and a fitted tank top, Brooke was much better prepared for tromping through Florida farmland than Olivia.

Since it seemed she was stuck making nice for a few moments, she asked, "Do you know Scott well?"

"Hmm... that's a tough question," Brooke said as she watched her dog run with the chickens. "I've known him for several months now, but I can't really say I *know* him. If that makes any sense."

Olivia nodded. She was similar in many ways. Letting people in could suck. After growing up in a superficial world and living with a fiancé she hated, she'd put up a wall and guarded it with designer clothes, expensive makeup, and bitchy quips.

"I know he was in the Army. Special Operations, which is why the guys here call him Spec." Brooke smiled. "I'm guessing something traumatic happened to him there, but he never speaks of it."

Spec. Huh, her brother would've liked that nickname. "Yes, he served with my half-brother. They were best friends for about twenty years."

Brooke's expression betrayed her surprise. "But you've never met him?"

She shook her head. "No. My relationship with my brother was... complicated." Not knowing him well would always be her biggest regret.

"Ahh, one word that says so much."

That had Olivia smiling. Usually, she found herself standoffish with new people, but something about Brooke drew her in. Maybe it was the open smile or the way she didn't seem to judge despite Scott's obvious hatred of her. Regardless, she allowed herself to relax—a bit.

"Is your brother here too?" Brooke asked.

And she tensed up again.

"No. He…" She cleared her throat as sadness swamped her. So many years had been wasted on family nonsense. Now she'd never get to fully know the brother she'd been forbidden to speak to as a child. "He was killed in action almost two years ago."

Brooke stopped dead in her tracks. "Fuck. I'm so sorry to hear that." Then she cocked her head. "It explains a few things."

"Like?"

"Oh, well, Spec seems to be struggling with some demons," Brooke said without elaborating further.

Demons?

Because of the Army? Sadness over Deke's death? Relationship troubles? Family drama? While she was dying to push, Brooke's tone didn't invite further discussion on the topic.

"We're here," Brook said with a smile as they stopped in front of what looked like an enormous and recently renovated barn.

"Oh, you have horses?" She'd taken riding lessons for years as a kid and loved horses as much as she loved all animals.

Laughing, Brooke said, "No, there aren't any horses there. Unless you wanna consider Spec a stallion." She winked. "None of us have any horse experience. This isn't used as a barn anymore. We tore down the old structure and built this.

It's twice as big and holds four studio apartments for future club members or prospects."

"Oh." And she'd brought Olivia there because? It didn't matter. The longer she talked to Brooke, the more she could put off figuring out the rest of her life now that her plan to seek asylum with Scott had blown up in her face.

"Right now, Spec is the only person living here. He's on the second floor, apartment on the right." She pulled the door open for Olivia, who walked into the building to find a long staircase directly in front of her and a hallway to its right. "Follow me."

She slowed. Were they going to Scott's apartment? After the way he'd screamed at her, that seemed like an unwise idea.

"Did you come to meet Spec because you wanted to talk about your brother?"

She got the sense Brooke was a sort of mother hen around here. She seemed protective of the men. While it was Olivia's instinct to tell her to mind her own business, she had a feeling she'd get the door slammed and locked tight if she pissed off Brooke, so she had to give her something. "Sort of. I... uh... had a lot of complicated stuff going on at home and needed a break." Understatement of the century. "I was hoping to lay low for a while and thought maybe I could get to know Scott a bit." She huffed. "Clearly, that didn't work."

"There's that word 'complicated' again," Brook said, but it wasn't spoken with malice or judgment.

"Right."

"Here we go," Brooke said when they reached the top of the stairs. She turned left, pulled a key out of her pocket, and opened the door. "After you."

Frowning, Olivia stepped into the undecorated studio apartment. It was small, tiny really, with an itty-bitty kitchen, a queen-size bed, a bathroom to the right, and a bite-size living area. The walls were bare, and the bed was naked. Scott didn't live there. Or if he did, he'd just moved in that morning.

"What's this?" she asked as she turned to Brooke.

"A place you can stay."

"What?" She turned back to the room. If she'd said the Pope lived there, Olivia wouldn't have been more stunned. The idea of it appealed to her on a bone-deep level. No more crappy hotels. No more exhaustive running. A place to stop and catch her breath. At least for a few days. Hell, her across-the-hall neighbor would be a former Army Ranger. How much safer could a girl get. "I... why would you offer me this?"

"Because it's what she does," a male voice said.

Olivia whipped around to find the curly-haired man snaking his arm around Brooke's waist. He kissed her cheek, then her jaw, then her neck.

Olivia averted her eyes as Brooke let out a breathy sigh.

"Brooke is the queen of rescuing wounded strays."

His words had her spine snapping straight. "I'm not a stray. And I'm definitely not wounded," she snapped. "I have money." She was in a sticky situation but not some damsel in distress.

He just raised an eyebrow as if to say, "Aren't you?"

"I'm not," she reaffirmed.

"Olivia, this is Curly," Brooke said as if sensing someone needed to step in. "He's the club's president and my ol' man."

"Old man?" Her forehead scrunched. Like her father?

"Just means we're together," Brooke said, waving it away. "I was offering Olivia a place to crash for a while."

"I heard," Curly said with amusement lacing his voice.

"She looks like she could use a place to crash for a bit. You cool with that?" Brooke asked, looking up at the handsome, rugged man.

His gaze bore into Olivia's. She challenged him with a raised eyebrow and proud stare as if to say she didn't give a shit either way, while inside she was praying he allowed her to stay. It'd solve the problem of where she'd lay her head for the next few nights, and something about having big tough bikers all around made her feel safer than she had when sleeping in a hotel by herself.

As the seconds ticked by, the urge to squirm under his intense assessment became unbearable. Just as she was about to ask if he'd rather take a photo, he spoke.

"You can stay tonight."

"Curly, that's not long enough," Brooke spoke to him as though he wasn't scary as hell.

He held up a hand. "You can stay tonight even if Scott pitches a fit." Glancing down at his woman, he continued. "Any more than that, she's gotta clear it with him, babe. Won't have him feeling uncomfortable in his own home."

"I'll take care of it," Brooke said, beaming up at Curly.

Well, that was surprisingly fair. It would only buy her one night of reprieve, but she'd take it. It was more than she had when she arrived. Knowing where she'd sleep and that it wasn't a sketchy roadside motel gave her tremendous relief. "Thank you," she said, swallowing some of that pride she'd been told she had too much of.

All part of her act.

Curly nodded.

"Don't worry, Olivia. I got this. I'll totally get Scott on board," Brook added with a quick kiss for her man.

Chuckling, he gripped Brooke's chin between his thumb and forefinger, tilting her head up before saying, "I have no doubt you will." Then he kissed her long and slow.

That was a hot kiss. She'd been engaged and never kissed like that. Her kisses with Lance were always more proper.

Not as unrestrained. But watching them made her shiver and long for something she'd never experienced and didn't fully understand.

Whew. Was it the Florida air, or had the temperature jumped about ten degrees?

"You remind me of myself," Brooke said after Curly left her standing there slightly wobbly. "When I first arrived in Florida, I also left a *complicated* situation behind, and I didn't know anyone here. It can be hard." She frowned and shook her head as though plagued by unpleasant memories. "It's why I assumed you could use a place to crash for a bit."

Being understood felt nice. Something about Brooke set her at ease and made her want to become friends. Before Olivia had a chance to respond, Brooke was smiling again.

"Let's get your stuff, and I'll give you the grand tour."

Feeling like Dorothy in OZ, Olivia followed Brooke over the dirt and crispy grass to the junky car she'd traded her baby in for.

She'd left behind a lot of things she'd loved—all material possessions that didn't matter.

What did matter was that she had a clean, safe place to lay her head for the night. She'd use the quiet comfort to come up with a plan for tomorrow. Scott wanted nothing to do with her, so she'd have to find a way to take care of her problems herself.

Chapter Four

Scott downed his fourth shot of whisky in as many minutes. Or was it the fifth?

Didn't matter. All he had to do when he finished blurring his mind was stumble to the barn and up the stairs. Hell, he could crawl if he got too shitfaced.

Either way, dragging his drunk ass across the farm was preferable to having those damn familiar eyes scorching his brain for the entire night.

Deke hadn't known his half-sister well. She'd been a toddler when their father disowned Deke for joining the Army and refusing to join the family's large corporate business. Olivia's childhood had been spent with an entire set of silver flatware in her mouth while Deke had been crawling through the sand defending his country. Deke wanted to form a relationship with his sister, but their father had filled her head with poison where Deke was concerned. When she'd aged enough to make her own decisions, the siblings had begun to repair their relationship. No one could call them close, but Deke being the honorable motherfucker he'd been, would've gone fucking AWOL if Olivia needed his help. No questions asked.

Fortunately, spoiled princesses rarely wanted for anything, especially someone to help them escape their cushy life of luxury.

Fuck, that dress alone probably cost more than he and Deke had made in a week their entire military careers.

He didn't have a damn thing to feel guilty about, sending her starchy ass away. What the hell had she been thinking showing up there in the first place, strutting into an MC clubhouse like she belonged there, then turning up that prissy nose at what she found?

And he'd have had no choice but to kick his brothers' assess if they'd pounced on her. He owed Deke that much and a million times more.

Don't you owe it to him to have a civil conversation with his sister?

Probably. And it was just one more thing to add to the guilt pile. He couldn't be around her without the weight of Deke's death grinding him to dust. So, Olivia could sashay her Botoxed face and her thousand-dollar shoes right back to Daddy's mansion.

"Another," he said, tapping the bar. A pleasant buzz hummed through his veins, but not nearly enough to obliterate the sight of Olivia.

Did she have to be so fucking hot? Christ, he'd popped a boner for his best friend's little sister. Sure, she was one hundred percent grown woman, but still. Too fucking messy.

"You sure?" JT, a hang-around hoping to prospect, asked. The kid couldn't be more than twenty-three. Scott felt even more ancient than the aches and pains he had courtesy of the US Army.

"Yes, I'm fucking sure. I'm also sure you won't make it as far as a prospect if you question shit I tell you to do." Sure, he'd been lucky as an original member of the chapter to avoid the misery of prospecting, but he'd spent plenty of time licking boots and kissing asses in his years of military service. He'd paid his dues.

The kid lifted his scrawny arms in surrender. "Sorry, Spec. My bad. Here, just take the bottle." He slid the bottle of whisky across the bartop. It stopped directly in front of Scott.

He'd swig right from the bottle if he were in his apartment, but Curly already had it in for him. Shouldn't piss off the club by putting his mouth all over their booze.

He poured, then swallowed another shot. Damn, that burn was epic—one of his favorite feelings. Meant numbness wasn't far behind.

"Well, well, well, if it isn't the stupidest member of our club." Tracker came up behind him, slapping a heavy hand on Scott's shoulder before sitting next to him. "You gonna share that, or should I just get you a straw?"

A straw wasn't the worst idea. With a grunt, he slid the bottle to Tracker as a chuckling JT delivered a shot glass.

"Who the fuck said you could laugh?" Tracker barked.

JT's eyes flared wide. "Uh, sorry, man. I just... it was funny."

"Eh, I'm bustin' your balls," Tracker said with a laugh. He filled the shot glass, sucked it back, then repeated the action. "Ahh, that's much better." He turned Scott's way and pointed a tattooed finger at him. "As I was saying, you're stupid."

"Assuming you're gonna tell me why." Scott poured another shot. Seventh, maybe? He didn't know why he was counting. Maybe the fact he could still count meant he hadn't had enough to drink.

"Oh, I sure am. You had one fine piece of expensive ass strut in here looking for you, and you didn't even give her a chance to turn down a fucking before you tossed her out on said ass. And in case you were too dumb to notice, it was a very fine ass, brother."

Of course, he'd noticed. He wasn't blind. Or dickless. But it didn't matter how hot her ass was. Or how lush those tits had been. Or how she wasn't a stick figure but had some mouthwatering curves. None of that mattered. She was his best friend's little sister, therefore off-limits no matter how many plastic surgeons had made her look that damn tasty. Except despite her millions of dollars, he suspected every one of those curves was natural.

"More to life than ass, brother." He poured another shot.

"Well, duh, there's tits and pussy." Tracker laughed. "Don't worry, I noticed those too. Well, the tits, at least. Mmm." He kissed his fingers. "Chef's kiss."

Scott ground his molars together. "Stop fucking talking about her like that. She was my goddamn best friend's little sister. And I meant there's more to life than fucking."

With a snort, Tracker grabbed the bottle and poured himself another shot. "Eh, not sure I agree with you there, brother. That's the kinda thing a guy says when he hasn't gotten laid in so long, he forgets what to do with his dick."

After polishing off another shot, Scott glared at his friend. Tracker's smirking face swam before his eyes. He was a cool guy—animated, pierced, inked, personable—the kind of guy who let shit roll off his back. Someone Scott could see becoming a damn good friend if he was in the market for that kind of thing.

Which he was not.

Considering he got his last friend killed.

Fuck. What the hell was wrong with this weak-ass whisky?

He downed another shot and took the bait. Better than talking about Olivia. "Fucked that waitress from Buck's not long ago." God, it had to have been three months by now. Pathetic.

Tracker frowned. "Jenny?"

"Fuck if I know." He'd known her name at one point. "Good lips. Sucked a mean dick."

"Yep. That's Jenny."

He grunted, not caring in the least that Tracker had also had her mouth on his dick. Maybe the alcohol was kicking in.

Finally.

Ty, Curly's cousin, and the MC's VP, sauntered up to the bar and dropped his ass on the other side of Scott. His shaggy hair needed a trim two months ago. The guy was getting downright scruffy. Ty didn't give a shit about it, though. He was about as low maintenance as they came. "JT, get me a beer. What are you hens clucking about?"

"Last time Spec got laid," Tracker quipped.

Ty accepted the beer from the hangaround. "What's it been three, four years? Sucks, buddy, but not everyone's blessed with a monster cock like me. Can't keep the honeys away for shit."

Tracker let out a boisterous laugh, slapping the bar. "Honeys? What year is this? Nineteen sixty?"

Even Scott laughed at that one. Yep, the booze was doing its job. Pretty much the only time he laughed these days was when his blood-alcohol level exceeded the legal limit.

They bullshitted for a few minutes before Tracker went off to text his next conquest. Scott stayed at the bar with Ty, who asked, "You okay, brother?"

"Dandy."

As Ty grunted his disbelief, Lock and Pulse burst into the clubhouse with Jinx trailing behind. That huge fucker worked for Ty and was the only one who'd been absent that afternoon when Scott lost his shit on Olivia.

"I'm fucking thirsty!" Jinx shouted. "JT, get me some vodka."

Pulse wandered over. "Nice thing you did, Spec," he said, clapping Scott on the shoulder.

"The fuck you talking about? I don't do nice shit."

Pulse was a nurse. He was the only one of them who'd

been a little wishy-washy about patching with the club. He was an intense guy. Most serious of the bunch. Probably the smartest too. They'd already needed his medical experience on more than one occasion.

And not just to mend guys Scott had beaten up, though there had been one or two of those.

Whatever, they'd all deserved it and more.

Chuckling, Pulse said, "I'm talking about the fancy lady. How you let her stay here."

An icy wave of rage crested over Scott in an instant. He shoved away from the bar and got in Pulse's face. The metal stool clamored to the ground, but he barely registered the loud clatter. "What the fuck are you talking about?"

Pulse lifted his hands and took a step back. "Jesus, brother, chill... not looking to piss you off. I'm talking about that woman who came to see you. Just glad you worked your shit out enough to let her stay."

"Let her stay?" The ice in his veins melted, replaced by boiling hot fury.

Pulse's gaze shifted back and forth between Ty, who'd risen from his stool, and Lock, who was approaching from the side. He was another one who stayed on the quieter side.

"Uh, she's crashing in the apartment across from you." Pulse's forehead wrinkled. "Did you not know?"

"What?" He exploded forward, shoving Pulse into the nearest table. She was in the apartment across from him? What the hell? Now he'd have to see her every day? To see Deke's eyes and be reminded of his failures even more than usual. Fuck, no. He'd rather die. He clenched his fist. One punch to Pulse's mouth would end the garbage spewing from it.

"What the fuck, man?" Jinx yelled as he and Ty grabbed Scott's arms and yanked him back. Lock jumped in the middle, holding a hand out to ward him away.

With the six-foot-six behemoth, Jinx, holding him back, Scott had no chance of smacking the shit out of Pulse. "He's fucking messing with me, and it's bullshit," he shouted, pointing a finger in Jinx's face.

"So you're gonna beat his ass?" Ty yelled. He and Jinx muscled him away from a furious Pulse. "You're wasted and need to simmer the hell down."

"You're goddamn right I'm gonna beat his ass." Scott lunged but couldn't escape the hold his brothers had on him. "Tell me you're fucking lying." How the hell was he supposed to function with Deke's little sister walking around the compound, reminding him of the worst moments of his life every day.

"Enough!" Curly roared into the mayhem. The room quieted as they all looked toward the entrance, where Curly stood with Brooke and none other than Olivia.

For fuck's sake.

He clenched his jaw. Why the fuck hadn't she left? And why was she so fucking pretty, standing there in that ridiculous dress with those long sexy legs and his favorite kind of tits—not too big, not too small, very perfect for his hands. Through the alcohol and even his dislike for her, his dick twitched.

Damn her.

Curly looked ready to rip his head off, probably for making Brooke frown so hard. A flash of humiliation crossed Olivia's face before she had a chance to school it.

He stumbled forward, ready to rip into her as Ty yanked him back. "Don't you fucking dare," he whispered. "Trust me when I say you don't want to see the prez truly pissed. He didn't do the crime, but he still spent thirteen years behind bars. Curly's no one's fool and can fight dirtier than all of us combined, Spec."

"Fuck this," he spat out as he wrenched out of Ty's hold.

Just as he was about to get the hell out of there, Brooke shouted.

"Hey! Knock it the hell off."

"You know," Olivia said to Brooke, gazing around the room with a pinched expression as though the place were covered in shit. Her voice was all throaty like people got when they were turned on. Except she seemed to speak that way all the time. "I appreciate you inviting me to hang out, but this isn't exactly my scene."

It amazed him how she could convey so much revulsion in one sentence. Her arrogantly wrinkled nose and the disgust in her tone were more obvious than if she'd worn a shirt that said, 'You're Beneath Me.' God, he hated women like her. Ones who thought they were better than everyone because they'd been born to parents with fat wallets and never struggled a day in their lives.

She gave Brooke a quick hug. "I'm going to turn in so I can get an early start out of here tomorrow."

Oh, thank fuck she planned to leave in the morning. One night he could handle. He'd get blackout drunk and pass out on a bunk there in the clubhouse. Eliminate any chance of running into her at his apartment.

"Get your shit together," Ty whispered in his ear. "Curly was in a fucked-up club before. One where the members turned on each other. Guarantee he won't put up with it this time."

He turned and stumbled his way back to the bar, where he immediately poured another shot. Over the next few minutes, people from around town began to file in. Women mostly, looking to bag a biker for the night or maybe even a permanent spot on the back of a motorcycle.

Everyone gave Scott a wide berth, which was how he preferred it. Sitting alone and drinking himself stupid worked fine for him. Or it did until Brooke sidled up next to him and sat her meddling ass down.

Fuck.

He peered over his shoulder to find a slightly blurry Curly hovering in the doorway of his office with folded arms and a glare that said, "You so much as make my woman frown, and I'll hang your nuts from the ceiling."

"Why?" he asked before she had a chance to tell him what an asshole he was.

She pursed her glossy lips. "Because I think she needed it."

He snorted. "She doesn't need shit. You got any idea how much money her family has?"

With a shrug, she said. "I didn't ask. I just got a sense she's going through some heavy stuff, and she needs a place to take refuge for a while."

"Heavy stuff," he said with a chuckle. What a joke. He'd been through heavy stuff. Deke had gone through heavy stuff. Olivia lived a life of privilege. "What? You think Daddy took her black card away?"

"No, I don't," Brooke said in a chastising voice that might have humbled him had he not consumed half a bottle of booze already.

"She's not one of your dogs, Brooke. You can't give her some treats, scratch her ears, and earn her loyalty." He stared at his empty glass. Speaking of drinking, where the hell had JT run off to?

"Gee, Spec, thanks for that. I was really hoping she and Ray would become besties." She huffed. "I'm not a fool, and I don't like the implication that I'm being taken for one. I saw myself in her and did what I wish someone would've done for me when I first got here. Olivia said she had some complicated stuff going on and needed to get away."

"Of course, she did." Why couldn't she have chosen any other location in the entire world to *get away* to? "Complicated like her boyfriend only owns one private jet?"

"Damn, you can be cold." With a frown, Brooke shook her head as though extremely disappointed in him. Deke would probably have done the same.

Join the club, sweetheart.

This was the least of his sins.

"Just so you know, Curly agreed she was more than welcome to stay tonight, but you'd have to agree for her to stick around longer."

"Well, I don't agree with that." Problem solved.

Brooke set her beer bottle down then spun on her stool until she fully faced him. He stared straight ahead. No way in hell would she guilt him into letting Olivia stay.

No. Way.

"She also told me you were her brother's best friend."

Great.

"That you served together, and he died overseas."

Fuck.

"And that he said if she ever needed anything and he wasn't around, she could turn to you, and you'd help her. You'd do it because you loved him like a brother." Her voice softened. "I imagine you'd have expected the same from him if your sister needed help."

Well, motherfucking fuck. The woman didn't play fair. Chloe's face drifted before his field of vision. Yeah, he'd have wanted Deke to help her if the tables were turned. And Deke would've done it too. Without a second thought.

JT came by and poured more whisky into his shot glass. He glanced between him and Brooke before backing away with wide eyes.

Scott turned his head to find Brooke wearing a wide, victorious grin. She knew she had him by the balls. His ingrained sense of honor and duty to his fallen friend wouldn't let him refuse her.

He stared at the full shot glass in his hand. His stomach

roiled with a mix of guilt, shame, and agony. Olivia would be there every day for who knew how the hell long. Every morning he'd leave his apartment knowing Deke's sister slept behind one thin wall. The woman who'd never get to fully know her brother because Scott hadn't saved him. Had her heart broken when she'd learned of his death? Had he broken her heart with his weakness and inability to keep Deke alive?

He'd joined the MC hoping a new brotherhood would give him a sense of purpose and something to think about besides how he failed his best friend. But his past caught up with him, and now he'd entered hell.

After tossing the shot back, he stood. "Just keep her the hell away from me."

Without another word, he stormed through the clubhouse to a back room that had been converted into a bunk room for guests. As of now, the only people who'd used it were visiting club members from their mother charter in Tennessee. The bunks didn't have sheets or blankets currently. Brooke probably knew where he could find some, but then he'd have to face her again.

With a growl, he pitched face-first onto a bed and prayed for the quiet peace of oblivion to take over.

He could escape Olivia in his dreams but not Deke.

Deke haunted him day and night.

Chapter Five

"You're serious, aren't you?" Brooke asked. She stopped walking and grabbed Olivia's arm. Her ponytail hung over her shoulder where it landed after she'd whipped her head around violently. "You've never been to a Target?"

With a shrug, Olivia shook her head. "Nope. Not once."

The other woman's mouth made a perfect O shape. "Oh, my God, how have you survived this long? What are you, twenty-three?"

Chuckling, Olivia began walking toward the store with the giant red bullseye again. "Twenty-five. And apparently, I've been missing out."

"Well, maybe not. I get the sneaking suspicion Target is below your budget. Based on your outfits, I'd guess you don't shop at many big-box stores."

She glanced down at her outfit with a frown. She'd paired a cream sleeveless silk blouse with a flouncy pink miniskirt and her favorite Jimmy Choo sandals. Nothing about today's clothes screamed fancy or over-the-top. She'd thought it was the perfect choice for a low-key shopping trip. "What's wrong with my outfit? You said to dress casually."

"Nothing," Brooke was quick to say with a soft smile.

"Nothing is wrong with it. Your clothes are gorgeous. Beyond gorgeous. Just not what we're used to around the club," she said, gesturing to her cutoff shorts, fitted cotton tank, and thin flip-flops. "Day-to-day, we're a little more accustomed to comfort than luxury. The guys' idea of high-end fashion is a T-shirt without holes and fifteen-year-old jeans." She gave a wry smile. "I'm not too different myself."

"Oh. Well, I hope this is okay." She never, *never* left the house without a coordinated outfit and styled hair. Hell, she never left her bathroom in the morning without a fully made-up face. Lance had only ever seen her barefaced in the dark. And you wouldn't catch her in a pair of sweatpants unless they were designer, and even then, sightings were rare. Looking put-together and polished gave her a sense of confidence she couldn't imagine having with a naked face or wearing scrubby clothes. Not that Brooke looked like a scrub. She pulled off the shorts and tank well, looking comfortable and gorgeous in the hot Florida sun.

"Of course, it's okay! You do you. Wear whatever the hell you want." Brooke nudged her with her elbow. "I can't promise the guys won't stare. They're a bunch of degenerates, but no one really cares."

They laughed together as they reached the store. "They do seem a little, uh, rough around the edges." Then again, she didn't know a person outside her social circle who didn't own a Porsche, let alone who rode a motorcycle and wore chains. And that one guy with the mohawk? Well, he also had a pierced lip, septum, ear gauges, and she'd probably missed a few other holes. It'd been near impossible to keep from staring at him. Not because she objected to his look but because it fascinated her like a unique animal at the zoo would capture her attention—unfamiliar and intriguing.

"They are that, but they're great." The glowing grin on Brooke's face spoke to her love of the men in the MC. "Loyal, protective, fun. Hot." She winked. "The club is new, but the guys became a family super-fast. I think they all needed that sense of brotherhood for their own reasons."

What were Scott's reasons? Didn't he already have a family with a few siblings? Deke had mentioned at least one sister. Why would Scott seek out this group of, well, criminals, technically? Shaking her head, she shoved those thoughts aside. Scott's motivations weren't any of her business.

"Thank you for this," she said with sincerity. "You didn't need to come shopping with me today, but I appreciate the company. I can't imagine how you convinced Scott to let me stay, but I'm grateful. I can't go... I mean, I'm not ready to go back home just yet."

Or ever. But she didn't want to get Brooke involved in her real problems. She just needed a few days to figure out where to go next and how to handle Lance.

Brooke grabbed a cart and turned left as though she knew the store's layout by heart. All Olivia could do was follow along in awe. This store seemed to have everything—office supplies on one side, feminine hygiene products on the other, and gardening supplies on the other end of the building.

"My pleasure." Brooke grabbed a candle off a shelf and took a whiff. "Ohh, no, eww. Smells too much like a soap my grandma used to use." She set it back down with a dramatic shudder. "And don't give up on Scott. He's a good man. I think he's just seen too much in his life. It's hardened him. I'm still trying to crack my way past his shell. I think Curly feels the same way."

Being a Ranger for over a decade? Yeah, he'd for sure seen and done a lot. But Deke had been by his side through all of it and hadn't acted like a dick. Not that she'd been very close with her half-brother, but he'd always treated her with kindness at the very least. Even when she'd believed all the horrible lies their father had said about him.

"Let me guess, Scott asked you to keep me away from him as much as possible?"

"What? No, definitely no. Nope, not at all." Brooke's face colored, and she shook her head with too much force. "That's silly."

Olivia snorted. "You're a terrible liar."

Linking their arms as she'd done the previous night, Brook tugged her toward a sign hanging from the ceiling that read, 'Kitchen and Dining.' "Enough serious talk. Let's get you some supplies."

Twenty minutes and much help from Brooke later, Olivia had most of what she needed to survive a few weeks in the studio apartment if she ended up staying that long. She wasn't convinced it would be wise but hoped it could work. Lance would never think to look in a place like the club. He'd never known about Scott and wouldn't expect Olivia to surround herself with bikers if the world was coming to an end and they were the only ones around to take her in.

She bought the basics—towels, toiletries, some simple plates, and flatware. This Target place really was a one-stop haven. She couldn't believe how easy it'd been to get everything on her list. Nor could she believe she now owned plates made from something called melamine that could be dropped on the floor without shattering.

She was trying, really trying not to come across as the spoiled princess so many people accused her of being. She didn't think she was better than anyone here. In fact, she often had low self-esteem from growing up under her father's hyper-critical eye and moving right in with a fiancé who was as superficial as they came. Perfection in her looks and actions had been demanded from both men. Twenty-five years of living with very wealthy men had made her who she was. Money and privilege were all she knew. She was trying to fit in but felt like a square peg trying to fit in a round hole.

Somehow, she managed to keep her flabbergasted reactions in her head and act like this shopping excursion was normal for her.

Which it wasn't. She and her friends shopped at boutiques and designer stores where appointments were required, and a liaison assisted them with whatever they needed. Shopping trips usually consisted of champagne in the dressing room, and she sure as hell had never seen panties come in a pack of three for the cost of a venti Frappuccino.

By the time they reached the bedding, Olivia's head was spinning, and she felt so out of her element, she could've cried. Toilet brushes, mops, squeegees? Her face burned with shame as Brooke recommended items Olivia had never touched, let alone used. At home, their housekeeping staff kept a rigid cleaning schedule, and if anything needed an extra shine or polish, Olivia only had to mention it once, and magically, the space was sparkling clean the next time she entered.

It was then the reality of her situation truly set in. She was alone—no family, no fiancé, no staff, no friends—no one to take care of her but herself. And she'd never done it on her own before. Thankfully, her grandmother had left a trust fund in her name alone, so she had money but no direction or purpose or clue where to start. What good was money if she had nothing or no one else? She'd landed among a very tight-knit group of men who'd all hate her once Scott got done with them.

And she was terrified.

But was she more afraid of the big bad world than she was of her ex-fiancé?

That was the question. Because she could return home, cast herself at Lance's feet, and promise to keep her mouth shut. She could vow to play the obedient, dutiful trophy wife who turned a blind eye to her husband's heinous extracurriculars.

She could have the security of an enormous house, staff, and millions of dollars at her disposal. This shopping trip would be a one-off, Scott's scorn could be forgotten along with Brooke's kindness, and she could be comfortable once again.

Couldn't she?

A memory of the drugged woman struggling against Olivia's fiancé flashed through her mind, making her stomach sour.

No. She couldn't return. Not if she wanted to look at herself in the mirror ever again.

So, she had to put on her big girl panties—she had two packs now—and learn how to live in the real world so she'd never again find herself entangled or reliant on a man who turned out to be a monster.

"Olivia?" Brooke asked in a soft tone. "You okay? You've been staring at those sheets for about three minutes."

She blinked. "Oh, sorry." Her instinct to snap with some comment about the low quality of the bed linens became strong, but she resisted. Brooke had been nothing but compassionate, and it wasn't her fault Olivia's life was a hot mess. She sighed. Maybe she should try for honesty instead of a snippy comment to mask her anxiety. "I'm a little overwhelmed, to be honest."

"Okay, here's what we're gonna do," Brooke said. She grabbed the nearest sheet set and tossed it in the cart. "Let's check out and hit up a nearby coffee shop for a break. Sound good?"

As her shoulders unwound, Olivia realized how tense she'd been. A break would be fantastic. A real break where she could forget her stress would be even better, but she'd take a coffee and a breather. "Sounds perfect. Thank you, Brooke."

"My pleasure." She winked. "Let's get moving."

After paying for a mountain of supplies that should last

her a solid few weeks, they walked to a small coffee shop in the same strip mall as Target. Armed with giant iced coffees and two-thousand-calorie muffins, they strode across the busy street to a picturesque park.

"Oh, this is peaceful," Olivia said as she sat on the warm park bench.

"I know. I love it here. Ray does too."

Ducks swam in a still pond, the sun heated her skin, and joggers ran by every so often. Olivia closed her eyes and soaked in the serene environment. For the first time since she left her home, she was able to take a full breath. She was safe and had a place to sleep for the foreseeable future. All she needed to do now was figure out what to do next.

One step at a time. Today's step had been getting necessities.

Piece of cake.

They sipped their drinks in silence for a few moments. Just as Olivia was about to dive into her cinnamon streusel muffin, Brooke stiffened and swore under her breath.

"You okay?" Olivia asked instead of sinking her teeth into her treat.

She followed Brooke's troubled gaze to find two men in leather vests similar to the ones Scott and Curly wore heading their way.

"Don't look at him," Brooke said as she turned to Olivia.

"What? Why? Isn't he part of the club?"

"No, he's not. Don't draw attention to us."

Olivia's heart rate climbed as she averted her gaze to the ducks in the pond. Tension radiated off Brooke, but she stayed outwardly calm.

From the corner of her eye, Olivia noticed one of the men staring their way. "I think it's too late," she whispered. "He noticed us. He's coming this way."

"Shit," Brooke said. "Let's go." She started to stand, but the man reached them before her butt lifted off the bench.

"Where you ladies running off to? Don't leave yet." A greasy-nailed hand landed on Brooke's shoulder, forcing her to remain seated.

She sent Olivia a worried side-eye that had a tremor of unease running down her spine.

An average-size man with shoulder-length blond hair and a matching goatee sat next to Brooke. He flashed a smile, showing a few gaps in his teeth. The motorcycle vest he wore had various patches but nothing to indicate involvement in a club like Scott's Handlers' patches had.

"Get the fuck away from me," Brooke said with force.

Olivia swallowed and straightened her spine. Is this what happened to people who hung around motorcycle clubs? Though the instinct to run had her leg muscles twitching, she'd never abandon Brooke. Plus, she could strut with the best of them in her heeled sandals, but a sprint was a different story. With as inconspicuous movements as she could muster, she slid her hand into her purse for her phone. Too bad she didn't have Curly's number. Or anyone's. Hell, she'd call Scott at this point.

The bench creaked as another man joined, this time sitting next to her. Immediately, the scent of deli meat and weed assaulted her nose, causing her to pull away reflexively. He draped an arm across her shoulders, keeping her close.

"Damn, Brooke, you got yourself a fancy friend here." He stuck his nose in her hair. "Smells fancy too."

Her stomach roiled. "Excuse me!" Olivia jerked her head. "That's disgusting." Who the hell did this neanderthal think he was?

He laughed hard, making his round face jiggle. He had a good fifty pounds on his friend. Most of it seemed to have landed in his gut which tested the strength of his T-shirt's fibers and parted his vest. His stomach molded to Olivia's side, soft and slightly damp.

"Could you back up?" she asked, wrinkling her nose. "I don't make a habit of getting close to men who can't be bothered to bathe or brush their teeth."

"Seriously," Brooke said with much less superiority and far more annoyance in her tone. "Back. The. Fuck. Up."

The man next to Brooke laughed. "You hear that, Dante? The fancy bitch thinks you smell like pig shit."

"Fuck you, Rag."

Rag? What kind of a name was Rag?

"How's Curly?" Rag asked Brooke as he brushed her hair behind her ear.

"Don't," she barked, lifting a hand to swat him.

He caught her wrist and must have been holding it too tight because Brooke flinched and shifted beside her.

"Nuh-uh," he said with a smirk. "Answer the question."

"Curly's fine," she said through clenched teeth.

"He's on his way here," Olivia rushed to add.

He wasn't, but if it'd get these creepers to leave, she'd tell them an alligator was about to crawl out of her ass. They couldn't be in any real danger, could they? It was broad daylight! All she had to do was scream, and someone would come running, right?

"And who are you, fancy bitch?" Rag asked, looking her up and down like she was for sale.

"None of your fucking business," she snapped. Whoops, there went her snooty but calm façade.

Brooke shot her a wide-eyed look as Rag laughed. When he finished finding her funny, he nodded at Dante, who grabbed her by the throat.

She made a choking sound as her air supply disappeared. Oh shit. She hadn't thought they'd do anything. She'd been dead wrong. Flashes of the helpless woman struggling in vain against Lance flashed through her mind. Would she suffer the same fate? Be violated by a man she couldn't fight off.

If only she could scream.

What the hell? Did no one notice what was happening to them, or were people so apathetic they'd had no plans to help?

"Hey!" Brooke reached for Dante's arm, but Rag tsked. "Don't fucking do it. Let's try this again, fancy bitch," Rag said as her eyes began to water. "What's your name?"

"Olivia," she rasped around the hand squeezing the air out of her throat. Her vision fuzzed, making it seem as though the pond had a wavy current.

"See how easy that was?"

The hand around her throat disappeared, and she sucked in gulps of air as she scooted as close to Brooke and as far away from Dante as she could get. "I'm Scott's gir—"

"She's Spec's ol' lady," Brooke rushed to say, shooting her a warning glare.

Right. He was Spec to the club. "Y-yes," she managed, throat aching. They'd never believe her if she called him Scott. And she'd already forgotten about the ol' man, ol' lady thing.

Rag and Dante exchanged a look she couldn't decipher, but they weren't nearly as cocky as they'd been seconds before.

"Damn." Dante chuckled next to her ear. "You must be some crazy pussy to shack up with that deranged motherfucker." He moved his hands to his crotch, groping as though they weren't out in public for all the world to see.

Olivia's eyes nearly fell out of her head.

"How 'bout you drop down on those knees and give me a little bit of what Spec likes."

Her mouth dropped open as panic surged through her veins.

"That's a good start," he said with a wink.

"You're disgusting," she said as she tried to shove him away. The damn man didn't budge. The fear she'd been feeling transformed into full-on disgust and outrage. "Sco... uh, Spec is going to be here any second, and he'll flip his shit if he sees you touching me." In reality, he'd probably shake the guy's hand and wish him well, thrilled she was someone else's problem.

"You think Spec is deranged now? Imagine what he'll do if he finds you with your hands all over his woman?" Brooke added. "It'll make what he did to your friend, Prick, look like child's play." Her words were forceful, but her voice trembled. She was as unnerved as Olivia.

A quick flash of worry sparked in Rag's eye. What the hell had Scott done to his friend?

"Tell Curly we were asking for him."

"Yeah," Dante said as he stood with a grunt of effort. He stroked a grimy hand down her cheek. "See you around, princess."

She narrowed her eyes as she wrenched her face away. That fucking nickname.

They lumbered off as though they didn't have a care in the world. Olivia blew out a breath and sagged against the bench. Her heart ran wild, and her insides felt like Jell-O. She curled her hands into fists so Brooke wouldn't see the shaking. "What the hell was that?"

"That was two guys from an MC Curly was involved with a decade and a half ago. They betrayed him and let him go to prison for a crime he didn't commit. Now that he's out and back in town, they're pissed he wants nothing to do with them." She stood and held out a hand.

Olivia blinked. Curly had spent more than ten years in prison?

Brooke shook her outstretched arm. "Come on. Let's get back to the clubhouse. I gotta tell Curly about this. He's gonna flip when he hears. Oh God, your throat is bruising already. They're all gonna lose their shit. Hope you can handle some fireworks."

Coffee and snacks forgotten, she gave Brook her hand. Together they dashed back to Brooke's car and broke every speed limit hurrying back to the clubhouse.

Running from one biker who propositioned her to another who couldn't stand the sight of her.

Fantastic.

She'd fled her home to find a safe place to lay low until her fiancé lost interest in her. Now she was fleeing a park with a woman she barely knew after being harassed by a pair of terrifying bikers.

On the positive side, she'd gone a full thirty minutes without thinking about Lance.

But what the hell had she gotten herself involved in now?

Chapter Six

Scott re-racked the barbell then used his fatigued abs to crunch to a seated position on the weight bench. He rotated his shoulder. Damn, he loved that burn in his muscles from an intense workout, even with a bitch of a hangover. When he'd left the military, he assumed to be ecstatic to leave behind the mandatory physical training, but not only did he straight-up like working out, he craved it—needed to channel his runaway thoughts into physical discomfort. As he pushed his muscles to the limit, the ache and strain gave him a few moments of mental peace. Thankfully, the rest of the guys had been all about his idea of adding a weight room into the design plans for the clubhouse. He spent hours there every day, mainly on the heavy bag, pounding his demons into fucking dust.

Or trying to. They were persistent motherfuckers.

"Hey, Spec," Lock called from the doorway.

"Sup, brother." Scott glanced at his new friend over his shoulder. The tension from yesterday hadn't lingered. "Need a spot?"

Lock shook his head. "Nah. Curly wants all hands on deck out by the bar."

"Uh-oh. Something happening?" As soon as he asked, the zing of needing action buzzed under his skin. Sixty minutes of pumping his muscles and taxing his heart hadn't done shit to soothe the beast inside.

"Think so. His ol' lady is here with that new chick, Liv."

Liv? Fuck that. "Olivia."

"Huh? Oh, no, man, she said it was cool to call her Liv."

"She's Olivia," he said through clenched teeth. No fucking way was she getting all chummy with his brothers. Not when every one of them was probably picturing what she looked like under all those designer clothes.

Lock shrugged. "Whatever. Prez wants us. Think the ladies ran into some trouble."

With a snort, Scott stood from the bench. "Probably needs someone to wipe the drops of sweat off the princess' forehead."

"What was that?" Lock asked over his shoulder as he walked out of the gym.

"Nothing." Scott grabbed his towel then mopped his face. "On my way."

He didn't bother tossing on a shirt. Wearing clothes when he was sweaty like this sucked. If his naked torso offended the princess' delicate eyes, all the better.

He was the last to arrive at the bar area. The rest of the guys stood clustered around what had to be Liv—Olivia—and Brooke.

"I'm fine." Olivia's highbrow speak came through loud and clear. "Seriously, Tracker, it's not a big deal."

"What'sa matter, princess?" Scott called out as he slung the towel around his sweaty neck. "You break one of your fake-as-fuck nails while you were shopping?" He'd never admit his first thought upon seeing her neat nails had been to wonder what they'd feel like raking down his back.

The group parted, giving him access to the ladies. The first thing he saw was Brooke's scowl directed his way. She didn't appreciate his opinion of her new, ritzy friend.

Too fucking bad.

"Jesus, you can be a dick sometimes," Pulse muttered as he hovered over Olivia like a mother hen.

"For fuck's sake, what's the big de… what the fuck?" Who the hell put their hands on her? Christ, Deke would kick his ass for letting his sister get hurt. And rightfully so.

Olivia sat on a barstool with her head tilted up as Pulse examined three round bruises ringing her neck like some fucked-up necklace. "I'm fine!" she said with a huff. "Why won't anyone believe that I'm fine? Seriously, it's just a few bruises. I'll live."

"It's not that we don't believe you," Pulse answered as he ran a finger over her throat.

Scott clenched his fists as the absurd urge to rip his brother's hand away plagued him. He wanted to be the one to make sure she wasn't hurt. Hell, he shouldn't have let her be in a situation where she'd be injured in the first place, if for no other reason than to honor Deke's memory.

God, he was a shitty friend.

He glanced at Curly, who had to have cracked a tooth with how hard his jaw was clamped. Beside him, Brooke worried her lip as she watched Olivia.

"There's important shit on your neck, sweetheart. Just lemme do a quick check to make sure nothing vital is injured." Pulse winked, and Scott's hackles rose.

Charming asshole.

"Be happy I'm not making you go to the ER." He probed around for a few moments, asking her to swallow. Eventually, he nodded and backed away. "You're good, sweetheart."

Sweetheart? The winks? "For fuck's sake," Scott muttered.

"What was that?" Pulse asked with a smirk.

Scott glared at him. "Nothing."

Olivia lowered her chin and shot him a haughty glare that made his dick plump and his stomach revolt. Bitch mode activated. Yeah, she was fucking fine. Not that he'd tolerate bruises on any woman. He shuddered as the memory of his sister's bruised and battered body tried to work its way into his mind. It fueled his rage to incendiary levels. "What the fuck happened?" he ground out.

"Rag and Dante from Curly's old club were harassing us," Brooke said. "They didn't really say anything. Just wanted us to let Curly know they're thinking about him."

Those pieces of shit. Narrowing his eyes, he swooped his gaze back to Olivia. Fuck it, he had to know for himself. He walked until he was within touching distance and grabbed her chin between his thumb and forefinger. As he tilted her head, she met his stare with one of her own. It dared him to make a big deal about the bruising. His lips quirked. The pretty princess had grit. And a backbone. Deke would be proud. Scott was too. Just a smidge. Not that he'd admit it to her in a million years.

"So what happened to your throat? Dante get pissed at you for telling him to pack sand because his boots weren't Lou Berts or whatever the fuck?"

"Louboutins?" Brooke asked around a laugh as Olivia gave him a death glare.

"What the hell are you talking about?" Curly asked with a scrunched forehead.

"They're shoes, babe." Brooke still chuckled as she patted Curly's arm. "Very, very expensive shoes."

"Why would bikers wear them?" Lock looked about as confused as Curly.

"They wouldn't." Olivia's voice didn't hold any of the humor the others did. "Scott thinks I'm an elitist who won't talk to someone based on the price of their footwear."

"Pretty sure I never used the fucking word elitist," he said, mimicking her uppity tone. Fuck, he hated it when she spoke like that. Worse than nails on a chalkboard. Little did she know his boots were his pride and joy, costing upward of a few hundred hard-earned bucks. Fuck, this woman got under his skin. To make matters worse, aside from the damn bruises, she looked as polished and put together as usual, which only made him want to mess her up.

And that had his cock waking up.

The traitor.

"Despite what *Spec* thinks, I don't judge people for what they wear. The guy was disgusting. He smelled like meat and kept pawing at me." She kept her pissed-off gaze on him as she spoke, daring him to contradict her.

Pawing at her? Scott clenched his jaw. Dante would pay for that a hundred times over.

"He wanted to know my name. You may think I'm a piece of fluff, but I'm not stupid. I refused to give him my name. He grabbed my throat and squeezed until I had no choice but to tell him. When I did, he released me."

To keep from tearing the room apart with his bare hands, Scott clenched his teeth and counted. "So," he said when he got to seven. Ten required more self-restraint than he possessed. "He got your name anyway, and you got a nasty purple necklace for your trouble. You're right. You're a genius."

"Spec, what the hell?" Brooke cut in, gaping at him like he'd lost his mind.

Maybe he had. This woman drove him to it. The sight of those bruises was making him murderous and guilty as hell. As if he didn't have enough of his own issues, Olivia fried his brain. He couldn't decide whether he wanted to bend her over his knee or fuck her from one moment to the next.

Maybe bend her over his knee, then fuck her…

Goddammit, now he was going to have a full-on chub in

front of the whole damn club. What a waste of a good boner. As nice as those fancy tits and ass were, the woman had to be an ice queen in bed.

Uh, Scott, you're sweaty.

Scott, I only do missionary sex.

Scott, I don't swallow. Actually, I don't really do blowjobs.

It'd all be accompanied by a scrunched nose and shake of her head.

His cock deflated. Much better. Oliva belonged in a nailed box with a sign that said Dead Best Friend's Prissy Little Sister. He had no business wondering how those tits felt and that pussy tasted.

And he was getting hard again.

"Spec!" Curly snapped.

Shit.

"Yeah, Prez?"

"The fuck's going on with you?" Curly folded his arms across his chest and glared.

Blinking, Scott scanned the room only to realize he and Curly were the only two people left. When had everyone else gone? "Sorry, boss. Zoned out for a second." It'd been happening occasionally, but usually when he was in one of his rages.

"Yeah, noticed that." With a sigh, Curly ran a hand through the thick mess of spiraled hair that gave him his road name. "Told the ladies they need to have someone with them if they go out."

The ladies. Like Olivia was part of the club family now? Snorting, Scott dragged a hand across the back of his neck. "Imagine they loved that."

"Yeah, you know how independent Brooke is. Pretty sure she'd rather just stay home than have a babysitter tailing her when she's out."

"Think she prefers to be home with all those pups anyway,

74

brother."

"I know." That got a chuckle from the gruff man, but it quickly turned into a scowl. "After what happened with Maverick, I'm fucking stupid to hope these assholes would lose interest in us."

Scott's gut twisted with guilt. "Fuck, boss, that shit was on me. I know it." He'd lost his shit after being confronted by two of Curly's old club brothers in a gas station. They were spewing all kinds of bullshit, and as usual, Scott's beast exploded, fucking one of the guys up pretty bad. In retaliation, they kidnapped Maverick and his ol' lady when they visited the area.

"We're gonna have to do something, but, damn, I was hoping we could fly under the radar a little longer." Curly had seen a fuck-ton in his life. The man lived hard and rough, breaking nearly every law in existence with his prior club. Thirteen years in prison for the one crime he didn't commit would affect any man. Curly valued his freedom above everything except Brooke. Scott knew the prez would gladly spend his days in a cell if it meant keeping his woman safe.

When he opened this charter, Curly said one of his primary objectives was to stay quiet and off the cop's radar for as long as possible. Being a one-percenter MC, the quiet wouldn't last forever, but the prez had no love for cops. War with another group of bikers would kill any chances of living a cop-free existence.

"Could get ugly," Scott said as he rounded the bar. Alcohol, they needed alcohol.

"It's already ugly." Curly sat on a stool and rested his forearms on the bartop. "For fuck's sake, Spec, they choked Olivia in broad daylight. Right out there while ducks were swimming in the pond and runners were jogging by. I know you don't like this woman, but you can't think she deserved that."

Scott held up his hand as ice formed in his veins. "I'm gonna stop you right there, Prez. My shit with Olivia is personal. Got nothing to do with the MC. I don't give a fuck who she is. Any man puts marks on a woman like I saw today, they deserve their fingers broken at the very least." Maybe some castration for good measure, as an extra punishment from Deke.

"Yeah," Curly half grunted, half spoke.

Scott slid him a beer, then popped the top off one for himself. The icy liquid tasted fantastic and helped cool his heated temper.

"You know, whatever the personal shit is, it wouldn't kill you to dial down the asshole when you're talking to her."

"Don't plan on talking to her."

Curly took a swig of his beer then stood. "She's living across the hall from you. And she's here because she's going through some shit."

Scott's head popped up at that. "She told you that?"

"No, but she gave Brooke that impression. Something's going on, and it's big enough that she fled home for a while. Maybe cut her some slack?"

With a snort, Scott shook his head. "I'm not giving her tantrum attention because she's pissed Daddy cut up her credit cards or whatever. She'll get bored of being in that tiny apartment without all her luxuries in no time." She'd shunned Deke for much of her life. Why the hell should she be extended any courtesies?

Deke would've bent over backward to make her feel welcome, but Scott wasn't as tender-hearted.

"You're a cold man, Spec. Fucking block of ice for a heart. Except when it comes to Chloe," Curly said of his sister. "Only time I've seen you thaw is around her. Think with what happened to her, you'd be more willing to help a woman in need."

Shit. That arrow hit its mark. Scott rubbed his chest as though the prez really had speared him in the heart.

Curly rapped his knuckles on the bar. "Catch you later."

"Later, Prez." Damn right, Scott was a hard motherfucker. He had to be to survive the shit he'd lived through, to do the things he'd done, and to keep from letting the guilt over Deke's death destroy him. If that made him cold, fuck it. It's the way it had to be.

"And, Spec?" Curly called from the door to his office.

Scott looked his way.

"Remember she showed up *here*. To find you, her brother's best friend. A rich girl like that?" He arched an eyebrow. "She probably had options. But she's here. To see you. Why do you think that is?"

The words bounced around in his head as Scott finished his beer. The prez straight-up didn't understand. Olivia and Deke hadn't been close. She'd grown up a pampered Daddy's girl. The same Daddy who kicked Deke out on his ass when he enlisted. Did the man even know Deke lived on the streets until basic training? Did Olivia realize it? Did either care? Probably not. They were too busy living the good life in their mansion, bathing in diamonds, and eating on solid gold plates.

Olivia stood for everything he hated. Rich jerks who lived in their ivory towers looking down on the regular folk. She had no idea what it was to struggle, to fight, to fear, and yet she thought herself better than him because of her clothes and shoes and wallet. She didn't deserve softness from him— someone who didn't put up with her bullshit for once in her life. That's one she needed.

And that's how it'd stay. He had no plans to change his attitude toward her. It kept her away and kept him from having some emotional heart-to-heart where he spilled his guts and details of Deke's death.

No way in hell would they be having that conversation. No matter how big of an asshole he had to become or how many times he had to overlook something about her that shattered his preconceived notions. Like the way she'd handled everything that happened today.

Maybe he didn't give her enough credit and perhaps he prejudged her too harshly, but he needed to stick to those judgments.

It was safer for everyone.

But mostly for him.

Chapter Seven

The weather was a dream.

Eighty-five degrees and, from what every person at the clubhouse had told her, a rare dry day for Florida. Even the humid days didn't bother her. Olivia soaked up the sun and heat like one of those little lizards she saw lounging all over Brooke's lanai.

And this lanai was just about the best thing in life. She could've happily spent the rest of her life sitting right there on the cushy chaise while the dogs scampered around in the yard and the gentle breeze blew through the screen.

Warmth filled her from within as well. Having Brooke trust her enough to ask her to watch the dogs while she and Curly went on a dinner date meant the world to her. Throw in the fact that Curly didn't force some poor club member to babysit her, and she was in tropical heaven.

Curly and Brooke's house was locked down tighter than most military bases. Last year, Brooke's ex-husband had broken in and nearly killed her, or so they'd told her. After that, Curly invested in an epic security system. The Hope Diamond probably wasn't as secure as she was at that moment. The assurance of safety put her mind at ease and allowed her to truly relax for the first time in a week.

Ray, Brooke's German Shepard, pushed through the doggie door snout first, lapped up some water from his dish, then scampered over to her chair.

"Hey, boy," she said with a huge smile. "Wanna snuggle? I'll move my legs." She shifted her legs to one side of the lounge chair. Ray sniffed her knee, managed an awkward revolution or two, then flopped down with a contented doggy sigh. The heat radiating off his furry body would have her needing a dip in the pool in no time, but she didn't mind.

Once she settled somewhere safe and permanent, she'd need to look into getting a pet. Not only would a dog like Ray help her feel safer if she lived on her own, but the companionship would do wonders for her psyche.

A pet had been the one consistent gifts she'd asked for every Christmas and birthday. Well, that and to visit her older brother. Both requests had never been denied, just ignored.

Her online classes had ended about ten days ago. She'd been taking one class at a time over the past two semesters. It'd be great to take more, but she'd wanted to fly under the radar. Thankfully, she had two months off until the next one began. Would she be somewhere she could continue her coursework? Hopefully. Two months would be long enough to have her life ironed out, right?

Glancing at Ray, she grinned. Oh, to be a dog with nothing more to worry about than when the next ball would be thrown. "Nice life you got yourself here, huh, Ray?"

The dog's ears twitched at the sound of his name, but he didn't lift his head.

"Though from what I hear, you deserve it, saving Brooke's life." She reached forward and scratched behind his massive ears, then flopped back in the chaise.

Her gaze fell to Brooke's laptop lying on the table next to her. "Ray, I need your help. Will you check my email for me?

You see, I ditched all my electronics when I left home so Lance couldn't track or contact me. It's been days, and I need to check my email, but I'm kinda dreading it. I'm sure Lance has sent many hate notes. So whaddaya say? Help a girl out? Read them for me?"

Ray lifted his head and let out one deep woof.

Sighing, she grabbed the laptop off the table next to her. "Yeah, yeah, I know having paws makes it difficult to type. But I'm pretty sure you're just being lazy."

Ray whined, then settled back down.

"Go ahead. Take a nap. I'll just be over here staring at the computer screen." Brooke had been nice enough to let her borrow her laptop. Not only did she need to check for messages from Lance, but she needed to email her father and let him know she was okay. She'd left him a voicemail saying she was taking a solo vacation to destress. She'd asked not to be disturbed but promised to check in periodically. Her father would find it extremely out of character, but he'd taken his latest young wife on a trip to the French Riviera for a few months and wouldn't worry too much. His being abroad meant Lance wouldn't get to him either, which was one less worry.

Like the house, Brooke's computer had the best of the best when it came to security, including an encrypted VPN. According to Curly, no way could Lance—or the FBI—track her activity.

Not that she'd let on to why she wanted a secure computer. She learned within moments of meeting him that Curly was perceptive. Too much so. If she didn't want him asking questions about her visit or her life, she'd need to be extremely careful not to tip her hand too far.

"All right. Enough stalling." She logged into the operating system using the guest account. A few clicks and typed keys later, fifteen hundred unread emails stared her down.

Not surprisingly, the first dozen or—

She scrolled down. Holy shit. Not a dozen, but the first thirty-two emails were from an anonymous account. Lance. Who else would it be? Her stomach twisted as she skimmed some of the subject lines.

You can't hide.

I'll find you.

Bitch.

You'll wish you were dead.

Fuck you.

The list went on. All thirty-two emails had different subjects, increasingly threatening. The most recent sent only eighteen minutes ago had her blood running cold.

I'm getting closer.

Closer to what? Finding her? Showing up in Florida? Bringing danger to the Handlers' door? Or was it all bluster designed to freak her out?

Maybe coming to Florida had been a colossal mistake. Scott didn't want her there, and she knew no one aside from him. Sure, Brooke was becoming a friend, but what kind of person brought baggage like hers to the home of someone they barely knew?

As though he sensed her distress, Ray whined and pushed his heated body against her leg. He provided a measure of comfort, but, man, she wished he could tell her what to do. Leave? Stay? Ask for help? Reply? Ignore Lance? The right decision eluded her.

Hand trembling, she clicked open the most recently received email. What was the point of reading them all? They'd only terrify her.

I just wanted to talk, but now I'm pissed. You have no money. No job. No house. I'm the son your father wishes he'd had. I'm getting closer to finding you. See you soon, my love.

* * *

What would he do if he found her? Hurt her? Kill her? Force her back to a life she'd never realized was stifling her? Would he expect her to marry him and stand by his side with a phony smile while he drugged and raped unsuspecting women as a weeknight hobby?

Never.

"Yo, Curly? Where you at?"

Oliva screamed. She slammed her hand to her chest, ready to catch her heart as it leaped from her chest.

Ray's head popped up as the French doors to the lanai opened wide. "Curly? You and Brooke better not be fucking naked out he... oh."

Scott.

Ray let out a delighted yip and practically flew over to the man.

"Some protector you are," she muttered as she breathed out.

"Where's Curly?" he asked without so much as a simple greeting.

Swallowing, she closed the laptop with trembling hands. Her insides shook even harder than her fingers. She hated knowing the angry six-foot-plus biker looming fifteen feet from her would sense her distress. "H-he and Brooke, um, they went to dinner." She cleared her throat to buy herself a minute to settle. "I-I offered to hang with the dogs."

Just at that time, a few of Brooke's rescue pups came through the doggy door to inspect the newcomer. He crouched to give each of the dogs some attention.

Olivia's gaze immediately zeroed in on his long, nimble fingers as they stroked over a chunky bulldog's head. This whole acting like she didn't care about him would be much easier if he weren't so large. And if he didn't smell like sunshine and man. Or if he was ugly.

"Well, fuck, I forgot about that." He narrowed his eyes her way. "What's wrong?"

"Nothing."

"Bullshit. What's wrong?"

She rolled her eyes. "Nothing. You startled me. That's all." When he didn't say anything, she huffed. "Curly gave me a huge talk about how secure the house was and how no one could get in under any circumstances. I wasn't expecting to hear a man's voice. It freaked me out, Scott."

He sent her an unconvinced glare from his squatted position. Thankfully, his dark glasses hid the hatred in his eyes. She wasn't sure she could handle it after reading Lance's email. She craved warmth and comfort but wouldn't find it here.

"I have a key. You're shaking. Curly's right, this house is as safe as it gets. You don't need to be scared. Promise nothing will happen to you here."

Her jaw dropped. Had he just reassured her and been kind about it?

He coughed an uncomfortable sound. "And it's Spec," he said, saving all his warmth for the dogs. "We're not friends. You're a guest with my club. You call me Spec."

So much for the kindness. "Come on, Sc—" This time, she felt the revulsion in his glare. "Spec. Isn't this getting a little old?"

He grunted. "Whatever. I'll catch my prez later. Bye, boy," he said, patting Ray's head a final time before turning and walking toward the house again.

Her gaze went to his ass as his long legs ate up the short distance. She couldn't help it. As much as she wanted to return the man's hatred, he fascinated her on many levels. Physically, he woke something inside her she'd thought she'd lacked. Lance had been handsome, and she'd been attracted to him, but never like this. Never this wild desire. She'd probably tackle Scott right there and give the poor pups a show they weren't old enough to see if he expressed interest. And the man hated her, but maybe it was because he hated her. Some confused mixture of hatred and desire were screwing with her libido.

Then there was his relationship with Deke. They'd been as close as brothers, according to her half-brother. Closer than she'd ever been to him, that was for sure. And she wanted to learn more about their friendship and her brother.

And there was the man himself. So angry. So cold. So capable. There were so many facets to him—the biker, the soldier, the friend, the foe. She'd only been privy to one side, but the others were hiding somewhere beneath his resentment.

"Wait!" she called out just as he stepped into the house.

He stopped and glanced back at her over his shoulder.

"Did he hate me that much?" God, she hadn't meant for her voice to sound so small. So pitiful and needy. "I tried to make up for the years we didn't have a relationship."

All she got in response was one eyebrow arching over his sunglasses.

"Deke," she whispered. It still hurt to say her brother's name. "Did Deke hate me so much that he made you hate me?" She'd loved her brother. Yes, for too many years, she'd listened to her father's lies about him, but over the past seven years, she'd tried so hard to make up for that.

A muscle in his cheek fluttered. He stared at the pool for a long moment then faced her. "No," he said. He closed the doors then looked at her with his hands on his hips. He was so handsome it made her insides twist. "He was much nicer than I am. He didn't hate you. All he wanted was a close relationship with you. Like I said, he was a better man than me, so I'll hate you for him."

Ouch. She'd been accused of never knowing when to quit.

Sometimes, it was an excellent quality to possess. This wasn't one of those times, yet she couldn't let him walk out like this. Something about the moment seemed so final like she'd never see him again if he walked out now.

"He wouldn't want that."

"What?"

"Deke." She straightened her shoulders and tried to speak with confidence she didn't feel. "He was good like you said. He wouldn't want you to hate me on his behalf."

"You think you know him well enough to speak for him? Fuck, you're arrogant." He shoved the glasses to his head and made a play of rolling his olive-green eyes. Then he let out a half grunt, half laugh. "Must run in the family."

Her heart skipped a beat. A joke? A softening in her direction?

He glanced out into the yard with a sigh for what felt like an hour but couldn't have been more than twenty seconds. "Why are you here?" he asked.

She opened her mouth, but he held up a hand.

"The real reason. Not some bullshit about wanting to get to know your brother or me. Why are you really here?"

Panic flashed through her. How much should she tell him? Not the truth. He'd either send her packing or take her problem on for the club out of some obligation to her brother. Neither option worked.

"I, uh, ended my engagement."

"Of fucking course. So why'd you come here? Daddy mad he lost his wedding deposits?"

She tilted her head and smirked so she wouldn't cry. "I didn't tell my father. He'd side with my fiancé over me as always. Deke wasn't the only recipient of his displeasure."

Something flashed in Scott's eyes. An understanding? An inch of give? Maybe a hint of compassion? But it disappeared as quick as it came, leaving nothing but a hardened

86

expression and cold gaze.

"Calling your father's feelings toward Deke displeasure is like saying Florida is a tiny bit warm."

"Yeah." Where did she go from here? Clearing her throat, she said, "Uh, my fiancé and I had been together since I was nineteen. Our lives were completely merged." She shrugged as she shifted her gaze to Ray. "I needed to get away for a while. Figure out my next steps."

"So you came to slum it with bikers in Florida?"

Anger flashed through her. Would it kill him to spare her one ounce of kindness? "No, *Spec*, I came to meet the man my brother said was his very best friend. The man who always had his back. The one he said to go to if I ever needed anything, and he wasn't around."

Her words hung heavy in the air. Even Ray seemed to pick up on the weight of the moment. He whined and nudged Scott's hand with his snout.

Scott exhaled, muttering something she couldn't make out and probably cursing her name. Then he walked over to where she sat and plopped down on the empty lounge separated from hers by a small end table. Her breath caught in her lungs. Was he staying?

"So what do you need?"

"From you? Just to know more about my brother, to know the man you knew."

He was quiet for a while, so long she wondered if he'd fallen asleep beneath those sunglasses.

"Deke ever tell you about the time he hooked up with a chick who robbed him while he was asleep?"

She chuckled, trying to ignore the fluttering in her belly caused by the timbre of his voice. "No, but I'd really like to hear that story."

He side-eyed her before saying, "I'll stick around until Curly gets back. You shouldn't be here alone anyway."

"He said I'm safe here by myself." She'd love it if he stayed. Being afraid all the time was exhausting, and with him there, she didn't have to worry.

Scott just grunted. He didn't face her but instead focused on the dogs running around the yard. "So, one night, Deke left with this totally whacked-out woman he met at a popular Army bar right outside the base. She had a purse with a stuffed cat that she talked to like it was real."

Olivia's eyes widened, and she laughed. "For real? Why would Deke go for her?"

"She was hot as fuck," he said as though it was an obvious conclusion.

She snorted. "Typical."

A shrug was all she got. "Anyway…"

As he spoke, the tension she felt began to bleed from her system. His voice was intoxicating when he wasn't using it to bark at her. It made her feel safe. His whole presence did. So she settled in to listen to a ridiculous story about her brother and pretend for a bit that her ex-fiancé wasn't hunting her and Scott didn't despise her.

This wasn't a declaration of friendship or even a ceasefire, but she'd take what she could get from the troubled former soldier.

Chapter Eight

Two days later, Scott was still kicking his ass for the hour and a half he spent regaling Olivia with story after story about her brother. In his defense, she'd looked hotter than sin sitting there in a dark purple bikini that deepened the green of her eyes. Those eyes had held a note of fear that brought out his protective streak. He hadn't been able to leave her there, and the desire to stay had nothing to do with an obligation to Deke and everything to do with him.

And his dick.

Idiot.

So now he was pissed. Mostly at himself, but he wasn't known for making the most rational decisions when angry.

He pounded on Olivia's door like he had a whole SWAT team there to draw her out.

"What?" Olivia's muffled voice came from behind the thin walls. "Um, just a minute," she called. "I'm coming."

The door cracked, and one eyeball appeared in the sliver. She still had the chain lock latched. "Scott? Is everything okay?" The sleep hadn't left her voice, giving it a rougher quality than usual.

With a huffed laugh, he shook his head. "You were

sleeping."

"Yeah. It's only eight-thirty, not that late. And it's Saturday."

"Open the door, Olivia."

"Uh, I'm not really prepared to receive visitors right now."

He grunted. "Prepared to receive visitors? What the fuck is this, the Victorian era?"

"Uh, no, it's not," she said, getting a little kick of that sass she loved to dole out.

He'd die before admitting it, but something about how her hackles rose got him hot. She didn't fear him but gave it right back.

"I'm not properly dressed, and I don't have any makeup on. That's all I meant."

Like he gave a shit? He could see a sliver of sweatpants through the cracked door, so she wasn't naked.

Wait, fuck. The word 'naked' stuck in his head. She'd be gorgeous naked. All that smooth skin she spent so much money caring for. Hell, he'd pay money to see her in those sweatpants too. And not because she'd look all cute and rumpled straight from her bed.

Wait, was there more to why she didn't want him coming in? Oh, hell no. He slapped his palm on the door. "Olivia, I swear to God, if you've got one of my brothers in there…"

The one eyebrow he could see wrinkled in confusion. "What? Why would one of your brothers be in here?"

"Oh, I don't know. Because you're fucking him?" Curly would be pissed if he murdered one of his brothers, but he could already feel the fury heating his blood. Fury, not jealousy. He wasn't sure he could control himself if Tracker or Jinx or hell, any of them, walked out of her apartment.

She gasped. "You're a pig. And not that it's any of your business, but I'm completely alone. Believe me, there are a million men I'd sleep with before lowering myself to a biker."

Part of him, most of him, wanted to kick the door in and show her just how little she meant by that weak declaration. He bet he could have her dripping for him in minutes, begging for his cock.

Of course, he'd have to melt that impenetrable layer of ice first, so maybe not.

It melted the other day while she laughed at your stories about Deke.

She had a gorgeous smile.

He scowled. "Just get your ass down to the clubhouse. Maybe try to show a little gratitude to the woman who gave you a free fucking place to stay, huh?"

Olivia's spine snapped straight, and the emerald eye glaring at him narrowed.

"What's a matter, princess? Not used to someone calling you out on your behavior? When you're staying at someone's house, and they invite you to a family breakfast, you get up and fucking go. Even if you miss an hour or two of your precious beauty sleep. And if you're not selfish, you get up even earlier and help with shit."

She pursed her pouty lips. If she'd been able to shoot fire from her eyes, he'd be burning for sure. Instead of blasting him as he'd assumed she would, she nodded once. "Please tell Brooke I'll be down in ten minutes. And don't call me princess."

The door shut in his face, and that was that. Shaking his head, he jogged down the stairs and over to the clubhouse. About fifty yards separated the two buildings. Enough for him to have some privacy but be available to Curly and the club whenever necessary.

As he entered the building, the smell of bacon and coffee had saliva pooling in his mouth. First to arrive, he went straight to the kitchen to see what he could do for Brooke. Anything to help get him back on Curly's good side after this shit with Olivia. And the shit with the guy whose ass he kicked at the bar last week.

"Hey, beautiful," he said as he strode into the kitchen. Curly stood at the coffee maker, filling his mug, so Scott made sure to plant a loud kiss on Brooke's cheek. She laughed and swatted at his arm while Curly glared daggers.

Okay, maybe he wasn't doing everything to get back on his prez's good side. It was just too much fun to mess with him and his possessive nature when it came to his ol' lady. Not that Scott would ever poach a brother's woman. Even if he was that particular brand of asshole, Brooke wasn't his type. She was far too kind for the likes of him. That and she'd been with a man who'd roughed her up. Scott wasn't a soft man. Occasionally, he liked to fuck hard, bordering on aggressive and couldn't be with a woman he'd be worried about triggering.

So Curly didn't have a damn thing to worry about. Yet he did. And it was a hell of a lot of fun to screw with him.

"Hope you're hungry," Brooke said as she blushed. "I'm making enough for an army."

"I'm always hungry. Why don't you put me to work? My mama raised me right."

Curly scoffed.

"Great." With a broad smile, she handed him a spatula. "Flip those pancakes for me." She pointed to two griddles loaded down with a dozen or so pancakes.

"Yes, ma'am." He went to work, flipping the delicious-smelling pancakes. "Oh, I woke up your new best friend. Can you believe she was gonna sleep through this?" Shaking his head, he muttered, "Rude."

When Brooke didn't respond, he peered over his shoulder to find her standing at the stove, biting her lower lip. "I didn't tell her about breakfast," she said with a grimace. "Shit, I knew it was the wrong thing to do. Sometimes she seems overwhelmed by all of you guys, and I didn't want her to feel pressured to show up if she wasn't comfortable. Not everyone is used to being around a group of huge growly bikers."

His stomach dipped. Well, shit. "So, she had no idea about breakfast?"

Another grimace. "No. Sorry." Brooke pinched the bridge of her nose. "Tell me you weren't a jerk to her."

"What?" He scoffed. "No."

She sent him a glare.

Geez, this was worse than getting scolded by his mom. "Maybe a little."

"Scott!" There was a definite whine in her voice. She looked to her ol' man. "Curly, can't you force him to be nice to her? This is seriously getting old."

The prez lifted his hands, "Babe, I warned you about this. Said you were on your own when it came to Livy." His words said one thing, but the glare he shot Scott said another. Plus, he was calling her Livy?

For fuck's sake.

Brooke's scowl would've made him laugh if Curly wasn't in the room. She was the sweetest woman but had a protective streak ten miles long for her rescues. And make no mistake, Olivia might not be a furry canine, but she was one of Brooke's rescues. However, if he laughed, Curly would skin his hide.

She pointed the deadly end of a knife his way. "You'll make nice when she gets here, you hear me? Whatever your issue is with her, put it aside for an hour so we can have a nice, drama-free breakfast." She shifted the direction of the knife down to his beloved motorcycle boots. "If you don't behave, I'll make you keep Clipper for the week."

"Damn, woman. You fight dirty." Clipper was this adorable mutt Brooke began fostering last week. He was damn cute but had a serious shoe fetish and had already tried to gnaw on Scott's boots. "How do you ever win an argument with her, Prez?"

Curly grunted, then took his coffee out of the kitchen, probably to go to his office and do whatever bullshit he had to do to keep the club running smoothly. "Scott, you're meeting with Devos later, right?"

"Yes, boss. In three hours." Devos was a contact who'd borrowed a cool fifty grand from the club. He was due to pay it back plus a disgusting amount of interest in a week. Scott planned to pop by and remind the man how important it was to meet that deadline. Though if he were honest, part of him hoped Devos would default. It'd give him a chance to beat on something other than the heavy bag that had taken quite a bit of abuse the past few days. Since his disastrous bar fight, he'd been trying to keep his hands to himself and needed a human outlet. And with Olivia around stirring up all sorts of shit in his head, he'd needed an outlet more than ever.

Speak of the devil, Olivia stepped into the kitchen wearing very short denim shorts that showed off her sexy legs and a yellow fitted T-shirt that outlined her breasts. What the hell happened to the fancy-assed dresses and ridiculous heels? Today she'd dressed like a Florida native, and she looked ten times sexier than she did in her thousand-dollar dresses.

"Morning," she announced, chipper as hell. She went straight to Brooke. The two of them embraced. "How can I help?" She was all smiles, but Scott saw the tension running beneath the mask. Tension he'd put there.

"The muffins are ready to come out of the oven. Mind grabbing them for me?" Brooke asked.

"You got it." After grabbing a mitt, Liv bent over and retrieved a tray of muffins.

Wait, Liv? When the hell had he started thinking of her as Liv instead of Olivia?

Scott groaned as those damn shorts pulled tight across her truly stellar ass. The kind of round ass he'd kill to get his hands on. Fuck, this was going to be a long breakfast. The pungent scent of burning food hit his nose. He glanced down at the griddle with a curse.

Scorched to shit.

Yeah, he definitely needed to punch something today.

"SERIOUSLY, BROOKE, I'M so sorry I overslept. I would've been here earlier to help," Olivia said as she set the piping hot pan of muffins on a cooling rack as instructed. She'd never tell Brooke she had no clue what she was doing and hadn't made a muffin, well, ever.

Fake it till you make it.

Brooke rested a hand on her forearm. "No, I'm the one who's sorry. I didn't want you to feel obligated to come if this group is too much for you, so I didn't tell you about the breakfast. But I should've let you make that decision. I really am sorry, Livy." She gave a gentle squeeze before releasing her.

The humiliation she'd felt crashing a breakfast she hadn't been invited to turned into affection for the woman who'd given her a safe haven, no questions asked. "I can handle them," she said with more confidence than she felt. At the very least, she could pretend. Her false bravado skills were excellent.

"Good. Then I'm glad you're here. It's nice to have another double X chromosome to balance all these Ys.

"Heard that," Scott muttered as he scraped a plateful of pancakes into the trash.

"See what I mean?" Brooke winked. "Can you please rescue that man before we're eating McDonald's breakfast sandwiches?"

Olivia hesitated. Her gaze went to the muscular expanse of

Scott's back, where he cursed at the griddle as he attempted a second batch of pancakes. She'd been up half the night scrolling Lance's social media accounts from her new phone. Convinced he was still in Chicago and nowhere near her, she'd finally been able to set the phone down but still couldn't quiet her mind enough to sleep until well past midnight.

"Sure," she said, straightening her shoulders. She could handle this. All she had to do was keep from giving in to her instinct to snap at him if he got grumpy with her.

And she could do that.

This should be a piece of cake.

With a fortifying inhale, she made her way across the large industrial kitchen to where Scott hovered over two griddles. "Need some help with that?" she asked in as friendly a tone as she could muster.

His back stiffened before he rolled his shoulders. A glance over her head, probably at Brooke, had him sighing. "Yeah. I'm a shit cook."

She gave him a half-smile then stepped up next to him. "I'm not the best either, but I think we can handle flipping a few pancakes between the two of us."

He grunted and handed over the spatula. She flipped the ones he'd poured onto the griddle, then grabbed the bowl and scooped more batter. Scott stayed quiet but kept that laser-sharp gaze on her. She had to consciously keep her hand from trembling, especially when he reached in front of her to grab his coffee, and she got a whiff of a clean, fresh, soapy male scent. God, the man smelled like some insane combination of strength and fresh laundry, if that was even possible.

They worked in silence as Brooke buzzed in and out of the kitchen. Given the way Scott felt about her, their proximity and the silence should've felt more awkward, but it was oddly comforting. His large, imposing presence had her feeling safer than she had since leaving Chicago. Nothing would happen to her while Scott was nearby.

Unless he killed her himself, of course.

Brooke disappeared through the doors again, prompting Scott to finally break the silence. "I'm sorry about this morning."

Her eyes bugged, and she bit her lip to keep her jaw from hitting the floor.

He huffed a laugh and rolled his eyes. "Accusing you of bailing on Brooke's invite. I didn't know she hadn't told you about breakfast."

Oh, my God, the man apologized. To her. Sure, his grimace made her think it physically hurt him to apologize, but he'd done it. "I… uh, it's fine." *Profound, Livy. Truly.* "I mean, it's all right. You were just looking out for your friend. It's admirable, really."

He was back to grunting his responses.

Or so she thought.

He rested his palms on the counter and turned his head her way. Those eyes, green like hers but such a different shade, seemed to see straight inside her. "Look, I was a dick. You don't need to excuse it."

She nodded. "Thank you."

Maybe this could be the start of a tentative friendship.

"I don't want you here."

Or maybe not.

"But I told Brooke you could stay, and Deke would beat my ass if I turned you away, the fucking softy, so I won't go back on my word. You can stay as long as you need to sort your… stuff. I won't give you shit about it. I'll even try to stop being a dick. Just keep outta my way as much as possible, and I'll do the same. Agreed?"

A painful lump formed in her throat. "Agreed," she

croaked. For a second, one fleeting, glorious second, she'd thought he'd extend an olive branch. But no. At least he wouldn't be openly hostile anymore as long as she kept her distance.

They reached for the bowl of pancake batter at the same time. She beat him to it by a fraction of a second, which meant his hand landed on top of hers. It was so much larger and so rough. Immediately, a shower of electricity buzzed up her arm, lifting all the little hairs as it traveled to her core. She yanked her hand back with a sharp inhale.

Had he felt it?

One glance at him confirmed that notion. He stared down at her, eyes swirling with something. Heat? Lust?

Her heart sped as he stepped into her personal space, forcing her to tilt her chin up. Her lips tingled under his gaze. Oh my God, was he going to kiss her?

Yes. Despite his words, he was about to kiss her.

He leaned in closer.

She might pass out.

The door swung open as Brooke strode back into the kitchen.

Scott jerked back as though he'd touched the hot griddle.

Olivia's heart stuttered to a stop in her chest. Face hot as the Florida pavement on an August day, she picked up the bowl and went to work on the next round of pancakes as though nothing had happened. She kept her gaze down, unable to look at Scott or Brooke.

Had that even happened? Or did she conjure his smoldering gaze up in her imagination? What the hell was wrong with her? Nothing had happened. Whatever attraction she felt was all in her head. The man had told her he'd tolerate her presence out of some misguided sense of obligation to the half-brother who barely knew her, but he had no desire to get to know her in any way. And there she was practically swooning like a teenager whose crush glanced her way for the first time. God, if his hot stare caused such a visceral reaction, she couldn't imagine how she'd react to having his naked body pressing her down into a bed.

Or the floor.

Or against a wall.

Gah! Get it together.

After the touch she vowed to forget, they finished the pancakes in stilted silence. Olivia measured every movement to ensure their skin didn't come in contact again. He probably felt the same as her, unwilling to cause a scene or mess up Brooke's plans for breakfast.

When they moved to a long table to eat, Scott took the seat farthest from where she sat.

As much as she should look at his offer of peace as a gift, she couldn't shake the heaviness in her chest. He'd closed and locked the door on any friendly association, and she'd be lying if she claimed it didn't hurt.

A lot.

To top it off, every time he smiled at something one of his brothers said, her stomach fluttered.

Leave it to her to experience some sort of wild attraction to a man who couldn't stand her. Her older brother's best friend, no less. Shaking her head, she bit into her pancake.

Huh, it'd turned out quite tasty.

It was time to put thoughts of Scott out of her head and use this reprieve to plan the next phase of her life. She'd spent the past few days in Florida more worried about her relationship with Scott than Lance. "You have some wires crossed, girl," she mumbled.

"Don't they say something about the first sign of losing your mind is talking to yourself?"

Her cheeks heated as she looked up into the face of the man sitting next to her, Tracker, she believed, stared down at her with an amused expression. "Sorry. Was I talking out loud?"

"Yes, ma'am, you were." He winked, then pointed to himself. "But as you can see, I'm not much of one for conventional thinking, so go right ahead and yammer away."

Conventional couldn't be used to describe the man, that was for sure. He had tattoos. Lots of tattoos. They covered his arms and peeked out from the collar of his T-shirt. Then there were the piercings—at least three on his face, two wide gauges in his ears, and who knew what she couldn't see. Dark hair fanned across his head in an impressive three-inch mohawk. Tracker was the type of man Lance would've bristled at on sight and refused to speak to. Yet, he seemed to be the most charismatic and friendly of everyone here.

"Conventional is boring," she said with a smile for the charmer. "Trust me." She'd been conventional, classy, and polite her whole life. Where had it gotten her?

Hiding from her fiancé with no plan for her future and no one to turn to for help except a man who hated her.

"Amen to that," Tracker said. He held his coffee mug out toward her.

With a laugh, Olivia lifted hers and clinked it to his. "Cheers."

Scott might not want her there, but Brooke seemed to like her as did Tracker. Though she hadn't found what she'd been searching for when she came to the MC, maybe it hadn't been a complete mistake. Being around this close-knit group gave her insight into what she'd like for herself in the future. And this was exactly it—friends, chosen family, meals together, laughter, and support—maybe with a bit more conventional group than a club of outlaw bikers.

Though these guys were nothing like she'd initially thought they'd be. All but Scott seemed to accept her without judgment.

She and Tracker chatted and joked for most of breakfast. After a few moments, Pulse and Lock joined in, then Jinx, who was the biggest man she'd ever laid eyes on, yet seemed to be as sweet as a teddy bear.

Tracker slid his arm across the back of her chair and left it there as he told a story about a frat boy who'd bawled like a baby during his first tattoo. Olivia found herself laughing more than she had in ages.

At one point, she met Brooke's gaze. The older woman winked, and Brooke smiled in return.

Damn, she was glad Scott had woken her up. She could've done without the heart-stopping pounding on her door, but it seemed to have ended well.

Thoughts of his name had her peering down the table to where he sat. As though sensing her attention, he glanced up and caught her gaze. Of course, her stomach did that stupid fluttery thing again. Maybe when she landed somewhere a little more permanent, she should see a doctor.

His eyes shifted to Tracker's arm behind her chair, and immediately, his smile flipped upside down, and the scowl returned.

So much for their truce.

Chapter Nine

Devos was the kind of man who needed to fall flat on his face and suffer a dozen or so kicks to begin to dent his ego. He was young, fit, cocky, and brash.

Annoying as fuck.

But he wasn't as rich as he wanted to be, hence the borrowing of fifty thousand dollars from the Handlers in the final push to get his tech company off the ground. He'd owe something like eighty thousand in a week with the added interest, but the company had mega promise and should be extremely lucrative in no time.

"Mr. Devos," Scott said as he ignored the receptionist and burst right into the man's spiffy office. "Hope I'm not interrupting."

The arrogant twenty-something with his slicked-back hair, pricy suit, and manicured nails jolted. He sat at his desk, phone to his ear, mouth open as though catching flies.

"Hello? Craig? You still there?" Scott heard a woman's voice coming through the phone.

"I'll call you back," Devos said before hanging up the phone despite the woman's protests.

The near trembling receptionist appeared at the open

doorway. "I'm sorry, Mr. Devos, he barged right in."

"It's okay, Sandra," the man said, waving her away. "Shut the door, please."

She nodded and scurried out as fast as possible.

"Spec." Clearing his throat, he straightened in his chair and smoothed the lapel of his fancy suit. "Did you have an appointment?"

Scott nearly snorted. "Is that little flex supposed to intimidate me?" Make him feel lesser because he was in jeans and a cut instead of an overpriced Armani suit?

"Excuse me?"

He strode forward, then planted his hands on the desk, hovering over the man. "I'm hearing rumors I don't like, Devos."

"I... uh, I'm not sure what you mean."

Scott cocked his head as he studied the man. Then he chuckled and dropped into one of the empty chairs opposite Devos' desk. "Ohh, nice," he said as he wiggled into the soft leather. "How much of my club's money bought these bougie chairs?"

Finally, the man paled. About time he realized this wasn't a friendly visit. "I'm not, uh, I'm not sure how much the chairs cost. I don't think it's real leather."

"No? Huh, feels nice," Scott said as he ran a hand along the leather. It was real, all right. "Smells like a fucking dried-out cow to me. You lying to me, Devos?"

"N-no."

"Hmm." Scott leaned back and kicked his legs up, propping his boots on Devos' desk. A neatly stacked pile of paper crumpled under his heel. "These are real leather. You like 'em?"

"What?" Devos' eyebrows drew down. "They're... nice."

"Thanks." Messing with this guy's head was the most fun he'd had in ages. If Curly hadn't said he wanted an update within the hour, Scott could've played this game all afternoon. But as it was, the prez didn't find as much joy in the potential delay of his cash.

"I still have a week left," Devos said.

Scott inspected his fingernails—blunt and uneven on rough, calloused hands. Nothing like Devos' soft-filed ones. "You do."

"So, uh, why are you here?"

"You like going to have someone file your nails and shit?"

Devos blinked. "What?"

"Never really got the appeal." Devos couldn't keep up with the conversation switches. Scott lived for this shit. Confuse and overwhelm before attacking, similar to tactics he'd used in combat. Only now, he didn't get to play with the fun weapons, but psychological warfare had its own perks.

He dropped his feet to the ground. "I'm hearing some concerning shit," he said as he slapped his palm on the desk, making Devos jump.

"Wh-uh, what do you mean?"

Scott stood and began to explore the office. "Well, for starters, I hear you don't have the money to pay us back." He picked a small modern knick-knack off a metal stand and pointed it at Devos. "And you promised us you'd have the money and more. Remember?" Grinning, he set the ugly thing down in the wrong spot.

Hard.

So. Much. Fun.

Devos' eyes bugged. The stupid piece of marble probably cost as much as they'd lent the idiot. He wanted to jump up and return it to its rightful home. Scott could feel the uncomfortable need to fix it coming off the guy in waves. But Scott intimidated him, so he kept his ass in his chair. "Yes, I remember. And you don't need to worry. I have the money. Y-you'll get it on time. Next week."

That subtle reminder of how he still had seven days to get his shit together had Scott laughing. "Oh, great. Phew," he said, placing a hand on his chest with a dramatic sigh. "Cuz a little alligator told me you might have given some of that money to Lobo. You know, maybe to have his guys harass our women in public. Keep us stressed and focused on what that bastard's up to. If we're too busy dealing with Lobo, we might give you a pass on returning the money on time."

Devos paled. Bingo.

Lobo was a small-time criminal, dreaming of making it big in the outlaw world. Basically, he wanted to be Curly, so he'd teamed up with some of the guys in the prez's former club. Guys like Dante and Rag, the fuckers who'd hassled Brooke and Olivia. Lobo didn't take it well when it became clear Curly had no intention of reconnecting with those motherfuckers. Poor guy wasn't man enough to handle a little rejection from the club.

Lobo became a prickly thorn in the MC's side. Since he wasn't invited to join, he'd decided to fuck with the Handlers instead. A few months ago, he'd kidnapped Maverick and his ol' lady when they were visiting Florida. He knew the Handlers were in the business of loan sharking and probably approached Devos with a little deal to fuck with the club. It bugged the hell out of Scott to think this guy might have used Handler money to pay Lobo to harass the women. Liv might annoy the fuck out of him, but he'd kill Devos before letting him hurt her.

He walked behind Devos' desk and kicked the seat of his fancy office chair. It spun in Scott's direction. He caught it by the armrests and loomed over Devos. "Did you pay Lobo's henchmen to harass Curly's ol' lady? M-my ol' lady?"

He'd nearly fucked that up. Christ, saying he had an ol' lady, in general, was weird as hell. And to pretend Olivia was that woman?

Hello, mind fuck.

But even he could admit she'd look hot as sin in a Handlers' cut with those tiny denim shorts she'd worn at breakfast.

Devos shook his head so fast, his cheeks rippled. "No! No. I didn't do that. You'll have your money. One... one week. I'll have the money. I swear it."

Scott stared him down. A bead of sweat rolled from Devos' temple. "Good to hear. Trust me when I say you don't want to know what'll happen to you if you're late." He grinned a smile he'd been told looked maniacal. Whatever worked. "See you next week, bud."

He patted Devos on the cheek, not quite as hard as a slap, but more than a friendly touch. Then he strode toward the door. About halfway there, Scott spun back, snapping his fingers. "Oh, one more thing." He lowered his voice to a deadly tone Deke used to call his *oh shit* voice. "I find out you had a hand in scaring my woman, and it won't matter if you pay the money back tenfold. I'll cut off your balls, paint 'em gold, and give them to my ol' lady to wear as earrings. She likes gold." He winked. "She's classy like that."

Any remaining color leeched from Devos' face. He swallowed hard.

Scott gave him a sunny smile. "See you in a week."

As he left the office and then the building, he forced himself to keep his walk light and bouncy, as though calling Olivia his woman didn't affect him when, in reality, it freaked him the fuck out. Mostly because his body wasn't rejecting the idea as he'd expected.

The moment he'd called her his woman, his cock had perked up and taken notice. Dammit, he knew he shouldn't have jerked off to thoughts of her bent over his bike last night. He'd been in the shower and horny, not because he'd seen her sitting at Brooke's pool in that skimpy bikini, but just plain hard because he was hard. Nothing more.

But he had thought of her in one of those flouncy little sundresses she liked to wear. She'd also been wearing a very sexy, very needy gleam in her eye as she stood next to his bike. So he'd mentally torn the straps of her dress, watched it fall to the ground, then fucked the shit out of her over his bike.

He'd come fucking hard too. So had she. The princess was the screamer in his filthy fantasies.

It had to be why talking as though she was his woman affected him today. Because there was no way in hell any part of him, even his cock, liked the idea as a legitimate possibility. She was bossy, snobby, superior, and lazy as hell.

Is she, though?

As he reached his bike, he glanced down. "No one asked you," he said to his cock, which was trying to bust its way out of his jeans. He scrubbed a hand down his face. "Jesus, I'm talking to my dick."

Thoughts of Olivia reminded him he wanted to warn Tracker off her. He'd noticed them acting all chummy at breakfast. And he hadn't liked it one bit. Not because he was jealous. Hell no. This was nothing more than having Tracker's best interest in mind. His brother didn't need a woman who was used to the finer things in life. The man owned a tattoo shop and lived in a one-bedroom bungalow five steps from the beach.

He couldn't even understand why Olivia appealed to Tracker. Sure, she was hot. Sexy as fuck, but Tracker had his hands on hot, nearly naked women every day. She was also damned adaptable, being able to jump into a group of misfit bikers without batting an eye. And there was a chance she was tougher than he'd given her credit for. And if he were honest, she hadn't once complained about the very basic accommodations, or the farm, or Brooke's horde of animals hanging around. So maybe she wasn't quite as prissy as he'd accused her of being.

Not that any of those things mattered. He'd wanted no part of her when she'd arrived, and nothing had changed, even if the rest of his club seemed to be falling under her spell.

He swung his leg over his bike just as his phone rang. "Lo?" He answered without checking the screen.

"Scotty!" His sister practically squealed into the phone.

"Christ, Clo, tone it down a bit. I was hoping to have my hearing for a few more decades. What's up?"

"Rocket and I are coming to visit!"

"No shit? When?" Visits from his sister and her ol' man never disappointed. Chloe was a kick-ass sister. She was a kick-ass woman in general. She'd survived a horrific trauma and came out on the other side stronger. Now that she had Rocket in her life, she smiled all the time. He and her ol' man hadn't gotten off on the best foot, but that was years ago, and now they were brothers through the patch.

"Pretty soon, we're thinking. There are a few details to work out up here, but I'll let you know before we head out to ride down there."

"Can't wait."

"So, what's new?"

Scott frowned. "Why do you sound weird?"

Chloe scoffed. "What do you mean?"

"Your voice is weird. Like you're trying to be all innocent when really—" Oh, hell no. "Brooke called you, didn't she?"

"Huh? I have no idea what you mean." Someone, probably Rocket, snickered in the background.

"You're a shit liar, sis. Is that what this surprise, very-soon visit is about? You want to come down here to meet Olivia? Make sure I'm not being too much of an asshole?"

"Told you he'd see through you," Rocket said.

"Pfft, you shut it." Chloe's muffled voice had Scott chuckling. "Fine," she said when she came back on the line. "Brooke called me. She said she thinks Olivia could use all the friends she can get. And she might have mentioned you haven't been the most welcoming person in the world."

Of course, she did. "Not your business, Clo."

"Told you that too," Rocket called out.

"Excuse me, are you looking to sleep on the couch tonight?"

Rocket snorted. Then there was some whispering that'd probably make Scott vomit if he knew what Rocket was promising to do to his sister, especially since he caught the words *tongue* and *hours*.

"Hey, pervs, can we focus?"

"Sorry." Chloe sounded a little more breathless than she had a few moments ago.

He'd be ignoring that.

"Look, everything's fine here. I'd love for you to visit but not meddle in my shit. Olivia's just slumming here for a few weeks, and then she'll head back to her fancy life in Chicago."

"Hmm."

He frowned. "What's that mean?"

"Nothing! Fine, I won't push. But I still want to visit."

"Door's always open, Clo."

"Great. Last thing I'm gonna say. Be nice to her, Scott."

He rolled his eyes to the sky and bit his tongue.

"You might not understand her world, but that doesn't mean her problems aren't real. The closeness of the club is one of the things that saved me. Don't deny her that if she needs it."

Ugh, way to lay on the guilt.

"Thought you were butting out?"

"I am! I said I was done. So how are *you*? You been controlling your anger?"

For fuck's sake. If he needed a lecture, he'd call his mom. "Goodbye, Chloe."

"Ugh! You're so annoying! Bye! I'll call you with the details. I love you," she rushed out before he disconnected.

Shaking his head, he hit the throttle and started the trip back to the Handlers' farm, but it wasn't the mind-clearing ride he'd been hoping for. Instead, it was fraught with thoughts of Olivia and questions about why she'd come to Florida and why the thought of her as an ol' lady wasn't horrifying.

In fact, it almost sounded good.

Chapter Ten

For the third time over the past week, Scott caught Olivia frowning at her phone. She sat on a picnic table outside the clubhouse, oblivious to his presence. He'd be lying if he didn't admit to being curious.

If he had to guess, he'd say texts from her ex-fiancé.

Were they pissed-off messages, cursing her out and spewing hatred?

Were they sweet words of love, hoping to win her back?

Were they hot? Full of raunchy promises of long erotic nights if she returned?

That's what he'd send, though. With the way she scowled at the phone, he'd guess it was the first.

The guy was an asshole. At least Deke had thought so the one or two times they'd met over the years. What was his name? Lucas? Larry? Something like that. Scott hadn't given enough of a shit to remember. He recalled the important details—Jerk who'd stared down his surgically enhanced nose at Deke and hadn't bothered to hold back on his disapproval of Deke's visit.

She was better off without the guy.

She huffed, making her shoulders rise and fall, then set the phone face down on the picnic table. Instead of leaving, she stared off into the distance. He didn't like the tension in her spine or the bunched shoulders.

Brooke made no attempt at hiding how much she loved Olivia. They hung out daily, and she'd been invited to every club event over the past week. It made it hard to avoid her, but he'd done his damnedest. Even if she'd seemed to lose the stick up her ass since she'd arrived, his head was too fucked up over Deke to attempt a friendship. Not to mention he popped a boner every time he got close to her like he was some high schooler who couldn't control urges.

It probably had something to do with the fact her uniform had changed from expensive dresses to tanks and cutoffs, much like Brooke. He'd still never seen her with a hair out of place or without perfect makeup and nails, but at least she no longer looked like she was heading to a church brunch every day.

Jinx wandered up to the picnic table and sat his huge ass next to Olivia. She tensed as the table creaked, then relaxed and smiled at him. Scott forced himself to ignore the hot twist in his gut as he watched her laugh at whatever the hell stupid shit Jinx was spewing. Within a few minutes, she was leaning her head on his shoulder as they chatted, and Scott was flexing his fists at his sides.

"Down, boy," Tracker said, snickering. "You look like a snorting bull right now, and Jinx is wearing a red shirt, so maybe chill out?"

"What the hell are you talking about?"

With a chuckle, Tracker shook his head. "Nothing, man. You need her to go inside?"

He glanced down the road where a shiny Mercedes was stopped, the driver talking to JT. The hangaround pointed toward the clubhouse, and the driver resumed driving.

"Nah. Pretty sure Devos was the one to hire Lobo, so I

want him to lay eyes on Olivia. He gave Lobo money to harass her and Brooke. I want him to know who she is and how serious I am about him staying the fuck away from her."

"Your ol' lady, right?" Tracker said, doing a shit job disguising his smirk.

"Fuck off."

"Hey!" Tracker lifted his hands. "You're the one who told Devos she was your woman."

His gaze shifted back to the table where Jinx and Olivia had noticed the car. Jinx held a hand out as though instructing Olivia to remain seated at the table. Her eyes immediately went to Scott's. He nodded once, and somehow, she seemed to understand he wanted her to sit tight.

He didn't want to think too hard about why he got a thrill from her looking to him for guidance. Nope. Not thinking about that at all.

Thankfully, Devos pulled up, drawing his attention. Scott made the tactical decision to have the guy return his money on the Handlers' turf. Devos needed to see the men who'd be removing his limbs if he so much as talked to Lobo again or breathed in the direction of the women.

He parked his expensive ride then got out, frowning as his fancy shoes sunk an inch into the slightly wet ground. It'd rained the night before, and the mud hadn't fully dried. Scott didn't greet him, just stood, arms folded as he waited for Devos to come to him. The guy carried a shiny metal briefcase, probably full of the money he owed like they were in a ransom movie.

Next to him, Tracker grunted. "This guy for real?" he asked as he watched Devos try to keep his shoes out of the mud.

Jinx sidled closer but lingered between Devos and the picnic table as a barrier to Olivia. Perfectly styled, as he'd been last time, the guy looked exactly like someone he could picture Olivia with.

Scott hated him even more than he had last week.

"That my money?" he called.

Devos' gaze shifted between him and Tracker before he nodded. "Yes. It's all here, with the interest."

"Fucking better be," Tracker said.

Devos' eyes widened, and Scott couldn't hold back his laugh. He'd kill to be in the guy's head right now, getting the unguarded reaction to Tracker. The two men couldn't have been more on opposite ends of the fashion spectrum with Tracker's mohawk, tattoos, and piercings.

When Devos reached them, he held out the briefcase. "Who wants it?" he asked with a slight tremor in his voice.

"That'd be me," Tracker said. Once he had the case with the cash, he said, "Gonna head in and count it all up. If it's good, you can go."

"Oh, it's, uh, it's good." His wide-eyed gawk stayed with Tracker.

Having Devos come to the farm was the right decision. This was so fun.

"Hope so." Tracker disappeared into the clubhouse, leaving him and Devos nothing to do but stare at each other. Scott didn't mind. Waiting he could do. Hell, he'd stayed in one place for days, prone in the desert sand for orders to move.

Devos, however, sucked at keeping his cool. He shifted side to side, ran his hands through his hair, and let his gaze wander.

To Olivia.

"That your girlfriend?" he asked.

Scott grinned as he reached out and slapped Devos' face. Not too hard, but probably felt like being hit by a truck to a soft guy like Devos.

"What the fuck, man?" he shouted, cradling his cheek.

From the corner of his eye, he caught Olivia's spine snap

straight and her hand fly to her mouth, but she kept quiet.

Admirable.

Jinx didn't. He laughed long and loud.

"I say you could look at her?"

"N-no." Devos' cheek was bright red and already swelling.

Whoops. Maybe he'd hit a little harder than he'd intended. Whatever. At least the guy would know he wasn't screwing around.

"So why the fuck are your eyes on her."

"S-sorry."

Scott grinned. Damn, this guy was too much fun. Bet it hurt like hell for him to apologize. Guys like Devos thought they were the shit. Top dogs in their little closed-off social circle of corporate cogs. Felt great to take him down a few rungs.

"Money's all there," Tracker called out from the door to the clubhouse.

"Pleasure doing business with you." Scott held his hand out.

Devos eyed it as though it was a snake ready to strike but reached out and took it. The second their hands met, Scott yanked him close. "Now you know what she looks like. She's mine, Devos. Stay the fuck away. I don't like it when my woman's upset. Makes me violent. Next time, I won't be as sweet. I'll make your head roll across the damn farm. Get me?"

"Y-yeah. Sure, man. Of course."

Scott straightened. "Get the fuck off club property."

Devos practically ran to his car. This time he didn't bother to try to save his shoes which had Scott and Jinx laughing as he slipped and skidded in the mud.

"Damn, brother, that was some beautiful work," Jinx called once Devos was driving away.

Scott grinned at him. "Fun as fuck too." Even though his

brain screamed at him to go straight into the clubhouse, he couldn't help but glance at Olivia. He was pretty sure Jinx filled her in on who Devos was and his connection to the man who grabbed her throat.

Would she be disgusted by what he'd done? Slapping a man unprovoked? Probably.

When he met her gaze, he got his answer, but not the one he'd expected. She stared straight at him then nodded and gave him a small smile. Almost as though thanking him for looking out for her.

That couldn't be right. The Olivia he knew would turn her nose up at the possessive display, even if it were all for show.

Then again, the Olivia he knew wouldn't wear those damn short cutoffs and that tight-as-fuck tank top.

So maybe he didn't know Olivia at all.

OLIVIA STAYED SITTING on the picnic table, watching the wind rustle the grass and the chickens running around long after the guys went inside. If anyone in Chicago saw her, they'd think she'd had a lobotomy.

But she loved it there. The warmth, the fresh air, the peace of nature. So many things she'd never bothered to enjoy all spread out before her. Taking advantage of it soothed her soul.

The quiet gave her much-needed time to think as well. Before Jinx had joined her, she'd been scrolling through Lance's social media accounts under her father's name. She had his passwords memorized since she'd set it up for her dad.

Careful not to inadvertently comment or like any of the posts, she'd scanned everything Lance posted in the past few weeks, searching for any mention of her. By now, people had to be talking, right? Wondering where she'd run off to? Curious as to why she'd bailed on her commitments and hadn't accompanied Lance to any functions.

The answer had come in the form of a tweet from Lance stating she was struggling with depression and had checked herself into a mental health wellness facility in Sweden for thirty days.

Comments had poured in. Love from hordes of people who didn't actually give a crap about her but wanted to be on Lance's good side.

Sickening.

But at least it gave her a few more weeks of reprieve before people would wonder where she'd run off to. Of course, if Lance found her and killed her, that would work to his advantage much more than hers.

That was enough. She rose from the picnic table. If she sat out there much longer, she'd think herself crazy because the next topic to analyze was the fact that Scott slapped a man across the face for looking in her direction.

Yikes.

She refused to dwell on the fact that she found him standing up for her sexy as hell because that was just plain insanity. And what the hell was that look he gave her before he disappeared back into the clubhouse?

No, time to find something to distract her from her thoughts. Maybe she could wrangle an invite to Brooke's. The dogs always set her mind right.

But first, she heard a rumor Lock had brought donuts when he'd arrived, and she could use a sugar fix.

She strode into the clubhouse's kitchen to find mayhem.

"Don't you fucking dare!" Jinx said. He held his hand in front of him, warding Tracker off while the other held a cream-filled donut high in the air. Tracker bobbed in front of him as though looking for the perfect place to attack.

"Swear to Christ, if you steal my favorite donut, I'll shave that fucking mohawk in the night."

Lock jumped at his side, trying to reach the donut, but Jinx was a mountain of a man, holding the treat way out of Lock's reach.

"Livy, help!" Jinx cried. "Make these assholes leave me alone."

Laughing, she lifted her hands. "Sorry, buddy, you're on your own. I'm just here for the sugar fix."

Scott came walking in from a side door. His eyes lit then as he took in the scene, then he crept behind Jinx, quiet as could be. The man had some impressive stealth skills.

Olivia pressed her lips together to keep from laughing and giving away his presence.

With the silent mobility of a ninja, he sprung up from the ground and onto Jinx's back, piggy-back style.

"Holy fuck," Jinx shouted as he jolted. "You almost made me piss myself."

Olivia gave up holding back her laughter. These guys were hilarious. Lance wouldn't even eat a donut without a knife and fork, let alone play keep-away with one. When was the last time she let loose like the guys and just had some fun?

Was it bad if she couldn't even recall a time?

Probably.

Scott stretched up and plucked the donut out of a sputtering Jinx's hand. With a victorious whoop, he tossed it to Olivia. Somehow, she managed to catch it. She took a huge bite.

"Mmm, that's good," she said around a mouthful of sugary goodness. She licked her lips, then looked up to find Scott's gaze locked on her mouth. Her insides clenched. How was it possible for one look to amp her up so much? She couldn't help it and slicked her tongue across her lower lip again, just to watch Scott's eyes flare.

And they did.

"You're all dead to me!" Jinx grumbled, killing the

moment. "Bunch of rotten thieves."

Laughing, Scott dropped down from Jinx's back with lithe movements.

She couldn't help but wonder if those moves translated to the bedroom. Ugh, the man needed to stay out of her brain.

Scott's gaze clashed with hers. They held, suspended for just a moment before Jinx let out a roar and attacked. He lifted Scott off his feet in a bear hug, which had to be a huge feat because Scott was over six feet tall.

But compared to Jinx, he was small.

"Got you now, asshole!" Jinx yelled. Laughing like a loon, he muscled Scott over to the walk-in pantry. "Now you're gonna sit in there and think about what you did," he said as he shoved Scott into the dark pantry and slammed the door. He used his bulk to keep the thing closed as Scott tried in vain to escape.

Olivia shook her head. "Why do I feel like a preschool teacher right now?"

Tracker chuckled around a mouthful of donut. "No clue."

"You gonna put me down for a nap, Miss Olivia?" Jinx asked.

"Ugh," Lock said, shaking his head. "That's just creepy, dude." He grabbed a donut from the box and took a bite in his typical calm manner.

"Thanks for the donuts," Olivia told him.

He lifted his snack in salute before heading out of the kitchen.

"Wait up," Tracker called to him. "I'm coming with."

Olivia frowned as she glanced toward the pantry. Her stomach wobbled with unease. "Uh, Jinx, why is Scott being so quiet?"

The big guy snorted. "Probably planning a sneak attack the moment I let him out. Not happening anytime soon," he hollered to the closed door.

Something wasn't right. She had no idea how she knew it, but her gut was screaming. "Jinx, I hate to be a buzzkill, but, uh…"

Think, Olivia. Scott would hate to show his brother weakness if something was wrong. And she really thought it was.

"Brooke asked me to bring her a bag of dog food. She ran out at the house and keeps extra here. I'm gonna need to get in the pantry."

Jinx let out a dramatic sigh. "Okay, fine. For you and Brooke, I'll let him out. But I'm not stupid enough to be here when he gets out. He'll kick my ass."

She snorted. "You're huge."

"Yeah, but you ain't seen Spec in one of his trance-like rages. Trust me, girl, he could take down the whole club at once."

Olivia frowned. Did it really get that scary?

"C'mere." Jinx dropped his voice to a whisper, waving her over. "Put your back to the door. I'm gonna run out, then you can release him."

Rolling her eyes, she did as asked.

Jinx scurried from the room, and a few seconds later, she stepped away from the door.

"Scott?" she called out. "It's open."

Nothing happened. Frowning, she walked to the pantry and pulled the door open.

Scott stood in the center of the huge walk-in, wide-eyed and trembling. Fear, like she'd never expect from a man as tough as him, was written across his face. He almost seemed in a daze, unaware of her presence.

"Scott?" she whispered as she lifted her hands. "It's okay. You can come out."

He jumped as though she'd shocked him. The fear disappeared, replaced by a steely furious scowl that had her stomach sinking. "Where'd Jinx go?" he asked as he stormed past her and out into the kitchen. "His ass is mine."

He played the part well. Said exactly what she'd have expected if he were still in the game. But his forehead was covered in sweat, his hands had a subtle tremor, and his face had paled to ghostly levels. His eyes darted around wild, uncoordinated swoops, scanning every direction of the kitchen.

Something was wrong. "Are you okay?" she asked, taking a step toward him. She had to clench her fists to keep from reaching for him. As much as she wanted to touch him, to soothe him, he'd never tolerate it from her. And she did want to touch him. Wrap her arms around him. Preferably when they were both naked and needy.

What was it? She'd seen Lance angry, sad, frustrated, sick, stressed, and never once did she experience a physical need to press her body against his and absorb his pain through her skin. But it was there with Scott.

He gave her a sharp glare that had her stopping in her tracks. "What the hell do you mean? Of course, I'm okay. Or will be once I kick Jinx's ass."

He shoved past her, bumping her shoulder with his. She couldn't help but notice his shirt felt damp with perspiration.

She frowned at his back as he stormed out of the kitchen.

Why the hell was Scott sweating like he'd been in a sauna instead of the air-conditioned pantry for two minutes?

And why did she want to wrap her arms around him and promise whatever plagued him would be okay?

Chapter Eleven

Though no longer openly hostile, Scott continued to avoid her, and she returned the favor. With Brooke inviting her to dinner or over to the house nearly every day, Olivia frequently ended up in his presence, but she did her best not to engage. If the others found it weird, they kept their opinions locked down.

There were three problems with the pretend-the-other-doesn't-exist plan. The first being her constant awareness of him. He entered a room, and she knew. Her stomach went haywire, her neck tingled, and she got turned on, which led to the second problem. She wanted him more and more each time she saw him. The man was sex in jeans. She'd caught sight of him shirtless, sweaty, and walking out of the gym the other day—instant wet panties for the first time in her life.

And the third problem—the man never took his eyes off her.

Never.

Even at this club party, Olivia felt the weight of his gaze tracking her as she chatted with Brooke by the bonfire. His stare burned her as she crossed the field to get a drink. Was it her imagination, or did that gaze grow colder each time a man spoke to her?

Well, fuck him. She could do whatever she wanted and talk to whomever the hell she wanted. Scott didn't get a single day in her life. Not as her brother's friend, nor as a big badass biker.

He disapproved of everything she did, from staying on MC property to helping Brooke with the dogs to flirting at a party. For fuck's sake, he'd sneered with a lip curl and everything the moment he'd caught sight of her at this party the second she'd arrived.

The rest of his club brothers rocked. It'd only taken them a few days to ignore his grumbling and warnings to keep the hell away from her. Now she jogged with Pulse in the mornings, had lunch with Jinx almost every day, and played pool with Ty each afternoon. Most nights were rounded out drinking a few beers in the clubhouse. Brooke quickly became a close friend, and even Curly seemed to enjoy having her around. Only Scott continued to ice her out and act like a royal jerk in her presence.

The only times he'd shown her anything but hatred or neglect had been that five whole seconds of concern after she and Brooke had an encounter with Curly's old club members, the few minutes he'd spend telling her stories about her brother, and a quick apology at breakfast. Other than that, he remained an ass the past few weeks.

Worst part of it all?

She was so wildly attracted to the jerk. She couldn't make it through a night without an erotic dream that left her drenched in sweat, aching, and reaching between her legs to get herself off to a man who hated her. How embarrassing.

A wolf whistle had her glancing over her shoulder. "Damn, woman, you're fine as fuck."

A smile curled her lips as Tracker approached her, weaving around a few partygoers. Of all the guys, he was her favorite.

So unlike anyone she'd known, he was covered in tattoos, didn't take life too seriously, and flirted with anything that moved. He also had an adorable dog who trotted by his side. "Thanks, Tracker. Hi, baby," she said to the dog as she crouched down to love on her.

"Uhh, yeah, don't do that." Tracker hauled her back up to stand with a hand under her arm.

"What's wrong?"

"Not about to get my ass kicked because I let you flash the whole party by bending over in that tiny skirt."

"What are you talking about?" She glanced down at her black denim skirt and equally dark crop top that bared a few inches of her stomach. Combined with the four-inch heels, she felt sexy and powerful. "I love this outfit. And I crouched. I didn't bend."

"Yeah, pretty sure every cock at this party loves that outfit. But someone is about to have an aneurysm, and I'm not willing to be the one to pay the price for it." He stroked a hand over his stubbly jaw. "This mug is too pretty to be all busted." Then he gestured with his chin in the direction she'd last felt Scott's stare.

Sure enough, he stood near the fire, drink in hand, lethal gaze locked on her.

A shiver ran up her spine despite the warmth of the night. Why was she so turned on by a man who hated her?

"He can't stand me," she said to Tracker. "Trust me, I could strip down naked and dance with every man here, and he wouldn't give a shit."

"Keep telling yourself that, sweetheart." He shuddered. "God, it'd be a bloodbath."

"I'm serious. He's just trying to intimidate me. Get me to leave sooner." Which she'd seriously been contemplating until checking her email yesterday. Lance ramped up the threats, describing in disturbing detail what would happen if she didn't return to Chicago. If she'd been honest, she felt as though she was in a bubble here with the club. Lance's threats via email or DM hadn't seemed real. But something about yesterday's shocked her out of her mild denial and into gear. It was time to put on her big girl pants and make some life decisions.

Tracker slid his arm around her shoulders and drew her to his side. Then he leaned down and pressed a lingering kiss to her cheek. "See, he wants to murder me right now," he whispered in her ear.

Laughing, Olivia playfully pushed him away. "You're crazy. Trust me, he's just afraid I'll get my hooks in you, and he'll be stuck having me here longer."

Tracker threw back his head and let out a long laugh. "Well, you got my vote, sweetheart. Stick around as long as you like. You fit in." With a wink, he headed off to the keg to fill his cup.

Olivia couldn't keep the smile off her face as she watched him leave. He thought she fit in. Strange as it was, and Scott aside, she liked it there with this rough-around-the-edges group. A lot.

Her entire life had been spent in comfort. Housekeepers, chefs, drivers, designer clothes, lavish vacations, you name it, she'd had it. But here with the Handlers, performing simple tasks such as helping Brooke with the dogs, cooking for herself, cleaning her bathroom, and giving Ty her two cents on the design of a car wash he was opening, she was helpful for the first time. Basic as it was, it felt incredible to be doing tasks others found value in. She was contributing rather than existing.

And she loved it. Even if it came with a studio apartment, lukewarm showers, and a farm. The only thing she'd change was Scott's attitude. Having to be on alert to stay out of his way constantly was exhausting.

She glanced at him to find him still watching her. God, those eyes. So intense, so full of secrets and pain. What would it be like to be the woman to crack that man open? To learn what tortured his mind and kept him awake at night because she heard him pacing, occasionally crying out, and punching what she hoped was a heavy bag well into the early morning hours.

So many times, she'd fantasized about knocking on his door and giving him another outlet for his insomnia. Letting him have her body to work out all that frustration and restless energy and to exhaust them both until their heads could finally be quiet enough to sleep.

But, of course, that would require he tolerate being in her presence for more than five seconds.

As she watched him watching her, a woman slithered up to him. She had lengthy legs made even longer with heels higher than Olivia's four-inchers. Her dress appeared to be plastered on, barely covering her ass or tits in any respectable way. Even through the darkness, Olivia could make out layers of caked-on makeup, shoddy hair extensions, and an empty brain.

She looked cheap, easy, and basic.

Scott smiled at the woman and a hot twist of jealousy burned through Olivia's stomach.

"Ridiculous," she muttered as she sipped her drink and shifted her attention to the dancing fire. She tried, really tried not to look again but failed after only a few seconds.

Winking in her direction, he knew this was getting to her, and he loved it. Scott leaned down to the woman's ear and whispered something, keeping his attention on Olivia. The woman giggled and wrapped her arms around one of his big biceps, smashing her tits against him. He laughed at something she said in return, and the jealousy in Olivia turned into something darker, something more depressing.

What the hell was she doing there?

Sure, she was hiding from her fiancé, but there were plenty of places she could go. Literally anywhere. Instead, she chose to stay where she wasn't wanted. Why? Because she felt close to a brother she'd barely known by being near his friend?

Or was the reason more pitiful, like this insane crush she'd developed on the man who hated her?

Regardless, it was time to go. Time to leave Florida and figure out her own problems.

She upended her drink onto the grass then turned away with a sigh before getting sucked back into staring at Scott. At least she wouldn't have to watch him and the woman walk off to find a dark corner to get down and dirty in.

She should say goodbye to Brooke. Her new friend would worry if she didn't, but she'd also try to talk Olivia into staying. And she might get Curly or the others involved. In her vulnerable state, Olivia would be inclined to throw her smart intentions out the window if someone expressed interest in having her stick around.

No, heading straight out was the wiser choice. She'd grab the few things she'd arrived with and get out of town tonight. Once she was far enough away to avoid turning back, she'd text her regrets and gratitude.

This time would fade to nothing but a blip in her memory —a time she'd stepped into an unknown world and learned new things about herself.

Slipping out ended up being easier than she'd expected. Most of the guys had paired up with women, drinking, dancing, or making out. Loud music helped hide her actions. Brooke and Curly weren't anywhere to be found. Hopefully, they'd snuck off to make a few naughty memories.

At least someone was having a good night.

She took her time walking from the clubhouse to the renovated barn. The thick, humid air reminded her of late summer in Chicago, yet May had barely begun in Florida. She'd almost reached the barn when the twig snap had her whirling left.

"Hello?" she called out.

A darkened figure emerged from around the barn, making her take a step back.

"Well, if it isn't the princess."

Dante. One of the men who'd confronted her and Brooke a week or so back.

Immediately the hairs on the back of her neck stood straight up, and she took a step back. This couldn't be good. "W-what are you doing here?" Instinct told her to run, but she'd make it two steps before breaking an ankle in her damn heels.

"I came for the party. Easy to slip in when the place is loaded with people." Much as he had the last time she'd seen him, he wore dark jeans and a T-shirt under an unaffiliated motorcycle cut. The same odor he'd given off last time—deli meat—wafted her way, turning her stomach.

"Party's that way," she said as she pointed toward the field behind the clubhouse where the bonfire could be seen raging away. Not that he'd been invited, but she only needed to divert his attention for a few seconds to get the hell inside the barn.

Didn't work.

He reached out and grabbed her arm before she could step away. "Where you running off to, princess?"

"Let go of me." She tugged but couldn't free her arm from his bruising grip.

"Come on," he said, pulling her to him. His damp shirt pressed against her bare stomach. "Night's just getting started. Since you don't seem to be in the mood for a crowd, how about we have a private party?"

"No thanks," she said as she twisted her arm back and

forth. Her skin burned where his fingers dragged across it.

Still grasping her wrist, Dante propelled her backward. She had no choice but to walk, or she'd fall on her ass. Her back hit the barn, startling a squeak from her.

With each passing second, her heart pumped faster, and her stomach sank lower. If she didn't get away from him, something awful was going to happen to her. She knew what it was but couldn't allow her mind to go there.

Think, think.

He grinned down at her, revealing a few gaps in his teeth.

"Back up. You smell disgusting." She tried to shove him, but he laughed and grabbed her hip. Rough hands landed on her bared skin below her crop top. Disgust crawled over her skin like a horde of insects, so different from when she and Scott had inadvertently touched.

Scott!

"My b... uh, my ol' man, Spec, is waiting for me upstairs." He'd been wary of pissing Scott off the first time she'd met him. She couldn't blame him for that one. Hopefully, his fear remained. "He was in a shit mood today and didn't feel like partying. I promised I wouldn't be long. He'll freak out if I'm not up there in the next two minutes."

As though she hadn't spoken, his hands inched higher until they rested just beneath her breasts. She froze for a split second, but then rage took over. She wouldn't end up violated like that poor girl Lance had taken advantage of. Hell no.

She shoved with all her might, screaming, "Get the fuck off me!" Her words disappeared into the night, drowned out by the loud music.

Dante laughed. "Feisty little, slut, ain't ya? Bet Spec loves that shit. Little pussy cat hissing and spitting at him." Leaning in, he pressed her against the wall with the heavy weight of his thick body.

Hot, rancid breath drifted over her ear, making her cringe.

"I like it too," he said before licking up the side of her neck.

She gagged and struggled for all she was worth, beating on his back and trying to kick him, but his heft rendered her ineffective. "Help!" she screamed. "Get the fuck off me. Help!"

One hand returned to her body, sliding under her crop while the other slapped over her mouth. He pressed so hard she couldn't move her lips enough to bite his palm.

A muffled scream left her as his fingertips grazed the undersides of her breasts.

She squeezed her eyes shut. Tears leaked out and rolled down her face. No way could she look at him as he touched her against her will.

A howl came from somewhere nearby an instant before Dante disappeared.

Olivia's eyes flew open. She blinked, then zeroed in on two men battling it out in the dirt. "Scott!" she yelled.

His fists flew, connecting with Dante's face again and again. Blood sprayed up in an arc before splattering across the ground. Olivia stared in a mix of relief, horror, and fear for Scott. Dante was huge and gave as good as he got.

"Scott!" she shouted again. When he didn't answer, she tried, "Spec!"

Nothing. He was in a trance. Blind to everything around him but the man he'd kill if he didn't stop hitting him.

Olivia rushed forward. If she had to risk a whack to the face to keep him from committing murder, so be it. As she drew close, a loud bark followed by a shout of, "Olivia, don't!" had her freezing a few feet from the deathmatch.

Lock rushed past her. He threw himself at Scott, grasping under his arm. Tracker tagged her around the waist and hauled her away from the danger zone. For his efforts, Lock ended up with an elbow to the nose.

"Calm the fuck down, Spec!" Lock shouted at Scott while blood dripped down his chin.

More men rushed over, but Olivia only had eyes for Scott. Her heart pounded, and her head swam with the implications of what was happening. Dante lay on the ground, bloodied and unmoving.

Had Scott killed him? Her stomach lurched.

Scott fought Lock's hold as he tried to lunge for Dante again.

"A little help here?" Lock called out.

Ty came out of nowhere, latching onto Scott as well.

"Get the fuck off me," he shouted, jerking his arms out of his brothers' hold.

He whirled around and stumbled a few steps back. His eyes were wild, unfocused, and full of deadly intent as they connected with hers.

If he hadn't shown up when he did, she shuddered, not wanting to go there. She'd rather focus on Scott. Whatever had happened, it was as though he'd disappeared into some out-of-control violent episode. Terrifying and heartbreaking.

"Scott," she whispered as she took a step forward.

"Liv, stay back," Ty said, his voice full of warning. Tracker still held her.

"What the hell is going on here?" a loud voice boomed from the gathered crowd. "Oh, fuck."

Olivia diverted her attention to the newcomer. A cop. In uniform. She sucked in a breath.

"This you?" he asked, looking straight at Scott, who had blood on his clothes and knuckles as well as bruising on his face.

All he got for an answer was a sneer.

"Knew when I heard there was a party here tonight there'd be trouble. Of course, it was you. Who the hell else would it be? Scott Hughes, you're under arrest—"

"No!" Olivia shouted, jumping forward without thought. Once again, Tracker held her back. "Fuck, Tracker, let me go!"

"Get her the fuck outta here," Scott yelled, pointing at her as he was pushed to his knees and then cuffed.

"You can't arrest him!" she shouted, flailing against Tracker's hold. "Tracker! Let me go!" This couldn't be happening. He'd saved her. He already hated her. Now he was going to be arrested because of her?

Tracker's arms came around her in a vice grip, stilling her wild movements. "Sweetie, let us handle it," he whispered. "Spec will be fine. He's fucking tough as hell."

"Get her in the fucking apartment!" Scott screamed over his shoulder as the young police officer dragged him off.

Tracker lifted her around the waist and carried her toward the house.

"No! Please, Tracker. He was only helping me." Her heel connected with Tracker's shin as she struggled to get down.

"Ow, woman! Chill the fuck out."

With a wince, she sagged. "I'm sorry. I just can't let him be arrested for helping me. That guy would have... he was going to... you know."

Tracker stiffened, then set her down. "Then I'm sorry Spec didn't kill him." Before she had a chance to make a break for Scott, Tracker ushered her into the barn. "Hey," he said, gripping her shoulders. "We'll work it out. Trust me, okay? He doesn't want you to see him like this. Go upstairs, pour a drink, and let us sort it. Okay?"

Freaking men. "Fine," she grumbled. "But I'm not happy about it."

Chuckling, Tracker hugged her. "Understood. I'll send Brooke up in a minute."

Olivia nodded against his chest, hugged him back, then trudged up the stairs. Pouring a drink involved more effort than she had the mental capacity to manage, so she grabbed an open bottle of wine from her refrigerator, yanked the cork with her teeth, and guzzled right from the bottle.

After a few good swallows, she headed to her tiny closet, kicking her heels off on the way. She couldn't sit around waiting to hear something. She'd go insane. So, she changed her clothes, washed off her makeup, and made her way back to the kitchen for the rest of the wine. Who knew how long she'd been standing at the counter drinking when someone finally knocked?

"Scott?" she cried as she yanked the door open.

But, of course, it wasn't him. Why the hell would he be at her door?

"Sorry, no. Just me," Brooke said with a sympathetic sad smile.

"Where's Scott?" Olivia asked as she stretched to see beyond Brooke into the hallway. "Is he okay?"

Brooke cringed. "Um… turns out that cop is a relative of a guy from Curly's old club. So, uh, Scott was arrested and taken in about fifteen minutes ago."

"What!" Olivia shouted. It felt like the entire world was crumbling around her, and she had no idea what to do. "That's bullshit. That asshole had his hands all over me even though I was screaming and fighting. Scott saved me from being assaulted! They *arrested* him? I'm going to the police station."

She scanned the ground. Dammit, where were her sneakers?

Brook grasped her shoulders, stilling her movements. "Liv, Curly and the guys are in church right now, talking to their attorney. She's good, and she'll get him out. What are you looking for?"

"My shoes! I need to do something. He can't spend the night in jail." He'd freak out. He hated small, enclosed spaces. No, he'd never told her, but she noticed things. He had a hard time riding in cars. The other day he mentioned something to Pulse about how he hated elevators. And that incident with the pantry? Total claustrophobic meltdown. "I'm going to get him the fuck outta there."

"Olivia, you're drunk. You can't drive there."

Shit. Brooke had a point. She didn't feel drunk, but she had inhaled half a bottle of wine in the past half hour. "Drive me. Please." She grasped her friend's arms. "Please, Brooke. He can't stay there. You know he's struggling with some things. Trust me when I tell you, a jail cell is the worst place for him right now."

Indecision crossed Brooke's face. She stared at Olivia for a long moment. Each of those passing seconds felt like hours as Olivia tried her hardest to keep from shaking her friend. "Fine," Brooke finally said, staring up at the ceiling. "Curly is gonna kill me. Gimme your car keys."

Relief hit fast and hard. "Thank you," Olivia said as she hugged Brooke. "Thank you. Thank you. Thank you. I promise I'll take all the blame. I'll talk to Curly." She spotted her sneakers near the kitchen. Releasing Brooke, she ran toward them, stuffed her bare feet inside, then grabbed her keys from the counter. "Here," she said as she tossed them to Brooke.

Two minutes later, they were speeding toward the local police station. Olivia breathed, counted to fifty, and called upon her inner bitch. The one she'd tried to bury over the past few weeks. There was no way in hell she was leaving that police station unless Scott was in the car next to her.

Chapter Twelve

Sweat. Heat. Stale air surrounded him.

Scott tried to breathe, but he couldn't. The air was too thick, too heavy, too familiar. He was back. In the desert. In the box. Waiting for pain. Waiting for torture.

Waiting to see Deke.

No.

He shook his head and clenched his fists against his damp thighs.

Deke was dead. He'd died almost two years ago.

And Scott had been rescued from the desert. He couldn't be back there. So why was he suffocating inside a sweltering box as walls closed in on him?

A harsh laugh ripped him from the past and deposited him on a hard bench in a tiny Florida jail cell. It had three solid concrete walls to his sides and back and one wall of bars in front of him.

Right. He'd been arrested for kicking the shit out of Dante. How the hell had he gotten on the compound? The fucker had dared to put his hands on Olivia. Christ, the panic in her voice as she pleaded with Dante to stop had instantly sent Scott into the uncontrollable rage he'd been experiencing

135

more and more lately. The kind of anger that demanded action and results. A fury he had no choice but to charge into and use his fists to destroy.

His only regret was that Dante still breathed. Or at least he'd been alive when that hick cop slapped the cuffs around Scott's wrists. Hopefully, Curly could get the club's attorney there quickly because he wasn't sure how much longer he could tolerate the cell. It didn't matter that he could see the entire tiny building between the bars. The cell was still a box he couldn't escape.

Last thing he needed was to lose his shit and give the cops a free show of his greatest weakness. No one knew about his issue with enclosed spaces. He didn't want their pity, didn't want their questions, and had no intention of telling anyone why he'd taken the door off his closet.

Fucking trauma. Sometimes he even struggled to close the door when he had to piss.

Another laugh made him glance up. Sweat dripped from his chin to the concrete floor.

The desk cop he'd been handed off to—a cocky little shit with a fucking mustache—stood at the front desk laughing. "What's wrong?" he asked with thick mocking in his tone. "Does the big, bad biker not like being locked up?" He sauntered over, grinning like this was better than Christmas morning.

Scott scowled. It was all he could do. His tongue had dried up, and his throat constricted. He'd rather be smothered in honey and left near a fire ant hill.

Officer Stache gripped the cell bars, giving them a rattle. "Better get used to it."

The door to the police station opened, but Scott kept his attention on the cop.

"Heard you fucked Dante up good. Unprovoked as I hear it. Get comfy. You're gonna be here for a—"

"Excuse me!" Olivia's voice, full of superiority and disgust, broke through the cop's rant. She stormed through the tiny lobby to where the officer stood. "Unprovoked? Did you just say unprovoked?"

Officer Stache shuffled his feet and stared at the floor. For the first time since the cell slammed shut, Scott's lips quirked.

"Uh, ma'am, if you need to file a report, I can help you at the desk," the cop said as he tried to usher her away from the cell.

"Don't you dare touch me," she seethed, stepping back. Her gaze flicked to him, concerned and furious before focusing back on the cop.

Scott almost felt bad for the guy. He'd been on the receiving end of her fury a time or two, but this seemed like another level. She was out for blood.

"Sorry, ma'am. Meant no disrespect." The cop lifted his hands.

Olivia snorted. "That's rich." She jammed her hands on her hips then walked until she was an inch from the cop. He towered over her, so she had to tilt her head way back. "Who do I speak to, to get him out of there? You? Or someone higher ranking?"

Scott would've laughed if he wasn't working so hard to keep the panic attack at bay. Officer Stache straightened and puffed out his chest. "I'm the only one here tonight, ma'am. But—"

"Great. Let him out," she said. "Now."

Clearly, the rookie cop had no idea how to handle the demanding female. "Uh, I can't do that, ma'am. He's been arrested for assault. He'll have to be arraigned and have bail set."

"Assault?" she practically shrieked. "You wanna talk about assault? This man saved my life tonight." She gestured toward the cell with a wild arc of her arm. "That putrid piece of shit, Dante, attacked me. He put his hands on me. Under my shirt." She placed her hands over her tits, and the cop's eyes nearly bugged out of his head. "Touching my body despite the fact I was fighting and screaming at him to stop. You understand what I'm saying? And do you know what that's called, officer?"

"Um, yes, ma'am." He shifted. "That's sexual assault."

Brooke quietly walked into the station and stayed by the doors. Her eyes widened as she took in the sight of Olivia confronting the cop.

She stood with her hands on her slender hips and fire shooting from her eyes. "That's right. It's sexual assault. Scott is the only reason I wasn't raped!" she screamed. "He shouldn't have been arrested."

"Fuck," the cop said. "Um, are you willing to make an official statement?"

"I'm willing to do whatever the hell I have to do to get him out of that goddamn jail cell as fast as possible."

"Follow me, please." The cop walked over to the desk.

Scott met Olivia's gaze. In the two weeks since she'd appeared at the clubhouse, he'd not once seen her in anything other than a coordinated outfit, pristine shoes, perfect hair, and flawless makeup. She always looked ready for a magazine shoot, no matter the time of day.

Except for tonight.

She wore olive green sweatpants and a Handlers' T-shirt one of the guys must have given her. Her face had been scrubbed clean of its party makeup, and her hair sat high on her head in a sloppy bun.

She was a mess and the sexiest woman Scott had ever seen. Christ, she was gorgeous all done up, but like this? All natural? She was stunning. An air of vulnerability clung to her. One she obviously hated and worked to mask with the armor of impeccable style and attitude. But there, staring at him through the cell bars, he saw it. The soft underbelly she hid with sass and snobbery.

He hadn't wanted her, anyone really, but her especially seeing him this way. Sweating, near shaking, exposed, and raw. She was too smart for her own good, and those damn shrewd eyes saw straight through his bullshit to the panic lying beneath. Fuck it, she knew he was hanging on by a thread, and she knew why.

Damn her.

"Go home, Olivia," he rasped.

She cocked her head. "No." Then she squared her shoulders and marched over to the cop's desk. Scott couldn't help the rush of pride that surged through him. She'd been through a lot tonight but rallied and now fought like hell for him. Much as he wanted her back at her apartment and away from his mess, he had to admit he admired the fuck out of the stubborn way she defended him.

He'd been wrong about her. So had her brother. She might have been raised as a pampered princess, but her spine was pure steel.

She was Deke's sister, all right. God, he'd have been proud of her tonight. Still, he'd make sure she knew not to involve herself in his shit again.

She sat at the desk, furiously scribbling away on a notepad, probably documenting what had happened with Dante. Fuck, if only he'd arrived sooner, it wouldn't have gotten as far as it did.

How the fuck did that asshole get on the property? As soon as he got the fuck out of there, Scott would be talking to Curly. This shit with his old club members needed to end. They had to make a statement, or they'd be seen as pussies. Curly's goal of not drawing attention to the club wasn't working. It was time to let his enforcer do his job.

It was time to try things Scott's way.

The door opened and in strode the club's lawyer with Curly hot on her heels. The prez took one look at Brooke, rolled his eyes, then pulled her to him for a long kiss.

Olivia's head popped up from her writing. She stood. "You must be Scott's attorney," she said with authority.

The lawyer stood an inch or so taller than Olivia and wore a maroon suit that gave her a sharp, competent appearance. Yet she had nothing on Livy's natural presence.

"That's right, I am. And you are?"

"Olivia. I'm the one who was being assaulted when Sc... Spec showed up and kicked that fucker's ass. I want him out of that damn cell in the next few minutes. Whatever it takes, whatever it costs."

Fuck, she was a bossy little thing. He'd love to see what happened when she channeled all that feisty energy into something a hell of a lot more sexual. He bet something wild and uninhibited lay beneath her polished veneer. Maybe she'd never let that side of herself out to play before, but if he ever got his hands on her, he'd make sure the vixen prevailed. Not that he'd ever be in that position.

She was Deke's sister, for fuck's sake.

He should be shot for even going there in his mind.

The lawyer smirked then held out her hand for Livy to shake. They continued speaking in much more hushed tones. Then his attorney pulled out her phone and made a call. She seemed all business, jotting notes and nodding along with whomever she was speaking to.

Office Stache spoke into the phone as well, arguing under his breath. He didn't wear the same confidence as the attorney. Hopefully, that meant something good for him.

Time slowed, and the cell began to shrink down on him again. Why the fuck did this have to happen now? He wasn't alone and could see everyone else in the police station. Air flowed freely in and out of the damn jail cell. Yet he might as well have been suffocating in that fucking hot box in the desert. His clothes were drenched in sweat, and his chest tightened until he feared a heart attack.

After a few moments, which felt like hours, his leg bouncing became more of a tremor. The trembling traveled up his calves, through his thighs, into his stomach until he had to clutch the edge of the bench with all his might to keep from shaking right off the damn thing.

Thankfully, no one paid him any fucking attention. No way in hell did he want the cop, his attorney, or any of his brothers to see him being a pussy. He just needed a second to get his body under control. Closing his eyes, he tried a technique the army psychologist he'd had no choice but to work with had taught him.

He listened to the clipped tones of his attorney barking orders into her phone.

He inhaled the musty scent of the jail cell.

He felt the cold, hard bench under his ass and beneath his fingers.

Shitty as this situation was, he wasn't in the desert. He was in Florida. Safe from torture.

Christ, nothing made him feel weaker than being forced to rely on these head-shrinking games. But they goddamn worked, and if he could pull it off without anyone knowing what the hell was happening inside his brain, he'd do it.

Because a full-blown panic attack would be the height of humiliation.

Once he had some semblance of control over himself, he opened his eyes to find Olivia's anxious eyes staring at him through the cell bars. She stood right there, her hands wrapped around the metal.

The woman had no idea how sexy she was. Standing there in a T-shirt and sweats, she was hotter than any of the women who came by the clubhouse dressed to entice. If shit was different, if he wasn't fucked in the head, and if she was the filthy rich half-sister of his dead best friend, he'd have been all over her, right then and there in the fucking police department. All he'd need was a few minutes to slip his hand between those bars and down her pants. He'd work her over until she was soft and breathy, creaming in his hand and pleading to come.

"Better?" she asked with concern bleeding from her tone.

That worry, that hint she knew he'd been struggling snapped him straight out of the dirty fantasy and back to the cold, hard, shitty reality. "The fuck you talking about? I'm fine."

She pressed those pouty lips together then shook her head. "Don't do that. Please. No more games. Not tonight. Tomorrow you can go back to hating me but be real with me tonight."

Be real with her? What? Tell her how he got her brother killed? How he wasn't strong enough to fight back? How he came out of that godforsaken desert with more screws loose than a rickety table?

He stood and met her with the bars between them. "Don't be so dramatic, princess. My attorney's here now. Why don't you take your fancy ass back home and let someone who actually contributes to society take over?"

Anger flashed in her gaze. He could literally see her hackles rising. And he was a sick man because all that fury only made him want her more. Christ, if she let all that passion out to play in bed, she'd be a goddamn animal.

He smirked, waiting for her to rip into him. Their typical interaction. Maybe foreplay were they any other people.

But she squared her shoulders and gave him a sad smile. "It doesn't work," she said. "Pretending to be okay all the time. Eventually, the truth catches up to you. And it seems like it's been chasing you pretty hard for a while now. Stop running, Scott. It's easier that way. Trust me. It's not pretty if it catches you on its own."

He gripped the bars hard, refusing to allow her words to penetrate the steel he'd reinforced his skin with. Who the hell did she think she was? And what the fuck did she know about anything? "I don't need a spoiled, pampered—"

"Mr. Hughes, Ms. Truitt." The attorney's heels clacked on the floor as she marched over. "I'm sorry about the tremendous inconvenience of this shoddy police department's handling of what happened tonight." She spoke loudly, so the cop would hear her. He scowled from the desk. "We'll have you out of here as soon as the paperwork is complete."

She turned to Olivia who'd stepped back. "I'm assuming you want to press charges on the man who assaulted you?"

Fuck. With all the bullshit happening in his head, he'd forgotten what got his ass tossed behind bars in the first place. Now that he looked at Olivia with something other than lust or frustration, he could see the toll the night had taken on her. Light bruising on her neck spoke to the incident he'd been lucky enough to fucking interrupt. If he'd had it to do over again, only thing he'd change would be how hard he'd hit that Dante fucker. Next time, he'd make sure the guy couldn't get up.

Ever.

"Absolutely," Olivia said with a nod. She wrapped her arms around her belly.

Scott frowned. The move made her smaller, meeker than he'd ever seen her, and it didn't sit right. Olivia wasn't small. She was bossy, superior, and fucking exuberant.

"Great." The club's attorney held out a card. "Give me a call tomorrow, and we'll get the ball rolling."

"Thank you."

With all she had at her disposal, wouldn't she have her

own attorney, or fuck, even a team of attorneys who could make Dante's life a living hell? Why would she use the club's?

"Great. Let me put a fire under the officer here so we can get you home and sleeping in your own bed." With a grin, the attorney turned and strutted her way back to the desk where Officer Stache worked, filling out papers.

"Olivia, go home," he said as Brooke and Curly approached the cell.

"I'll take her." Brooke wrapped an arm around Olivia's shoulders. "Come on. You've gotta be exhausted."

"Yes. I am." Her voice held a note of sadness it hadn't had when she'd spoken with him. Maybe even disappointment. Well, she could join the club because that's exactly what he was to himself as well. One big giant disappointment, and if she thought he was going to cut himself open and bleed his emotions all over her or anyone, she was insane.

Curly stopped them from leaving with a hand on Brooke's arm. "I'll hang around and take Scott back. See you at home, baby. Don't wait up."

Brooke smiled at him. "You know I will anyway. Love you."

"I love you," Curly said before kissing her the way he always did, with passion and hunger. No pecks on the cheek for those two.

Olivia watched them with naked longing on her face. It only lasted a second or two before she caught herself and averted her eyes.

Scott frowned. Did she want something like Curly and Brooke had? He sure as hell never considered it for himself. Who the hell would put up with his issues?

"Bye, Spec. I'll probably see you tomorrow." Brooke waved and guided Olivia toward the exit. Halfway there, Olivia glanced over her shoulder. The concern was back in her gaze, and it kicked him square in the nuts. Aside from his sister, who worried over him?

Not a goddamn soul.

And that's how he liked it. It was much harder to disappoint people when you didn't get close to them.

Yet despite pushing her away with every weapon he had at his disposal, Olivia still cared.

He frowned.

Why the hell did that make him feel warm inside?

Chapter Thirteen

He'd returned home twenty minutes ago.

And Olivia had been standing outside his door for five of those minutes. The shower ran, meaning he wouldn't come to the door if she knocked. So why wasn't she going back inside her little apartment?

Well, that was because he'd left the door unlocked and for four and a half of the past five minutes, she'd been alternatively talking herself into and out of barging into his apartment.

Why did she care how he was holding up? He'd made his dislike of her clear on every occasion possible—almost every time they were in the same room together. So why the hell couldn't she leave him alone? Why did she feel this draw to him she'd never experienced with another human being?

Was it the connection to her brother?

Was it how he'd helped her out of a terrible situation tonight?

Was it the inner struggle she sensed in him? Like a wounded animal needing a safe home?

Or was it because he appealed to her physically the way no other man ever had?

It didn't matter. She needed to walk away. Leave the man alone and worry about her own problems, which no one in the club was aware of yet.

But instead of doing all that, she grasped the doorknob and turned it, letting herself into his private space.

His studio mirrored hers, so she knew exactly where the bathroom was. As though possessed by some unknown entity, she walked straight toward the open bathroom door. He was in there. Naked. Wet.

Suffering?

Or had he written the night off as a crappy one and moved the hell on.

As she should be doing.

With each step closer to the bathroom, her heart sped and her knees shook. Her body reacted to his nearness in the most reckless ways. Beneath her T-shirt, her nipples tightened and ached. Her skin tingled like it did when she was about to be touched by someone she wanted. It'd been so long since she experienced that electric buzz of anticipation, and it had no place in that room.

Nothing of the sort would happen.

She'd poke her head in the bathroom, make sure he was okay, and be told to get the hell out.

Despite a voice in her head warning her over and over that this was a horrible idea, she kept moving toward the bathroom. With only a few more steps, she found herself staring into the steamy space.

Her breath hitched, and her sex clenched at the sight that greeted her.

Scott stood in the shower with the sliding glass door open.

Naked.

Muscular.

Tattooed.

Scarred.

So many scars. Her heart plummeted at the sight of them. What the hell had he endured? And how had he survived? No wonder he fought monsters in his head. One of which seemed to be small spaces. First, the way he reacted in the pantry, then the cell, and now he kept the shower door open despite water spraying into the bathroom.

He faced the showerhead with one arm braced against the wall and his head resting on his forearm. Water sluiced down every dip and ridge on his body, making her jealous of hydrogen and oxygen.

The man was a work of art. Sexual power and temptation celebrated in one very erotic man. His other hand played with his very stiff erection. Not jerking it but fondling his balls and teasing the tip of his dick.

Olivia's mouth flooded with saliva, and her sex grew damp as the two orifices fought over which wanted him more.

She stood frozen, staring at him with her body rioting for fulfillment and her brain screaming at her to run.

But she'd never leave. She couldn't. Wouldn't. Because right alongside his sex appeal was a cloud of despair, and all she wanted was to chase it away.

"S-scott," she whispered. Hopefully, her presence wouldn't startle him or make him slip.

His eyes popped open, and he stared at the wall in front of him for a beat before slowly turning his head in her direction.

Olivia swallowed.

Lust blazed in his eyes, along with anger, frustration, and even resignation.

"If you're not planning to strip down, climb in, and drop to your knees, what the fuck are you doing here?"

The question alone nearly sent her to the floor. She grabbed the countertop for support. "I-I wanted to make sure you were okay."

"That doesn't answer my question." He wrapped his hand around his length, then gave a few firm tugs.

She knew what he was doing. He was trying to scare her away so she couldn't peek beneath his protective veneer to the damaged man at his core. But she'd never had this reaction to the sight of a naked man before and didn't feel an ounce of fear. There was this raw need to touch and be touched, no matter the consequences. And regardless of the fact, he didn't even like her.

She took two steps forward in what might be the stupidest decision of her life. Scott smirked. With the way they fought, he probably assumed she'd tell him to go to hell. The smirk fell right off his face as she whipped the T-shirt over her head.

His gaze instantly went to her bare breasts, and heat flared in those eyes. Instead of feeling exposed or helpless, a surge of power rushed through her veins. He liked what he saw. He wanted it and her despite their differences.

Just as she wanted him.

Without looking away, she curled her thumbs inside the waistband of her sweatpants and panties and shimmied them down over her hips. When she straightened, she found Scott's hand had stilled on his cock. His expression held a mixture of challenge and disbelief, daring her to continue while not actually believing she would.

The appreciation in the way he stared at her gave her a thrill like no other. Scott was easily the most attractive man she knew, and the fact she affected him sent her soaring.

She swallowed down the sizzle of nerves reminding her she might not be able to handle a man like him and slowly closed the distance to the shower.

She stepped in, maneuvering herself into the small space between him and the wall. He didn't bother stepping back to give her additional space. Immediately, the heat of the water mixed with the intense heat radiating off him, her head spun.

Neither of them spoke. Words weren't necessary. Their gazes met and held for long moments, saying everything they couldn't voice. They both needed this.

A release.

A connection.

To feel something deep and powerful.

Scott reached out and slid the shower door closed. They were enclosed in their steamy world, just the two of them and whatever burned between them. She checked his face for panic or signs of claustrophobia, but all she saw was desire.

As slowly as her trembling thighs would allow, Olivia lowered to her knees while keeping her gaze fixed on Scott's face.

"Open," he said in a gravelly command, still baiting her, still testing to see if she'd follow through or if she was just that good at bluffing.

He had no idea how much she wanted this. She'd given Lance plenty of blowjobs over the years. And a few other guys before him. Some were fine, some eh, and some she'd even enjoyed. But this was the only time she'd craved the feeling of a man's cock between her lips. She wanted his taste on her tongue. She needed his groans in her ears. Hell, she even wanted to feel his hands dominating and holding her head while he took what he wanted from her mouth. Anything to keep him looking at her like she was the most desirable woman in the world. The need to be the woman who could make him forget whatever had been tormenting him back in that jail cell had become an obsession she couldn't shake.

So she'd give him this. And maybe it'd give him some measure of peace. Some relief from whatever haunted him. She'd never acted this way before. So brazen with her sexuality. Offering herself for what would be a purely physical, borderline aggressive sexual encounter with Lance wouldn't have been fathomable.

But she craved it with Scott.

She lowered her jaw and waited at his feet for whatever he was about to do.

"This isn't romance," he said, sounding as though he was fighting for air. "There won't be anything sweet or tender about this. This ain't nothing like that kiss you watched between the prez and Brooke."

Yes. Exactly what she wanted—to feel something other than fear, confusion, anger, helplessness. She wanted to feel powerful, sexy, wanted. To use her body to ease his anguish and give him relief as well.

The tip of his cock hovered an inch from her wide-open mouth. Instead of answering, she leaned forward and circled it with her lips, sucking the head and tonguing his slit.

"Fuck," he shouted as his hips jerked forward. He slapped the shower wall and let out a groan.

She popped off him then cast her gaze upward. "You have demons that torture you."

His eyes narrowed in warning. What the hell was wrong with her? She was literally baiting the beast. She'd seen him flip out on more than one occasion. Just tonight, he'd almost beaten a man to death. He lived on a hair-trigger, and the gun was always loaded.

And yet she didn't feel any hesitation. Only an erotic desire so strong she nearly vibrated with it.

"Use me. Give them to me. I'm at your mercy. I'm not here for romance." This was in no way a pity fuck or gratitude for saving her earlier. She knew what she was in for.

Rough, raw, and primal.

"Don't say I didn't warn you." He slid his thumb into her mouth then curled his other fingers under her jaw and pulled it down. "So pretty like this," he said in a husky voice. "Waiting for my cock."

Electricity zapped down her spine. Her nipples were so tight, they ached for his touch. What was happening to her? She was in the most vulnerable position possible. On her knees before a man who struggled with his anger. Whose strength dominated hers. Who could hurt her if he wanted.

And she was more turned on than she'd ever been.

He removed his thumb, replacing it with his dick. Olivia held her breath. Any trepidation took a back seat to the fire in his gaze. The man was one hundred percent with her.

Much slower than she'd expected, he pressed his hips forward and guided his cock into her mouth. Immediately, she closed her lips around him, giving him the drag of wet, hot friction as he thrust.

"Jesus," he whispered. The muscle outside his jaw fluttered as he clenched his teeth. His nostrils flared, and his abs rippled.

Olivia slowly lifted her gaze, locking onto his. So much desire smoldered in his eyes, she felt it pumping through her blood, driving her on. Despite his dominant position, she held all the power.

His dick slid deep, bumping the back of her throat. She gagged, but his appreciative groan made it worth any discomfort. As he began to withdraw, she grabbed his ass and held him in place.

It took a few seconds to relax and adjust to breathing through her nose, but his shouted curse when she swallowed made her feel like a powerful goddess.

She sucked hard as she drew her head back, dragging her lips along his cock. Before she could tease the tip, he plunged back in. Again and again, they played this game, her retreating and him chasing. His thrusts grew harder and more desperate after a few minutes.

"Fuck!" He fisted her wet hair but didn't steal her control. Water ran down her body and over her sensitive breasts, ramping up her desire as much as his constant grunts of pleasure.

His eyes were slits, as though he fought to keep them open, and his chest heaved with every breath.

"Fucking sinful mouth," he ground out as his fingers flexed against her scalp.

She hummed, and he slapped the wall. If she could've smiled around his thick cock, she would have. Saliva coated her lips and pooled at the corners of her mouth, driving the man out of his mind.

"You fucking love it, don't you?" he asked, sounding as though he was mid-marathon. "Love me fucking your pretty face."

She hummed her agreement.

"Get your fingers in your pussy," he ordered as he continued to pump in and out of her mouth. Her rhythm faltered, and he rammed against her throat, making her gag again. But, hell, she didn't care. Relief from the incredible tension twisting her lower belly was on the way. After giving his ass a firm squeeze, she ripped her hand away and shoved two fingers into herself. A muffled moan escaped around his cock.

Since discovering Lance cheated, she'd avoided sex with him and had become quite proficient in getting herself off. But this was next-level.

"Fuck, that's as hot as your damn mouth."

Overwhelming sensations bombarded her from all angles. Fingers played in her pussy, stroking exactly where she knew would get her there fastest. Scott was huge and hovered over her with that intense, sex-filled gaze. His cock shuttled in and out of her mouth. Her head spun, and her body buzzed while she worked herself over.

The closer she got to coming, the sloppier the blowjob became. Soon, Scott let out a strained mumble. "My turn," he stated as his grip on her hair tightened. There went her control. He took it easily, though she didn't put up an ounce of fight. "You concentrate on petting that pussy, and I'll drive up here."

He was rough, deep, and borderline too much but so attuned to her that he never crossed the line. He held her head still, taking what she'd offered. Olivia kept up as best she could, sucking, licking, and swallowing, all while riding her fingers.

Her entire body began to tremble. How could this feel so incredible? It was raunchy as hell. The filthiest sex she'd had but also the hottest. Scott didn't hold back on letting her know he loved it too. His curses, groans, and words of encouragement gave her an emotional pleasure that matched what her fingers were doing in her pussy.

"Stroke your clit, Liv. Fucking get yourself there. I'm close. Want you to come when I shoot down your throat."

She whimpered and did as he asked, pressing her thumb to her clit while she curled her fingers. The bite of pleasure-pain from her scalp joined the sensations stealing her ability to process anything but the physical.

"Fuck, so damn sexy. Such a hungry mouth."

Her toes tingled, and as she circled her clit, the white-hot pleasure exploded inside her. She cried out around Scott's dick as the orgasm blurred her vision, and she swore the pleasure reached her soul. Shaking and dizzy, she worked herself through it.

Scott shouted, "Fuck yes," then grabbed her face with both hands. He held her still, shoved deep, and came with a powerful cry. Olivia swallowed reflexively, trying to keep up.

"Take it all," he growled down at her. "Fuck."

Damn, watching him find his release nearly made her come again on the spot. His muscles flexed, and his eyes grew near black. Those tattoos danced and tempted her to stand and run her hands over his skin. But he wouldn't want that, it'd be too tender, too sweet, too emotional.

This had been nothing more than a reprieve from the screwed-up night.

The reality of what they'd done crashed around her as he slipped from between her lips. The water had cooled, no longer fogging up the shower. Gone was the intimate little world they'd created.

What the hell had she done?

That had been the most primal sexual experience of her life, and it happened with a man who despised her. She let her guard down and exposed her vulnerable underbelly in a way she hadn't even with her fiancé. And he turned out to be a monster. Would Scott spew cruel words that would humiliate her and turn something she didn't fully understand but had loved into regret and embarrassment? Would he send her away?

As he came down from the high, his eyes blinked open, and he pierced her with his laser gaze.

She waited, wet, chilly, and somewhere between sleepy-sated and terrified. Without so much as a flicker of a smile, he reached under her arms and hauled her up to stand, pulling her flush against him. She rested her chin on his chest, staring up at him. Heat from his muscular body soaked into her, chasing away the cold.

"You won't do what I expect," he said in a thick voice as he stared at her lips.

They tingled under his appraisal. What would she do if he kissed her right then? Not that he would. This wasn't romantic. Wait, he'd just said something. "What?"

"I keep pushing you away, and you keep destroying all my barriers no matter how much I bark and growl." He pushed her damn hair out of her face. "I don't understand you."

"I—" Words failed her. How did she explain the connection

she felt with him?

"Thank you," he whispered, and her eyes nearly fell out of her head. He chuckled. "Come on. You're shivering, and it's late."

As he guided her out of the shower, grabbed a towel, then rubbed her dry, she stood there gawking like she'd lost her tongue. Even though they weren't talking, this was the most relaxed and open she'd ever seen him. Even when he interacted with his brothers, he always appeared on edge.

He pressed his lips to her forehead in a gentle kiss so in contrast with the rough sex in the shower, and his heart went soft and gooey.

Pride swelled inside her. She'd done it. She'd given him what he needed to feel good.

But now she'd opened a door she wasn't sure would close again. Panic began to bubble up. What did this mean for them now? Would they go back to the cold animosity? She couldn't imagine it. Would he demand further answers as to why she was there? What would happen if she told him?

She'd been ready to leave Florida just a few hours ago. Now she wanted nothing more than to crawl into bed with Scott and beg him to hold her all night long. Instead, she grabbed her clothes and hightailed it across the hall to her apartment like the coward she was.

She stared into the darkness until her eyes grew too heavy to remain open and her brain finally began the slide into sleep.

And then her phone chimed.

Chapter Fourteen

Scott stared at the ceiling long into the night.

Olivia had blown his mind. Literally. He worried his brain had melted and blasted out his cock with the strongest orgasm he'd enjoyed in years, if ever. Christ, his bones had nearly liquified, and for a moment, he'd wondered if he'd slip right down the drain with the water as the shower cooled.

And to watch her get off on getting him off? Something he'd never bothered to give much thought to, but Liv was fucking captivating in her pleasure.

Fuuck. What the hell happened to the stuck-up woman who stared down her nose at him even though she was a good six inches shorter?

The nagging itch at the back of his mind made sleep impossible, wondering if he'd misjudged her all along. If he were honest with himself, he'd taken one look at her gorgeous face, expensive clothes, and prickly attitude and slammed his walls down. When combined with what he thought he knew of Deke's family and guilt and other fucked-up shit in his head surrounding Deke's death, he couldn't stand the idea of her. She was a walking representation of how he'd failed Deke.

So, he'd become a massive asshole to keep her the fuck away.

But she'd seen through his antagonistic exterior to the disaster inside and tried to help.

Hell, she had helped more than anything he'd tried. More than therapy, pills, and alcohol. Even more than beating the piss out of motherfuckers. And that was saying something because he'd discovered the easiest way to quiet the demons in his head was to let them have control over his fists for a while. They'd quiet in the aftermath of a violent fight. At least for a time.

But Olivia, Deke's fucking sister, the woman he'd pushed away with every ounce of his strength, saw through all that shit. She'd stripped herself bare, dropped to her knees, and sucked out every ounce of anguish through his dick. And even though it should've been as temporary a fix as fighting or fucking anyone else, he felt altered on a cellular level.

Why?

Why the fuck had she done it, and why had it rattled him to his core?

The question kept him awake most of the night. Eventually, he fell into his typical nightmare-plagued sleep but woke when the first sliver of sun passed through his blinds as usual. The two and a half hours of sleep he'd managed hadn't done shit to solve the mystery of Olivia. Instead, he woke agitated and wanting to know what kind of game she was playing.

Taking a piss, drinking some coffee, and brushing his teeth did nothing to settle his mood.

He stared across the tiny apartment. The answer to his question resided two doors and thirty feet away. If he didn't get it, today would be another bloody day. The need for another release simmered under his skin, and if he didn't get relief, he'd pound it out of someone. Curly would strip his patch if he didn't find a better outlet.

Olivia's face mid-climax popped into his head. Goddamn, that had been a sight.

"Fuck it." He stomped across the small apartment and out the door. Two steps later, he was pounding on Olivia's door.

"It's open. Come on in."

Seriously? She'd been attacked outside last night and didn't bother to lock the damn door? He twisted the doorknob. Sure enough, it turned, admitting him into her apartment. "Fuck," he whispered.

Just as he was about to berate her for the dangerous move, she called out from the bathroom. "Hey, Brooke, just washing my face. Grab a seat. I'll be right out. Oh, there's coffee if you want it."

He frowned. Brooke must have planned to check on her this morning.

The club's first lady was a damn good woman.

If he were a good man, he'd announce himself, but no one would accuse him of being good these days. He took the few steps to the small bathroom that mirrored his own. Olivia stood in front of the mirror with her palms on the counter and head bowed.

Not washing her face.

Just staring.

She wore nothing but the oversized Handlers' tee she'd worn to the police station last night. The same one she'd ripped off and tossed to the floor before sucking his cock. Long sexy legs extended below the hem of the shirt.

Were her knees sore? The tile floor wasn't forgiving. Fuck, he hoped she'd woken with aching knees. He was a sick man.

After seeing her in that shirt, he was doomed to get at least semi-hard at the sight of his club's logo for the rest of his life. The strange thing was the twist he felt in his chest along with the jolt to his cock. Something akin to pride at the sight of her representing the club that meant the world to him.

As though she sensed his presence, her head whipped up, and her eyes flared wide. "Scott," she said with a gasp. "You startled me. I thought you were Brooke. She said she'd check in this morning."

"Your door wasn't locked."

Straightening, she smoothed down the shirt. "I know. I left it open for Brooke."

Tension thickened the air. Olivia's eyes shifted left and right, focusing everywhere but on his face. Damn, she looked good. Fresh-faced and natural like she did last night. How did the woman not recognize how gorgeous she was without all the expensive potions?

"Uh, can I get you a coffee or something?"

"Okay."

She stepped forward then paused as though waiting for him to give her space. He didn't move, forcing her to squeeze past him. Their bodies brushed, making his abs tense and his balls tighten.

His dick jumped for joy while she sucked in a sharp breath. Her eyes widened and met his gaze for an instant before she quickly side-stepped away. "Uh, have a seat. I'll get the coffee."

She hurried into the small kitchen and over to the full coffeepot. Keeping her back to him, she filled two mugs. "Black, right?"

He grinned. She knew how he took his coffee.

"Yeah."

Instead of heading to the couch, he followed her into the kitchen. After two decades in the military, most of that being in special operations, he had no problem with stealth. He could walk softer than a kitten, especially barefoot as he was now.

Olivia seemed oblivious to his presence directly behind

her. After pouring the coffee, she blew out a breath, planted her palms on the counter, and bowed her head, pretty much assuming the same position he'd found her in.

Only this time, his gaze went to the sliver of ass cheek peeking out beneath the hem of the T-shirt.

He groaned, unable to keep from imaging his hands full of that sexy ass.

Olivia jumped, but before she had a chance to turn, he pressed against her back and splayed a hand across her belly.

She gasped. "W-what are you doing?"

"You're tense as fuck this morning. Need to come again?" Hopefully, she did. Sex was so much easier than untangling the mess in his head.

"What? No, I uh… I'm fine."

Slow as he could manage, he walked his fingers, gathering up the T-shirt. She froze in his arms, but he could feel her racing heart against his chest. A warm and spicy scent tickled his nostrils. She smelled like a fucking dessert, and he was a man who never passed on dessert.

"Regrets?" he whispered in her ear.

"N-no." She shook her head quickly. "Just a, ah!"

He flattened his hand over the silky skin of her lower stomach and tucked his fingertips under the elastic of her panties. "Just a what?"

She shook her head, panting. "A, uh, text. Um, a concerning text. It's nothing."

"Hmm." A concerning text? From whom? The ex? Her asshole father?

Scott ordered himself not to give a shit, but whatever it was, it'd clearly affected her. So he shoved it aside to be returned to later because he had something much more pressing to attend to.

"Sure, you don't want to come again?" he whispered in her ear as he inched his fingers down her panties. He loved that she had a neatly trimmed patch of hair. She seemed like one of those women who spent hours at the spa each week, ridding themselves of every strand of body hair and trying to preserve every ounce of their youth.

But he'd never preferred the hairless trend.

"Hmm?" He dipped his finger through her folds, finding her wet. His rigid cock pressed into the soft curve of her ass.

"Y-yes," she said. She arched her back, rubbing against his erection and making him groan. Damn tease.

"Yes, what?"

"Yes, I want to come." The words rushed out of her mouth. He rimmed her slippery entrance with his middle finger, teasing but not nearly enough to give her what her body was begging for. She thrust her hips forward, clearly trying to coax his fingers inside her.

"Ask nicely," he growled as he played with her.

"W-what?"

"Ask. Nicely."

She squirmed against him. The feel of her ass bumping his cock repeatedly almost had him shoving her forward, yanking her panties down, and burying himself to the hilt. But fuck, he wanted to feel her come all over his hand first. Feel all that hot, creamy arousal coating his fingers as she squeezed and pulsed around him.

"Scott, please!" It came out as a whine, and he fucking loved it. "Please make me come."

"That's better. Let's give this needy pussy what it wants." He shoved two fingers inside her. The way she cried out had him nearly coming in his jeans.

Her pussy clamped down as he stroked her walls. She was hot, scorching, and so fucking wet.

"God, yes," she said on a breathy exhale as her head fell back on his shoulder.

He worked her, fucking her on his hand as she rocked her

hips to help him out. "Feel good?" he whispered before nipping her earlobe.

She moaned and turned her head so their gazes met. She gazed at him through blown pupils. "So, so good," she whispered.

"You gonna let me fuck you after I get you off?" He might die if she said no.

Her eyes darkened with lust, and she nodded.

"Say it."

"I..." He pressed his thumb over her clit. "Oh, shit. I'm gonna let you fuck me."

They hadn't kissed last night, but her lips hovered right there. One inch away. Two little indents from where she'd bitten her lip called to him. He closed the distance, taking her mouth the way he wanted to take her body—hard, harsh, ravaging.

She gave as good as she got, opening for him and accepting the onslaught with enthusiasm. She tasted minty and intoxicating. Her curious tongue explored his mouth. When he bit her lower lip, she moaned and ground her ass against him.

He continued fingering her. Her hips sped, egging him on. After a few moments, she placed her hand over his, keeping his fingers deep inside her. He took the hint, rubbing her walls with fast, rough strokes.

She whined into his mouth, making him chuckle. "That's it, baby," he said against her lips. "Tell me what feels good."

"Scott," she groaned as she rode his hand. She squeezed her eyes shut. "I'm close."

Grinning, he strummed her clit. She jolted hard at the first touch.

"More."

Damn, what was fucking sexier than a woman demanding what she wanted? The Army taught him how to follow orders, and he did it well. "Yes, ma'am." He thumbed her clit again and again. On the third pass, she tensed and dug her nails into his hand. Her mouth opened, and at first, no sound came out, but then her back bowed, and she let out a long wail. She vibrated against him, still holding his hand in her pussy.

"Wow," she said as the shaking became gentler tremors.

He chuckled.

Her head still rested on his shoulder, only now it lay heavier. Her eyes had taken on that slightly drunk post-orgasm haze, and her smile was crooked. His cock was hard as fucking iron against her ass. She shifted, and intense pleasure had him grunting.

Olivia's smile turned wicked. "Something wrong?" she asked with mock innocence as she wiggled that perfect fucking ass.

He grabbed her hips to still the erotic torture. "Yeah, something's wrong. My cock's hungry as fuck."

She straightened, then turned to face him. The sultry look she gave him spoke of pure sex. "Well, we can't have that, can we?" She made quick work of his button and zipper.

Before she shoved them down, he grabbed the condom he kept in his back pocket.

"Guess the army taught you good preparedness."

"Among other things." He'd have winked if he wasn't dying from the gentle brushes of her fingertips against his cock. Instead, he spun her around and pushed between the center of her shoulder blades. She immediately bent forward, sticking that delectable ass out and bracing on the counter with her elbows.

"God, woman, that ass is sinful."

With a light laugh, she hiked the T-shirt up over her hips and shook her ass. He groaned as he pushed his pants down to his knees. "Fucking stop, or I'm going to come from putting the damn condom on."

Her laugh had him smiling despite his desperate need to fuck. She peered over her shoulder, watching with heat as he ripped open the foil and sheathed himself. The minx licked her lips as though recalling the taste of his cock on her tongue. This was the woman he assumed would be a block of ice in bed. How wrong he'd been. She was the hottest fire, and he never could resist a flame.

He rolled the condom down his length, fully aware of her eyes on him. Fuck, it felt too damn incredible. He clenched his teeth and thought of sleeping on the hard ground in freezing temperatures. Anything to keep him from unloading before he got inside her pussy. With the condom in place, he fisted his cock and glanced at her face.

"Scott?" she said in a husky voice.

He raised an eyebrow and rubbed the head of his cock through her soaked folds.

She exhaled, and her eyes fluttered closed as she bit her lower lip. When she opened her eyes, need shone bright and hot.

"Fuck, you want this cock, don't you?"

With a nod, she said. "Yes, Scott." She spread her legs wide and stuck out her ass.

He couldn't help but grab it and knead the soft flesh. His mouth watered to take a bite.

Later.

"Forget what you think you know of me," she said. "I'm not soft. I don't need it easy. I won't break."

Her face was flush with arousal. With her hair in a sloppy bun, he had a full view of the slope of her neck. She'd be walking away with his mark on her skin. He'd make sure of it.

"You saying you want me to fuck you hard, Livy?"

"The harder, the better."

Fuck. The harder, the better. Who was this tempting woman? He didn't do soft. Hadn't for years. Softness left him a long time ago with the shit he'd seen and done. He fucked as he fought with fierce determination and no holds barred, trying to drive away his demons.

His brand of fucking wasn't for all women.

But he'd been willing to try to temper himself if it meant getting inside Olivia.

To know he didn't need to? That she once again saw him through her nonjudgmental gaze and understood what he needed? And maybe to have it be what she needed as well?

He couldn't even call what he'd done to her as misjudgment because it was so far beyond. Whatever she'd been through in her life brought her here, to this same place as him. She needed the same escape.

Wanting the same raw fuck.

"Wish granted, baby," he said as he snapped his hips forward and entered her in one fierce thrust. She tossed her head back and shouted her pleasure.

"Jesus fucking Christ," he ground out. The hot, tight clasp of her pussy made his eyes cross.

Olivia blew out a breath. "So big," she whispered under her breath with praise he probably wasn't meant to hear.

"Why, thank you, beautiful," he said, sounding like someone had run his vocal cords through a woodchipper. "You holding on?"

Her hands moved to the edge of the counter. "Yes."

"Then let's ride." He pulled out and slammed back in with just as much force as he had the first time. Before Olivia could finish crying out, he did it again. He dug his fingers into the soft flesh of her hips as he fucked her with furious thrusts. She pushed back against him, meeting every thrust and increasing the force. Fuck, he wished he'd had the foresight to rip that T-shirt off her. He'd fucking love to watch her tits bounce as he pounded into her.

"Scott," she moaned. Her arms shook with the effort to keep up with him.

"That's right, baby." He grabbed her shoulder with one hand and her hip with the other, holding her in place to accept what he gave her. She whined and tried to move with him, but he had complete control.

"Please, Scott."

He lost all sense of time and place as he dominated her body. She made the most incredible sounds every time his cock bottomed out inside her. Whimpers, shouts, mewls, sexual praying, and his favorite, his name falling from her lips repeatedly.

"Tell me how much you love this fat cock tearing you up?" he asked between pumps. Sweat ran down his back and poured off his forehead. Her back glistened and hair stuck to her neck. He leaned forward and licked a long line up her spine.

"Yes! God, Scott, yes, I love it! Keep fucking me. Don't stop!"

He couldn't talk anymore, too lost in the tightest, hottest pussy he'd ever been in. Olivia's entire body undulated as she tried to work herself on his cock. He kept her as still as he could, giving him what he wanted and taking everything she had to offer. Their grunts and groans rang in his ears with their harsh breathing. They became two animals focused on nothing but discovering the ultimate pleasure in each other's bodies.

"Harder, Scott," she shouted just as he wondered if she could keep on taking him.

He growled and pistoned his hips even faster. Sweat flew off his body.

"Touch my clit!"

"Fuck, yes," he said as he shoved his hand between her

legs. He pinched her clit.

Olivia screamed, and her pussy strangled his cock with powerful contractions.

"God fucking yes," he shouted as her orgasm sent him spiraling into outer space. Colors flashed before his eyes. His balls exploded in white-hot pleasure so intense his knees buckled, and he collapsed onto her back.

Beneath him, she breathed as though she'd run a race. Her pussy continued to flutter around him, and she twitched every few seconds. He glanced up, seeing that spot on her neck he'd vowed to mark. Summoning whatever strength he had left, he stretched up and latched onto her neck with his mouth. He sucked hard.

Olivia groaned but didn't shy away from him. Instead, she tilted her head, giving him easier access. He sucked until she gasped, then licked over the spot. The woman purred beneath him. If his cock weren't completely drained, he'd fuck her all over again.

He pressed a kiss to the hickey, then straightened off her back. She let out a little sigh of pleasure that twisted his insides with a strange warmth. Once upright, he gathered her into his arms, turned her, and kissed the hell out of her.

She melted against him as though they'd never had a cross word between them. When he finished ravaging her mouth, he stared down at her. She gazed up at him with sleepy eyes. "We probably need to talk at some point," she said, but there wasn't anything worrisome in her tone.

"Yeah." He both craved and dreaded time to talk with her. There were so many things he had to say. So many things she might not be ready to hear. He'd faced the worst kind of enemy combatants without batting an eye for two decades, but the thought of revealing his secrets to Liv terrified him. "Why don't you go clean up? I'll get us some fresh coffee, then we can talk. Okay?" He stroked her damp hair away from her face before kissing her again. What would he even say? He owed her an enormous apology to start, but after that, he had no idea if he could voice his thoughts.

"Mmm. That sounds good."

A knock at the door had her spine snapping straight.

"Livy?" Brooke called out. "Just wanted to check on you."

Olivia tried to jump out of his arms, but he held her firm. "Scott! I need to get dressed," she whisper-yelled. "How could I have forgotten she was on her way here? She could've walked in on us. Look at me. I'm a mess. My hair isn't done. I don't have makeup on, and I'm in sweats!"

He chuckled. "I'm still wearing a condom, so I think I have you beat."

She chuckled even as she slapped his arm. "Go in the bathroom while I get myself presentable." Then she called out. "Be right there, Brooke! My God, I never let anyone see me like this."

He frowned and grabbed her wrist before she had a chance to dart to her dresser. "Throw on some shorts, but otherwise, stay like this."

Her eyes bugged. "What?" She ran a hand through her hair. "No. I can't."

He tugged her close. "You're beautiful like this. Brooke doesn't give a shit what you're wearing or if you have makeup on. I guarantee she isn't wearing any. You're stunning like this. All soft and warm." He slid an arm around her waist under the T-shirt, stroking the soft skin of her hip. "Please. It reminds me of fucking you, and I don't want to think of anything else."

She chewed her lower lip, but he saw he'd won.

"Livy, you okay?" Brooke called.

He kissed her.

"Okay fine." Rolling her eyes, she waved at his crotch. "Just get rid of that thing, please!"

Chuckling, he slapped her ass as she turned toward her dresser. She yelped and shot him a glare. "Coming, Brooke!"

He slipped into the bathroom to dispose of the condom.

Much as he loved his president's ol' lady, Brooke better make it fast because he planned on spending the rest of the day buried in the best pussy he'd ever had.

After they talked.

And that thought took care of the re-emerging boner he'd worried Brooke would notice.

Chapter Fifteen

Oliva shimmied her jeans up one leg the second after her bathroom door snicked shut, concealing Scott.

Tingly pops of energy skittered across her skin from head to toe. The orgasm had shaken her to her core. Even Brooke's intrusion hadn't dampened its powerful effect.

So that made twice in less than twelve hours she and Scott had ignored their awkward tension in favor of out-of-this-world pleasure. The universe had to be playing a prank on her. Why else would she have climaxed harder than ever at the hands and cock of a man who hated her?

Though he did seem to be moving past the hatred.

But what the hell did it mean, and where did it go from there? She was keeping a very large secret from him about why she'd fled to Florida. And now that Lance had discovered her new phone number, she might be in danger. Was this time to tell him?

A headache began at her temples.

"Coming!" she yelled at the door as she hopped on one foot while trying to get the other in the jeans. The irony of screaming that word wasn't lost on her. Somewhere in there hid a damn good joke.

As she buttoned the jeans, she closed the final distance to the door. "Hey, sorry!" She opened the door to find a frowning Brooke. "I was in the middle of getting dressed." She glanced down. "If you can call this dressed."

That earned her a smile. "Yes, Liv, you can call that dressed. Jeans and a T-shirt are pretty much my uniform," Brooke said as she indicated to her own denim shorts and T-shirt. "What you wear every day is *dressed up.*"

Laughing, Livy moved aside. "Come in. Want some coffee?"

"I'll take a whole pot." Brooke followed her to the small kitchen. As she dropped into a chair at the two-seater table, she yawned. "Sorry."

"Please," Olivia said as she poured a cup of coffee for her friend. "I'm sure you got about as much sleep as I did... maybe three hours." She walked the beverage to the table before grabbing sugar and creamer and taking a seat.

"Yeah. Curly was up with Ty most of the night, fixing some security holes and planning. We need a way to know if and when someone like Dante gets on the property. Or better yet, make it so they can't." She yawned again, then shook her head. "Anyway, I don't sleep well when Curly isn't there, so I tossed and turned. You?"

"Yeah." Olivia tapped her aching right temple. "Couldn't turn it off."

At Brooke's innocent question, the reason for Olivia's lack of sleep came rushing back with a vengeance. Sex with Scott gave her a few moments of reprieve, but this was a problem she couldn't hide from or shove under the rug. Not without putting others in danger. Her friend would assume she hadn't slept because of what had happened to her the previous night. She'd be correct, only not about which event had kept her up. What had her life become that a near assault and the arrest of Scott pale in comparison to a pre-dawn text message?

"I hear that." Brooke sighed, then gazed toward the door. "Seems quiet across the hall. You heard any movement from Scott? I'm planning to check on him next."

Instantly, her face heated to match the temperature of the Florida sun. "Oh, um, I—"

Her bathroom door opened, and Scott strolled into the room with extra swagger in his steps. The morning orgasm seemed to have done him as well as it did her. He oozed confidence as though strutting around shirtless in the apartment of a woman he claimed to hate was an everyday occurrence.

Shit. How had she forgotten he'd shown up shirtless?

"Oh." Brooke's eyes widened, then narrowed. She pursed her lips. "Huh." A sassy grin grew across her face. "Well, this is new."

Scott folded his arms across his impressive chest as he propped his ass against the counter, looking much too comfortable in her space. Right there where he'd fucked her senseless less than ten minutes ago.

God, what she must be thinking. For weeks, they could barely stand to be in the same room, and now he was making himself at home in her apartment.

Shirtless.

Why the hell did he have to be shirtless? Olivia could barely tear her eyes away from all those delicious muscles even as her face continued to burn with embarrassment.

Scott pushed off the counter. "I should check in with Curly," he said to a smirking Brooke.

"He called church for ten this morning. Gives you an hour or so to get dressed."

Scott closed the distance to the table. "I'll be there." He plucked Olivia's coffee mug from the table and took a sip. The tongue that had been in her mouth and on her neck only moments ago swiped across his lower lip as though grabbing an extra taste. "Mmm. Second best thing I've tasted this morning."

Olivia's mouth dropped open. He did *not* just say that.

A strangled sound of amusement left Brooke.

"Thanks for the coffee. Got distracted before I had a chance to drink mine." Then he winked before sauntering toward the door. "I'll find you later."

Who the hell was that man, and what did he do with grumpy Scott? If it were possible for a human to burst into flames, she'd have done so right then. But from embarrassment or lust, she couldn't say.

The second the door closed behind his very fine ass, Brooke zeroed her astonished gaze on Olivia. "Girl, you better start talking because either you and Scott had some naked fun, or I woke up in the Twilight Zone. Come to think of it, those aren't mutually exclusive. So, spill. I need details. Like, all the details."

Pressing her hands to her heated cheeks, Olivia shook her head. "Brooke, I have no freaking clue what the hell happened in the past twelve hours."

"But you know you want more of it, don't you?" She leaned forward, literally on the edge of her seat as she asked the question.

Did she want more? More of the orgasms? Sure.

More time away from Chicago? More time to think and plan her future? More time with the MC? More time with the broken man who drew her to him like the most potent drug?

None of it scared her away as all of it should.

"Shit, Brooke, I think I do want more."

"Hell yeah, you do!" Brooke raised her hands in the air and shimmied as though someone had scored a touchdown. "I can't tell you how nice it's been to have another woman around here the past few weeks."

Though she smiled, Olivia couldn't get quite as ecstatic about the admission. Her thoughts remained with the man who'd nearly killed someone to protect her. What happened next? Retaliation? And which Scott would come back from church?

The raging former special ops soldier?

Or the hungry man couldn't keep his hands off her?

And the question that should be at the forefront of her mind is what did she do now that Lance knew her phone number?

SCOTT FELT ON top of the world. For the first time since he'd been discharged from the army, hell, for the first time since he'd stepped foot in Afghanistan on that final deployment, the weight in his chest dwindled to an annoying press, not a crushing elephant.

He'd like to credit the sex, but it wasn't merely fucking or getting off. When he'd first left the army, he'd made it his mission to try to heal his mind by fucking his way through the female population.

It hadn't worked.

He might have more issues than the damn newspaper, but denial wasn't one of them. He knew damn well this morning's mood was courtesy of the specific woman more than the general fucking. Olivia had blown through his bullshit, seen *him*, and still got down on her knees.

And bent over the counter.

If he were smart, he'd walk the fuck away now before shit got even more complicated. She still had no idea how her brother died and that Scott had been the cause. When she found out, because that shit couldn't stay buried forever, she'd likely drive one of those spikey heels she loved straight through his nuts.

But now that his cock had a taste of her sweet pussy, he

couldn't walk away. Combine it with how goddamn alive he felt right now, he knew she had her hooks in him.

The woman who acted opposite to everything he'd judged her to be.

Fuck.

"Hey, brother," Tracker said as he walked into the chapel.

"Hey, Track. Want a beer?" Sure, it was early in the morning but fuck it.

"Thanks." Tracker grabbed a beer from the icy bucket Scott had set in the center of the table.

He'd arrived first. After last night, Curly probably wanted to roast his ass over an open flame. The least he could do was show up early for church and make an effort to be a team player.

The prez worked his ass off to keep the cops away from his club. After spending thirteen years behind bars, partly because of his old club and partly because of a dirty fucking cop, Curly didn't play nice with the police. His showing up at the station last night had been a huge fucking feat, one he was probably pissed as hell about today. Shit, thoughts of the police station had him recalling the way he'd nearly lost his shit. If it weren't for Liv and the brave way she'd marched her sexy ass in and demanded his release, he'd have fallen into a full-on panic attack in front of the officer.

"You doing all right?" Tracker asked as Pulse walked into the chapel.

"Yeah, I'm good." Scott held his fist up for Pulse as he came around the table. His brother tapped it with his own, then plucked a beer from the bucket.

Locke arrived next, followed by Jinx, laughing to himself about something.

"You sure?" Tracker asked with narrowed eyes. He took a long pull from his beer. "Figured you be even more of a cranky asshole today than usual after all the shit that went down.

"Seriously," Jinx cut in. "You seem fucking different." He waved a hand. "Almost, I don't know, bouncy."

Different? Bouncy? Scott snorted. Thankfully, he didn't have a mouthful of beer. "The fuck? You still trashed from last night? I'm sitting on my ass drinking a beer. I've barely said two words. What the hell makes you think I'm different? Or bouncy? For Christ's sake, what does that even mean?" he asked, laughing.

"Jinx is right!" Tracker straightened and pointed his beer bottle in Scott's direction. "He's fucking laughing. Who the hell are you, and what have you done with Spec? You know the guy. Looks just like you, chews nails, drinks gasoline for breakfast."

"Barks at everyone," Pulse added.

"Kicks puppies for sport," Jinx said.

"Shaves with a chainsaw," Tyler said around his laughter.

Snickering, Scott shook his head. This group was a bunch of idiots.

"Ooh," Ty said as he joined them in the chapel. "We listing Spec's finer qualities? Don't forget how he makes small children cry for kicks and giggles."

"Very funny, assholes, I get it. I'm an irritable bastard." He lifted his hands in surrender as he settled back in the chair. "Put your weapons away."

"This is so weird," Tracker pretended to whisper to Lock. "He's still not getting pissed."

"Sorry, I'm late," Curly announced as he strode into the room. He closed the thick double doors behind him. Made of dark wood, they spanned the ten-foot-high ceiling and were heavy as fuck. A local metal worker had made the Handlers' logo into an impressive set of door handles, split down the middle. It was badass, and Scott loved walking through those doors into the chapel.

All of them had collaborated on the clubhouse's design. Curly could've done the whole thing himself, but that wasn't the kind of prez he wanted to be. He'd wanted all his guys to view the clubhouse as home. So they'd pooled their ideas and created a haven for all of them.

Inside the chapel, an oval table made from the same dark wood as the doors filled most of the space. Fifteen men could easily fit around it. Someday, they'd have a larger membership, but Scott had no problem with a small club and taking their sweet time to find prospects.

Not just anyone could patch, and Curly planned to be one picky bastard when it came to letting men prospect.

Halfway to his seat at the head of the table, Curly paused. "You look different, Spec." A frown scrunched his face. "Can't figure out what it is, though."

"For fuck's sake," Scott grumbled as the rest of the guys burst into laughter.

It was damn good to hear everyone laughing after the stress of the previous night, even if he had to be the butt of the joke.

"What'd I miss?" Curly asked as he reached his leather chair. "You know what? Forget I asked. Not sure I wanna know." His ass hit the seat. "Okay, this shit from last night…"

He lifted his gaze and speared Scott with a lasered assessment. "You square?"

Nodding, Scott leaned forward and planted his forearms on the table. "Yeah, Prez, I'm good. I, uh, lost my shit. Saw Dante with his hands on Livy, and I—"

He blew out a breath. Fuck, remembering it threatened to destroy his post-fucking high.

Curly lifted a hand, making Scott bite off his next words. "Not looking for an apology. Don't need it. Don't want it. Pretty sure any of us would've reacted the same way if we'd gotten there first."

"Damn straight," Tracker murmured. The guy was fun and, on the surface, more chill than the rest of them, but he had a steel core.

"You might have gone overboard but fuck it. Dante was on our property, putting his hands on a woman who didn't want it. One of our women at that. He's damn lucky to be breathing. And he's still breathing this morning. At least as of two hours ago when Pulse checked with his nurse."

One of their women? They viewed Liv as one of them? Did they think she was his? Why the hell did that light him up inside? Scott lifted his chin toward his brother in thanks. Pulse must have called in a favor to get Dante's nurse to reveal patient information and break the strict medical privacy laws. Much as he'd have loved to hear he'd sent Dante down to hell, Scott didn't need a murder charge mucking up his life. Pulse nodded back.

"Y'all know I've been trying to keep this club under the radar. I want no part of the men I used to ride with, and I don't trust the cops for shit," Curly continued. "But that's not possible, and I should've been prepared for something like this. I knew my return would stir up shit in the area, but I underestimated how much." His troubled gaze met Scott's head-on. "Last night is on me."

When the guys started protesting, Scott the loudest, Curly lifted his hand. "No. It is. I should've done more after all that shit went down with Maverick and his ol' lady a few months ago. Lobo's gone dark, but the rest of them have been a pain on our collective asses. That ends today."

Lobo was a young and hungry biker responsible for the kidnapping of Maverick and his ol' lady around Christmas time. They'd been down in Florida visiting from the Handlers' mother chapter in Tennessee. The club had rescued them before they suffered worse than bruising and cuts, but Lobo escaped. Since then, no one had seen hide nor hair of the fucker, but his errand boys made themselves a nuisance.

Until last night. Dante crossed the line from irritant to threat. And now shit was on.

"Here's what we know about them. Lobo's old man was in my club over a decade ago. He died of an overdose a few years before I went away. You all know that club fell to shit, but anyone who lingered in the area seems to be coming out of the woodwork now that I'm back."

The state awarded Curly a multimillion-dollar settlement for his wrongful imprisonment. It was hush money. Something to keep him quiet about the crooked cops and horrendous management of his case. Little had they known, Curly wasn't one to run his mouth to the media, but the money sure as hell didn't suck. Especially since he'd been able to afford the Handlers' property and renovations without batting an eye.

His old club caught wind of that cash, and the members who still lived in the area wanted a piece of the pie. They were butt hurt to be excluded from the Handlers MC and had banded together to form a disorganized club with Lobo at the helm.

"We have two women living on the property right now," Curly continued. "And while they're both pretty kick-ass, Lobo had made it clear he has no qualms about going after ol' ladies." His eyes shot to Scott. "Or any woman. So here's what I'm thinking."

Scott leaned back in his chair as he absorbed Curly's plan to keep the property safe and rid themselves of Lobo and his crew. The guys might have thought he was in a fucking *bouncy* mood, but they'd find otherwise really quick if anyone else tried to put their hands on Olivia.

She might not be his for the long term, but she was for today, and he'd be damned if some piece-of-shit biker wannabe laid a hand on her again.

Chapter Sixteen

How had he gotten her phone number?

Olivia had been careful to cover all her tracks. Or so she'd thought. Before leaving town, she'd ditched her cell, left her computer behind, emptied her checking account, ditched her car, and paid for everything in cash. A quick how-to-disappear-yourself Google search gave her step-by-step instructions to hide from an abusive ex.

Money wasn't an issue, at least not yet. The cash she'd withdrawn would hold her over for quite a while, especially since Curly refused to let her pay rent. None of her new possessions were the luxury designer brands she'd grown up owning. She rarely spent money, and once the cash ran low, she had the secret trust left by her grandmother.

The trust account had enough money to live comfortably for years, maybe even the rest of her life. Lance wasn't aware of its existence, but she hesitated to tap into it too much out of an abundance of caution.

Despite it all, a text from Lance came through at two that morning. Not an email or a DM but a text, which meant he was actively hunting her and making progress. The unfamiliar number and vague threat meant nothing. This was all Lance.

Lance: *A princess can't survive outside the castle. I'm getting closer to finding you. See you soon.*

Not long ago, as in a few months back, she'd have agreed with him. She never imagined she'd be happy without her designer shoes and purses. Or without her luxury mattress, spa-worthy master shower, or thousand-dollar espresso machine. But it turned out she could live without her weekly spa trips, mimosa brunches, extravagant shopping trips, and oversized mansion. She could live without all that and not even miss it. She'd discovered that mani-pedis with vapid friends, endless party planning, and flashing her pearly whites from the side of a powerful man didn't fulfill her as much as living in a shoebox with people who respected and appreciated her for who she was. People who had real conversations, real problems, and real lives they loved.

Minus Scott. Until last night.

"Jesus," she whispered out loud as memories of Scott's hands and mouth tortured her senses. Would it happen again? Should it happen again? Those questions potentially had very different answers, but neither was more important.

"One man problem at a time, Liv." As much as she'd rather dwell on her issue with Scott, Lance had the power to destroy her life in a very real way. What did she do now? Get another phone number? He'd probably find that one out as well. Clearly, she'd overlooked something when covering her tracks. If he found her phone number, could he find her just as easily?

"Shit," she whispered as her stomach soured. Lance had the power to rain down hell on the MC. He had legal contacts, judges in his pocket, cops on his payroll, and government officials bowing at his feet. He could destroy the lives of men she'd come to value more than her own family. "What have I done?"

"You know, talking to yourself is the first sign you're losing it."

Oliva jumped, then whirled around to find Tracker standing in the open door to the clubhouse's kitchen. "Holy crap, you scared me," she said as she stuffed the phone into her short's back pocket.

"I know. That's what made it fun." His unrepentant smirk and chuckle had her rolling her eyes. "What are you up to in here?" he asked as he sniffed the air.

The man had more tattoos than anyone she'd ever met. Sure, she had friends with a tramp stamp or knew guys with some ink on a shoulder, but in her world, that was it. Tattooed skin wasn't considered high-class enough, especially if it couldn't be hidden under a simple jacket. Tracker had sleeves on both arms, and she guessed plenty of ink under his clothes. If it weren't for his easy smile and chill personality, he'd have intimidated the hell out of her.

Maybe it was this whole transformation from rich girl to woman on the run that had her relaxing her uppity standards.

"I'm making dinner," she said, wincing as she heard the words come from her mouth.

Tracker raised an eyebrow. The left side of his mouth curved up in a smirk. "Do you know how to make dinner?"

"Shut up!" She grabbed a dishtowel off the counter and threw it at him. "I can handle it. I've been practicing."

"It was an innocent question!" He caught the towel before it made contact, then raised his hands. "I'm not stupid enough to speak ill of the chef or turn down a free home-cooked meal. Whatcha making?"

"Pulled pork sandwiches, cornbread, and a few veggies. Nothing fancy." She held up the recipe on her phone.

"Huh," he said, lowering his arms.

"What?"

"Kinda figured you'd be serving us caviar and foie gras, whatever the fuck that is."

"Okay, that's it!" She rushed forward, making a shooing motion with her hands. "Get out of my kitchen. And keep your brothers out too."

Laughing, Tracker backed out of the kitchen.

"And foie gras is liver of a chicken or duck," she yelled after him.

"Fucking gross!" he called through the door.

Oliva giggled as she continued working on dinner. After the way the club rallied around her last night, she wanted to do something to say thank you. A meal seemed so inadequate, but these guys liked to eat and couldn't cook for shit. Not that she could either, but she could read and follow directions. Hopefully, those skills translated to pulling off an edible meal. Brooke would also appreciate a second set of hands helping with family dinners, as she called them.

If it was a flop, pizza delivery was only a few clicks away. These guys had never met a pizza they didn't devour. Even if her meal crashed and burned, at least this experiment gave her mind and hands something to occupy themselves for a few hours besides stressing about Lance or swooning over Scott.

She forced her troubles from her brain, popped in her earbuds, then got to work. A few hours and three or four minor missteps later, she had the kitchen smelling like a five-star restaurant. Okay, maybe four stars. Probably three. Sure, the corn muffins were a little dry, and she'd added way too much pepper to the pork, but everything was edible and was ready to be plated.

The best part of it was she'd only thought about Lance six times and Scott ten. It might not sound like much of a win, but when they'd both been on her mind constantly since the previous night, she'd take the slight reprieve.

As she turned off the music, a strong arm banded around her waist. Her brain immediately went to Lance. She stiffened until Scott's familiar scent floated under her nose. Silly, Lance would never make it on the property and into the clubhouse unseen, especially not since the guys ramped up security after last night.

How had she not noticed how good Scott smelled before? A little spicy, a little sweet, a little dark. His scent matched his personality.

"I gotta say, this is the last place I expected to find you," he whispered after pulling out her earbud. His teeth nipped her earlobe, making her knees wobble.

"Behave," she said, lightly rapping his knuckles with her wooden spoon.

He chuckled. "Mmm, I had no idea you were into that kinda thing. Gimme that spoon. I'll keep it for later."

His scruff tickled her cheek and sent shivers across her nerve endings. She refused to acknowledge the heat expanding across her lower belly at the thought of his hand landing on her ass. "You need to back up so I can give you things to carry to the table. Is everyone here?" She tilted her head up to see him better. There was a lightness about him today that she'd yet to see. Selfish as it might be, she liked to think she contributed at least a little to his newfound peace.

"Yeah. You told Brooke to have the guys here by six, so the men are here. And we're hungry," he whispered before taking a quick bite of her neck.

"Ugh," she groaned and squirmed to try to relieve the building ache between her legs. "You're a little bit evil. You know that?"

Releasing her, he barked out a laugh. "You've seen me beat a man near to death, lose my shit on my brothers at least a dozen times, and I've treated you like shit since you arrived. But now you decide I'm evil."

The acknowledgment of his animosity toward her had her stomach twisting with anxiety. "Well," she said, forcing what was hopefully a sexy grin. "With your hands on me, it's easy to forget everything else."

"Hmm." He frowned, then grabbed the enormous platter of prepared sandwiches from the counter. "Come for a ride with me after dinner? There's somewhere I'd like to take you. It's quiet, and we can talk."

He'd admitted he'd misjudged her and treated her poorly. The man before her was one-hundred-eighty degrees away from the man she'd been pissing off by breathing the past few weeks. Could she trust it? Was this because she'd sucked him off and spread her legs? Or was it real? Could she trust the change in him?

"Yes," he said.

Her eyes widened. "What?"

"You asked if you could trust the change in me. The answer is yes."

Well, crap. "I'm sorry, I didn't mean to say it aloud." She swallowed, waiting for the anger and recrimination she'd come to expect from him.

His eyes held profound sadness but no anger. "I know. There are reasons for my reaction, and I'd like the chance to give them to you. I'll keep my hands to myself, and once I'm done talking, you can decide whether you want to stay here."

She gasped. He'd make her leave?

He shook his head. "Don't misinterpret me. *I* want you to stay. I'm just not sure you'll want to once we talk."

Frowning, she took in the broken man before her. He'd been an Army Ranger for years. Decades even. He'd seen and done things she couldn't even imagine in her nightmares. Same as her brother. Whatever plagued Scott's mind, it was big. Men like him didn't struggle with trivial annoyances. They'd spent too much time witnessing the shadowy side of life.

"Okay. I'd like that."

"Great." He flashed her a rare and genuine grin that transformed his features from fierce to irresistible. "Just wear something comfy and bring your gorgeous self. Leave everything else to me." With a wink, he turned and disappeared into the dining area with the platter.

Olivia pressed a hand to her stomach and sagged against the counter. "Damn that man," she whispered. Was he that potent to all women, or was it her? Did she have something inside her that weakened when he shot her one of those sexy winks or mischievous smiles?

Within seconds, he returned for another armful of food. Before she knew it, he'd set everything out on the table, leaving her with nothing but the corn muffins to carry. As she walked into the dining area, cheers and applause sounded from the table full of hungry men and Brooke. A few dogs chomped bones while lying on their beds in the corner. Everyone was dressed casually in jeans and T-shirts. Bottles of beer sat half consumed at each place except for her's and Brooke's. They had glasses of wine she knew wouldn't be fancy or expensive but surprisingly delicious. Smiles graced each face, directed at her while everyone clapped their hands.

All this for a meal they hadn't even tasted yet. It could taste disgusting for all they knew. There were no white gloves, no servers, no crystal glasses, or gold-rimmed place settings. Nothing about this meal said fancy or gourmet. But she'd never attended a more special dinner in her life. Her face heated, and her eyes watered as she waved away their praise. "Maybe you all should taste it first."

"Pretty sure you could serve these guys some of Ray and Harley's kibble, and they'd fight over it," Brooke said with a beaming smile. She sat right where she belonged—beside her ol' man at the head of the long rectangular table—an integral part of the family.

Tracker grabbed a sandwich and took a huge bite. "Fuck yes, this is delicious," he said around a mouthful of food. "Come sit, girl. You've outdone yourself."

Whether he was serious or only polite, it didn't matter. She'd never felt more appreciated or accepted than she did sitting with this rag-tag family of bikers. Scott steered her toward her seat, next to him and across from Brooke.

Once they were seated, he picked up the quickly dwindling plate of sandwiches and held it for her. She grabbed one, then reached for the cornbread. After his plate was full, Scott grabbed his fork and dug in. Without missing a beat, he settled his left hand on her thigh and let it stay there throughout the meal.

The feel of those calloused fingers resting on her bare skin, shifting and occasionally stroking, had her wanting to melt into a puddle on the floor. Scott chatted, laughed, and ate as though nothing had changed, but Olivia found it hard to concentrate on anything beyond the warmth of his skin on hers. She faked it well, laughing along with Tracker's ridiculous stories, oohing and aahing over the dogs' antics, and gossiping with Brooke, but the entire time a large piece of her awareness stayed on Scott's warm, strong hand.

"Damn," Curly said as he leaned back and rubbed a hand over his stomach. "That was a seriously good meal, Olivia. Thank you."

"Truth!" Brooke added. "We might have to get you on the rotation." She winked.

Olivia couldn't have kept from grinning if she tried. How nice was it to be appreciated for something she'd created? The last time she'd cooked for Lance, he told her the chicken was bland and overcooked while the veggies were raw and salty. They might have been, but still, no one here had a negative word to say about the crumbly corn muffins. How hard was it to spread a little kindness to the woman he was supposed to marry? It was one of the many red flags she'd ignored in favor of a cushy life. It'd taken Lance sticking his dick in another woman to wake her up to the fact their relationship had died long before he cheated. Well, long before she knew about the cheating, anyway.

And there went her thoughts, skipping down a dark path.

"You good?" Scott asked. "You got all tense."

She glanced down to his hand still on her leg, then relaxed. The words, I'm great, nearly fell from her lips after years of being programmed to respond as such. But Scott's expression held a sincerity she wasn't accustomed to. The question wasn't an obligation or a throw-away. He legitimately wanted to know if something was bothering her. And that had her answering with more truth than she'd given her fiancé in years. "Rogue, unsettling thought. Nothing to do with anything here." She smiled. Though he couldn't know the whole truth, she could at least give him a little vulnerability. Maybe he'd do the same tonight in return. "It passed, though."

She could be forced to flee Florida at any point. Who knew when Lance would find her? Right then and there, she vowed that no matter what Scott told her tonight, she wouldn't waste a moment of her time here with him. Every second deserved to be soaked up and every experience reveled in.

"Hmm," he said, leaning in.

Just when she thought he'd kiss her and give his brothers a real jaw-dropping show, he winked.

Her belly fluttered. God, she loved it when he did that.

"Ready to get out of here?"

"Soon as I help clean up."

"Fuck that," he said with a snort. "You cooked. No way are

you cleaning this shit too."

"And you?" she said, trying to keep from laughing.

"Fuck that too. I carried the shit to the table. You assholes are on clean-up duty," he called out as he stood, pulling her up with him. "Except you, Brooke. You're neither an asshole nor on clean-up duty."

"Knew you were my favorite, Spec," Brooke shot back.

"Come on, babe, let's go." He tightened his hand on hers and towed her toward the door. "We're out, fuckers! Don't wait up."

"Have fun, you two!" Tracker called. "Don't you bring her back here knocked up!"

Olivia gasped while Scott flipped Tracker the bird, and everyone else laughed their stuffed faces off.

Once outside in the balmy evening air, Scott pulled her close and wrapped his arms around her waist. Then he took her mouth in a kiss that left her lightheaded and weak-kneed. "Damn, I love your mouth," he said before kissing her again.

She surrendered to the rise of passion, pushing all thoughts besides pleasure out of her mind. Everything else could wait until later. The evening had been the best of her life, and with how his hands squeezed her ass and his mouth devoured hers, the night promised to keep getting even better.

And then, for the second time in twenty-four hours, her phone buzzed.

Chapter Seventeen

As though the last day hadn't rattled his world enough, it turned out Olivia had ridden a motorcycle before. If anyone had asked him ten minutes ago, he'd have put money on the fact that she'd never been within five feet of a bike before coming to Florida, let alone ridden one.

Good thing he didn't make that bet. He'd be out a chunk of change.

That'd show him to bet against her.

But then he was quickly learning everything he'd thought and assumed about Olivia Truitt was dead wrong.

Part of him hated that he wasn't her first, but on the flip side, a massive surge of pride tore through him at what an excellent fucking rider she turned out to be. She held his sides, grip loose and confident as she leaned into each curve with him. Much as he loved those sexy thighs bracketing his hips and her tits smashed against his back, he couldn't help but imagine her riding alongside him on her own bike instead of at his back.

Christ, she'd look smoking hot in tight leather pants, totally in control of the powerful beast between her legs. The thought made him hard as hell, which was damn

191

inconvenient when maneuvering a hundred of pounds of vibrating metal through dark beach-bound roads.

"Are you taking me to the beach?" Livy yelled in his ear as they slowed for a stop sign. Her question jerked him from his dirty fantasies.

He smiled at the enthusiasm in her voice. She looked so fucking cute in his spare helmet with her hair hanging down. It'd been all he could do to keep from jumping her right there in the clubhouse parking lot.

"Yeah," he called back. "Figured you've been in Florida for a few weeks and haven't seen the gulf yet. We need to fix that."

"You'd be right. Yay!" She squealed a thrilled, high-pitched sound that had him smiling. Her enthusiasm for simple things like dinner with his club brothers, playing with Brooke's crew of dogs, or a nighttime trip to the beach made him want to introduce her to everything she'd never been allowed to enjoy from her ivory mansion on the hill. All the things she'd have been told were beneath her or low-class.

According to Deke, she traveled by private jet, owned a bedroom-size closet full of designer clothes, and spent summers in Europe. Scott expected her to look down her nose at the no-frills way he and his brothers lived, but it was yet another incorrect assumption. However, visiting his world for a few weeks wasn't the same as living in it. Not that he planned for or wanted her to stick around long-term. Eventually, she'd return to her life.

Hopefully, she'd spill the truth about why she'd popped up in Florida in the first place. He didn't buy her bullshit about needing time away because of a breakup. Sure, he believed she'd dumped her fiancé, but there was more. He'd bet his bike on it. Not once had she mentioned communicating with anyone from home. Who cut off every person in their life? Someone who didn't want to be found.

That's who. And why the hell wouldn't Olivia want to be found? Had her fiancé cheated? Humiliated her? Did her friends take his side over hers? Probably something along those lines.

With a sigh, he tried to shift his focus from the woman draped all over him to the allure of the ride. Typically, he loved each mile for its freedom and power to clear his mind. Tonight he couldn't clear his thoughts, and they all revolved around the gorgeous sister of his best friend.

He had to stop obsessing about it. She didn't owe him any explanations. And if she was there hiding from the embarrassment, who was he to judge? Hell, maybe she'd decided to slum it with an MC as revenge. Fucking a biker would send a strong message of how pissed she was. The guy would show up with flowers and something sparkly in a few weeks, wooing her back. Hell, it didn't matter anyway. Once he told her about his role in Deke's death, she'd run back to her world, leaving Scott in his.

It didn't matter why she was there. Scott didn't do long-term, and even without his part in Deke's death, Olivia would never want long-term with a motorcycle club. They'd have a few weeks of hot sexy fun, repair the divide between them, share stories of Deke, and that'd be that. A hot memory to look back on.

There you go making assumptions again.

The ride passed too fast, and before he knew it, he'd parked in the empty beach lot under a streetlamp.

"Is the beach even open to the public at this time of night?" Olivia asked as she glanced around the carless space.

With a shrug, he climbed off the bike. "Don't know. The place isn't blocked off so, yes?" He turned to find her scanning their surroundings. "Do you care?" While he waited for her to answer, he unclipped the helmet she'd borrowed. When he removed it, static made her hair grow in volume.

"No, I guess not," she said, still not looking convinced.

He winked, then smoothed her hair back in place. "Promise I won't get your pretty ass in trouble."

"Hmm, I was hoping it could get in at least a little trouble." She tilted her head and gave him a playful grin. "If you know what I mean."

Chuckling, he grabbed her around the waist and hauled her off the bike. She squeaked and clutched his arms but laughed loud when he set her on her feet. "Think I can figure it out." His hands went to her ass, and he squeezed. "I promise that kind of trouble is always part of the plan."

He kissed her unglossed lips. She opened for him immediately, letting his tongue claim her mouth. She tasted of the wine she'd had at dinner. The throaty whimper that escaped her had his cock twitching. With a growl of regret, he wrestled his mouth away from hers. "C'mon. I've got a blanket. Let's sit."

After retrieving the blanket that lived in his saddlebag for impromptu beach visits, he grabbed her hand. Together, they strolled onto the sand halfway between the parking lot and the surf. "This spot good?"

Livy faced him. The light breeze blew her hair around her face in a gentle dance. Her eyes glowed in the moonlight. Clear skies and a full moon made for the perfect amount of light. "This is wonderful. It's so beautiful here. So peaceful at night. I haven't been to the beach in forever."

Exactly why he'd wanted to bring her. "Help me spread this out."

With a squeak of happiness, Livy grabbed the other end of the blanket and helped him spread it on the sand. She kicked off her shoes and plopped down with a hum.

He stood like an idiot staring down at her as she dug her pink-tipped toes in the sand.

She beamed up at him. "You gonna sit or stare all night?"

"I'll sit. Gonna stare for a few more seconds first."

With a snort, she shook her head. "Creeper," she said, but the word held no heat.

That had him laughing. He liked her sass and that she wasn't afraid to dish it out to him. Since leaving the military, he knew what an ornery asshole he'd become. And how his temper lived on a hair-trigger. And how the grown-ass men of his club often kept a wide berth. But not Livy. She had no problem getting in his face with teasing or even telling him off. It reminded him of Deke.

There were many things he was learning he liked about her. Things beyond her perky tits, tight ass, and wet pussy. And that's why he had to tell her the truth about what happened to her brother.

But then she let out a little hum of delight. "You know, even with the creeper act, this is kind of perfect."

SCOTT'S DEMEANOR CHANGED in an instant. He'd gone from watching her with appreciation to a stiff block of ice seated beside her, staring out at the Gulf of Mexico.

Frowning, Olivia replayed the past few moments in her head. Had she said something to set him off? Piss him off? Sure, she'd teased, but he'd seemed to take her joking in stride. In fact, that was something she liked about him. He could handle her sarcastic personality. The natural inclinations she'd been suppressing for years.

She'd seen Scott in various moods since she'd arrived in Florida—pissed off, raging, aloof, laughing, maybe even mildly happy. But this tense, pensive version was unfamiliar to her, and she had no idea how to proceed. Should she try to draw him out of wherever he'd disappeared to in his head? Or should she leave him be to process his stuff?

In the end, she landed somewhere between the two. Scooting closer, she rested her head on his shoulder and followed his lead, watching the water flow over the shoreline. Hopefully, he'd understand the silent support. She was there to listen if he wanted, but no pressure.

The gentle lapping of the water lulled her into a relaxed, nearly hypnotic state. So much more serene than the ocean, the Gulf provided a calm that felt like a warm hug. Eventually, her eyes grew heavy, and she leaned heavier on Scott.

"Deke didn't know you well," he said out of the blue.

Her eyes flew open, and her heart jackhammered in her chest. He was talking. "Well, you know our father exiled him from the family when he was eighteen. He told me Deke left on his own and wanted nothing to do with us. That he was rebellious, and maybe even a little dangerous." She'd been so dumb to believe the lies but also young. "So, we saw each other only when I was older and understood the lie for what it was... my father trying to keep me on his side when he was the one with the problem."

Scott shook his head. "No, I mean, he didn't know *you*. He had no idea that you're adventurous, sweet, funny, and would do anything for the people you care about."

Her stomach twisted with regret. No, her brother wouldn't know any of those things about her. They'd met a handful of times over the years and talked occasionally, but sadly, she'd always shown him the sides of her that he'd expected. She'd been too immersed in her own world to let him see the real Olivia.

"No," she said, unable to keep the sadness out of her voice. "He knew me as the rich Daddy's girl who was a spoiled brat."

"Because you wanted him to."

That had her insides stilling. "What do you mean?"

"It's how you protect yourself."

"No—"

"Yes. The expensive clothes, the makeup, the perfect hair… the prickly attitude."

This conversation was hitting uncomfortably close to the truth. "Okay, Dr. Freud, I think this conversation is over." She lifted off his shoulder. Who the hell did he think he was? This was the talk he'd wanted to have? One where he insulted her?

He turned his head and speared her with a look that went straight through her skin to the years of damage beneath. "It's all armor. It's to keep you from getting hurt. Or more hurt. If no one sees your soft, sweet, gooey core, they can't damage it."

Her mother died when she was a small child. Her brother had been banished. Her father was a man who doled out material items instead of affection. He'd gone through multiple wives throughout her life, bringing in women who tried to win her over only to leave her motherless again. Her fiancé cheated. Yes, she'd been hurt and tried to keep it from happening again.

Years were wasted with Lance, and her fiancé didn't understand this fundamental component of her personality. He'd never bothered to lift her mask and peer beneath. Neither had her brother. But in a few weeks, Scott not only saw beneath her armor, but he yanked the damn thing off and exposed her vulnerable underbelly.

The instinct to stand up, barrage him with insults and strut back to the bike hit her so strongly that she almost gave into it. All her other shields were missing. She wasn't wearing makeup, wore frayed denim shorts, an off-the-rack T-shirt, had messy hair, and flip-flops. She didn't have any of her physical defenses. Scott stripped away her emotional disguises as well. And now she was bare before him in a way no one had ever been.

Terrifying as it was, it also felt incredible to have someone see her for who she was and understand the motivation behind her actions.

She opened her mouth to say something. Maybe confirm his analysis, but before she had the chance, he looked out at the water again.

"I'm the reason Deke is dead."

Chapter Eighteen

"What?"

Her gasp of shock didn't bother him in the least. Neither did her outrage at his previous words. He was too terrified he'd find hatred and disgust in her eyes to worry about her other reactions.

Following his return from the goat-fuck of a final deployment, he'd been debriefed by the Army. Exhaustively. They'd demanded details, no matter how small, of every second during his captivity. Even the special team sent to rescue him had been grilled on his state of mind, actions during the rescue, and whether they trusted him. Reporting that he hadn't cracked, that he hadn't spilled a single classified nugget of information—hell, he hadn't so much as told them his full name—should've filled him with pride.

It hadn't. Not even a little. The Army's investigators hadn't believed him. "Everyone cracks under torture," they'd said so many times he'd heard it in his sleep.

So, what the fuck had been the point of all that miserable training?

Then there was Deke's death. All he'd had to do was betray his country to save his friend's life. A country that didn't believe him.

Talk about a kick in the nuts.

After he'd left the debriefing room, he'd vowed never to speak of his captivity again.

And here he was about to vomit that experience all over Deke's sister. The one he'd fucked and wanted to fuck again more than he wanted to keep this horrifying story in his head. But he knew he couldn't touch her again until he'd purged the poison inside him.

She had the right to slap him and run back to Chicago.

"Scott?" she barked, pulling him away from the coarse desert sand to the humidity and soft white sand of the Florida beach.

He swallowed the burning acid rising from his gut and then forced himself to face her. She hadn't moved, still sitting close enough to touch but no longer did. Where he'd expected to find hard, appalled eyes, he saw nothing but compassion and confusion.

That would change soon.

"I don't believe you," she said, her voice steady and with that slightly bitchy tone he hadn't heard from her in a few days.

He grunted out a laugh that had nothing to do with humor. "What were you told about how Deke died?"

"He'd listed me as the point of contact for the Army since our father wanted nothing to do with him, and his mother isn't alive. I spoke directly with the officer and chaplain who came to inform us. They said he was taken hostage and killed by enemy combatants in Afghanistan. Details beyond that weren't discussed. Are you saying that's not the truth?"

"It is," he said. "But it's a dumbed-down and G-rated version of what happened." It took everything he had to keep his eyes open and stay in the moment instead of being dragged back to the hell that had been their captivity. His heart tried to pound but felt so heavy it could barely beat inside his tight chest. Air wouldn't flow, getting trapped in his lungs and causing a harsh choking sound.

"Hey." Olivia shifted to her knees. She cupped his face between her soft hands and held his head where she wanted, giving him no choice but to keep eye contact.

The gentle touch opened a pressure valve in his chest, allowing him to breathe easier.

"I'd say you don't have to tell me anything, but I think you do, Scott. I think you need to get this poison out of your system so you can start to find some peace. So take as much time as you need. I'm here, and I'm not going anywhere."

"You will."

"I won't." The bitchy tone was back in full swing, and he actually smiled. Releasing his face, she settled on his lap sideways. She kissed his cheek, then his lips, then his chin before resting her head on his shoulder like she somehow knew he couldn't look her in the eye while he told the story. "Ready when you are. We can sit here all night if it helps you."

They could wait a lifetime. He'd never be ready. "We were captured together and held for a week, me and Deke. Seven days. I can't tell you anything about who they were, but it doesn't matter. They split us up immediately. I was kept—" He shuddered as the heat rushed back, making him sweat as though he were there.

"Hey, it's okay." She stroked up and down his arms. "You're here. With me. In Florida. All of that is long over."

Long over, perhaps, but still alive and living rent-free in his head. Her softly spoken words, gentle touch, and weight on his lap helped keep him from slipping into a debilitating flashback.

"I was kept in a box. Small enough I had to curl up. They left me there about twelve hours at a time. In the hot sun. It got over a hundred and ten degrees in the daytime and fucking cold at night."

Her breath caught, and she swallowed as her eyes watered. "Jesus," she whispered.

He nodded. "They decided to try to break us in different ways. Every twelve hours, I was dragged from the box, given one glass of filthy water and a few bites to eat, then brought to the room where they kept Deke. Fuck." His stomach lurched. He closed his eyes and breathed through his nose. "Trying not to puke."

She remained quiet, lending support through her touch and steady presence. How the fuck had he ever thought this woman was a princess? She was proving to be as strong as any of the Rangers he'd served with. Deke would be fucking proud and probably damn surprised.

"They'd interrogate us. When we refused to answer, Deke would be…" he swallowed "… he'd be tortured. They made me watch as they hurt him over and over. Each time they said it would stop if I just told them what they wanted to know. Each day it got worse. He was so… God, Liv, he was so fucking strong. He never broke despite the horrifying shit they did to him."

Tears rolled down her cheeks, landing somewhere between them.

"Scott, I'm so sorry you were forced to suffer like that. So sorry." She cupped his face again, swiping tears he hadn't realized he'd shed. "I'm not sure how you survived torture like that, but I'm so grateful you did. You're the most amazing man I've ever met. The strongest. The bravest."

What? No. Her words tried to worm their way through the thick layers of damage to his heart. But he couldn't let them. He wasn't the one who needed her sympathy. He wasn't the one who'd endured the unimaginable torture. Deke had. He was the one who deserved her attention. Why wasn't she railing at him and crying over the injustice her brother suffered? Why didn't she blame him for not protecting Deke?

"Liv, you don't get it. What happened to me was nothing like what they did to him. Nothing! Every moment for him was complete agony. They never let up. Never gave him a break. All I did was fucking watch! He died in front of me because I couldn't find a way out. Couldn't think of a way to save him. I kept quiet, and he paid the price!"

He tried to keep from shouting, but it was the only way he knew to get through to her.

"Fuck!"

Olivia remained calm. She didn't yell back, lose her shit, or berate him. Sure, tears still flowed from her eyes but no hysterics.

She smiled at him, so sad it'd have broken his heart if he had anything left to break.

"I don't think anyone has said this to you, so let me be the first." She swiped her tears away, straightened her shoulders, and said, "I still believe you're the most amazing man I have ever met. I'm in complete awe of your strength and resilience."

He shook his head. The panic he fucking hated tried to claw its way out. How the fuck could he make her understand? "No, I—"

Her soft hand landed over his mouth. "Shhh," she soothed. "You need to hear this. *Really* hear this. "If you thought this conversation would change how I feel about you, you're right."

Here it comes.

"It's made me realize I had no idea just how remarkable you are."

What?

When he tried to speak, she shook her head and smashed her palm against his lips.

"I'm not sure I can put into words what I'm feeling for you right now... pride, admiration, respect, devotion, compassion. All these words seem so inadequate."

He couldn't have looked away from her if the world was on fire. Every syllable out of her mouth was spoken with a fierce sincerity.

"You were tortured as much or even more than my brother. Scott, you were held in a box that must have gotten as hot as an oven. You were dehydrated, starved, folded up like a toy, and forced to watch someone you love suffer unspeakable pain. I'm sure you've left out plenty of things they did to you. I know you have scars, and they didn't come from nothing.

"I love Deke and will forever be haunted by his death. I'll always regret the years I spent without him in my life. And I will always wish I did more to be family to him. But he's at rest now. His wounds are gone, and his scars no longer exist. He's found peace. You're still suffering every day."

A rogue tear escaped, sliding down his cheek. It landed on Olivia's finger. She removed her hand from his mouth. As she leaned in close, the citrusy scent of her expensive lotion swirled around, perfect for the warm Florida evening. It helped. Nothing about the desert had smelled even remotely appealing. Scott clung to these tiny sensory details that kept him in the here and now.

With Olivia.

She kissed the corner of his mouth. That was all it took to have his cock filling with blood. If she noticed it harden against her leg, she kept it to herself. But she did press her lips against his ear. He clenched his fists to avoid grabbing her and rolling her beneath him.

"You don't have to suffer anymore. We'll find a way for you to have peace, Scott. I promise. And we'll do it together. You aren't alone."

Did he dare reach out and take the lifeline she offered him?

Would Deke approve?

Fuck, this woman was everything his soul needed but didn't deserve. He turned so their lips rested a breath apart. Her pupils dilated, and her breath caught. "Let me make you feel good," she whispered as she settled her palms on his chest. His heart hammered as though trying to leap from his chest straight into her waiting hands.

Shaking his head, he captured one of her hands just as she began to push him onto the blanket. She froze.

"It's my turn, baby," he said. His voice felt wrecked from the effort of not breaking down in a pile of a shattered man. Olivia didn't seem to care. Just like she didn't care that he'd cried. Or spilled his guts. Or acted like an ass to her when she arrived. Only her beauty eclipsed her capacity for forgiveness and understanding. "Lie back, Livy. Let me have you."

Eyes wide, she obeyed without a second's hesitation. She shifted off his lap and then maneuvered onto her back on the small blanket. "Christ, you're beautiful like this," he murmured. "Under the stars with the moonlight shining down."

"Who knew you were so poetic?" she asked with a sly smile.

"I'm not." Not even close. He'd never felt or acted like this around anyone. Even his sister, who knew him better than anyone, or the man he'd called his best friend, who'd been privy to his inner thoughts and fucked-up feelings, never saw him exposed.

The grin slid off Olivia's face, morphing into a serious expression. She understood what he meant. How big this was. What her acceptance meant to him. How important this moment was. Thank fuck because he couldn't have put it into words to save his life. That wasn't where his talents lay.

But he could strip her down and use his mouth, hands, and cock to show her just how much she meant to him.

She gazed left then right, which made him smile. "Ever been fucked outside like this? Exposed for anyone to see?" Not that they'd encountered a soul since they'd arrived.

Biting her lower lip, she shook her head.

"You like it? The idea that someone might walk by and discover how good I'm making you feel? Might hear you begging me for more? Might see that beautiful face twist with pleasure when I make you come? Over and over?"

Her chest rose and fell fast, showing him his words' effect. When she didn't answer, he raised an eyebrow.

"Yes," she whispered with a quick nod. "I like it. I feel… wanted. Like we can't even wait to be somewhere more appropriate."

His nostrils flared, and his cock jumped. "You're fucking wanted, Liv." He pressed the heel of his hand to his dick. The damn thing was going to need to chill the fuck out because he had plans for Olivia before he got to sink inside her. "And I haven't had an appropriate thought about you since you waltzed into my clubhouse."

Her eyes flared, and she licked her lips.

He groaned. "You're fucking killing me already. Reminding me what that tongue can do."

With a grin, she said, "I love that I can do this to you."

He shifted, straddling her legs. Her eyes stayed with him, taking in his every move. Slower than he'd have thought possible, considering how his dick ached and how he wanted to fuck her more than he'd ever wanted anyone, he raised her shirt, exposed her stomach, and then unsnapped her jeans. Next came the zipper—one tooth at a time.

Her stomach quivered beneath his fingertips as he hooked them into the waist of the denim. Olivia bent her knees and lifted that stellar ass off the blanket. No further instructions were necessary.

He shimmied the jeans and her panties down her hips, past

her knees, and straight off her pretty feet. It probably would've been wiser to keep them around her ankles, but they'd done the quick and dirty fuck. This go-around, he wanted to be able to spread her legs as wide as possible and take his sweet time with that pussy.

With her pants heaped in the sand, Olivia sucked in a breath. Her eyes flicked left and right before landing on him.

"We're alone. Do you trust me?"

She shouldn't. He was a fucking mess. But one thing she could be sure of, he'd keep her safe and protected. They might be out in the open, but he'd rip the eyes out of any man who dared to set them on her.

"I do," she whispered.

"Lift your shirt," he ordered, ignoring how her trust warmed something long dead inside. "Wanna see those tits."

She did him one better, curling up to a sit, then whipping the T-shirt off her body. That left her in a lacy light-colored bra that did fuck-all to conceal her pebbled nipples. Her gaze fixed on his, she reached behind her back to unclasp it. Once it was off, she smirked and tossed it in his face as she lay back down.

He caught her bra with a swipe of his hand. "Fuck," he said as he brought the fabric to his nose, inhaling. Her perfumed scent made his eyes roll back in his head. "Wish I thought to do this with your panties."

"Jesus, Scott."

He winked, then dropped the bra somewhere in the sand.

As he looked her over, his playful mood vanished. "Look at you lying there. Legs bent, nipples hard for me, pussy wet and on display." And was it ever. The moonlight made her arousal glisten. He'd struggle like hell to keep from coming the second he got his mouth on her. "You're fucking stunning, Livy."

Her tentative smile didn't match the brazen way she

spread her legs wide and tilted her hips. "I could send you a picture if all you want to do is stare."

His neck arched as he belted a laugh into the quiet night. If anyone were strolling nearby, they'd be glancing his way. Not that he gave a shit. It felt good to laugh after such a serious conversation. Sex for him typically involved a race to get off. A killer orgasm was the end goal. What the hell was the point otherwise? Connection? Emotions? Fuck no. Laughter, banter, the whole playful vibe, it'd just never been a part of fucking for him.

At least until Liv. Now he found himself in no rush to get to the climax. Sure, he wanted to fuck her and blow his load as much as the next guy, but it'd happen, and there was a ton of fun to be had along the way.

What a crazy mindfuck. The last thing he needed was something else screwing with his gray matter, so he grinned and focused on the physical, which was going to be hot enough to steam the fucking gulf.

A serious blanket once again settled itself over them. Scott circled her ankle with his fingers. Soft skin greeted him. All those damn potions and creams she used paid off. Hell, he'd rob a damn lotion factory for her if this was the result.

Taking his time despite the raging need pumping to his cock, he slid his palm up the back of her shapely calf. Olivia's breath caught right before goosebumps broke out all over her leg. He kept going, wanting more skin with each second that passed, to the back of her knee, a tiny scar above her kneecap, back down to her ankle, and over the delicate bones of her foot.

He lifted her leg to his mouth this time, pressing a lingering kiss into the arch. Five perfectly manicured toes curled against the side of his face. Next, his lips met the prominent bone of her ankle. He trailed up the inside of her calf, brushing his lips along the skin. Livy's breaths could be heard above the gentle lapping of the gulf.

"Scott," she breathed on a sigh as he tongued the back of her knee. She shivered, and he watched as her fingers curled into the blanket beneath them. Her face held a mix of lust, anticipation, and wonder.

Her inner thigh slid like butter along his tongue. She squirmed as he drew higher to her sex. For fuck's sake, he could smell her arousal and might die if he didn't taste her in the next few seconds.

Hands inside her thighs, he pushed wide, spreading her out like a feast before him. He inhaled the groan as though truly enjoying the seconds before an incredible meal began. Olivia propped herself up on her elbows and gazed at his head lingering right above her pussy.

"You wanna watch me eat this dripping pussy?" he asked. How he spoke around the thickness in his throat would forever remain a mystery.

She nodded.

"Dirty girl. Mmm." He shifted his attention between her legs. "So wet. All for me, huh?"

"Yes."

"I like that," he said before swiping his tongue through her sex. Her flavor hit his senses, and like the most potent drug, he was instantly addicted. "Fuck," he mumbled as he licked her again.

Olivia whimpered and arched her back, putting those incredible tits even more on display.

The way she surrendered to him. How she trusted him. How she seemed to care. It fucked with his head, but he'd be lying if he claimed to hate it.

He knew one thing, though—her power over him grew with each taste of her pussy.

Their eyes met. Hers were hazy and full of need, but he was afraid to know what his revealed to her. "You're gonna fucking ruin me," he whispered.

Her eyes flared with shock a second before he lowered his head and ate the fuck out of her like he'd been dying to do.

Even with desire at an all-time high, one thought lingered.

It might be too late.

She might have already ruined him.

Chapter Nineteen

The man could do things with his tongue she'd only ever read about.

Within seconds, he had her trembling, and the need to come more imperative than ever. Every cell in her body responded to him in ways it never had to another man. Something in her called to him, and now that he'd had her, would any other man compare? Lance sure hadn't. Even in the beginning, when she'd wanted him and enjoyed being with him, it hadn't been like this. She didn't crave Lance's hands on her. She'd never been willing to beg, steal, or kill to feel his touch.

Her arms shook from long moments of supporting her weight, but the idea of losing sight of his head creating magic between her legs was unfathomable. In the past, she'd squeezed her eyes shut and concentrated on the pleasure to get herself to orgasm, but here, that wasn't necessary. The sensations overwhelmed her nearly to the point of too much.

He sucked at her clit, making her whimper. He kept at it, adding the occasional flick of his tongue. She couldn't control the needy sounds flying from her throat in the same way she was helpless to keep her sex from producing so much wetness. If he weren't lapping it up with so much enthusiasm, she'd have been mortified. As it was, he acted as though he'd never had anything so good.

After one final swirl of his tongue, he abandoned her clit. Olivia groaned in protest.

"Don't worry, my needy baby, I'm not going anywhere." Two thick fingers slid into her, giving her that almost full sensation. Incredible, but not quite enough. Only his cock could fully satisfy the emptiness.

His lips shone in the moonlight, glistening with her arousal. Curling the fingers deep inside her, he licked his lower lip and then made a hum of approval. Hands down, the move would forever live in the top three hottest things she'd seen. Olivia clenched around his talented fingers. He didn't go down on her as some obligation to make her come or strictly because he thought she'd enjoy it. He loved it as much as she did, and that only made it sexier.

Who wouldn't want a man who got off on eating her out?

Olivia moved her hips with him, encouraging him to keep fingering her. Every time he thrust in, she pressed her pelvis up, making the heel of his palm bump her clit. Sparks shot through her body, lighting her up.

"You fucking love this," he growled. He was so attuned to her every breath and shiver that he caught onto what she was doing. Holding his fingers deep inside her, he curled them, rubbing the walls of her pussy as he ground his palm against her clit.

She cried out and worked herself on his palm. "Scott, please!" Her head thrashed back and forth. It wasn't enough. She needed more, harder, and fuller.

"What do you need, baby?" he asked wickedly. Teasing her. He knew exactly what she needed but wanted to hear her say it.

"You!" she yelled as he found her G-spot. Her arms gave

out, and she landed flat on her back.

"You want my cock?"

"Yes!" God, yes. Nothing had felt as good as him drilling into her that morning.

"You'll get it. But first, you're gonna come on my mouth." The words barely left his lips before he was licking her clit while still plunging his fingers in and out of her.

"Scott, please." She couldn't have kept quiet to save her life. Her stomach felt tight. Too tight. Pressure built and built until she thought she'd die if she didn't get her release. Her hips shot off the blanket, slamming into his face.

He chuckled against her. "Fucking love making you beg," he mumbled against her, or at least that's what she thought he said. It was hard to hear over her panting. "So fucking desperate and wild for my cock."

"Yes," she said. It was practically a sob. "Give it to me." She wanted nothing more than to feel as full as possible and have the thickness stretching her and taking over her senses.

"Soon."

She growled, making him laugh a split second before he grazed his teeth in the lightest rake across her clit. The sharp shock of it sent her spiraling into a powerful orgasm. She squeezed her eyes shut as she shouted his name and welcomed the tremors. They went on and on, prolonged by his continued fingering and licks. Eventually, she calmed, and when she opened her eyes, it was to find him stripping out of his shirt.

All those delicious ripples danced before her eyes. She tracked his movements as he flicked the button on his jeans, then lowered the zipper. In the next second, he shoved them down and then yanked them off his feet. Fully naked, he kneeled between her splayed legs. Her body thrummed with an odd mix of lethargy and desire.

"You look fucking ravaged," he said with a sexy smirk.

She smiled back. "And you look fucking hard." She mimicked the way he said *fucking*.

Laughing, he ripped open a condom she hadn't seen him produce. "I'm that." He rolled the condom down his stiff length, clenching his jaw as though the slightest touch drove him crazy. Once the latex was in place, he released himself only to wrap his large hands beneath her thighs. Quick as lightning, he yanked her closer.

Olivia yelped as she flew down the blanket.

Before she had time to register the new position, his fingers found her slit. She groaned as he swirled them around and then stroked himself with the evidence of her arousal. It was so filthy yet so erotic she couldn't keep from staring at him. But the tantalizing show didn't last more than a few seconds. Maybe someday, he'd let her watch as he jerked himself to completion.

Scott leaned forward, bracing himself on one elbow above her. She gazed up into his hungry face. "Kiss me," he ordered.

Their lips collided in an urgent meeting. Her flavor lingered on his tongue, new and not unpleasant. The head of his cock nudged her entrance as though asking for permission.

"Please," she said into his mouth on a whine she'd be embarrassed about if he didn't seem just as hungry for her.

When he didn't advance or shove into her, she popped her eyes open. He stopped kissing her and stared down, seeming lost for words. But there was a vulnerability in his expression. One she'd never thought he'd show her, given their original animosity. But there he was, telling her his secrets, confiding in her, and looking at her like she was the most precious woman on earth.

This was more than sex. More than comfort. More than tension release. Even more than mutual pleasure. This was something deeper. Something terrifying, yet it drew her in like the most potent drug. "You don't need to say anything," she whispered. "I feel it too."

He nodded once and then kissed her again. This time, he pushed his cock in so slowly and with so much care, she nearly wept.

When he bottomed out, she arched against him, pressing her breasts into his firm chest. His hand went to her ass, pulling her even tighter against him as though he couldn't bear for even an inch to separate their bodies.

He fucked her slower and with more tenderness than she'd thought possible for a man like him, one so powerful who'd seen violence and lived in a dark world.

They never stopped kissing. Their mouths lazily played and mimicked the rest of their bodies. When the need became too much and her roaming fingers dug into his back, he seemed to understand without words.

The leisurely pace vanished in an instant.

She cried out against his mouth as he slammed into her with so much force, the hand on her ass dug in to keep her in place.

Again and again, he hammered into her while stealing her breath with mind-melting kisses. Her head spun, and her body sang with pleasure. The fullness she'd craved moments before satisfied her in a way she didn't understand. It was as though he belonged there inside her.

A key fitting in a lock.

The final puzzle piece.

She'd come to Florida looking for sanctuary and found something that exposed her to a more terrifying danger. One that could destroy her worse than any punishment Lance could drum up. Yet she wasn't attempting to protect herself. A mistake that could end in crushing heartbreak if she didn't wise up.

Scott squeezed her ass with a grip bound to leave marks, chasing away thoughts of anything but how amazing his body felt against hers. Inside hers.

"You feel like fucking heaven," he rasped as he powered into her. His gaze held an intensity she'd only seen from him during a fight. Sweat coated his forehead, and his jaw clenched with tooth-breaking tension.

"You too," she managed.

They kissed again, sloppy and without skill, trying to absorb each other. She wouldn't have thought she could come again so soon, but the tension rebuilt with a vengeance. She grabbed his ass and held on for dear life, moving with him. Beneath her fingers, his muscles bunched and flexed as he worked his hips.

Air became necessary, so she ripped her mouth away only to shout when he held her against his pelvis and ground into her clit. He thrust, then held her close again, repeating the move three or four times.

The cataclysmic orgasm slammed into her, catching her by surprise. She buried her face in his neck and sunk her teeth into a cord of muscles beneath her lips.

"Fuck!" Scott shouted as she bit down. He crushed her to him and roared as he came inside the condom.

She loved how his formidable body shook in her arms as he gave himself over to the pleasure. It was the only time he let down his guard. With a final grunt, he collapsed on top of her, but his heavy weight only pressed down for a second before he was rolling them to their sides.

Drowsy, contented eyes met hers. "Thank you," he whispered as he cupped her cheek. "You—"

"You're welcome," she cut in.

If he said anything else, she was likely to reciprocate with foolish emotions and sentiments she couldn't afford to share. Florida was a stop on the way to figuring out her life. Lance would find her eventually, and she'd have to leave. That'd be an impossible task if she gifted her heart to Scott. Both because she wouldn't want to go, and he'd never let her. After all they'd done for her, she wouldn't lay her problems at the feet of the Handlers MC. They had their own troubles with Lobo and Curly's former club brothers. She refused to add her issues to the pile and would rather die than introduce more violence or trauma to Scott's life.

"I'm naked on the beach," she said with a smile.

He frowned but let her change the conversation to lighter topics. With a grin, he palmed her breast, making her exhausted body attempt to come back to life. "You say that like I haven't noticed. Trust me, if you're naked, I know it." He winked, thumbing her nipple.

"Mmm."

With a sigh, Scott kissed her lips. "We should roll outta here. I got church early tomorrow."

She pouted, which had him laughing. Even though she was fully exposed to anyone who happened to wander by, it felt as though they were cocooned away in their own little bubble. "I suppose," she said as she sat up.

Ten minutes after getting dressed and groped by Scott, she comfortably rested against his back as he navigated the trip home.

To his home, rather. The Handlers' compound. She didn't have a home at the moment.

It was dangerous for her to think of the studio apartment as hers, even if the Handlers' compound felt more like home with each passing day.

But it wasn't home.

They passed a sign that read, *Lithia ten miles*. Part of her never wanted the ride to end. Being on the back of his bike as they flew down the road was almost as satisfying as sleeping with him.

Almost.

A loud rumble rose behind them as they pulled up to a stop sign.

Beneath her, Scott's body tensed. He glanced in the small side mirror. "Fuck. Pull out your phone and call Curly," he yelled. "Now! I'm gonna fucking floor it." His voice was sharp, in full command mode. Gone was the open and giving lover she'd spent the last few hours with. In its place was the deadly Army Ranger and one-percenter. As she reached for her phone, she risked a glance behind her. A pack of single headlights grew closer along with the deafening roar.

Motorcycles.

Gaining on them fast.

Her heart lodged in her throat.

Scott hit the throttle, and they shot off with jarring force. She bobbled the phone but somehow managed to keep it from flying out of her hand while clinging to Scott. With one arm banded around Scott's waist, she clutched him as tight as possible and tried to operate the device. Her hand shook as she scrolled to Curly's contact.

Hearing anything from the phone proved an impossible task between the rushing wind, the thunder of the bikes, and the thick helmet. "Curly?" she screamed when she thought, hoped, prayed he might have answered. "We need help! A group of bikers is chasing us," she shouted directly into the phone's mouthpiece without bothering to put it to her ear. There wasn't any point. "We're a few miles out of Lithia on the way back from the beach." Jesus, she should've paid more attention to the roads on the way there.

She peeked over her shoulder again. The bikes were close. Too close. Scary close.

"Hurry!" she screamed before stuffing the phone in the pocket of her hoodie.

"Hang on tight," Scott shouted.

She squeezed around his waist so hard, it had to hurt, but the thought of flying off the bike as they raced along sent a wave of terror coursing through her. Plastering herself to his back, she fought to calm her breathing and keep from losing control. Freaking out wouldn't help him or their situation.

Easier said than done when his heart pounded beneath her body just as hard as hers. He took a sharp right so fast that the bike tilted. Mere inches separated her from the abrasive road. If she'd been able to unlock her arms from around her waist, she could've touched the ground, and had her skin ripped off.

Olivia squeezed her eyes shut and held her breath. When the asphalt never shredded her clothes or tore into her skin, and the bike righted, she was finally able to breathe.

The thunder grew louder and closer despite their speed. Scott's bike was huge but not as agile as some.

Two bikes sped past them, one on each side. They veered toward each other at the center of the road, cutting Scott off. Two more appeared at their sides, matching pace.

If she weren't clinging to him like a monkey, he'd be able to escape. She had no doubt he'd try some daredevil move to get away. But her presence hampered his ability to push the bike to its limit. His unwillingness to risk an accident with her at his back kept them from outrunning their pursuers.

He slowed the bike. It was either that or crash into the motorcycles in front of them. Suddenly, she wished he'd been in some monster truck club instead of a biker club. He could plow these assholes over and never look back.

But they were on a motorcycle and vulnerable to the world. She was so scared she could hardly breathe.

When they came to a complete stop, Scott kept the engine running, same as the other bikes.

"Get off the fucking bike," someone yelled.

Beneath her, he was rigid as a log.

She really tried to let him go, but her arms wouldn't obey. They stayed locked around his waist in a death grip.

Flashes of the night she discovered Lance's crimes flashed through her mind. The same fear had kept her immobile, staring at the computer screen for long minutes. She'd never experienced paralyzing terror before or since that night.

"I said get off the fucking bike!" a man in front of them shouted. She couldn't make out his face beneath the dark helmet and face shield, but she sure as hell understood what it meant when he pulled out a pistol and aimed it their way.

"Baby, breathe," Scott murmured. "You're shaking."

She couldn't respond. Her mouth dried up, and her tongue thickened, blocking her throat.

Scott's hands landed on hers, where they were locked against his stomach. He gently pried her fingers open, then lifted one trembling palm to his mouth and kissed it.

"Follow my lead and do what they say. You're strong as fuck, baby."

She pressed her forehead to his back and then nodded. His words bolstered her with confidence. If nothing else, she wanted Scott to be proud of her. To know he could count on her at his side in a crisis. The man had suffered more than any person should. She couldn't contribute to his torture by making him worry she'd freak out or shut down.

"I'm good," she whispered, pulling from his grip. She pressed her hand over his heart and counted five solid and steady beats before climbing off the bike. He followed suit, removed both their helmets, then took her hand.

Together they turned toward the man who'd shouted at them.

Olivia took one look at his face, and her stomach dropped.

Pure evil stared back at her.

"Grab 'im and bag 'im," dead-eyes ordered.

Four men converged on them.

Olivia whipped her head around as Scott's grip tightened. "Don't fucking touch her," he snarled.

One of the men tagged her around the waist, yanking her from Scott's side while the three others attacked him. She screamed and kicked but was no match for the strength of her captor.

Scott never had the chance to fight. Immediately, a black bag was yanked over his head. He had to be paralyzed with panic because he didn't kick out or attack.

"No!" Olivia screamed. She fought like an animal—a lioness protecting her pride. As Scott's hands were yanked behind his back, she raked her nails down her abductor's arms. Skin balled up under her nails.

"Fuck!" he shouted. The grip on her loosened just enough for her to break free. She sprinted toward Scott, who was being shoved to his knees. "Get that off him!" she screamed like a madwoman. He had to be panicking, unable to breathe. They hadn't talked about the claustrophobia specifically, but after hearing his story and witnessing him in the jail cell, she couldn't fathom how he felt with a bag over his head.

Just as she was about to reach out and rip the bag from his head, she was caught again.

"Fucking bitch," the asshole growled.

"No! Get that off him now." She kicked, scratched, flailed, and screamed as loud as possible. No one came. The road remained deserted, and Scott remained on his knees. His chest heaved—she could see the tremors wracking his body. She'd kill each one of these men with her bare hands if she got the chance.

"Enough!" the man who seemed to be the ringleader shouted. "Shut the fuck up, or he gets a bullet in the brain."

She froze.

"Fucking finally," the man holding her mumbled.

"Don't shoot him! I'll be quiet," she cried. "I'll stay calm.

I'll do whatever the hell you want—"

"No!" Scott growled.

"Anything. Just get that fucking bag off his head."

The man laughed, transforming his face from evil to vicious. He loved every second of this. Her fear evaporated, and a fiery rage took its place, burning through her veins.

"Not sure what you have to laugh about," she called out. "You may have one Handler, but there are many more. And they're going to tear you to fucking pieces."

His laughter disappeared instantly. He settled the gun on the back of Scott's head. "Good to know," he said with smug arrogance. "Guess I need to kill this one while I have the chance."

Icy terror seized her lungs.

What had she done?

Chapter Twenty

The motherfucking heat.

Would it ever end?

The heat, torture, and goddamn sand stuck in his wounds and on his sweaty skin. It irritated like a bitch. His whole body had become a red, itchy mess of mini scratches and discomfort.

A furious feminine wail sliced through his desperation.

Olivia?

Scott blinked in the darkness.

Fuck! Deke was dead. He wasn't baking in a box in the desert. Sure, the air was warm, but not fry-an-egg-on-the-pavement scorching. And it was humid. There was a thick heaviness to the air only Floridians understood.

More shouting and panicked pleading helped clear the fog. Until the telltale click of a bullet being loaded into the chamber of a pistol made an eerie stillness settle over him.

He'd been here before, seconds from death, his life in someone else's hands. Only those other times, he'd been on active duty and prepared to sacrifice his life for his country. And he hadn't had a gorgeous woman burrowed under his skin counting on him to keep his shit together.

"Don't shoot him! I'll be quiet," Olivia screamed. "I'll stay calm. I'll do whatever the hell you want—"

"No!" Scott ground out. Fuck that. He'd gladly take a bullet to keep these motherfuckers' hands off her.

Olivia continued yelling until the hard barrel of the gun settled against the back of his head. Then she fell deathly quiet. Goddamn, he was so proud of her. Though blinded by the bag, he could see the look on her face clear as day— terrified yet furious.

"They aren't going to kill me," he said, voice strong and steady.

"No?" whomever the fucker was with the gun at his skull said with a laugh. "And why's that?"

"You pulled me over for a reason. You want something. She can't get it for you." He'd die before giving these assholes her name, though they probably already knew exactly who she was. "She's a woman. Curly won't listen to fuck-all from bitches."

Man, she'd skin his balls for that sexist remark.

Unless Brooke got to him first.

Curly would just laugh his ass off.

The gun stayed in place. Though he couldn't see Olivia or anyone, he felt the waves of anxiety wafting off her. He couldn't do a damn thing to ease her fears, which twisted him up more than having a gun to his head. Only one other time in his life he'd felt so helpless, and it ended with Deke's death.

No one would fucking die tonight.

Well, maybe the fucker holding him at gunpoint.

"You know," the guy said as though an idea had just popped into his head. "There's something I'd like. Actually, something my boss wants."

"Lobo?"

The responding grunt was all the confirmation Scott

needed. Lobo had sent these assholes. "Where's that motherfucking coward been hiding out? This seems to be his style, kidnapping innocent women and shit. Your boss a one-trick pony? This the only way he can get a woman's attention?"

The gun nudged his scalp. Hard.

"He wants a meeting with your president."

"Seriously? He never heard of a phone? A fucking text message?"

"Tomorrow night. Nine o'clock. Grim's Bar."

Scott had heard of the place. Biker bar a few towns over. Closer to the beach. Supposed to be a shithole run by a guy Curly used to ride with. "Want us to bring anything? Bottle of wine? Roses? A fucking cake, maybe?"

The gun cracked against his head again. "Fuck off with the smart-ass shit. Prez, VP, and your stupid ass. That's it. Anyone else gotta wait outside."

Scott spent his entire military career training for every possible scenario. Every brand of sensory deprivation, resisting torture, evasion, escape—everything. The time he spent in captivity fucked with his psyche, but it hadn't erased years of intense drills. He'd also been trained to observe his surroundings. With his vision blocked, his ears went on automatic alert. They twitched, picking up on a tiny vibration that would eventually become the thunderous roar of approaching motorcycles.

The club was on the way.

His family had his back. That knowledge chased away any lingering panic. He wasn't alone. Used to functioning in a team, he fucking loved this new brotherhood.

"Can't promise he'll accept this lovely invitation, but I'll pass it along."

The gun moved. Not far, but it shifted away from his head and down toward the ground. Scott didn't think as there wasn't any need. He trusted his instinct and training above anything else.

He swept his leg out, twisting so his back took the brunt of the fall. His shin collided with his captor's legs.

"Scott!" Olivia's scream quickly turned into a yelp of pain.

Oh, fuck no.

He heard the gun clatter to the road as the bastard fought to keep his balance. Scott thrust his bound hands upward. They whacked into skin, and a second later, he heard a grunt as the guy hit the ground. Scott wasted no time, scrambling to his knees.

Sounds of Olivia struggling spurred him on. He needed this asshole unconscious right fucking now.

The rumble of approaching bikes grew loud enough to be heard by everyone.

Blind, Scott dove toward the spot he'd heard the guy fall. His shoulder collided with something hard—the guy's head.

Perfect.

He flipped to his back and reached out with his tied hands. As he caught the gun under his chin, he pulled as hard as he fucking could. The shout of pain was music to his ears. Bending his arms, he immobilized the guy in a headlock.

The approaching bikes got so fucking loud he couldn't hear a damn thing over the roar of the pipes.

The cavalry had arrived.

Still squeezing with the crook of his elbow, he held firm against the guy's throat. His prisoner struggled, flailing as he tried to escape. But he didn't know shit about fighting, and Scott had been training in jujitsu since he was six.

The bikes quieted to a low hum as shouting overwhelmed his senses. At that moment, he realized just how much he trusted his brothers with his own life and, more importantly, Olivia's. They'd take care of her until he got this fucking hood off his head.

He counted to ten as he tried to block out all the noise. The body on top of him went limp.

"Thank fuck," he whispered as he lifted his arms. Two hundred pounds of man squashed him to the ground.

"I'm fine!" Olivia shouted. "Forget about me. Scott!"

Light footsteps smacked on the pavement. A soft breeze blew from her body as she dropped down to his side. She grunted. "Fuck, this piece of shit is heavy."

A chuckle he thought came from Tracker loomed above.

"Baby, don't hurt yourself," Scott said. "Track, that you? Get this fucker off me."

The weight disappeared but was immediately replaced by a much lighter one as Olivia scrambled on top of him. She went to work on the hood, yanking it off his head.

He blinked as the glare from the row of bikes seared his eyes. "Fuck, I'm glad that thing's off." Olivia's tear-stained face came into view.

"Are you okay?" she asked in a rush. She ran her hand over his body even though she knew he hadn't been beaten.

"Shh, baby, I'm fine."

"But the hood!" Hysteria tinged her voice.

Lifting his hands, he called out. Someone get these fucking things off me. Lock appeared seconds later with a master key and released his wrists. A locksmith was a good friend to have. As soon as his hands were free, he rotated his wrists, then sat up with Olivia in his lap.

"I'm okay," he whispered as she threw her arms around him and squeezed until her muscles shook. "Promise."

"We gotta get the fuck outta here," Curly said. "Someone's gonna drive by and call the cops."

Nodding, Scott stood without letting Olivia go. She crossed her ankles at his back and clung to him, clearly okay with the public contact. "They get away?"

"We got the one you knocked out. Locke's bringing a cage,

and we'll load him up."

"You know him?" he asked his president.

Curly shook his head. "Don't recognize him."

"Lobo wants to meet you tomorrow night. Grim's Bar."

Curly winced. "Fucking hate that shithole. At least it was a shithole a decade and a half ago."

"Worse now, if you can believe it," Ty called out.

With a snort, Curly turned toward his bike. "Let's roll. I know it's late, but I want everyone in church. Liv, Brooke and Ray are at your place. I figured neither of you would want to be alone. You did good calling me, honey."

Olivia straightened in his arms. "Thank you." Her smile was genuine, but Scott barely noticed.

"What the fuck?" he growled.

"Oh shit," someone murmured.

He set Olivia down and cupped her face. Worry and a hint of pain swirled in her eyes.

"He fucking punched you?" Familiar rage simmered in his blood. The same fury that had him beating the fuck out of Dante the other day. The same white-hot, murderous impulse that had him shooting the kneecaps off Curly's rival a few months ago. His pulse thrummed, sending blood to the muscles he ached to put to work. His breathing sped, and his vision blurred.

Someone dared to put a bruise on his woman's beautiful face.

His woman.

He glanced to where Ty hovered over the still body of the man he'd knocked out. That asshole wasn't the one to bruise her, but he was the only one they'd captured. And beating him to a bloody pulp would go a long way toward soothing the beast. Scott dangled off the ledge by one pinky finger. And that finger was weakening by the second.

"Hey." Olivia's gentle yet firm voice coaxed him back into

the moment. She wrapped her smaller fingers around his wrists where his hands held her face. He flinched as she touched his abraded wrists. "Stay with me," she whispered.

"Olivia, we need to go. You got him?" Curly cut in.

"I do." She nodded but didn't tear her gaze away. "Scott, we have to go. I can already hear sirens in the distance. Someone must have seen us."

"They hurt you."

"Yes. That stupid goon punched me. But I'm here, and I am all right. What's more important right now is for us to leave." She glanced at the guy on the ground before looking back at him. "You'll get your time with him. But it's not right now. Please get me out of here."

The gentle plea worked its way into his chest and around his heart. He nodded as the fog cleared. Oliva stood before him, bruised and terrified but calm. The angst inside him shifted its focus from intense fury to the imminent threat of being arrested again.

He'd never understand how those slender arms hauled him over the ledge and back on solid ground. Nothing and no one else had been able to accomplish that since he returned from Afghanistan. When he'd fly into a rage, justified or not, it only settled when he'd worked the venom out of his system, usually through his fists.

But Olivia managed it with a few softly spoken words and a gentle caress. He tightened his grip on her face and tugged her to him, where he kissed her hard and fast. They didn't have time for it, but he rested his forehead against hers. "Fuck, you're amazing."

"You okay?"

"I'm okay, baby. Let's get the fuck outta here."

It'd been too damn close. Shit would have to change, starting with Olivia sleeping in his bed every night. His club had a target on their back, which meant Olivia wasn't safe.

The only way to guarantee her safety was to keep her close. Very close. So close he could wrap his arms around her. She'd have to be naked too.

For her protection. No other reason.

Chapter Twenty-One

"Hey." Brooke tapped Olivia's knee.

She turned from where she'd been staring at the still water in the pool. "Yeah?"

"You okay?"

Was she okay? Amazing how a two-word question could necessitate such a complicated answer. "Am I okay?" She took a sip, a gulp, of her wine, then pushed her plate of fish tacos aside. "In the last few days, I've been mauled by a nasty thug, gone to the police station to bail out a man I thought hated me, had more sex with that man than I've had in years, been attacked on the road by a group of renegade bikers, and now I'm sitting here with you pretending I'm not freaking out about this meeting the guys are at. So, the answer is no. I'm not totally okay. I kinda feel like I'm living in a movie, but I'm not at the end where everything works out. It's right in the middle where everything's going to shit, and you have no idea what the hell will happen."

Okay, that was a lot. And she hadn't even mentioned the ongoing texts from Lance.

Brooke blinked at her. "Um, not to be insensitive to everything you've gone through, but do you think you could expand on the sex-having part?"

She snorted, which turned into a giggle, then a full-blown belly laugh. Brooke laughed along with her. The combination of wine and stress had her emotions on a hair-trigger. Thank God they finally bubbled out as laughter instead of the tears that had been threatening all evening. She had no idea what the hell she and Scott currently were to each other but making him proud was important. Blubbering in the corner wouldn't help accomplish that. Staying strong would. Strong like Brooke, who, in her mind, was the perfect ol' lady.

Not that she envisioned herself staying in Florida as Scott's ol' lady. She had no idea what the future held, but she didn't think Scott wanted her to envision a life with him.

"Not sure what's so funny," Brooke said, laughing right along with her. "I was dead serious."

"Oh, God." She set her wine glass down and shook her head. "I have no idea what the hell we're doing, but ever since Scott got home from jail, we can't keep our hands off each other. We've moved past hatred to… something else."

"What is it they say? There's a fine line between love and hate." Brooke pursed her lips. "I think that's it. Someone said something like that anyway."

"Yeah, don't think love is the word I'd use. Lust, for sure. Pent-up aggression. High stress? Whatever it is, it's freakin' hot." Her face heated as she said the words. She'd never had a girlfriend she'd been comfortable enough to confide in like this. They all tried to one-up each other with their sexual exploits and purse purchases.

Giggling, Brooke closed her eyes and nodded.

"What are you doing?"

"Imagining it. You're right. Dayum, girl, that is hot."

"Hey!" She threw the cork at Brooke. "Keep your thoughts on your own man and away from Scott."

One of Brooke's eyes popped open. "Is that jealousy I hear?

Might there be more than lust?"

Her face flamed. "No. I'm just trying to save you from Curly's wrath."

"Please." Brooke waved a hand in front of her face. "I'm not scared of that man. His punishments always come with extra orgasms for me." She winked then got a horrified look on her face. "Sorry. I think I had too much wine. My mouth and brain are no longer connected."

"No, it's good." Any distraction worked. "It's keeping my mind off this meeting." And Lance.

There went any lightness in the conversation. Brooke seemed to sober up in an instant. "Curly and I haven't been together that long. Not quite a year, so I'm not the most experienced at club conflict, but there was some initially. I have no idea how this meeting will turn out tonight, but what I do know is that these guys trust each other and have each other's backs one hundred percent. They'll keep each other safe no matter what happens."

The words didn't erase all the fears, but they reassured her enough to lose much of the tension in her spine.

"Scott can handle himself and probably everyone else in that room," Brooke added without a hint of doubt in her voice.

She was right. Of all the Handlers, he was the one with the training on conflict resolution, offensive maneuvers, and general ass-kickery. "Thank you, Brooke. I needed the reminder that I trust him and his skills."

"Good." She winked. "More wine?"

The two glasses she'd already sucked back had a light and floaty feeling coursing through her veins. One more might push her over the edge from tipsy to drunk. "Sure, what the hell."

"Yay!" Brooke topped them both off, killing the second bottle. She wasn't shy with the pouring. "You know, he trusts you too, Liv. You said you needed the reminder to trust him. I want you to know that he trusts you too."

An unsettling feeling fell onto her shoulders. "What do you mean?"

"I know things were, let's say, unpleasant with him when you first got here, but I'm pretty sure that had much more to do with him than you."

She stared into the full wine glass, unable to take a sip. "Yeah." That was an understatement. Now knowing all he'd endured and the misplaced guilt he suffered, his hostility toward her and volatility made sense. But she'd never betray his confidence by divulging his secrets.

"Look, I can't give you details of club business, but we've all been concerned about Scott for months. The mood swings, the violent fights, the over-the-top reactions to any aggressive situations. It's been clear for a while that something serious is going on with him, and it's only natural to assume it's a result of his career in special forces. Then you came along, and we find out his best friend was killed on their final mission, and it doesn't take a detective to determine something traumatizing happened to him."

"He's been through a lot." Understatement of the century. What Scott suffered, no human should ever hear about, let alone experience. If those events were able to break a man as strong and capable as Scott, they'd destroy most people.

"I'm sure it's worse than anything I can imagine." Brooke reached across the table and squeezed her hand. "I'm so glad he's been able to confide in you, Liv. In just a few short days, I've seen a lightness in him that was never there before. You're so good for him. And to him."

This conversation caused a physical ache deep inside her. While she'd been living a cushy life surrounded by luxury and wealth, Scott and her brother existed in hell. She'd forever regret the years she'd spent believing her father's lies about her brother and how he'd been the one to sever ties to their family. As she'd grown, she learned the truth, but so many years had been wasted by then.

She wouldn't make the same mistakes with Scott. She'd cherish every moment, every kiss, every touch. Part of that meant trusting him with her story as much as he trusted her with his. Even the buzz of wine couldn't stem guilt from pummeling her.

She hadn't outright lied, but she hadn't been truthful either. Scott thought she was there, maybe nursing a wounded heart or making a petty statement. What he didn't know could bring an enormous and deadly problem to his club's door.

She shook her head and withdrew her hand from Brooke's grasp with a heavy sigh. "You give me way too much credit, Brooke. Credit I don't deserve. I haven't been anywhere near as forthcoming with Scott as he's been with me. He doesn't even know the real reason I'm here."

Brook cocked her head and studied Olivia. After a few seconds, it became difficult to keep from squirming under her assessing stare.

"If I had to guess, I'd say you and your fiancé didn't break up. You ran from him for whatever reason. And you're terrified of being discovered."

Olivia gasped. She glanced around, suddenly feeling exposed and unprotected.

"It's okay," Brooke said, reaching out again. "I've pretty much thought this from the first time I met you. There's a reason my house is like a fortress. And I'm not judging. I've been there."

The house was safe. Right. Lance had no idea where she was. Despite the increasing text messages and emails, he didn't know. Because if he did, she wouldn't be receiving typed communication. She had no doubt he'd make an appearance in person.

"H-how did you know?"

Brooke's smile saddened. "I've been there, Liv. And I recognize some of the signs. Every time your phone chimes, you get this terrified look on your face. And you never talk about your ex. Usually, after a breakup, some man-bashing is expected. But you've never once brought him up. You don't contact anyone who was in your life before you showed up here. And you shut down any conversation about your life. At first, I wondered if you kept things locked up because of Scott, but then I remembered how I was when I first moved away from my psychotic ex-husband."

"I'd like to hear your story sometime if you're willing to share."

"Sometime, yes. I don't think either of us is up for another heavy conversation tonight."

"Yeah." She sipped her wine. "I'll share mine as well. I'd like to tell Scott first, though." He deserved to know before anyone else and to be the one to tell her to leave if the risk to his club was too great.

Brooke released her hand and rested back in her chair with a nod. "As you should." Then she smirked. "I know it's premature of me to say this, but I like you a lot, Liv, and I think you'd make a fantastic permanent addition to our rag-tag family."

Those words caused three simultaneous reactions in her.

The warmth of acceptance and friendship.

Excitement at the fantasy of sticking by Scott's side as his woman.

And terror.

Because as much as she'd tried to convince herself their intense connection was fleeting and merely sexual, deep down, she never wanted it to end. Scott had come to mean so much to her in such a short period. And the idea of losing it scared her almost as much as Lance finding her.

"You know he'll help you. The whole club will."

Her laugh sounded harsh and bitter. "That's part of my worry," Olivia said. "At first, I didn't say anything because he wanted nothing to do with me, and I didn't know who I could trust. Now I know I can trust all of you, and things with Scott have… well, progressed."

Brooke smirked and bobbed her eyebrows.

That had Olivia huffing out a laugh. "Thank you for trying to make me smile. If my ex finds me, it could be dangerous, not only for me but the whole club. I'm not sure I can lay that possibility at your feet. You've all become important to me. If anything were to happen—"

Brooke held up a hand. "Trust me when I tell you I understand. The club went through an embarrassing amount of drama because of me. Hell, Spec killed my ex-husband."

Holy shit. Olivia gasped.

Nodding, Brooke said, "It was horrible. But you have to give them the information so they can decide for themselves, as a club. It's just how it works around here. No one will think poorly of you. Everyone here has baggage. It's why we're drawn to the life. And if you're one of us, you're all the way one of us. Good, bad, ugly, and crazy exes."

There it was again. The warm and cozy feeling of acceptance. Friendship. Family. When was the last time she'd felt it? When had she experienced such support, nonjudgment, and care? She couldn't recall a time her father or fiancé had made her feel so safe and accepted. And the group of superficial ladies she'd called friends? Hell, they'd have dropped her the instant they caught her wearing shoes from Target.

"Thank you, Brooke. I wish I could make you understand how much your friendship means to me."

"You don't need to. I was in your shoes not long ago, so I

completely understand. You have no idea how much it means to me to be in a position to pay it forward."

Chuckling, Olivia said, "You really do like to rescue strays, don't you?"

Brooke barked out a laugh. "Guilty, but you're not a stray anymore. You have a family now."

With that, they clinked their glasses and fell silent. They'd succeeded in taking her mind off the Handlers' meeting with Lobo. Now that they were finished dissecting her life, the anxiety returned. Only now, it was coupled with worry over talking to Scott about why she'd come to Florida in the first place.

Hopefully, one day soon, this would be nothing more than an image in her rearview mirror. She could pursue veterinarian school. She could do anything she wanted. But where would she be then? Back in Chicago? Somewhere new? Florida?

And what were the chances she'd be at Scott's side?

Chapter Twenty-Two

If two decades of special forces training had taught Scott anything, it was how to focus amid distractions and discomfort. He'd spent hours lying in cramped positions, waiting and watching with his entire attention devoted to one spot. He'd ignored painful injuries in the name of completing a mission. He'd fought through snow, heat, bug-infested jungles, and bone-dry deserts with a single-minded focus.

Complete the mission.

And then he started sleeping with Olivia, and in just a few days, his concentration had been shot to shit. He kissed her goodbye at Curly and Brooke's place two hours ago and had spent most of the time since thinking about her. In church, Lock had to ask him the same question three times before it registered. On the ride to the meeting with Lobo, he'd nearly blown a red light while reliving the three times he'd made her come that morning.

And now? He still couldn't get his head in the game, and he was about to accompany his prez into a potentially hostile meeting.

"Fuck's up with you tonight, brother?" Tracker asked with a smirk as though he knew damn well where Scott's mind was.

"Nothing. I'm good."

"Thinking about a little brunette firecracker?"

He shot Tracker a death glare. Of course, the asshole just laughed.

Curly watched the exchange with a flat expression. Once Tracker was done razzing him, Curly strode over. "Need your head in the game, Spec, in case shit goes south in there. Your brothers need to trust you're at your best when you have their backs. I'm not sure you're the best one for this tonight."

That sobered him up quickly. He narrowed his eyes at his prez. "Are you questioning my loyalty to the club?"

A grin broke out across Curly's face. "Nah. Just fucking with you. Pretty sure you could fall asleep during the meeting and still kill the whole room if necessary." Curly slapped him on the back. "Just try to wipe that lovesick look off your face before we go in."

Lovesick? What the fuck?

"That ain't a lovesick look, prez," Ty chimed in.

"Thank you," Scott muttered. "Finally, someone's making sense."

"That's what we called pussy-whipped."

"For fuck's sake."

They laughed together for a moment before falling serious. Most civilians would think they were crazy for joking at a time like this, but dark humor had helped get him through tenser situations than this, and the joking kept his anxiety down. It seemed the rest of the guys agreed.

"Okay," Curly announced. "Spec and Ty are with me. The rest of you hang out here until we get back. Stay vigilant. I'm sure Lobo will send someone out to babysit you. Don't make me walk out to a blood bath, okay?"

Rolling his eyes, Tracker nodded. "Got it, boss."

Pulse and Lock nodded their agreement. Jinx didn't, which

had Scott's senses on alert.

"Let's do this." Tracker held out a fist they all bumped with as they walked toward the bar.

A handful of cars and bikes sat parked in the lot. Other than that, the place was quiet. Was the bar open to patrons? Maybe Lobo shut it down for the evening, or perhaps they did shitty business. Either way, the lack of civilians worked in their favor if this meeting took a downward slide. They'd all be fucked if bullets started flying and some drunk college kid took a wild one between the eyes.

He stayed fully alert, scanning high, low, left, and right. He clocked everything from the number of cars to their positions in the lot to the location of the windows on the building and possible evacuation routes. As they neared the front entrance, the door opened, and a bald giant stepped outside.

"Jesus," Ty muttered. "Guy's fucking huge."

Seriously, it was as though someone shaved the Hulk's head and painted him. This guy could crush skulls in one hand.

Scott rolled his eyes. "It's a stupid fucking show of force," he whispered. "Sure, he's huge, but he's probably slow as a fucking sloth. Bet you fifty bucks you'd have time to run back to your bike and grab a gun before he got his hands on a single skull to crush."

Hulk didn't speak. Instead, he grunted and jerked his head toward the door.

"If you didn't catch that, it was neanderthal for, 'Welcome, thanks for being on time. Please head inside,'" Scott said.

Ty coughed to cover up his laugh while Tracker laughed loud from a few feet back. For his part, Curly tried to play the no-nonsense president by shooting Scott a glare, but his quirking lips gave away his amusement.

Scott shrugged at the prez. They were dealt these rotten lemons, so they might as well make some shitty lemonade.

With a glower their way, the Hulk grunted again and puffed out his barrel chest.

Scott barely resisted rolling his eyes. "Yeah, we get it, big guy. You're huge. You're tough. You ate a dozen raw eggs and took an extra testosterone shot this morning. Stand down."

Curly gripped Scott's cut as the guy opened his mouth, most likely to eat some small children. "Get the fuck inside," he muttered.

"Sure thing, boss. Catch you later, Hulk," he said as he strode into the building.

"Christ," Curly muttered to Ty. "Think I liked it better when he was in a shit mood and lost his temper every five minutes."

Huh. Scott frowned as he walked into the bar. The prez had a point. If Hulk had flexed and postured a few weeks ago, Scott would've lost his shit, flown into a rage, and ended up bloody. Tonight, he was throwing witty quips instead of fists.

What the fuck was that about?

The question would have to wait.

They stepped into the bar, and Scott instantly went on alert. His nerve endings tingled, and a buzz zinged through his blood as well-honed senses kicked into full alert mode. Without needing to think about it, he began clocking every inch of the room, starting with possible exits.

A man, big but not as huge as his buddy, Hulk, hovered by the back door, arms folded across his chest and a bored expression on his mustached face. The double steel doors behind the bar would lead to a kitchen, which probably had its own emergency exit to the outside. No one guarded that door, but it didn't mean someone wasn't waiting in the kitchen. Behind them, another thug lingered at the door they'd entered through. And, of course, Hulk waited outside, keeping an eye on the other Handlers.

Next, the significant players fell prey to Scott's assessing gaze.

Two men sat at a table in the far-right corner of the bar. One had to be Lobo, and the other Scott didn't recognize. One man stood behind the bar, but he went about his business, drying glasses. The owner, maybe? Low on the threat scale. There were the two guys guarding the exits and two others. One sat at the bar, watching Scott and his brothers with a keen eye, and another stood near Lobo's table. All were armed and wore pinched expressions like they hadn't taken a shit in a week.

Fantastic.

"Pat 'em down," a man with a Hispanic accent spoke from the back table. It had to be Lobo.

"We're unarmed," Scott said. It was the truth. They hadn't bothered with weapons, knowing they'd be searched. Okay, fine, Scott had a hidden compartment built into his favorite boots. He kept a knife in it. Not that it mattered. He knew more than a dozen ways to kill these posers with his bare hands. But he spread his arms and legs like a good boy—no point in pissing all over this meeting before it got started.

Curly and Ty mirrored his stance. After a quick and frankly ineffective pat-down, the guy nodded at Lobo. Scott snorted. He could've had half a dozen weapons stashed on his person, and this joker would've missed them all.

"Welcome," Lobo said with a smarmy smile. "Have a seat."

A quick unspoken conversation went on between Ty and Curly, where Ty nodded then hung back while Scott walked to the table with his prez. He kept his expression tight and menacing, but when Lobo pulled out a Colt revolver and placed it on the table, it took all his strength to keep from laughing. This guy was a child, playing at being an outlaw— someone who'd seen too many mafia movies and now thought he owned the goddamn streets.

A hundred snarky comments tried to burst from Scott's mouth, but he was there as the muscle, so he kept fucking quiet. Curly got to do the talking.

The prez scooted along the bench seat. After a final sweep of the room, Scott followed.

"Curly," Lobo said with a nod. His gaze shifted Scott's way. "And you must be Spec. You've put more than one of my men in the hospital."

"The fuck you talking about? I'm a goddamn teddy bear." Okay, maybe he couldn't completely keep quiet.

Lobo's expression hardened. "Watch yourself, Spec. You're in my house now."

"Are we here to fucking socialize, or did you have something to discuss?" Curly cut in. "Because I've got shit to do, and having a playdate with you toddlers wasn't supposed to be part of it."

Scott kept his attention on Lobo. The man didn't enjoy being insulted. Who did? But this was more. Fire flashed in his eyes, and his jaw ticked. On the table, his fingers curled into fists. Had to be the toddler comment that pissed him off. The asshole was young to be in charge—late twenties, maybe.

Scott would bet his left nut the men he commanded were about as loyal as a rock. Any sign of weakness in their juvenile leader, and they'd either mutiny or flee. This whole situation was a ticking time bomb. Something would fucking blow soon. It was just a matter of what would go first. Would Lobo's guys fight for his spot at the top of their food chain, or would the man himself make a critical error in judgment?

"You have one of my men," Lobo said with ice in his voice.

Curly nodded. "I do. But that's not why we're here. We took him after he told us about this meeting. After he stopped my enforcer and his ol' lady on the road. So why the fuck are you wasting my time?"

Lobo vibrated with the kind of anger that could flip to

violence in a blink—Scott's specialty. He shifted, muscles tensing in anticipation of action. But Lobo kept himself in check. Barely.

"I have a deal for you," he ground out. "One-time offer. You agree now, or it's off the table."

Curly leaned back against the bench, folding his arms across his chest. "Let's hear it."

His apparent interest cooled Lobo's anger. A grin broke out across his face, and he leaned across the table, beady little eyes hungry with greed. "Money, Curly. I want to offer you money."

"I have money," Curly said in a bored tone. "A fuck ton of it, but you know this."

Lobo wasn't deterred. "I'm talking a steady stream for you and your men. Good fucking money coming in every goddamn day."

"And I'm guessing to get his money, I'll need to patch you and your crew into my club?"

"Nuh-uh." Lobo shook his head with a wry grin. "I like being in charge. I'm not interested in bowing down to you. All I want is a business arrangement. Use of your guys for transport, meetings, pick-up."

"Ah, and what will we be transporting, meeting about, and picking up?"

"Methamphetamine," Lobo said with glee, as though describing a chest full of gold bars. "Pure as the fucking snow. I'm talking incredible shit like you've never had."

The words hardly left Lobo's mouth before Curly said, "No."

Lobo blinked. "No?"

Curly nudged his leg, so Scott hopped out of the booth. "I'm not interested, and my club's not interested." He shrugged. "Guess the meeting's over. See ya around, Lobo." He climbed out of the booth.

Lobo sat there, stunned, mouth partway open.

Scott had to press his lips together to keep from laughing. And fuck, how much did he want to give the prez a high-five? Damn, that was fun.

Together they made their way toward Ty and the exit.

"This is happening. You can be a part of it, or you can be in my way," Lobo called out.

Without bothering to turn around, Curly snorted. "Consider me a human roadblock then."

"I'll go to your men on my own. Bet half of them will walk away from you when they hear the kind of cash I'm offering."

"Knock yourself out," Curly called, still giving Lobo his back. It took fucking balls to stand with his back to a potentially hostile room. After being in prison and even injured at one point, Curly's skin had to be crawling with discomfort.

Maybe that was just Scott's.

"Challenge accepted," Lobo answered.

That was the final needle working its way under Scott's skin. What the fuck did Lobo know about how the MC worked? Not a damn thing. The stupid asshole had no idea the hell the Handlers could rain down on him. If that asshole thought a few dollar bills would break their loyalty, he had another think coming. Scott's nostrils flared as the familiar hum of anger began to pump through his veins.

"Keep your shit locked down, Spec," Curly muttered for his ears only. "Let's get the fuck out of here. You got a woman waiting for you. She'll skin you alive if you come back busted to hell."

A woman waiting for him? His steps almost faltered. Shit, it was true. Olivia was at Brooke's. Waiting for him. Worrying about him. Maybe even wanting him. All he had to do was leave this shit behind, walk through that door, and hop on his bike. Then he could collect his woman and spend the rest of the night buried inside her.

His blood rushed faster.

Damn, that sounded worlds better than heading home to clean split knuckles and apply ice to new bruises.

"I'm cool," he whispered.

Curly nodded. "Let's get the fuck outta here. What a bunch of bullshit."

Following Ty, they pushed through the door and out into the night. Neither of them paid Hulk any attention as they strode by.

"You know this might escalate tension between us," Scott said as they approached the bikes. "If he forms an official club, it could turn into war."

Curly stopped walking and met his gaze. "Good. Let them bring war. Lucky for me, I have a fucking special ops soldier on my side, huh?"

Scott grinned. "Ooo-fucking-rah, Prez."

The rest of the guys sat astride their bikes. No discussion of the meeting would occur there. They'd hash it out back at the farm. "Church at nine tomorrow morning," Curly said as he threw a leg over his motorcycle. He revved the engine and then sprayed an arc of gravel toward the bar as he peeled out.

Scott made eye contact with Tracker, who nodded then followed the prez. One by one, they left Lobo and his band of assholes behind.

The ride home passed in a blur of anticipation and a fucking semi-hard dick. It took everything in him not to push his bike to its limit to get to Olivia faster. He'd never experienced this before—an intense need to see a woman. To be in her presence. To get his hands on her to touch her and be connected to her. But the need was a living thing inside him now, and if he didn't feed that craving, he'd lose his mind.

As soon as they pulled into Curly's driveway, the women

came flying out of the house. Brooke ran straight to her ol' man, throwing himself in his arms. Olivia kept running past the embracing couple and right to him. He wrapped his arms around her and fused their mouths in a hot, claiming kiss. She tasted of wine, fear, and relief. They kissed for long moments. Her hands roved all over him as though checking for wounds.

They broke apart when air became scarce but stayed as close as possible. "I was so scared. But you're okay. Brooke said to trust you, and I do, Scott. I was terrified, but I knew you'd be okay because you're so strong. And so skilled."

He kissed her again to stem the flow of compliments he didn't want or deserve. She moaned into his mouth, then tightened her embrace. Pulling back, she stared deep into his eyes. "Take me home, Scott."

Home.

"Take me home and fuck me for the rest of the night. You have no idea how badly I need you." She pressed her hips into him, nearly humping him right there in Curly's driveway.

"Don't worry, I get it," he said on a gasp as her pelvis rocked over the iron rod of his dick. Her eyes closed, and a soft puff of air left her mouth.

Fuck, he needed inside this woman more than he'd ever needed anything.

He grabbed her hand. After pressing a kiss to her knuckles, he said, "C'mon, baby, let's go home."

The whole way home, she held him tighter, pressed closer, and stayed that way even when they slowed. It was only because she was exhausted and worried about dozing off on the bike.

At least that's what he told himself. Because thinking she might need to feel as close to him as possible was stupid.

And thrilling.

And so fucking appealing.

Chapter Twenty-Three

He was on her before the door snicked shut. Nothing could've stopped him from getting his hands all over her.

Olivia moaned into his mouth, completely shameless in her desire for him. He got it. This insane urge to have each other was the strongest and most intoxicating pull. It wouldn't be ignored.

She shoved her hands under his shirt, making him groan as those soft fingers glided up his stomach and over his chest. She pressed, molded, and nearly clawed his muscles as though trying to climb inside him.

His cock ached something fierce, and his balls hung heavy and full. When he finally came, it'd be fucking epic. He grabbed Olivia's ass and lifted, lining her up perfectly as he ground his cock against her.

They both groaned long, tortured sounds of half satisfaction and half need.

Kissing her like he'd die if he didn't, he worked one hand between their bodies. In seconds, he had his jeans unsnapped and the zipper down. Olivia helped him shove them down just enough to free his cock. Instead of moving to lower her pants, she wrapped her hand around his cock and squeezed.

"Fuck!" he shouted into her mouth as rockets went off in his brain. Pleasure hit him so hard, it nearly buckled his knees.

Liv's lips curled against his. Then they were kissing again. By some miracle, he managed to endure her mischievous hands without embarrassing himself while yanking her shorts over her ass, just enough to expose her saturated sex.

"Fuck me, you're drenched for me," he spoke against her lips as he dragged his fingers through the wetness.

She bucked into his hand. "Please, Scott!"

"What's wrong, baby?" He fingered her entrance, chuckling as she groaned in frustration. "Don't you want to play first?"

"No! I don't want to play. I want you to fuck me. Now!" The desperation in her voice turned him on as much as her hands fisting his cock.

"Hell, yes." Neither needed foreplay. The only thing that could satisfy the hunger was to get inside her. He knocked her hand off his cock, gripped the base, and pushed into her with one smooth, hard snap of his hips.

"Yes," she hissed. Her head fell back, hitting the wall as her eyes closed. "Yes. Feels so good." She grabbed his ass, holding him as deep as he could get inside her.

Good didn't begin to capture the astonishing feeling of the slick heat squeezing his cock. Even better than the last—

"Fuck, condom!" It was a weak protest because he honestly didn't know if he possessed the strength to pull out.

Olivia's finger's dug into his ass. He couldn't resist flexing his gluts and pulsing into her.

"Don't care," she said on a breathy exhale. "I'm clean. And protected."

His forehead met hers, and he inhaled her breath. "Thank fuck."

"Please don't stop. Please keep fucking me." The sassy,

defiant, sophisticated woman disappeared, leaving behind a raw, vulnerable, needy version of Olivia. He had a feeling she didn't show this side of herself to many, if anyone else. And fuck if that didn't make him feel unstoppable.

He kissed her, ending the plea. "Shh. I'm clean. I'm not stopping." Usually, he'd be fucking her into oblivion right now, but out of nowhere, a fullness entered his chest. Unfamiliar, terrifying emotions bombarded his brain.

And came flying out his mouth.

"What the fuck have you done to me, Olivia?" he whispered with their foreheads pressed together and their noses bumping. "You're all I want, day and night." He rocked his hips into her, making her whimper. "And not just for this pussy. I just want to be with you, look at you, talk to you, and listen to you talk. I can't stop it, Liv."

As she stared at him, her eyes grew watery.

"I don't think I wanna stop it. Christ, baby, I'm so fucked up, but if you can bear with me, I want us to try to be something."

"Scott," she whispered, then swallowed as a tear escaped. Every so slightly, she shook her head against him.

His heart sank straight to the floor.

But then she gave him a gorgeous but shaky smile. "Whatever you think I've done to you, you've done it to me tenfold. Scott, I want you more than anything. You have all of me."

His throat clogged. Words failed him. They stayed that way for a few more seconds, joined intimately while they did nothing more than share breath and absorb the moment.

But then Olivia's mouth curved up into an impish grin. She squeezed her pussy around his cock.

He saw stars. "Oh, fuck me." The need to pound into her came rushing back with startling force.

So he did just that. Widening his legs, he bent his knees,

almost making a seat for her to rest on. Her thighs had no choice but to widen. She squeaked as the move shifted him inside her. Then he grabbed her hands off his ass and plastered them to the wall above her head.

"Oh God," she whispered. A tremor ran through her that he felt in his dick.

He kissed her hard. If his heart stopped right then, it'd have all been worth it for a few seconds spent like this.

Olivia was entirely at Scott's mercy, pinned to the wall, spread wide, and speared by his cock. Never had she let a man have this much control over her physically. There wasn't a single thing she could do to stop him if he wanted to hurt her. Yet not a single inkling of fear found its way in—only excitement and anticipation.

And desire.

While his mouth worked hers open and his tongue slid inside to steal her mind, he shifted his hands from her wrists. He interlaced their fingers, holding her arms up in willing surrender. Something about the move had her near tears all over again. Who the hell knew why? He was as deep and connected to her as possible, yet a simple holding of hands got her all mushy inside.

Her eyes rolled back in her head as he dragged his dick most of the way out. His grip tightened on her hips one second before he slammed back inside.

Olivia cried out. Her body felt like a live wire, popping and buzzing with electric energy.

Scott fucked her like he'd been pining over her for years, and he'd never get another taste when he knew full well he could have her whenever he wanted.

Over and over, he hammered into her. Her ass hit the wall with every thrust. She tried to keep up and move with him, but her legs were spread so wide, she could do nothing but take the rough fucking.

And she loved every second of it. He dominated her, driving her closer and closer to the edge with every pump. Sweat dampened both their bodies, making them slide along each other. She forgot where she was. Forgot the year. Forgot her own damn name.

Olivia forgot everything beyond the feel of Scott owning her. She'd be happy to live in this moment for the rest of her life. But then, greed took over, and as much as he was giving her, she wanted more. With a whimper, she nipped his chin, then his lower lip. Scott took the hint, kissing her until her head spun.

Tighter and tighter, her center coiled until it felt she'd die if she didn't get relief.

Or oxygen.

She ripped her mouth away and sucked in air. Scott's lips found her neck, sucking so hard, the pressure sent a jolt to her core. Those ravenous lips trailed up to her jaw, where he bit. She loved it. Once, Lance had left a small hickey on her neck, and she'd freaked out at him. Now all she wanted was to wear marks left behind by Scott's mouth. The world needed to know she was his, and he took damn good care of her.

Finally, he released her hands. She immediately wound her arms around his neck and sought his mouth. Somehow, he managed to shove his hands under her shirt and bra. His fingers plucked and tugged at her nipples. Each time, her pussy clenched.

"Jesus Christ," Scott said. "Fucking hottest, tightest pussy. Heaven."

Her head spun. Breathing ragged, she could only mewl and moan. Her arms clenched around his neck began to tingle. So did her toes. The buzz traveled up her arms and legs until it met in her center. "Scott!" she yelled. "I'm gonna come." It'd be big. Huge. What barreled down on her would be a mind-melting orgasm, so enormous, it scared her.

"I got you, baby. Come. All over my cock."

That filthy mouth took things to another level.

"Please."

His hips moved faster. Harder. Deeper. They were two animals lost to everything but the primal need to mate and claim. The orgasm engulfed her like a tsunami obliterating everything in its path.

She shouted and squeezed Scott so tight if she'd had the ability for conscious thought, she'd have worried she'd broken his neck. All she managed to do was to cling to him and ride out the wave. Her thighs shook, and her pussy contracted at least a dozen times.

Scott lasted one or two breaths before his harsh curse hit her ear, and he came deep inside her.

Inside her. With no condom.

It was the hottest moment of her life. And she wanted a million more just like it.

Each time his muscles spasmed, he pressed her harder into the wall. It took him as long as it did her to calm down. As their breathing eventually leveled and the sweat began to cool, she shivered. Cold didn't matter. She'd gladly stay just like this outside in a blizzard.

After a few moments, his cock softened, allowing wetness to trickle out onto her thighs.

"Oh, my God," she whispered. "I can feel it. You."

"Mmm. I'd watch it drip out of you and then rub it into your skin if I could move. So fucking hot."

Wow. That would be sexy as hell. Her face heated, and her sex fluttered with renewed interest.

He grunted a half-chuckle with his face in the crook of her neck. "You know I'm thirty-nine, right? Gonna need at least a few minutes, babe."

Like she had any control over her body when he was around? Laughing right along with him, she gave him a playful whack on the back. And that took every last ounce of energy she had.

He shifted, banding his arms under her half-naked ass. "Let's go to bed. You mind if we wait until tomorrow morning to talk about how the meeting went?"

He planned to talk about it with her? Her heart nearly exploded. His words about not wanting her only for her body weren't merely words. Here he was, following them up with action, including her in his life, his club, and his family. "That's perfect," she managed around the lump of emotion in her throat. "Uh, but I should probably shower?"

He shook his head as he walked them the few feet across the studio apartment to his bed. His grin was pure evil. "Want you to fall asleep with me all over you. And in you."

Okay then. Wow. She wanted it too, but who the hell knew why?

When they reached the bed, Scott set her down on the mattress. Without needing words, they both removed the rest of their clothing. Once fully naked, a way she'd never once slept the entire night, Olivia scooted until she was settled in the bed. Scott followed seconds later, pulling her into his arms as soon as he was horizontal. The sigh that left him was so full of satisfaction and contentment that it made her smile against his firm chest.

This man was everything. She wanted to spend every night she had in Florida right there in his bed.

Dammit, the thought had her mind shifting to the limit of her time there. And that reminded her of the secrets she kept. Secrets Brooke told her she should divulge. How would Scott react? Not positively. She knew that for sure. But would he send her away? Because at this point, she lo—liked her time with him so much, she'd be devastated if he shunned her.

But then he'd once gain opened himself up to her tonight, telling her he wanted more than sex, and he planned to share the details of his meeting while she'd shared nothing of herself or her past. Guilt was a nasty little emotion that tended to sneak up on someone and infiltrate their consciousness.

It was now or never.

Swallowing a mouthful of fear, she pressed a kiss to the tattoo on his chest and then gazed up at him. "Scott?"

"Mmm? Yeah, babe?" he slurred without opening his eye. So near sleep. Another reason to feel guilty.

Waking him sucked, but if she chickened out now, she'd never get the words out. "I need to tell you something. It's about why I'm here in Florida. About my fiancé."

His visceral reaction came immediately and put a tiny fissure in her heart. His arms tensed around her, and his heart sped where it was pressed against hers. His strong jaw pulsed, and those eyes she loved on her turned hard and cold.

Abort! Abort!

This was a mistake. A huge screwed-up whopper of a mistake.

But it was too late to turn back. She'd opened the box, and all her horrors were primed to escape.

All she could do now was hope Scott didn't revert to hating her because, after the past few days, she couldn't stand being around him and not being close to him.

Chapter Twenty-Four

Olivia grounded him. She smoothed his jagged edges and anchored him in the present when the ghosts of his past fought to control him. No one else did that for him. No one could. Respecting her and just generally wanting to be around her only added to how incredible their connection was. Throw in mind-blowing sex and a near-constant erection in her presence, and well, fuck, he was one hundred percent sure he'd never meet another woman who ticked all those boxes.

In thirty-nine years, she'd been the only one. Where would he find another?

So if she were about to tell him she'd decided to return to Chicago and her rich-as-fuck sugar daddy, he couldn't be held responsible for his actions.

Not after he'd carved his heart out of his chest and handed it over to her.

He rolled to his back, letting go of her. The loss hit him hard. How was it possible to be so used to the feel of her against him so quickly? To need it as much as he liked it?

"What is it?" he asked as he fixated on the recently painted white ceiling. If he looked at her, he'd crack. Possibly beg her to choose him like some kind of pussy.

Her presence shrank. Olivia wasn't small in personality. At first, he'd assumed it was narcissism or an overly inflated ego. Now, he suspected her outward confidence and standoffish behavior hid a world of hurt and insecurity. So to feel her deflate as he pulled away killed him.

"What?" he asked again, this time with a venom he couldn't mask.

"Um." She cleared her throat, then propped herself up on her elbow. The beautiful face he lov—liked so much stared down at him with agony in her eyes. "I've thought about this so much. What to say. And now I can't figure out where to begin."

He wouldn't let those sad eyes pull him in. Not until he found out how deep she was about to drive the knife into his heart. "Just fucking say it. Cut to it."

"Okay." Pressing her lips together, she nodded. After a prolonged inhale and exhale, she spoke. "I left Chicago because I witnessed my fiancé on a security camera raping a woman in the garage of his office building. If you want all the details, I'll tell you the whole story, but the bottom line is that she was drugged. He paid money for her, and she was in absolutely no position to consent to anything. He caught me. He knows I saw."

What. The. Fuck!

Ice crystals formed in Scott's bloodstream as his brain tried to catch up to her words.

She wrung her hands and stared at the mattress between them. "Uh, so, I ran. Literally. I ditched my phone, bought a crappy car, and emptied my accounts. I have money in a trust he wasn't aware of, so I have security and sufficient funds to keep running, but he's searching for me."

"Jesus Christ." She'd been dealing with this shit for weeks? He pushed her onto her back, then rolled on top of her, pinning her arms above her head. Nothing but trust shone in her eyes. "So you came to me because Deke told you I'd be here if you needed someone and he wasn't around?"

Those beautiful green eyes held worry and uncertainty, but the trust remained. She bit down on her lower lip and nodded. Normally, he'd find the move sexy and go in for a taste, but her story rendered his dick lifeless.

"And I treated you like shit." Christ, he was a fucking asshole.

"No," she rushed to say, squeezing his hands. "Scott, please don't feel—"

He kissed the words right off her mouth. "Don't defend me. Deke would've whooped my ass and rightfully so. Don't fucking defend my shitty behavior."

"It's in the past. We're past it," she said with a hint of desperation as though she needed him to agree.

They'd moved beyond those first few weeks, but the shame of how he'd treated her would linger for a long time. "We're past it." He kissed her again. Fuck, he'd never get enough of those lips. "Doesn't mean I can't feel like an asshole for how I treated you." But they had a more pressing issue than his piss-poor attitude. "What are the chances this motherfucker will find you here?"

Sagging into the mattress, she shook her head. "I don't know. He somehow found my new phone number and has been texting me the past few days."

"What?" He exploded off her body and ran to her purse. His swinging dick, still coated in her arousal, barely registered. "This fucker has been contacting you? Threatening you?"

"Uh, yes," she squeaked.

He grabbed her phone from the tiny purse that probably cost more than everything he owned, not including his beloved boots. After thumbing it open with the passcode she'd shared the day before, he went straight for the text messages. Normally, he wouldn't violate her privacy by reading her personal shit, but a rapist ex-fiancé changed the game.

Miss me yet? See you soon.

Getting closer, bitch.

The longer you run, the worse it'll be.

Can't wait to get my hands on you.

The texts went on. Hundreds of them over the past three days. Fire heated his blood. He clenched his fist around the phone so hard, he worried the screen would crack. Who the fuck did this rich prick think he was? A million scenarios passed through Scott's head in the span of five seconds.

Olivia hurt.

Olivia scared.

Olivia at this man's mercy.

Olivia battered.

Olivia bruised.

"Fuck!"

His vision grew hazy as fury and the recognizable need for violence overtook his rational side. This motherfucker would die. By his hand. The club could help, but Scott would be the one to pull the trigger. And that would only happen after a nice, long... chat.

Fuck, yes, he liked that idea. His breathing quickened as the fantasy played out. Yanking fingernails, spilling blood, breaking kneecaps, shattering cheek bo—

"S-scott?"

Liv's shaky voice cut through the fog but didn't burn it away. He turned her way to find her seated naked in the center of the bed, knees drawn up and arms around her legs in a position of comfort. She looked so small, so worried, so scared.

Of him?

Christ. There it was—the shock he needed to keep him from flying into a blind rage. The thought of her being afraid sickened him. He'd rather Curly hogtied and tossed him in a trunk than have Olivia fear him.

"I want to kill him," he said in a voice destroyed by whatever emotions she evoked in him. The feelings were so deep, complicated, and terrifying that he had no name for them.

Love? Maybe. Who the hell knew? Did love feel half wonderful and half nauseating?

"I know," she said with a miserable half-smile. "But that's one of the reasons I've been so hesitant to tell you. I don't want you to take this on. I don't want your c-club to take this on."

The trembling lower lip did him in. "Baby, who are we if we don't protect our family? If we don't fight our family's battles?"

"I'm not f—"

"You are," he said as he strode toward the bed. After tossing the phone on the mattress, he climbed up. Olivia wasted no time, crawling into his lap and wrapping her arms around him. His heart fucking flipped.

"I'm so scared something will happen to one of you. I know it's only been a little while, but you all mean so much to me."

"Shh, baby, we've got this. We've got you." He smoothed his hand up and down her back.

Her arms tightened, and wetness soaked his shoulder. Christ, was she crying? "It'd be better if I just leave. Go somewhere random. Maybe out of the country."

Every cell in his body rejected that idea. "Fuck, no."

"I won't be able to live with myself if you get hurt because of me. Or if Curly is hurt, or Tracker. Any of you."

"Baby, we're tough as fuck. Do you think your pansy-ass,

live-in-luxury, Armani-wearing fiancé has anything on a former Ranger, a man who spent over a decade in a max security prison, and the rest of those fuckers?"

She stayed quiet for a moment, then said, "Ex-fiancé."

"That's my girl." He kissed her shoulder. "Trust me. Trust my club. I'll keep you safe, Liv. And my club and I will eliminate this problem for you." He didn't expand upon that, but guys like this douche, Lance, only went away when they were sent away. Like down to hell.

"I do trust you, Scott. More than anyone."

"I'm gonna need the whole story, babe. I need all the info. Then tomorrow, we need to bring it to Curly."

She sighed. "I hate this."

"I know, but it's how we do things here. There's no 'I' in motorcycle club."

That had her laughing. "You're making jokes. I thought I lost you for a few minutes there. But you're making jokes." She straightened out of his tight hug and looked him right in the eye. "Thank you."

He fingered the ends of her hair. "I'm fucked-up, Liv. Real fucked-up. I don't know if my head will ever get completely right, but I'm gonna work on it. I never want you to fear me or have to visit me behind bars again."

Through her tears, red-rimmed eyes, and stuffy nose, her smile lit up the fucking room. "I lo... um, I could never be afraid of you, Scott."

Christ, had she been about to say love? She loved him? What the fuck did he know about love? Not a goddamn thing. He'd have to worry about it later because learning the details of precisely what happened the night she left trumped everything right then.

"Tell me."

She nodded, then launched into her story. They sat there, naked and wrapped up in each other for a long time as she scared the fucking life out of him with her words. There were tears, anger, shaking, determination, and regret. By the time she finished, he had his arms wound tight around her again to keep himself in check. If it weren't for her soft, warm body keeping him on the bed, he'd light his ass out of there and up to Chicago. Her fiancé wouldn't see tomorrow's sunrise.

"You did everything right, baby." Especially making a flash drive with the footage. Though that's probably what put her in the most danger, it's what would eventually bring her fiancé to heel. Because after tonight, Olivia wouldn't be responsible for that flash drive any longer. It'd have a new home tucked away in the MC's safe. He'd fucking love to see Lance try to bust his way into the clubhouse.

"I don't know," she whispered. "I keep replaying it. Maybe I should've sent the footage to the media or the cops. Something to get justice for that girl."

He grabbed her shoulders and pushed her back so he could see those gorgeous green eyes. "First of all, like you told me, the cops live in Lance's pocket. Look at Curly's experience with the police. It's not always the best option. And second, going to the media would've created a shitstorm that would have painted a target on that girl's back and a bigger one on yours. We'll get justice, Liv. MC style. It'll be swift, and it'll be harsh. Then we'll find her and let her know she's safe too."

"Thank you," she said, cupping his face between her hands. He nuzzled into her palm.

There was more she wanted to say. He could see it in her eyes. The way she gazed at him like he wasn't a broken man with demons he'd battle for the rest of his life, but someone worthy of her. But she didn't speak. Instead, she brought her mouth to his as she shifted until straddling his lap.

He couldn't help it. He'd grown hard all over again not long ago. What the fuck was he supposed to do when the sexiest woman in the world was naked in his lap?

Olivia kissed him like she was starving. Like she wanted to crawl inside and merge her soul with his. He kissed her back just as hard, tangling his fingers in her hair to keep her mouth where he wanted it. He wanted nothing more than to stay just like this for the rest of the night.

But Liv had other ideas. Without breaking the kiss, she reached between their bodies and encircled his erection with her soft hands. He bucked and groaned into her mouth. She swallowed the sound as she positioned her soaked pussy over the head of his cock.

Instead of taking him inside like his leaking cock demanded, the minx teased the fuck out of him with tiny brushes of her pussy. Just as he was about to tear his mouth away and beg her to put him out of his misery, she sank hard and fast.

"Fuck!" he shouted as his eyes crossed.

Oliva giggled the happiest sound he'd heard from her yet.

Then she winked and rode him to fucking paradise.

Chapter Twenty-Five

For one solid week, life was perfect.

Seven days of riding on the back of Scott's bike, helping Brooke with the dogs, meals with the club, evenings having drinks by a roaring bonfire, and so many laughs, her stomach cramped.

Then there were the nights. If the days were perfect, a word hadn't been invented to describe the nights—hot, sexy, orgasmic, passionate, intimate, remarkable—some compounded combination of those descriptions.

Olivia climbed out of bed each morning with wobbly limbs, achy muscles, and a cheek-splitting smile on her face.

The texts from Lance stopped. Harassment from Lobo disappeared. If the rest of her life could've played out as those seven days spent with Scott and his family, she'd have signed on in a heartbeat.

But someone in the heavens had it out for her because precisely eight days after she realized she'd fallen head over heels in love with Scott, her phone rang at two in the morning.

Scott shot straight up in bed. "What the fuck?"

Olivia was slower to rouse, but Scott's distress had her

focusing on him over the blaring cell. "It's okay," she said, rubbing his back. Beneath her palm, his heart slammed against his ribcage. "It's just my phone."

"Fuck," he whispered. "I'm not cool with being startled awake like that."

"It's okay." She wrapped her arm around him and kissed his cheek. "Let me check it in case something's wrong with Brooke or the dogs." Really, who else would it be? Occasionally, one of Scott's brothers called her, but there wouldn't be any reason for it at this hour.

As the fourth ring pierced the quiet apartment, she snatched her phone off the nightstand. Her stomach cramped. God, no.

"It's Lance," she whispered as her hand began to tremble.

"Gimme," Scott said, making a grab for the phone.

She jerked it out of his reach, hopping off the bed. As much as she'd love to hand it over and let him deal with it, Lance would lose his shit if Scott answered the phone. Best to feel out the situation first. "Hello?" She held it to her ear and answered in a flat tone.

"I'm a very busy man, Olivia."

He'd always hated calling her Liv or Livy—said it sounded low-class. Her father wasn't a huge fan of the nicknames either. Now, after weeks of being around the Handlers who never used her full name, she hated the formal way it sounded coming from Lance's mouth.

With a fierce scowl, Scott advanced on her. She held up a hand and shook her head, but, of course, it didn't dissuade him.

"I don't have time to keep playing games with you, Olivia."

"Great," she said, backing away from Scott. A little growl left her man. "Guess that means you'll leave me the hell alone." Her back hit the wall next to his dresser.

Scott raised an eyebrow in a silent *where are you going to go now?* Then he planted his hands on the wall, boxing her in as he stared down at her.

"Not exactly," Lance said in her ear.

She had no doubt Scott could hear every word.

"That girl you saw in the garage?"

A wave of dread washed over her. "Yes? What about her?" God, if he'd done something to that poor girl, Olivia would never get over the guilt. Was this what Scott felt like when it came to Deke's death? If so, he was stronger than even she'd given him credit for.

"Well, I know her name, where she lives, and where she works. I know everything about her."

She glanced up at Scott in horror. Was Lance saying what it sounded like?

"If you're not back home in two days, I'll pay her a little visit. The tricky thing is you might not recognize her afterward, but I promise to send photos."

Pain tore through her stomach. "You wouldn't," she whispered.

"Oh, I definitely will. You underestimate how far I'll go to protect what I've built. What your father and I have built."

A second threat. More subtle than the first but nearly as potent.

Some of her horror morphed into anger. It bled from Scott to her and bolstered her confidence. "I'll send the video to every media outlet in the country. It'll go viral on social media within hours."

"Sure," he said as though bored with the conversation. "You could do that. But it won't help her. I have eyes on her and access to her at all times. You willing to take that risk?"

How had she not known she'd been living with the devil for so many years? It was one thing to have a business arrangement where they weren't in love, but it was quite another to lay her head down next to a monster each night. She swallowed, unable to form words. Bile burned in her esophagus. Hadn't he done enough to that poor, innocent woman? To threaten her further and put her fate in Olivia's hands went beyond. Monster wasn't an evil enough word for him.

She pressed a hand to her mouth as her stomach heaved.

"Fuck this." Scott yanked the phone from her hand. "Listen up, motherfucker. I don't know what the fuck you're thinking, but Olivia's not getting anywhere near you, and she's not alone. You're not the only one with eyes out there, and if you take one step in her direction, we'll rain hell down on your ass."

He ended the call before Lance had a chance to respond. Then without looking, he tossed the phone over his shoulder. Miraculously, it landed on the bed. "I know what you're thinking, and you need to get that shit out of your head right now."

"Scott—"

"No!" He slapped his hand against the wall, making her jump, but she wasn't afraid. He'd cut out his own heart before hurting her. "It's a trap, babe. A fucking trap because he knows damn well you'd rather give up your own safety than have something else happen to that girl."

"But—"

"No! I won't let you do it." He gripped the back of her head in his large palm and brought her face close to his. "I just fucking got you, babe. Please trust me to handle this."

Her hesitation had nothing to do with trust. Of course, she trusted him. But he was biased when it came to her. Maybe even blind. He'd choose her over someone else every time, and she loved him for it. But would it unwittingly put an innocent woman in jeopardy?

"I need to go talk to Curly. You're safe here, but I need to know that you're not gonna freak out and start getting insane ideas the minute I walk out that door. I need to know you'll be here when I get back."

As she gazed up into his stormy eyes, there wasn't anything she'd deny him. "I'll be here."

He kissed her long and deep until her knees weakened along with her resolve. "Go back to bed, baby. I'm going to call Curly to meet me in the clubhouse."

"Now? Will he be upset if you wake him?" She'd almost forgotten it was the middle of the night.

A wry smile curved his lips. "Baby, when are you gonna understand that Curly's the head of this fucked-up family? He'll fry my ass if I don't wake him up with this. Okay?"

"Okay." She nodded and kissed him this time. God, what did she do to deserve people like this in her life? She wasn't a bad person, but she'd never been particularly good. Materialism and status ran her days for most of her life. She'd been selfish, concerned with her looks and possessions, and hadn't been a great sister to Deke. Yet somehow, when she fell, she'd landed here among incredible people who took her in and made her their own.

Suddenly, the words she'd been suppressing for days wouldn't stay down any longer. Ending the kiss, she pressed her forehead to his chest and took a breath. Then she lifted her gaze. "I love you, Scott."

He blinked as though shocked. Had she not put her entire heart on the line, she'd have laughed at the look of panic that crossed his face. It didn't matter. She had no doubt he felt strongly for her. So, she covered his mouth with her hand. "I just needed you to know I'm not here because I want your help or I have a problem for you to solve. I'm here for you. For us. So go meet with Curly and come up with a plan because I want to go back to how things were twenty minutes ago when life felt perfect."

With a nod, he kissed her palm. She removed her hand and curled her fist, keeping the sweet gesture close.

He kissed her once before grabbing his cut and jeans. "Try to get some sleep," he ordered as he pulled up the jeans. "You'll need to be rested for what I have planned for you later." Then with a wink, he was out the door.

She sighed and sagged against the wall until his voice came through loud and commanding. "Lock the damn door, babe."

A chuckle left her tired body. "Sorry!" She hurried to the door and flicked the locks.

After a quick trip to the restroom, she was back under the covers loving the chill in the air-conditioned air.

But sleep eluded her.

She stared at the ceiling so long her eyes dried, and her brain felt like mush. But one thing remained clear.

She couldn't let an innocent woman suffer because she was too cowardly to do the right thing. She knew what she had to do even if it turned her stomach, terrified her to her core, and would wound the man she loved.

Scott wanted her to trust him.

Well, she trusted him all right. She trusted him to get his ass and the rest of the Handlers to Chicago and rescue her before Lance could do too much damage.

"I'M DONE WAITING around for this hemorrhoid to make a move," Scott said later that morning as he shoved Olivia's phone across the table toward Jinx. "As far as I'm concerned, he already made the first move when he called my woman this morning and made her go so pale, she was practically fucking see-through." As he spoke, he slapped his palm on the table, reveling in the sting. "This shit needs to end today. I propose I go to Chicago, slice this prick's nuts off, fry them up, and feed them back to him."

Scott dropped into a chair and folded his arms across his chest while waiting for Jinx to peruse the slew of vulgar, threatening, downright sadistic texts that had been coming in from Lance since he'd called hours ago. As soon as he was done, he passed the phone off to Tracker.

The prez hadn't given a shit about the three o'clock wake-up call, but he refused to make any decisions until the entire club could be briefed. Since he'd set church for nine that morning, he'd sent Scott home furious and fuming to wait until later in the damn morning to make any decisions.

Sure, he'd understood that a few hours wouldn't make a difference in the outcome, but fuck! Every second this Lance douche breathed was another second Liv worried for her safety and the safety of another woman who'd already been violated in the worst way by Lance.

"Look," he said while Tracker passed the phone over to Ty with a fierce frown. "When he called this morning, he told Livy he'd go after the woman she saw him rape. He's a motherfucker who knows how to manipulate Liv's soft heart. She doesn't give a shit that he's threatening her, but the second the twat mentioned going after this other woman, Liv was ready to hop on a plane and hand herself over to him." The thought of it had Scott cracking his knuckles, ready to pummel anyone who stood between him and Lance. "I can't let her do that." Fuck it. If he sounded like a caveman, so be it. "I *won't* let her do that. After what Brooke went through, I hope you'll all have my back."

Curly's jaw ticked, and fire flashed in his gaze. Scott would play it as dirty as he had to, to keep Olivia safe. If reminding the prez how he'd nearly lost his own woman to a psycho got the job done, then that's where he'd place his bet.

Instead of outrage from his brothers, them pumping him up and preparing to wage war against a motherfucker, someone snickered.

Scott whipped his head to the right to find Tracker doing a shit job of covering his mouth and his amusement. "Something funny, *brother*?" The ass was about five seconds away from one hell of a nosebleed.

Another snorted laugh came from across the room. Lock, of all people, stared down at the table with his damn shoulders shaking.

Scott's blood boiled. He hopped to his feet, slamming his palms on the table as another of his supposed brothers began laughing. "What the fuck is so goddamn funny?"

Tracker gave up trying to hide his glee. The mohawked dickhead pressed a hand to his stomach and let out a belly laugh that was apparently more contagious than the clap because the rest of the club laughed along with him.

Were they serious? Scott glanced from traitor to traitor, unable to come up with a reason to find a shred of humor. Yet even Curly's lips slanted up in a half-smirk.

Tracker lifted a hand. "Sorry, bro!" He took a freaking minute to catch his breath before continuing. "It's just... who are you?"

Scott blinked. "What?"

"Seriously," Lock piped in. "Two weeks ago, you'd have burst in here throwing shit and flipping tables, then gone AWOL, and we'd be burying a body right about now. Now here you are, falling in love and shit while bringing your problems to the table like a goddamn mature adult." He shrugged then snorted. "It's funny."

"What he said." Tracker pointed to Lock while still laughing.

"Seriously," Ty added with a choked chuckle. "You think you'll get hitched before Curly?" He glanced around the table. "Should we put money on it?"

"Jesus Christ." Scott sank back into the chair and let his face fall into his hands. Here he was coming to his supposed family of badass bikers with a very real problem, and all they wanted to do was gossip about his woman like a bunch of high schoolers in the locker room. "We're not getting fucking married," he said through his fingers. "We're just fucking around."

The second the words left his lips, the betrayal in them hit him in the back of the head like a car rear-ending him. Liv told him she loved him, and what did he do? Not only did he fail to return the words, but he just told the most important people in his life, aside from his sister, that she was nothing but a hot piece of ass.

Fuck.

"Mm-hmm," Ty said. "Just screwing around. Right. Keep telling yourself that, brother," Ty said, rolling his eyes.

"Seriously," Tracker added. "I've fucked a lot of women. Like *a lot* of women. And not once did one of those lucky ladies have me trying to act like a better man or some shit." He gave a dramatic shudder. "That is some rom-com level commitment."

Nothing about this damn meeting made sense. "Tracker, what the hell are you talking about?"

"He's right," Ty said, with a pensive purse to his lips. He scratched his three-day-old graying beard. "Since you guys stopped sniping at each other and gave in to the sexual tension, you're like a new man. You're a team player, you're calmer, you control your temper… kinda, and you're fucking communicating. Either it's Livy's influence or aliens kidnaped you." He smirked. "Any dreams about being probed that might not have actually been a dream?"

Scott flipped Ty off.

"Yeah, man," Tracker said. "It's freaking us out, you being all in love and shit."

"I'm not—" The rest of that lie lodged in his throat like a hunk of steak.

"What's that?" Tracker cupped a hand around his ear. "Didn't hear you."

Scott closed his eyes and pictured Liv's face. It was that or rip Tracker's smug face off his body.

Enough with this shit. He had a legitimate problem, and if his brothers couldn't take it seriously, he had no problem taking his ass to Chicago alone. The only reason he'd come to the club in the first place was out of respect for Curly and the club. And because it's how Liv would want him to handle it. She'd worry herself sick if he ran off on a solo mission. Hell, before he met her, he'd have…

Well, shit. That was his brothers' point, wasn't it? Pre-Liv, he'd have run off half-cocked and gotten himself in a world of shit for killing her ex-fiancé in a blind rage.

He opened his eyes to find Tracker smirking at him with a raised eyebrow as if to say, "Catching on yet, asshole?"

"All right." Curly lifted his hand. At least someone had gotten control of themselves. "Settle down. Look, Spec, we're giving you shit, but we know the problem with Liv's ex is serious as fucking dick warts. Okay?"

Scott nodded while Tracker shuddered.

"Here's the thing. We all love Liv, and Brooke will skin my hide if we don't help her in every way we can. But to make this club business, we gotta be formal about it and get a unanimous vote. Unless she's your ol' lady. Then she's official family, and we've got her back no matter what. So, Spec, what's it gonna be? You making her your ol' lady, or are we voting on helping?"

His ol' lady. Like Brooke was Curly's or his sister was Rocket's. Damn, he'd never even considered having an ol' lady—a woman who belonged to him and vice versa. It was a declaration of long-term commitment, not recognized by the government or God or whatever, but in the MC world. It was as good as a marriage. A patch didn't make his fuck buddy an ol' lady. Hell, he didn't make a girlfriend an ol' lady. That honor was reserved for a partner.

Someone to stand by his side and ride at his back—always.

They hadn't discussed it, but Liv said she loved him. And he was through pretending he didn't feel the same. "Yeah. I'm making her my ol' lady. Any objections?"

"Gentlemen?" Curly asked.

Scott glanced around the table at his brothers, who all wore grins and shook their heads.

"All right, then. Spec has an ol' lady, poor woman."

He flipped his prez off.

Curly snickered, then held his hand out. "In all seriousness, congrats, man. She's a damn good woman, and I know I'm not the only one who thinks that."

Warmth spread through his chest as his brothers nodded their agreement. "Thanks," he said as he shook his president's hand. Thankfully, no one called him out on how he had to clear his throat before speaking and still sounded choked up.

"I want a few of you on a plane to Chicago to deal with her piece-of-shit ex," Curly said. "I can't send everyone because I'm not convinced Lobo has gone dark, but half of you can go. Now, let's hash this shit out."

An hour and a half later, they had the details hammered out. He, Tracker, and Lock would head out the following morning. He preferred to ride over flying, but that would take days he wasn't willing to waste. By the time they finished planning, Scott's head throbbed, and his nerves were strung tight. These symptoms of giving Lance hours of focus could only be alleviated by one thing.

Olivia.

After a promise to check in with Curly later that evening, he practically sprinted to the barn and up the stairs. "Liv?" he called as he flung his door open. "Sure hope you're naked cuz my dick is hard as hell." Seriously, he hadn't come so much in such a short period since he'd been a horny teenager. Something about that pussy of hers de-aged his cock by two decades at least.

Eerie silence met his announcement. "Liv?"

More silence. Unease slithered through his gut. Decades of relying on it to keep himself and his team alive had taught him to trust his gut every time. And something was off. The place was never this quiet when Liv was over. She was either humming, playing music, or mucking around with something.

Maybe she went across the hall to her apartment?

Even as he posed the possibility to himself, he knew it wasn't correct.

A handwritten note lying on his tiny kitchen table verified it.

I can't live with myself if I take the coward's way out. This is something I HAVE to do.

I'm sorry.
I trust you.
I love you.
Livy

"God fucking dammit!" he screamed as he crushed the paper in his fist.

She'd left.

She was gone.

The table became his next victim. A half-full coffee mug and the turquoise vase his sister bought went sailing to the floor as he flipped the table across the room. Both shattered, but he didn't so much as flinch.

Liv left. She put herself in danger. He and his brother would've taken care of it.

Why the hell did she leave?

Did she not fucking trust him?

Bracing his hands on the wall, he hung his head. Betrayal flowed through him, twisting his insides until he could barely breathe.

He'd made her his ol' lady. And she walked out, back to her ex.

Curly's voice sounded in his head. "She's a damn good woman."

He stared down at the crumpled note lying on the floor between his feet.

This is something I HAVE to do.

I'm sorry.

I trust you.

I love you.

His breath stuck in his lungs.

Jesus Christ, he was such a stupid shit. There he was throwing an epic pity party while his woman was out fighting the battle without backup.

He straightened, pushing away from the wall as he made for the door. Her leaving had nothing to do with a lack of trust and everything to do with the fact she was a damn good woman. A woman who couldn't live with herself if she condemned someone else to a traumatic fate if there was a chance in hell she could prevent it.

She did trust him.

She trusted him to get his ass up to Chicago and rescue her gorgeous ass.

He raced down the stairs and out the door. "Curly!" he screamed as he sprinted back to the clubhouse across the field. "Curly!"

His prez burst out the door with Tracker hot on his heels.

"The fuck?"

"We gotta go now!" He ran to his bike. "Liv left. She's trying to take care of it on her own!"

"Fuck!" Tracker darted down the stairs calling for Lock over his shoulder.

"I heard!" Lock flew out the door toward his bike.

"Get your asses to the airport, and I'll get you flights," Curly called.

Scott didn't spare a second to wait for his brothers to mount their bikes. He had enough trust in his brothers to know they'd be hot on his tail.

He tore out of the lot, spraying a cloud of dust in his wake.

The men speeding after him had dropped everything and rushed to his aid without a single question or second's hesitation. They'd help rescue his woman no matter what it took.

A woman so selfless she'd sacrifice her safety for that of another.

The woman who loved him.

The woman who'd saved him.

Now it was his turn to save her, and he wouldn't rest until Olivia was back in his arms, and her ex was rotting in the goddamn ground.

Chapter Twenty-Six

Once she'd decided to go, physically leaving was the easy part. While the guys planned and plotted in church, Brooke had an appointment to pick up a rescue a few towns over. That meant quiet on the farm aside from one prospect standing guard at the entrance.

Lucky for her, the guy blushed and stammered every time she spoke to him. One flirty smile, a compliment about how good he looked in his prospect's cut, and a bullshit story about making a super quick run to the store for feminine products, and she was cruising toward the airport in her crappy car.

Easy as getting wet in the ocean.

Physically.

Emotionally was another story. The second the farm faded from view, a choked sob tore from the depths of her soul. She'd managed to put on a good show for the prospect, smiling, winking, and pretending she wasn't about to shatter. Thankfully, he didn't know her well enough to notice how tightly she gripped the steering wheel, how rigid her posture was, or the despair in her eyes.

Alone and heading straight for her ex, she didn't have to

pretend anymore.

She was as terrified.

Whatever happened with Lance, it wouldn't be pleasant. He'd be furious at best, murderous at worst.

Would she make it in time to spare an innocent woman more trauma?

And would Scott ever forgive her for running away?

He'd come. She didn't have a single doubt about that. He'd rescue her for Deke if for no other reason. But would he forgive her?

She hadn't thought it possible for her heart to fracture further, but somehow the tiny fragments splintered into tinier pieces.

The trip to the airport ended way too fast. After sobbing the entire way, Liv arrived at the private gate with a red nose, puffy eyes, and a broken heart.

"Name?" the gate guard asked as she shoved sunglasses over her eyes.

"Olivia Truitt. Lance Hamilton is sending his plane for me." She hadn't been able to find a commercial flight out of Tampa until the following morning. Fear for the woman Lance threatened had her calling him and informing him of her decision to return to Chicago. Anything to buy her time. He'd insisted on sending his private jet. She assumed it would take a good few hours, meaning she'd be worrying herself sick in the lounge until the jet arrived.

"Yes, ma'am. The plane is here and ready for you. You'll be leaving from the second runway in thirty minutes."

"What?" She blinked up at him. That couldn't be correct. "My flight was arranged forty-five minutes ago. How did the plane arrive so fast?"

"Hmm?" The guard glanced up from his clipboard. "Oh, Mr. Hamilton's plane has been parked here for a week since he arrived. He's rented it out a few times, but mostly it's been here."

A week? Lance had been in Florida for a week? The hairs on the back of her neck rose. She glanced around, suddenly feeling Lance's eyes on her, but that was impossible.

Wasn't it?

"Ma'am, I'm going to need you to drive through. You're getting a line behind you."

"Oh, yes, sorry." Without bothering to raise the window, she pressed the gas and made her way toward the small, exclusive parking lot.

Maybe she'd heard wrong. Lance couldn't have been in Florida for a week. Right?

And what did it mean if he was there?

Had he seen her with Scott? Had his spies been to the farm? Had he been watching her the whole time? So many questions, but one fact stood out. She'd be seeing Lance a lot sooner than she'd anticipated.

She was going to be sick.

"Jesus," she whispered, gripping the steering wheel as though it was a life preserver—the only thing keeping her afloat after being tossed overboard into the choppy ocean. Her hands shook as she opened the car door and stepped out into the hot, steamy Florida morning.

Every cell in her brain screamed at her to get back in the car and return to the itty-bitty apartment where she'd found love and acceptance. Back to Scott. If she drove fast enough, she might even be able to get home before he discovered her note.

Before he noticed she'd left him.

Home.

Never in a million years would she have thought a five hundred square foot efficiency apartment would feel more like home than her mansion in Chicago, but Scott and his family taught her home wasn't a place. It wasn't square footage or décor. It wasn't expensive crap no one would give a shit about when she died. It was the people who loved and respected her.

The man she loved.

Instead of giving in to the instinct to flee, she forced her legs to move in the direction of Lance's plane. As she drew close, a male flight attendant stepped onto the steps leading to the jet. Tall, dark-haired, and thin without being scrawny, she recognized him at first glance.

"Great," she mumbled.

"Good morning, Ms. Truitt. It's nice to see you again." His smarmy grin never failed to make her skin crawl. As Lance's favorite, he'd served her on countless flights. "Almost didn't recognize you dressed like that."

"Hello, Roddy," she replied with the polite mask she'd worn for years. True, he'd probably never seen her in anything but designer clothes, a full face of makeup, and styled hair. The denim cutoffs, ribbed tank top, and casual sandals had to be a bit of a shock as did her naked face and sloppy ponytail. Truth be told, she'd grown to love this dressed-down look for more than just comfort.

She thought she looked cute. And Scott sure loved it when her legs were bare. The man rested his hand on her thigh all the time.

Scott.

God, how was it possible to miss him so fiercely already?

Roddy stepped aside to let her pass but the second she came through the small door, he moved closer. His body brushed hers.

What the hell? Was that an erection she felt against her hip?

When she drew back on instinct, he chuckled beneath his breath.

What the hell?

"Take your seat, ma'am," he said, his voice laced with

humor. We can leave as soon as you're settled."

"Thank you," she muttered as she scurried away from him with a shudder. She settled into a plush chair on the left side of the plane. The buttery soft leather cushioned her bare legs with a luxurious touch she hadn't felt in weeks. Yet despite her extensive history with expensive materials, she suddenly preferred the cheap polyester of the mini couch in her apartment.

At least there, she wasn't afraid.

Liv closed her eyes, blocking out Roddy as he moved about the cabin, preparing for takeoff. His leg bumped her shoulder as he passed. Probably some lame attempt to intimidate her. Hell, Lance could've put him up to it for all she knew.

Unfortunately, with her eyes closed, the only thing she could see were the countless mental pictures of Scott she'd taken.

Scott, laughing with his brothers.

Scott's face full of supreme happiness while riding.

Scott naked.

Scott's hands on her.

Scott, coming.

God, this was torture.

Roddy's movement stopped, and Liv could've sworn he settled down in the chair opposite hers.

"Don't you have a job to do?" she asked. The bitchy, superior tone she'd shed in Florida returned with a vengeance.

When he didn't reply, she frowned. "Roddy?" She opened her eyes, blinking the man across from her into view.

Her heart stopped dead in her chest.

"Hello, Olivia," Lance said with bone-chilling calm.

Her breath seized, and words wouldn't come.

Her heart pounded as her gaze flicked to the emergency

exit. She thought she could face him, but one second in his presence and every instinct she had screamed at her to run. Could she make it? If she shoved him? Kicked him in the nuts?

Maybe.

"Don't bother," he said with a chuckle. "Everything is locked. I'd say you look good..." he continued, with a sour expression as though he'd bitten into something spoiled, "... but you look cheap. Not quite like a whore but close. Luckily, I have appropriate clothing for you."

Months ago, that comment would've sent her into a tailspin. She'd have revamped her entire wardrobe to make sure she had the trendiest, most high-fashion outfits to earn his favor. Now his disapproval thrilled her.

"Thank you," she said with a smirk. Damn, it felt good to find her voice. "I'd say it was good to see you, but we both know I'd be lying. And by the way, I don't give a shit if you like my outfit. I'm not wearing it for you."

"Oh no?" One of his perfectly shaped eyebrows arched. "This for *Spec*?" he said the name as though it were a dirty word.

How did he know that name? She swallowed the shock, smiled, and nodded as though she wasn't rattled by how much he knew. "It is. He loves when I wear these shorts. Something about being able to slide his hand up my thigh and under—"

The strong crack of his palm across her cheek came so fast that she didn't stand a prayer of preparing for it. Her head whipped to the side. He was so strong that her entire body slammed against the seat's armrest, especially her hip, which took the brunt of it against the armrest's wooden bottom.

Pain lanced across her face and hip at the same time, but she couldn't determine which was worse. To her every lasting shame, she cried out. But, damn, it hurt so bad.

Instantly, her hands came up to cradle her injured cheek. She blinked. Thankfully, her eyeballs hadn't popped out of the sockets.

Much as she wanted to stand her ground and spit in his face, her body took over, curling into a protective ball in the seat.

Glancing over his shoulder, he called out, "Roddy, please go to the lounge and find the captain. Tell him we'll be ready to leave in thirty minutes. And leave us alone until then."

"Sure thing, boss." Roddy nodded from where he stood near the prep station, watching her be abused. Her eyes pled with him to help, but he paid her no mind as he left the plane.

As soon as the door slid shut, Lance sprung from his chair. He loomed over her, bracing himself with a hand on each of her armrests. A thunderous expression she'd never seen in all the years they'd been together met her gaze. "Do you have any idea what you've fucking cost me these past few weeks?" he growled.

She didn't bother to answer, just stared up at him with what she hoped was defiance but feared was terror.

"Paying PIs, sending my plane all over the goddamn country looking for you, missed deadlines, canceled meetings, millions of dollars down the goddamn drain because you're jealous of a stupid whore." He screamed those last words in Olivia's stunned face.

Was that how he saw it? She'd run from him out of jealousy? Could he be that delusional?

"Jealous?" she said with a high-pitched, slightly hysterical chuckle. "You think this is about jealousy?" Fear seeped out of her blood, transforming into anger. "You fucking raped someone! You drugged and raped an innocent girl, and you think I'm jealous?" Her bark of laughter sounded harsh. "You're out of your fucking mind. Even if it hadn't been a crime, your dick is nothing to get jealous over."

She rose on wobbly legs. Rage had her confidence inflating and her muscles trembling. Channeling every bitchy instinct she'd ever possessed, she straightened her shoulders and ignored the throbbing in her cheek. "Now let me off this fucking plane."

"Your language is disgusting." Lance made a disgusted half-laugh and then grabbed her by the throat. She gagged and choked as air disappeared. "You're more stupid than I assumed all these years if you think I'm letting you go anywhere."

She clawed at his hand, trying with every bit of fledgling strength to loosen his grip. His eyes shot fire and hatred that terrified her.

"You think you're in control here? You think you have any say in how I conduct myself? Who I fuck?" He turned, slamming her back against the wall.

Thankfully, the move loosened his grip a fraction, allowing her to suck in small gasps of air. She raked her fingers over his hands, tearing the skin with her blunt nails, but he didn't even flinch. Instead, he shook her, rattling her brain.

"S-s-stop." She managed to squeeze the word past her vocal cords, but Lance was too far gone to notice. Even though she'd seen him rape someone and read his threatening texts for weeks, the violence and hatred shocked her. He'd claimed to love her once. Who was this dreadful man she'd spent so many nights next to? And how had she missed this for so long?

"You think she didn't want it, you stupid bitch?" he shouted, shaking her again. "You think she wasn't begging for it? You think they aren't all begging for it?"

Oh, God. He'd done it more than once. Maybe even countless times.

Her vision grew fuzzy, and a strange sense of calm washed over her. She was running out of oxygen, and instead of panic, her body and mind seemed to accept the inevitable unconsciousness.

The last thing she heard before blackness engulfed her was Lance whispering in her ear. "You think I couldn't have you begging for it in seconds?"

Olivia came to with a startled gasp what had to be seconds later.

Her mind took a moment to catch up even while her body fought the man hovering over her. She was back in the now-reclined chair, sprawled out with her legs spread. Lance stood between her legs. His slacks were pooled at his knees, and his dick, harder than she'd seen it in years, pointed up toward his stomach.

"N-no," she rasped through ruined vocal cords as he reached for her shorts. "No!" She swatted his hand away.

His laugh made her blood run cold. "There's nothing you can do to stop me from taking what's mine, *fiancée*."

As soon as he said the word, a strange sensation registered on her left hand. She glanced down to find the enormous engagement ring she'd left in their house back on her finger. Her stomach jolted at the sight of it. "No," she whispered.

This wasn't happening.

When his hands touched the button on her shorts, she completely lost it. Screaming, kicking, flailing her arms, she tried everything to keep him from touching her. No one would hear the weak cries coming from her sore throat, but she managed to clip his lip with the toe of her sandal.

"Fuck," he shouted, taking a step back.

She froze as he pressed a hand to his mouth, then drew it away covered in blood.

"You fucking bitch." He spat, spraying her shirt with red. He jammed his knees into her legs, pinning them to the chair. Then he grabbed her hands and wrenched them above her head in an unbreakable iron grip.

She struggled, thrashing back and forth in a wasted effort to escape.

He reached for her shorts with his free hand, but she couldn't block him this time.

"No," she whispered. "P-please."

He let out a dark chuckle. "Told you, you'd be begging me."

With a rough jerk, he pulled her shorts down enough to expose her underwear. "Cheap shit," he said with a dissatisfied grunt.

"After fucking a biker, I bet your pussy is just as cheap as the fucking panties. Too bad the motherfucker isn't here to see how a real man fucks his woman. Bet he could use the lesson, seeing as how you came crawling back to me."

Tears leaked from her eyes as her chest heaved with more terror than she'd ever experienced. But she fought like hell. "Get the fuck off me!" She bucked in the seat.

Damn, even the adrenaline firing through her blood couldn't keep her from hurting. Her wrists burned like hell where the skin twisted and stretched beneath his forceful grip. Her throat felt like it'd been rubbed raw on a cheese grater. The pain in her cheek disappeared beneath a pile of other aches, and her shin bones felt seconds from cracking, wedged between Lance's knees and the wooden base of the chair.

All her struggles earned her were more bruises and abrasions. She could barely see through the tangle of hair hanging in front of her eyes. Her voice weakened with each attempted scream until it was barely above a hoarse croak.

"Done yet?" Lance's smirk held amusement. His dick hadn't softened a bit during his struggles. The sick bastard was as turned on as she'd ever seen him.

Hot and bothered by the fight.

Aroused by her pain and fear.

Slumped in the chair with her top riding up and a leering Lance above her, a strangled sob burst forth. There was nothing she could do to stop him.

Would Scott be able to look her in the eye again?

How could he want her after this?

Why the hell hadn't she just stayed in his bed?

I'm sorry, Scott.

She squeezed her eyes shut as Lance lowered himself toward her.

Chapter Twenty-Seven

By some miracle, Scott and his brothers made it to the airport without a trail of cops flying after them. He'd pushed his bike harder than ever before, topping out at ninety-eight on the highway. Cars honked, trucker drivers flipped him off, and one soccer mom in a minivan screamed obscenities out her window, but he'd rocketed by so fast that all he'd caught was the word 'motherfucker.'

His brothers stayed hot on his ass the entire time, risking their licenses, hell, probably their freedom at those speeds.

When they reached the airport, they were forced to slow down. Scott wasted ten precious minutes finding a place to leave his bike. The second he killed the engine, he called Curly. "Get us on a flight?" he asked as he sprinted toward the terminal without bothering to look over his shoulder. The pounding of boots behind him let him know Tracker and Lock hadn't fallen behind.

"Nothing 'til fucking tomorrow," Curly said, voice thick with disgust.

"Shit! Fuck. You tried every fucking airline?"

"Yeah. I'm working on chartering a private jet, but even that shit's booked. I know this is time you don't have but give me fifteen minutes. I think I'm getting somewhere with this fucking asshole agent."

Christ. Scott came to a complete halt near the parking garage's exit. A private jet costs big money. Money Scott would never have. Curly had it, but that didn't mean the prez was under any obligation to shell it out for Scott or Liv. "Thank you," he said, sincerity thickening his throat. Those two words didn't begin to convey his appreciation, but he had no idea what would.

Curly wasn't one to need flowery words or praise, though. He grunted out an "Anything, brother," then the line went dead.

"Any luck?" Tracker asked from a few feet behind him.

"No. Fuck!" The urge to hurl his phone across the parking garage hit strong, but he needed the damn thing. "Nothing until tomorrow. Dammit."

This was Deke all over again. Helpless while someone he loved was in danger.

His blood surged through his veins and his fists balled of their own accord. The need for violence rose swift and sharp. Liv had been the one to help him tamp it down, to find a different outlet for his stress and trauma. Fucking her, talking to her, hell, just looking at her grounded him in a way nothing else could.

But now, she was gone on her way to a man who wanted to hurt her.

"Fuck!" he screamed, slamming his fists against his thighs as he bent over, and the world spun out of his control. He could feel it creeping down his spine. In the next few minutes, he was going to lose his shit. He'd freak out on someone who looked at him sideways. Beat the tar out of someone. Anyone.

God, even his brothers weren't safe.

"Spec?" Lock's calm voice penetrated his fog, but not

enough to erase it. "Can you look at me?"

Scott lifted his gaze. He literally saw red. A haze of red clouded his vision. Maybe he'd burst a blood vessel in his eye. Or perhaps he'd lost it for good. The idea of Olivia suffering was too much for his fractured psyche to handle.

Lock approached with his hands up. "You said there aren't any flights today?"

Breathing as though he'd just run there from the clubhouse, he could only nod once.

"Maybe Liv couldn't get one either. Maybe she's here waiting. Or holed up in a hotel."

Scott's spine snapped straight. Christ, Lock could be on to something. "Jesus," he whispered. The red evaporated, leaving Lock and Tracker clear as day in his sights. "You could be right. Let's split up. Search for her."

Tracker clapped him on the back, then took off running.

"Thank you," he said to Lock, who nodded and then headed in a different direction from Tracker.

Scott ran as well, toward a third area of the airport with his phone at his ear. "C'mon, baby, answer the damn phone."

Liv's chipper voicemail picked up on the sixth ring.

"You don't have to do this, Livy, please don't do this," he said after the beep.

He pocketed the phone and then continued into the airport.

Scott searched every area he was permitted to enter. As he ran through the baggage claim, he rammed at least five people with his shoulders and even knocked down a man scanning the arrival-departure screen. A few pissed-off travelers cussed him out, and others mumbled their annoyance, but he didn't slow.

He couldn't afford to waste a second.

When he burst into the women's restroom, a lady at the counter screamed, "What the hell? Get out of here!"

"Liv?" he called. "You in here?"

"Get out!" the woman shrieked.

He ducked back out, then continued to run through baggage claim, weaving through the crowd.

After a solid ten minutes of nothing, his phone rang.

"Liv?" he called into the phone without checking the screen.

"No," a voice said. Scott slowed and pulled the phone away from his ear. What the hell? "Devos?" he asked as he picked up the pace again. "Not really a good time, man." Dammit, he'd never have answered if he'd known who was on the other end.

"Listen to me, Spec. This is serious."

"Hanging up, Devos. This is shit timing."

As he was about end the call, Devos shouted. "It's about Olivia."

Scott stopped dead in his tracks. A woman smacked into his back. "Nice, mister. Just stop right in the middle of the walkway. Asshole," she grumbled.

He didn't give two shits who he pissed off. "What about Olivia?" he barked.

Devos lowered his voice. "I'm at the airport. In the private terminal, getting ready to head out of town. There's a man who just walked out to his plane. Real sketchy, man. He was on his phone, and I heard mention of the Handlers... you specifically. And something about a woman named Olivia. This guy is pissed, man. Thinks you're fucking his fiancée and was saying some seriously scary shit about what he wanted to do to you. And her."

Lance. Holy fuck. "Devos, you may have saved my woman's life." Scott glanced all around but didn't see any signs of the private terminal. "I owe you one, man."

"No, you don't. I fucked up with Lobo. This is my way of repairing the damage. I'll meet you at the terminal and tell them you're my passenger so I can get you through the gate."

A baggage claim service counter with one attendant wasn't too far away. "Consider it repaired. I'm on my way." Scott hung up, then raced toward the baggage counter. "How do I get to the private terminal?" he yelled from ten feet away.

A thin woman with sculpted eyebrows glanced up from her computer. "Excuse me?"

"The private terminal. Where is it?"

"Do you have a reservation, sir?"

He slammed his fist down on the counter. "For fuck's sake, where's the goddamn private terminal?"

Her eyes widened, and her lip trembled. She pointed a shaking finger. "G-go outside those doors and to the right. It's about a five-minute walk, then you'll see a big sign pointing it out on the right. But they won't let you in without a—"

He took off. Hopefully, she wouldn't have security on his ass in a matter of seconds. His thighs burned as he ran flat out. Motorcycle boots weren't made for running, the leather pulled and rubbed his ankles raw, but he ignored the discomfort. He'd suffered far worse for far less.

Crowds parted with shrieks and yelps as he sprinted outside. Most people probably thought he was simply late for a flight. Thankfully, as he ran outside toward the private terminal, the number of travelers thinned to a mere few.

Not too many people with enough cash to fly private.

Within ninety seconds, the sign for the private terminal came into view.

Still sprinting, he rounded the turn with a wide arch. After throwing the entrance door open, he skidded to a stop.

A small TSA checkpoint with only one agent stood between him and the private tarmac.

Fuck. How the hell was he supposed to get through— Devos appeared from the small, posh lounge next to the gate. He spoke with the agent, pointed to Scott, then spoke again.

The agent nodded and waved Scott over.

"Good afternoon, sir. Mr. Devos tells me you'll be his guest on the jet this afternoon."

Scott's heart hammered. He wanted to punch this guy in the face and rush outside, but he held back. "That's correct."

"Okay, come on through."

That's it?

He must have looked as confused as hell because Devos smirked.

No ticket? No boarding pass? No weapons scan? Shit, the other half lived a nice life.

He kept his face neutral so the TSA agent wouldn't uncover exactly how frantic he was to get the fuck outside and on Lance's plane.

Without speaking, Devos guided him outside onto the tarmac

Three planes were near the building. One single-engine prop plane and two impressive jets that must have set some rich people back quite a few million bones.

Which was Lance's jet? Was he on it now? Was Liv on it with him?

"That one," Devos whispered, gesturing to the farthest plane.

Scott shot a text to Tracker, Lock, and Curly, letting them know exactly where he was and which plane he'd be boarding.

"The guy is on board, not sure about the woman. Do you need help?" Devos asked.

"No." If he were smart, Scott would wait for backup. At least wait until Tracker and Lock arrived, no one had ever mistaken him for Einstein.

Waiting wasn't an option. Now was his best chance to slip onboard the jet unnoticed.

A few airport employees scurried around, but none paid

him any attention. They all seemed far more concerned with their jobs than two passengers seemingly enjoying the sunshine as they waited to depart.

"I may need help after, depending on how this goes down." Translate, he might need help or a distraction while the Handlers removed a dead body.

"Anything you need. I'll push back my departure time."

Scott held out his hand. "Thank you."

"Any time. I mean it." Devos shook it, then turned and walked back into the lounge.

Scott ran across the tarmac to the stairs outside the jet, scanning the area the entire sprint. Not for the first time, he wished he wasn't wearing clunky boots, but kicking them off would be fucking stupid and eliminate the possibility of a quick escape should he need one.

He took the stairs with as much stealth as possible. As he reached the top, he frowned. Where was the flight attendant? And what the fuck was that ragged, gravelly whisper?

He stepped onto the plane.

One glance of the pasty white ass standing, legs spread over one of the plane's seats was all it took for Scott to know he'd walked in on his worst nightmare. He didn't need the sight of Liv's sneakers to realize it was her. The sick feeling in his gut told him all he needed to know.

Scott had been in plenty of fucked-up situations before. His entire time in special forces trained him to deal with the most fucked conditions. None were more fucked-up than the days spent in captivity with Deke.

Until now.

Every ounce of training he'd suffered through flew out the window. He couldn't think. He couldn't plan or temper his actions.

He could only feel and react.

And what he felt was a flash of blinding rage so white-hot

it burned through him and propelled him toward Lance.

With the roar of an enraged animal, he charged Lance. The man jumped and spun around just as Scott reached him. He grabbed the front of Lance's pressed shirt and flung him away from Olivia with so much force that Lance hurtled into the opposite wall of the plane.

"What the fuck?" he screamed as he crashed to the floor. He looked up, sneering as his gaze landed on Scott. "You."

Behind him, Olivia scrambled to right her clothing. The fact she had to do so made Scott's need for violence shoot off the charts. This man would die today.

By Scott's hand.

And fuck the consequences.

Lance clambered to his feet. His dick hung soft between his thighs. He was a big guy, but Scott was bigger. And he knew dozens of ways to inflict pain or kill a man. But he didn't have the patience for anything fancy.

"S-scott," Olivia rasped from behind him as Lance yanked his pressed slacks up.

"Go outside, baby," he said. He followed Lance's every move. "Tracker will be there."

Fury flared in Lance's eyes at the pet name, and Scott loved it.

"Come with me," she whispered. A soft hand landed on his back. Her touch was magic, siphoning out his need for blood. "Please."

It almost worked. He was seconds from turning, gathering her in his arms, and leaving Lance for his club. But then the asshole snorted.

"Please," he said, voice dripping with mockery. "You got here too late to hear her saying that to me. 'Please, Lance.'" He mimicked Olivia's voice. "'Fuck me, Lance. Tear me up with your cock, Lance.' I was just giving the bitch what—"

Scott launched forward with a lightning-quick strike Lance

never saw coming. His fist connected with Lance's face in a satisfying crunch he'd play on repeat in his mind.

"Scott, no!" Olivia cried, but it was too late. The violence won. Scott was gone. Spec was gone. All that remained of the man she loved was the animal instinct to kill or be killed.

Lance crumbled to the ground, cradling his face. The man wasn't a fighter. He shot his mouth off, threw his money around, and used his size to intimidate those weaker and smaller than he was, but he was fucking soft as a baby lamb.

Were Scott a better man, he'd leave it at that. He'd won. Lance wouldn't hurt him. Couldn't hurt him.

But it wasn't enough. What Scott craved now was the man's fear. His pain. His regret.

His blood.

He grabbed Lance by his starched collar holding his face at the perfect height to receive punch after punch. It wasn't long before the pussy slumped. Scott released him, letting him flop to the ground.

He didn't stop.

With one knee on Lance's chest, he rained hell down on the man. Blow after blow connected with Lance's face until Scott's knuckles were so slick, they slid along Lance's mangled face.

Behind him, Olivia's weak cries of protest barely registered.

A pitiful groan came from Lance's busted lips, making Scott smile. He stopped the barrage of fists and sat back on his heels, letting satisfaction flood his veins. Then, he pulled a long knife from the sheath on his belt with a wicked grin.

With an eerie calm, he leaned over Lance's limp body. Who knew if the man could even see at this point? His eyes had blown up like two bubblegum bubbles. Scott pressed the tip of his blade to the left side of lance's torso.

"Scott," Olivia whispered, her voice thick with tears.

He leaned close to Lance's fucked-up face. "Your spleen's right under here. My knife's plenty long enough to reach it. There's no talking me out of it."

"Oh shit. Fuck!" Tracker's voice sounded through the hull of the plane.

"Any last words, motherfucker?" He dug the blade in, nicking the skin.

Lance moaned.

"Scott."

"Liv, don't!" Tracker yelled. "He's too far gone. It's too dangerous, sweetie."

Clearly, she didn't listen as her entire front pressed along Scott's back. Her slim arms came around, grabbing onto his. "I love you," she whispered in his ear as though they were home in bed, and she wasn't trying to soothe a rabid beast. "I need you. Please come with me."

The woman's power over him should've terrified him. But instead, her soft weight at his back made the need to have her in his arms override his need for vengeance.

He lowered his arm and dropped his head.

Olivia stood, pulling him up by his waist. He spun and engulfed her in his arms. Christ, she was there. And warm. And alive.

But what had Lance's assault done to her?

How far had the fucker gotten?

Over her head, he nodded at Tracker to let his brother know he was back and in control of himself.

Tracker winked then turned toward the exit. "I'll call Curly. This is gonna be a fucking mess to sort out."

"I'm sorry," Olivia said into his chest.

"Shh. Not now, baby. Let's get you home."

"I'm sorry," she said again.

Her destroyed voice hurt his heart. "Shh, Livy, save your voice.

She looked up at him with tearful eyes, shaking her head. "I'm—"

He kissed her to prevent another apology. When it ended, he rested his forehead on hers.

"Fucking scared me," he whispered.

"I love you."

"Fuck, baby, I love you so—"

Her eyes widened, and she yelled, "No!"

Scott's training took over. In the blink of an eye, he spun around and thrust the knife upward before he even registered Lance behind him with his own smaller but no-less-deadly knife.

His blade slid easily into Lance's stomach. The man's mouth dropped open in a silent scream.

Scott grinned.

Fuck, yes.

He twisted the knife and jerked right before releasing it.

The life was already draining from Lance's eyes.

He'd love to watch it completely die out, but Olivia clung to his back, trembling. So he gave Lance a little shove, sending the man down on his ass.

Liv shook so hard, he didn't know how she'd walk down the stairs. So he scooped her up in his arms and kissed her. "Let's go, baby. There's nothing here for us."

Chapter Twenty-Eight

She couldn't get warm.

Ninety degrees under the intense Florida sun, and Olivia was freezing cold. She was so cold she shivered the entire ride from the airport to the Handlers' compound. She soaked up Scott's heat as she clung to his back, but even that couldn't chase the chill away.

No one bothered them or even spoke to them when they returned to the clubhouse. There'd be questions and debriefs. Maybe a lecture because of her impulsive behavior or chastising due to the way she'd run off on her own. Hell, Curly might lose his cool on her for forcing his club to put themselves in danger and at risk of arrest.

Scott had killed a man. To save her. And maybe a little because he just plain wanted to. Liv had no problem with it. Lance had been a monster who'd only have hurt more women if he'd been allowed to live. Had Scott been thirty seconds later, she'd have been raped.

Tears stung her eyes. It'd been so close. Way too close. Terrifyingly close.

She shivered again, but it wasn't all because of the cold this time.

Curly might not agree with her belief that Lance needed to die. Now he was stuck cleaning up a royal mess that included the dead body of a wealthy man in a public airport. She'd be lucky if he didn't kick her ass off the compound.

She should ask what the plan was. Check with Scott to ensure everything was being taken care of without risk to anyone in the club. But she was exhausted. Keeping warm and blocking out the feel of Lance's hands pinning her to the chair had sapped her energy.

Scott rode his bike past the spot he usually parked it and straight to the barn. He killed the engine right outside the entrance, then climbed off the bike. The trembling ramped up the second his hot body disappeared.

"I d-d-don't know wh-what's h-happening to m-me." She shook so hard. If it weren't for Scott rounding the bike and standing before her, she'd have vibrated right onto the dusty ground. "I'm s-so c-c-cold."

"Shock, baby." His mouth was set in a grim line. "Let's get you inside and under a hot shower."

That sounded heavenly.

Thankfully, he reached up to unclasp her helmet. Her clumsy hands could never have managed it. As he reached toward her face, she caught one of his hands. "S-scott," she whispered on an exhale.

His knuckles were a disaster—raw, split, and bleeding. A few had clotted over, but most still oozed. Her heart ached at the thought of him getting hurt because of her.

"Hey," he whispered. He pulled his hand from hers and removed the helmet. "I'm good, baby. Your ol' man is a tough motherfucker."

She sucked in a breath. "Ol' man?" Did he mean that? He wanted her that way, or was he just saying words?

"If you'll have me."

Olivia swallowed a lump the size of a tennis ball in her

throat. "Y-yes." She nodded through her tears.

His eyes flared with heat as he stared down at her. He stroked his thumb over her bruised cheek. She could only imagine how swollen and purple it looked. God, she wanted to kiss him so badly right then, but his hands weren't the only part of him covered in blood. It had splattered all over his shirt and even on his face.

Mostly Lance's.

She wore his blood as well, all over her shirt from where he'd spit on her. They needed a shower, and they needed it an hour ago.

No more words were spoken as he scooped her up off the bike and cradled her against his muscular chest. She relaxed in his capable arms, letting him carry her up to his apartment. After locking the door behind him, he walked straight into the bathroom and then set her feet down on the floor.

"Steady?" he asked.

She nodded, still shivering. The chill from the air conditioner did nothing to stop her chattering teeth.

Scott didn't say anything. No empty platitudes or promises that it would all be okay. He didn't tell her not to worry or be upset, but he did reach into the shower and flip the water to hot.

She appreciated the lack of small talk. She wasn't okay. He probably wasn't okay either, and that was fine. They'd get back there, but for today, things were about as fucked as they could get.

The small bathroom filled with steam. They were back here again about to head into Scott's shower. So much had changed in the weeks since she'd dropped to her knees and taken care of him in the most intimate way.

She stood there, arms dangling limply at her sides while he undressed her with a fierce scowl. If it weren't for his gentle, near-caressing touch, his expression would've intimidated the hell out of her.

As soon as her filthy clothes were in a heap on the floor, he ushered her under the spray. The water coasted down her skin, drawing a satisfied groan.

Warmth.

It felt beyond incredible.

Ten seconds later, he stepped in with her. He didn't waste any time grabbing a loofa and squirting a massive amount of his intoxicating body wash on it.

Olivia stood there exhausted, wilted, and in a daze but warm. She felt a little foolish not helping as she let him wash the blood off her arms and the essence of that plane from everywhere else. It felt so good, but lifting her arms to assist seemed an impossible task.

She groaned as his large hands smoothed her skin and washed away the day.

The fierce scowl never left his face, but he didn't complain or seem to mind washing her. In fact, he lingered in his favorite areas and dropped kisses on the top of her head every so often, making her swoon. As soon as she was clean, he moved on to himself. Olivia watched his every move. The way his soapy hands roamed over his pecs. How he scrubbed hard to remove the blood from his forearms. The lingering way he cleaned his hard cock.

Seeing him touch himself had her body clenching. The need to be filled by him hit her hard and without mercy. It became vital—the only way she could think to begin to heal the day's wounds.

"Scott," she said, wrapping her arms around his neck. There was no way he missed the needy whine in her voice.

His eyes darkened with lust, and he tossed the loofa to the shower floor. "Need you," he growled, grabbing her ass and hoisting her up.

"Yes!" Their mouths met in a deep, drugging kiss she

never wanted to end.

Somehow, Scott managed to turn off the water and walk them out of the shower. They didn't bother with towels. He walked straight to the bed and sat on the edge. When she settled on his lap, she crossed her ankles at his back and rocked her drenched sex over his hard cock.

"Please," she whispered. "Please fuck me, Scott. I need you so badly." The fullness, the stretch, the way he filled her brain with thoughts of nothing but him and pleasure.

He pulled his head back. "Are you sure? He—"

She shook her head. "He didn't." Lance didn't belong in their bed, but reassuring Scott that she hadn't been raped was worth bringing him up.

His eyes narrowed as though assessing the truth of her statement.

"I promise. If you hadn't gotten there when you did..." She shrugged. "But you did."

He had to know she was downplaying the horror of what had happened. They could discuss it until their tongues dried up later. Now all she wanted was to feel as close to him as possible.

"You're sure."

"Sure, I need you. Sure, I want you. Now. Please."

He nodded once then kissed her again. She maneuvered herself until she was hovering over his cock, then sank in one swift, hard motion.

They gasped into each other's mouths as tears sprang to her eyes. This was right. This was where she belonged. "I'm sorry," she said with a garbled sob. "I was so stupid. I shouldn't have left." Shaking her head, she fought to keep from bawling. "I'm sorry."

He cupped her face and kissed her damp lips. "Shh, baby. I get why you did it. I get it."

Her eyes closed, and he kissed her cheek, then eyelid, then

the other cheek. The soft kisses went on, mending her battered soul with each gentle press of his lips. She loved that this man, this rugged, lethal, often hard man had a side only she saw. She treasured that he showed her all the parts of him.

Good, bad, ugly, and loving.

He moved his lips to her ear as one of his hands slid down her back. "But if you ever, *ever* scare me like that again, you won't be able to sit for a month." He punctuated the playful threat with a firm squeeze of her ass cheek.

A blast of heat shot through her, making her pussy clench. They both groaned as she rippled around his cock.

"Ride, me, baby," he said right before retaking her mouth.

Slowly, they rocked into each other. Neither had anywhere to be and no concept of time. They could've been there moving together for days for all she cared. It was lazy, sensual, and luxurious. She'd have been happy to stay there wrapped around him for the rest of her life.

But her body had other ideas, and soon the need to come became too strong to ignore. She moved fast, lifting her hips and dropping down on him again and again. Each time they came together, she rolled her pelvis, putting the most delicious pressure on her clit.

"You're so fucking sexy," he growled as she began to pant and bounce with more frantic need. They were both still wet, but not a smidgen of her was cold anymore.

Her sensitive nipples rubbed across his chest. All her senses were tuned into and surrounded by Scott. She was so close, vibrating with electricity and pleasure. "Scott," she whispered in a needy plea.

"Got you, beautiful," he said, working his hands between them. One firm press of his thumb to her clit was all it took for fireworks to explode behind her eyes. She squeezed him with her arms and legs, grinding into his finger to capture every ounce of pleasure.

"Another," Scott growled before she'd even finished coming. He worked her clit with fast, skillful strokes.

"No," she said with a groan. "I can't. It's too much." A strange mix of lethargy and hypersensitivity buzzed through her. "Scott." God, he hadn't come. He was still so thick and hard inside her. Holding back had cost him.

The corded muscles of his neck strained as he clenched his teeth. His nostrils flared, and his rough voice made her quiver the same way his calloused fingers did. "You can," he said, breathless. "And you fucking will."

Jesus, that sexy, commanding voice could get her to do anything.

"Lean back," he ordered. "Give me those tits."

Olivia released his neck and braced her hands behind her on his knees. The position thrust her breasts up toward his face.

"Fuck, yes," he said right before sucking onto one of her nipples.

She shouted and arched her back.

He thrust hard into her.

His fingers played with her clit.

His hot mouth sucked her like she was the tastiest treat.

Within seconds, she was hurtling toward another orgasm. Faster than ever before and, impossibly, more powerful than the last.

Using her arms for leverage, she pumped her hips in time with his thrusts.

"Fuck, yes," he shouted after releasing her breast. "That's it, baby. Ride my thick cock. Tell me how much you love me fucking you."

"Y-yes. I love it. You feel amazing." Words were almost impossible.

He looped an arm around her neck and then yanked her to

him. One hand stayed between her legs, circling her clit and occasionally pinching it. He tilted her head to the side and latched onto her neck with his mouth.

He sucked hard. Olivia cried out even as she tilted her head to give him full access to her neck. "Scott," she said with a gasp. Jesus, she'd be marked for days.

And why was that so hot?

"I don't want there to be a single doubt who you belong to," Scott said in her ear. "Any motherfucker who glances your way will know you've been claimed. By me."

Those possessive caveman words shouldn't have so much heat spreading through her. They shouldn't have her teetering on the edge of a monster orgasm, but they did. Because as much as he owned her, she owned him right back.

"Yes," she cried out. "Mark me. Do it again."

He let out an animalistic snarl and then sucked her collarbone at the same time he captured her clit between his thumb and forefinger. Her pussy clenched hard around the stiff cock inside her.

Scott ripped his mouth away and shouted a slew of curses that were vulgar even for him. His body shook with wild convulsions as he filled her. If only they could stay right there, joined so intimately forever. Forget the rest of the world.

But his orgasm triggered hers.

It rushed at her with an intensity that stole her breath. She couldn't yell, couldn't think—all she could do was cling to him and let the pleasure devastate her in the best way.

When her wits returned, it was to find herself still engulfed in Scott's protective embrace. His lips brushed over the mark he'd left on her neck.

She sighed at the gentle ministrations to what he'd done in a primal fit of passion. After a final kiss to the side of her neck, he met her gaze.

Much as she'd love to lock the door, bury her face against his chest, and block out reality, too much had happened to pretend otherwise. With her muscles still twitching from the staggering orgasm, she sighed and forced herself to ask, "So what now?"

HE COULDN'T STOP staring at the impressive hickey he'd left on her neck. No doubt his brothers would give him shit over it for years but fuck it. They'd only see the mark because Liv was alive and in his bed where she belonged.

He'd have walked away from Lance without killing the dickbag. Almost had. But he couldn't regret Lance's final act of stupidity and how it forced Scott to end him.

For the rest of his life, he'd remember how his knife slid like butter into the man's gut. It'd be a memory he called up whenever he needed to fucking smile.

Liv was free now. She could return to Chicago, to her home, or go anywhere in the fucking world. But she'd told him she loved him, and unfortunately for her, he was a possessive neanderthal who'd tie her to the bed and keep her prisoner before letting her walk away.

"Now we take Curly up on the offer he made me."

She tilted her head as her nose scrunched up in confusion. "What offer?"

"To build a house on the farm's land. I think he wants all of us to live on the property eventually."

"A house?" she whispered. "Are you sure?"

He grunted. "I'm sure there's no way in fucking hell you're living anywhere except with me, and this place is too small for a flea, so yeah, I'm sure."

"I meant more, what happens now with the club? With the..." she leaned in and whispered, "... body? Will you be arrested? Do I need to go to the station and make a statement? Make sure they know it was self-defense." The pitch of her voice rose as her words sped up.

"Breathe, baby. You don't need to do anything."

He ran his hands up and down the silky-smooth skin of her back. Not touching her wasn't an option. Thankfully, she craved his touch because he needed it to remind himself she was safe. His nightmares would be plagued by the moment he walked in and found Lance standing over her, pants down, about to fucking rape her.

"Curly is handling it. Money can make even the ugliest shit disappear."

"But there's a body in an airplane. How can you hide that? The pilot? That slimy flight attendant?" Her eyes filled with panic. "Scott, I'll die if you're arrested because of me."

"Shh, Livy, breathe with me." He inhaled slowly, nodding as she copied him. His breath came smooth and easy where hers stuttered. "Now blow it out. Good, again. Okay, you gotta keep this shit locked in a fucking vault, okay?"

She nodded and traced her fingers over a tattoo on his arm. "Of course. I'd never jeopardize you or the club that way."

"I know, babe." He hated to give her details, but she was so worked up over the thought of him being arrested. Probably because of the mess he'd been in when the cops hauled his ass in a few weeks ago. "The easiest way to get rid of evidence is a fire."

Her eyes widened. "What?" she whispered. "You're gonna set the plane on fire?"

"It's already done."

"But... but it's a twenty-million-dollar plane."

Scott shrugged. "Lance won't care."

She pressed a hand to her chest. "What about TSA? And security cameras? I'm sure they're everywhere at an airport."

He pursed his lips as he thought of how much to tell her. Fuck it, she deserved all the details. Curly certainly didn't keep shit from Brooke. "We have a guy, a hacker, who can take care of all that shit. I promise you no one will be arrested. You don't need to worry about that. Okay?"

She stared up at him with so much love and trust in her eyes that it punched him in the gut. Christ, this woman was everything.

"Okay," she said with a half-smile. "Thank you for telling me."

He cupped her face. "I fucking love you, Liv. I'll do anything to protect you, which means keeping myself here with you."

Her slight smile grew until she was beaming up at him. "Then I guess we better start working on a plan for a house, huh?"

"Yeah, baby, that's exactly what we should do." He drew her face to him and kissed her until he grew hard again. Then he flipped Liv onto her back on the bed, grinning like an idiot as she shrieked.

He'd never be who he once was. Not after all the shit he'd endured and the horrors he'd seen. During their calls, he wouldn't ever be the fun-loving, carefree man Deke told her stories about.

Liv got that. She'd witnessed his darkness, his suffering, and his demons.

And she loved him.

After today's trauma and what she'd witnessed a few weeks ago, she'd changed too from the woman who grew up with that silver spoon. She'd have her demons to conquer or learn to live with.

And Scott would be right by her side for every moment.

Loving her the way she loved him.

Epilogue

"He's a different man. I can't tell you how worried he had me. Liv, you're exactly what he needed, and I can't thank you enough for loving and accepting him, struggles and all."

Olivia turned toward Scott's gorgeous red-haired sister. Chloe and her ol' man had arrived the day before with a few other men from the club's Tennessee chapter. After a fun night of drinking, dancing, and laughter, the men were meeting inside the clubhouse while Brooke, Chloe, and she sat in the sun with cocktails.

The sun would soon set, leading to another perfect evening spent with family.

She smiled at Chloe. "It makes me so happy to know that I've been good for him, but please don't thank me. He's given me as much or more than I've given him. I'm not doing anything but loving him. I couldn't stop that if I tried. He's it for me."

"Damn, girl, you should write greeting cards," Brooke muttered.

"Seriously." Chloe wiped her tearful eyes. "We've both been through a lot in the past few years, and to know we've both found a soft place to land is more than I could've ever asked for. I really like you, Liv, and I know this might be premature, but I hope we'll become family one day. Well, even more than an MC family."

Now it was Olivia's turn to have wet eyes and a tingling nose. "Stop, you're gonna make me cry."

"Okay, enough schmoopy stuff," Brooke said. "I get it. You just met and have all these squishy feelings to share, but if the guys walk out and you're all blubbery and snotty, I'm gonna get in trouble for not keeping you happy."

That had them all laughing. "Good point," Chloe said. She winked. "Though why do I feel like you enjoy getting in trouble with your man?"

"Because you're a smart woman." Brooke's sly smile disappeared behind her margarita glass as she sipped.

Chloe laughed while Olivia smiled.

"Okay, one last serious question, then I'll be ready to talk about frivolous stuff," Chloe said, eyes on Olivia. "How are you holding up after everything that happened last month?"

And there went her mood. She could almost hear the shrill whir of the rocket crashing to the ground. Thirty-five days had passed since she made the terrible mistake of returning to Lance. Thirty-five sleeps since he'd nearly raped her and since Scott killed him. Most of those nights were interrupted by nightmares. Always one of the same three nightmares.

Scott didn't rescue her on time.

Scott found her, but Lance killed him.

Scott killed and had an entire SWAT team waiting for him when he stepped off the plane.

Every time she woke sweating, gasping for air, and crying, Scott was there to wrap her in his arms and remind her they were alive and safe. Either the man stayed up waiting for her to freak out all night, or he was so attuned to her that he woke at the slightest whimper.

Regardless, his presence, kisses, and strong arms were

slowly healing her from the trauma.

"I'm holding up okay," she said with a half-smile. "Not great, but okay. I have nightmares, and sometimes I feel crappy during the day. Anxious, I guess. Scott has been my rock. I should probably speak with a professional too, but I'm not ready for that."

"You'll get there," Brooke said. "Don't rush anything. You know what you need."

"Yeah. We're flying to Chicago soon to close the sale on the house. I'm nervous to go back, but Scott will be with me." She shrugged. "It'll just be hard to be around people who knew us together."

Lance had been a stickler about financial and estate planning. Early on in their engagement, he'd drafted a will naming her sole beneficiary of his property. She planned to donate all six-million dollars she'd be receiving from the sale of their ridiculous mansion to organizations helping victims of sexual assault and human trafficking—a fitting way to memorialize Lance.

Nodding, Chloe pierced her with a solemn look. "I'm assuming Scott hasn't told you because he's very respectful of my privacy, but I was raped a few years ago. It's too hard to go into details, but I'll just say it was really bad. Rocket rescued me. It's how we met." She took a long sip of her margarita. "Anyway, I went through a scary dark time afterward. And again, Rocket saved me. So I understand how difficult it can be to heal from trauma. Most of the women in the club have been through their fair share of trauma and tragedy. You have a wonderful crew of strong women ready and willing to help anytime you need it."

All she could do was reach out and squeeze Chloe's hand in gratitude. This was the first time she'd had unconditional support from her family and friends.

"You're welcome," Chloe said with a watery smile.

"Now I'm crying too!" Brooke sniffed as she wiped her eyes.

"Okay, okay. I'm done. Does anyone want to talk favorite sex position? Maybe how much they love their guy's dick?" Chloe turned toward Olivia and then wrinkled her nose. "Never mind. There are some things about my brother I never want to know. Eww."

Olivia choked on her margarita. Her nose burned, and her eyes watered. That had the other women cracking up.

They sat there for the next half hour, talking and laughing about anything and everything, building their bond as women in the club.

Olivia couldn't have loved it more. Soon Scott would come out, and they'd make a bonfire. She'd spend the rest of the evening wrapped in his arms before they headed to their bed in the very small apartment they'd be moving out of next week.

Her life wasn't perfect, but it was full of love, and she couldn't ask for more than that.

And the best part was she'd have it forever.

"WE'RE SEEING A huge increase in drug-related admissions at the ER," Pulse said as they sat around the table in church. "Meth in particular."

No surprise there. Lobo had warned them. He'd been quiet, suspiciously quiet, but the product was moving and selling.

And apparently fucking people up.

Curly nodded. "I've heard the rumor that the area is becoming a hotbed for meth sales and trafficking."

"I know you hate the idea, Prez, but we might benefit from having a connection to the local PD," Scott said. He'd been thinking about it for a while but hadn't wanted to rock the boat after all the drama he'd caused killing Lance. Getting rid of the body of a rich man from Chicago hadn't been easy and took a shitload of club resources and time. Pissing his prez off by suggesting they try to buy some cops had to wait. "Maybe we need to start vetting whom we can get on our payroll. At least so we can be in the know and not blind to the players and the cops' plans."

A heavy sigh left Curly. "You're right," he said, shocking the shit out of Scott. "Look, how I feel about the cops is no secret. This department was corrupt as fuck back in the day, and I'm pretty sure it still is. But I'd be stupid not to use any resource at our disposal. And if we can find a safe way to get intel that won't land any of us in jail, then we should take it."

"I've got an idea," Tracker said from across the table.

Scott lifted an eyebrow.

"Let's hear it," Curly said.

"They've got a new hire. A rookie. Woman in her early thirties. She's... different."

"Different?" Curly asked with a frown.

Tracker's grin grew wicked. "She's fucking gorgeous. Word on the street is that she was a fucking beauty queen back in the day. Came from a family of dudes who were all cops. As the lone female child, her family doted on her and tried to raise a princess. But guess what the little lady wanted her entire life?"

"Let me guess," Jinx cut in. "She wanted to be like her daddy and brothers."

"Mm-hmm. And granddaddy, and great-granddaddy. You get the picture. So when she got ballsy enough, she told them all to fuck off, moved from Alabama to Florida, and joined the department."

Curly's eyes narrowed. "How do you know all this?"

Tracker winked. "Met her at a bar last week. The woman's a bit of a man-hater and was looking to take some of that hatred out on a bad boy's dick." He shrugged. "What can I say? I'm always down for helping someone out."

Jinx barked out a laugh. "I'll bet you are."

Tracker winked. "Wasn't wearing my cut, so she had no idea who I am, but I'm thinking I get her addicted to my cock, I can get all sorts of info from her."

Scott snorted. "You think pretty highly of yourself, don't you, brother?"

Tracker winked and nodded. "Just facts, man."

Curly tilted his head. "What makes you think she isn't planning to use you in the same way?"

"Huh." Tracker scratched his chin. "Hadn't thought of that. Maybe she knew exactly who I was." His grin grew. "That just makes it all the more exciting."

"Fuck, I'm going to regret this," Curly muttered. "Okay, keep seeing her. I don't have to tell you to keep your fucking lips sealed about club business, right?"

"Of course not, Prez," Tracker said with all joking gone.

"All right, see if you can get her to give up any info." Curly rubbed his forehead. "God, Brooke will kill me if she hears about this."

Shit, he wasn't kidding. Liv would rip him a new asshole when she found out Tracker was fucking a cop for intel. He chuckled. Angry Liv tended to get all passionate, and he had no problem with that.

"All right, meeting adjourned," Curly announced. "I need some time with my woman."

Scott didn't need to be told twice. He practically flew from his chair and floated outside. These days, he often felt like his feet didn't hit the ground.

Thank you, Liv.

He stepped outside into the twilight to find three very tipsy women laughing so hard they could barely breathe.

"Scott!" Olivia shouted, throwing her arms in the air like she was cheering for a touchdown. "You're done. I missed you." She stood and stumbled. "Whoa."

He grinned. Maybe a little more sloppy than tipsy. Damn, she looked cute in those tiny white denim shorts and the navy-blue tank. "Hey, baby. Having fun?" he asked as he reached her.

"Yes! So much fun. Chloe is amazing. I love your sister." She threw her arms around his neck.

Over her shoulder, the sister in question beamed and gave him a thumbs up. "She's amazing," Chloe mouthed.

Scott grinned. Shit, the two most important people in his life got along as though they'd been friends forever. "Help me get the bonfire going?" he whispered in Liv's ear.

"Yes! Let's do that." She unwound her arms, grabbed his hand, and towed him around to the back of the clubhouse toward the huge firepit.

As soon as they were out of sight from everyone else, he backed her against the building and kissed the ever-loving hell out of her. Liv melted against him. That was one of his favorite things about kissing her. Every time. She fully surrendered herself to him. The rest of the world disappeared, and they lived in their own bubble of bliss.

"Wow," she said, sounding dazed. "That was one hell of a kiss. What did I do to deserve that?"

"You love me," he said.

She grinned. "I sure do."

"I'm glad you and Chloe are getting along. It means a lot to me."

She wiped his mouth with her thumb, probably getting rid of her lipstick. "I know. And I mean it when I say she's great. Everything go well in church?"

"Yeah, baby. It's all good."

"Hey, Scott?" she asked.

He gazed down into her glassy green eyes. "Hmm?"

"In case I haven't said it yet, I'm not leaving. Ever. You're stuck with me because I love you."

He chuckled. Tipsy Olivia cracked him up. "Hey, Liv?"

"Yeah?"

"If I haven't said it yet, you're the best goddamn thing that's ever happened to me, and I'll love you to the fucking end of the road."

She grinned, and he couldn't resist another kiss.

"You've told me," she said with a grin. "Lots of times. But it gets better each time."

He couldn't have said it better. Each day, each second with Liv was better than the one before, and that was saying something because each second he spent with her was paradise.

First Comes Loathe Preview

Michaela figured she would either vomit or pass out cold on the floor.

It was a toss-up which of the mortifying acts would happen first, putting a quick and final end to her dreams.

She shifted back and forth as she stood there gnawing her lower lip. No one had said anything yet and she'd been standing there at least a full minute. Every person in the room seemed busy with whatever tasks they had to complete.

Should she start? Launch into the scene? Or was she supposed to wait for instructions? Maybe she should have asked one of the other girls sitting in the long line outside the audition room for some advice, but she'd been going for confident and experienced, not the unsophisticated noob that she was.

"Name?" A man had a placard in front of him with the words *Casting Director* on it. He didn't even look up from a clipboard. The man looked like he walked straight off the cover of GQ in trendy black jeans, a metallic button-up with rolled sleeves. Black nail polish, an eyebrow ring, and perfectly gelled hair completed the look.

"M-Michaela." She cleared her throat. "Michaela Hudson,"

she amended in as strong a voice as she could muster with her legs shaking and insides bubbling with anxiety. Standing in an audition room at a real Hollywood studio for the first time made her high school audition nerves laughable.

A bright light flashed and she blinked and jumped back. "Wh-uh..." She ran a damp palm over her shoulder-length and newly blond hair. The hair she'd spent more time perfecting that morning than ever before.

"Sorry, casting photo," a tall, thin woman said from behind a camera.

"Oh, uh, sure." Michaela blinked a few more times to get the spots in her eyes to disappear.

Stand tall, look them in the eye, and be the star I know you were born to be.

Her mother's words rang loudly in her ears as the urge to shrink in on herself and curl into a ball grew with each passing second. Her very first memory was standing on a chair in her mother's kitchen around age four, holding a bottle of Mrs. Butterworth's syrup and thanking the stuffed animal Academy for the award.

All through Michaela's childhood, her romantic of a mother had been in awe of Hollywood. The glitz, the glam, the magic of being loved by the entire world. Michaela had fallen hard for the allure of movie star life as well. Acting was the only thing she'd ever wanted to do. Not just acting but excelling at it. Becoming a star. Living in one of those jaw-dropping mansions in the Hollywood hills where she'd never have to wonder where her next meal would come from or how her mother was going to pay her medical bills. They'd live the ultimate life without any cares, concerns, or hardships. How could anyone have a moment of unhappiness when they had the entire world at their feet?

Even before her mother had passed away six months ago, Michaela decided their dream would live on, so she'd done it a few weeks ago. Moved from a tiny spec of a town in West Virginia to big-city Hollywood to begin her career as a starlet.

"You waiting for an engraved invitation?" the casting director barked, again not so much as glancing her way. "You may have all day, but I don't. Get started."

"Yes, sir." Michaela closed her eyes, inhaled a shuttered breath, and launched into the short scene the talent agent instructed her to memorize. The one she'd practiced no less than eight hundred times over the past four days—in front of the mirror, while eating, sitting on the toilet, when she should have been sleeping, and even while waiting tables at the coffee shop. She'd kill to have the opportunity to act this captivating scene on a real set.

Three lines in and one heartfelt attempt at sophistication, the casting director dropped his pen and finally gave her his eyes. His gaze stayed focused on her as she ran through the scene, pouring every ounce of her soul into the cheesy dialogue. From the same table as the director, another man without hair and skinny as a rail with thick, square glasses read the male parts in a bored tone.

Michaela gasped and pressed a hand to her chest in response to rejection from her fictitious love. The more he spoke, the more she fell into the character. Before long, she'd fully immersed herself in the role, feeling the character's personality wash over her and chase away the poor, small-town girl, replacing her with the high-maintenance socialite she portrayed.

Her heart soared. The director sat with his chin propped on his hand, watching her every move. Sure, he wasn't smiling, but he didn't frown either. That had to be good. Though a minuscule role in a made for television movie, she'd be in a film if she got this part. A real live Hollywood movie. With her name in the credits and face on screen for all the world to see.

"I'm not canceling this trip," she spat out, channeling her inner diva with a flip of her long hair. Hiding her slight southern accent was the hardest part of this process, but she'd been practicing for weeks and thought she had it down pretty well. "Do you have any idea—"

"Cut!"

Huh?

Michaela snapped her mouth closed at once, and her arms slumped limply to her sides. That was it? She'd only made it through half the assigned script.

"What is this shit, Bob?" The casting director stood with a mighty frown and aimed the question at a talent agent seated at the back of the room.

Michaela peeked over her shoulder in time to see Bob shrug. "Don't know. She ain't one of mine."

"Who got you this audition, kid?" the director asked with an expression akin to someone drinking spoiled milk.

"Um, E-Elvira with Star Finder Incorporated." The eclectic agent with snowy white hair and enormous cat-eye glasses had promised Michaela would be *absolutely perfect* for the role.

"SFI." The director snorted. "Figures."

Her face heated under the stare of everyone sitting at the table.

"I-is there a problem, sir?" Trying to speak louder than the pounding of her heart had her nearly yelling.

"Yeah, there's a problem." He slapped his palms down on the table as he rose. "There's a huge fucking problem. Have you even looked in a mirror today?"

Michaela blinked as every person in the room abandoned their tasks and fixed their curious gazes on her. She felt as though she were naked, standing in front of a panel of hypercritical judges all taking pot shots at her in their minds. Though only the casting director slung the insults, agreement with his assessment shone on projected from every other person's face.

The tip of her nose tingled with the urge to burst into tears.

Had she looked in a mirror?

Seriously?

Only the stark fear of disrespecting a man who held her fragile future in his hands kept her from laughing out loud. She'd spent approximately four hours in front of the mirror, bleaching then styling her hair, giving herself a homemade oatmeal and honey facial, and slapping on more makeup than she'd ever worn. That was after countless hours of YouTube tutorials on how to apply Hollywood-style makeup.

"I'm sorry, sir, is my makeup smudged?" She ran a quick finger under each eye, proud of the way her voice didn't waver. Because inside, she was a quivering mess of fear and anxiety.

He sighed. "No. Look, I'm gonna save you a lot of time, trouble, and heartache, okay, kid?"

The quiet in the room somehow rushed louder than the roar of an angry sea.

Michaela nodded. What else was she supposed to do with the spotlight on her? Argue?

Flee?

Tempting.

"Go to college. Get a degree and a real job. Move on with your life."

What?

Her chest constricted as though a band tightened with each word he spoke. Move on with her life? This was her life. At least, her life's dream.

"I-uh, I'm not interested in college," she said in a small voice. The bleach blond female clones and eclectically dressed men's gazes morphed from interested to pitying, as if they all recognized what the casting director meant while she was still in the dark. "I want to be an actress."

He sighed and ran a hand down his face as though weary from the conversation. "I've sat through thousands of these auditions in my career. And here's the thing, we usually know within five seconds of you walking in the door whether you have it or you don't. And I'm sorry, kid, but you don't. It's a look. A vibe. An attitude. Some girls are Hollywood, and some aren't. You can dress up a turd and all that..." With a shrug, he sat and began shuffling through a stack of papers as though he hadn't destroyed her life. "It's an expression for a reason."

A fat tear wavered in the corner of her eye, blurring her vision and threatening to roll down her face at any second. She blinked rapidly. The man would not get the satisfaction of seeing her crack. He would not go out tonight and laugh with his buddies about how he made the simple country girl cry by wrecking her dreams with a few cutting words.

She was too ugly to be a serious actress. That's what he'd said. Not pretty enough, maybe not skinny enough, or glamorous enough. Regardless, the message was clear.

You're not good enough.

"You may go." He was back to speaking without so much as glancing in her direction.

Dismissed.

Michaela swallowed a painful lump as she turned and began to walk toward the exit with measured steps. The sound of her thrift-store heeled boots clacking on the tile floor rang out like shots of a gun in the silent room.

Her arms hung heavy and lifeless at her sides, not swinging as she strode on stiff legs. She felt like a doll with a plush, vulnerable center and rigid plastic limbs that couldn't bend. She didn't so much as blink as she held the fake smile and focused straight ahead on the door. But with each forward step, she grew closer to losing her composure.

Just a few more feet.

Finally, her hand gripped the door, and she yanked it open with enough force to have it hit the wall with a loud bang. Her heart was too heavy to cringe at the unexpected clamor. Michaela walked down the long hallway past the line of girls with nerves in their bellies and hope in their eyes. Same as she'd had ten minutes ago.

How many of these girls would walk out of that room with shattered dreams and demolished self-esteem? All? Some? Only her?

As she emerged into the heat of the California sun, the weight of despair sat heavily on her chest. The idea of climbing onto a stifling LA city bus and returning to her depressing shoebox of an apartment made her nauseous, so she turned in the opposite direction of the bus stop and walked.

And walked.

And *walked*.

Michaela strolled through the city until her feet blistered and her calves cramped.

What was she supposed to do now? Continue working hours upon hours serving coffee to ungrateful tourists? Tuck her tail between her legs and return to West Virginia? God, the thought of it had her wanting to grip her hair and scream at the top of her lungs. Small-town life wasn't for her. After eighteen years of living it, she could say that with certainty. Her heart wanted more, bigger, grander. She wanted the world to know she was so much more than a penniless girl from West Virginia whose family had never amounted to anything. Not a single person in her family had ever left their town. Every relative as far back as she knew had lived and died in the same town. It hadn't been enough for Michaela's mother, but she'd been too afraid to take a chance. Now she never could. Michaela vowed she wouldn't reach the end of her life with more regrets than accomplishments.

After hours of aimless wandering, she found herself on Hollywood Boulevard surrounded by tourists squatting next to the stars and taking hundreds of selfies. Their smiling faces and undisguised delight reminded her of herself just yesterday. Oddly enough, it seemed like years since she'd shared their wonder and awe though it had been less than twenty-four hours.

With an audible sigh and throbbing feet, Michaela stared down at the ground in front of her.

"Meryl Streep," she whispered aloud as she gazed in reverence at the pink star at her feet.

A laugh bubbled up from her gut, pouring out into the air. A few of the sightseers glanced her way with scrunched brows before returning to their business.

Meryl Streep? Of all the places she could have ended up, Meryl Streep's star it was.

Michaela's lips curled in a genuine smile. This had to be a sign.

Early in her career, many told this multi-award-winning actress she'd never amount to anything in the film world because she wasn't attractive enough. And look at her now. She sure as hell showed all the ignorant chauvinists who judged her.

What's to keep you from doing the same?

Nothing. Not one damned thing.

Michaela straightened her shoulders.

Screw that casting director.

Screw the rest of those uppity jerks peering down their noses at her.

She'd show them. She'd show everyone.

She laughed again, longer and louder this time, drawing the attention of dozens of tourists. Let them look. She'd need to get used to people gawking at her as she walked down the

street.
Michaela Hudson was going to be a star.

Thank you so much for reading **SPEC**. If you enjoyed it, please consider leaving a review on Amazon or Goodreads.

Other books by Lilly Atlas

No Prisoners MC
Hook: A No Prisoners Novella
Striker
Jester
Acer
Lucky
Snake

Trident Ink
Escapades

Hell's Handlers MC
Zach
Maverick
Jigsaw
Copper
Rocket
Little Jack
Joy
Screw
Viper
Thunder

Hell's Handlers Florida Chapter
Curly

Spec
Tracker (coming soon)

Blue Collar Bensons
First Comes Loathe
Shock and Aww

Audiobooks
Audio

Join Lilly's mailing list for a **FREE** No Prisoners short story.
www.lillyatlas.com
Facebook
Instagram
TikTok
Twitter

Join my Facebook group, **Lilly's Ladies** for book previews, early cover reveals, contests and more!

About the Author

Lilly Atlas is an award-winning contemporary romance author. She's a proud Navy wife and mother of three spunky girls. Every time Lilly downloads a new eBook she expects her Kindle App to tell her it's exhausted and overworked, and to beg for some rest. Thankfully that hasn't happened yet so she can often be found absorbed in a good book.